A
ZERO-SUM
GAME

—

Eduardo Rabasa

TRANSLATED FROM THE SPANISH BY

CHRISTINA MACSWEENEY

DEEP VELLUM PUBLISHING

DALLAS, TEXAS

Deep Vellum Publishing
3000 Commerce St., Dallas, Texas 75226
deepvellum.org · @deepvellum

Deep Vellum Publishing is a 501c3
nonprofit literary arts organization founded in 2013.

ISBN: 978-1-941920-38-1 (paperback) · 978-1-941920-39-8 (ebook)
LIBRARY OF CONGRESS CONTROL NUMBER: 2016945227

Cover design & typesetting by Anna Zylicz · annazylicz.com

Text set in Bembo, a typeface modeled on typefaces cut by Francesco Griffo
for Aldo Manuzio's printing of *De Aetna* in 1495 in Venice.

Distributed by Consortium Book Sales & Distribution.

Printed in the United States of America on acid-free paper.

What Max noted was the inverse: despite its hyper-realistic pretensions, political narrative was acquiring an increasingly fictitious character. The point of departure and the end met to close a circle that no longer even bothered to take into account some of the most manifest features of any attempt to explain the social sphere. In years gone by, the graybeard who signaled the disenchantment of the world proposed setting out from "what is" as it presents itself, even as a point of departure for those who wanted to transform reality. In present times, the reverse process was followed: to set out from a list of indisputably good desires, and to assume that—with sufficient will on the part of those with power—one could reach a just Utopia where everyone would stay in the place corresponding to him.

"Villa Miserias is, of course, a microcosm, but Rabasa's novel is anything but your simple society-in-miniature story. It's an emphatically political novel, and willing to embrace theory, rather than just practice: there's a discourse-framework here—some telling, rather than just showing—but Rabasa has a few tricks up his sleeve in this respect as well, and *A Zero-Sum Game* is decidedly (and for the most part successful as) an elaborately constructed fiction... A very impressive piece of work, in particular also in its creative approach to the concept of 'political fiction,' and in suggesting what fiction can still do."
—MICHAEL ORTHOFER, *The Complete Review*

"When I heard that Deep Vellum were publishing this translation, I was ecstatic. Rabasa comes with much praise. Channeling both Orwell and Ballard, his dizzying and intricate dystopia exposes the demagoguery and inequality, the individualism and false democracy of the way we live now. *A Zero-Sum Game* is not only a brilliant novel—it's the novel we need right now."
—GARY PERRY, bookseller, Foyles Bookshop (London, England)

"How can a satirical farce be so dourly realistic? How can a precise and theoretical evisceration of neoliberal democracy also have such bloody guts and viscerally real characters? How did Eduardo Rabasa manage to make such a personal account of an individual's crack-up into an anatomical sketch of political deadlock we find ourselves trapped in? And how did he make it so funny? Don't answer these questions: just read the book."
—AARON BADY, *The New Inquiry*

International Praise For A Zero-Sum Game

- *Shortlisted for the* PREMIO LAS AMÉRICAS, (*for Debut Novel*), given by the Festival de la Palabra from Puerto Rico to the best Spanish-language book of the year
- Selected among the 10 best books of the year by Nadal Suau, *Periódico ABC* (SPAIN)
- Selected among the 6 best books of the year by the literary blog, *La medicina de Tongoy* (SPAIN)
- Selected among the 10 best books of the year by Sergio González Rodríguez, *Periódico Reforma* (MÉXICO)

"*A Zero-Sum Game* is an outstanding political fantasy. Eduardo Rabasa has written a futuristic novel set in the present; its inventiveness is not based on new technologies but rather on new kinds of relationships. It's a novel about the most complicated of extreme sports: cohabitation."
—JUAN VILLORO, author of *God is Round and The Guilty*

"An amazing novel. On reading it, I felt myself to be immersed in a world that, as in certain works by Bolaño, transcends the characteristics typically associated with the Latin American novel. *A Zero-Sum Game* carries readers to regions of the imagination which subtly suggest the best of the Central European tradition. The sensation is as real as it is unsettling and, somehow, after a time, gives rise to an awareness of where we actually are. The prose rests firmly on a set of coordinates that can only be Mexican, revealing a totality of truths that reflect the complex texture of a country and a society immersed in a moment of violent convulsion. Few recent novels have managed to surprise me so greatly as *A Zero-Sum Game*."
—EDUARDO LAGO, author of *Call me Brooklyn*

"The comparisons to *Nineteen Eighty-Four* are inevitable (…) However, *A Zero-Sum Game* is closer to *A Brave New World* than to the Orwellian dystopia."
—VICTOR PARKAS, *El País*

"Meticulous, written with a harsh language, this is the portrait of a suffocating microcosm in which hierarchies are fixed by the illusion of a social progress that will never arrive. Rabasa dismantles with precision the mechanisms of a false democracy, in which no political alternation is possible (...) A mirror of some Latin American countries, this dense novel offers a pertinent reflection about the ways in which a regime can exercise violence today: less by outright repression and more through it's capacity of imposing a deadly lethargy on people."
—ARIANE SINGER, *Le Monde*

"This is an important novel. In terms of narrative, what the literary critics might call the central theme—power, our relationship with power, the power of power—is very deftly handled, and is combined with stories that interweave in perfect harmony. Rabasa's decision to set the novel in an insignificant place, which works as a mirror to anywhere in the world, was a very wise one; more wise still is the satirical tone which reveals itself in his functional prose (that is, prose that functions well). Nowhere in recent times have I read a better portrait of how things are shaped – or how those things, over time, shape us."
—JUAN BONILLA, author of *Prohibido entrar sin pantalones*, awarded the first PREMIO BIENAL DE NOVELA MARIO VARGAS LLOSA

"[Rabasa's] first novel, *A Zero-Sum Game*, collects outbursts of passionate love, of the conflicting relationship between a father and a son, and, above all, of a critique to democracy in the shape of political satire...Rabasa gives an unexpected turn to the genre of novels of social criticism, a literary tradition from which the author hopes to obtain the formula that allows him to think and understand the present...A demolishing piece of work, perfectly suited for Rabasa, an eternal restless soul, and one who invites to share in the pleasure of literature from his double role as a publisher and writer."
—LEONARDO TARIFEÑO, *Revista Vice*

"Rabasa's satirical vocation is cristallized in a cumulative effect that at times recalls the transversal cut with which Georges Perec sketched the life of the tenants of a building in *La Vie mode d'employ*, or the eagle-eye with which Damián Tabarovsky followed the comings and goings of a leaf that glides over a street of Buenos Aires in his novel-essay *Una belleza vulgar*."
—GUILLERMO NÚÑEZ, *Frente*

Table of Contents

PART ONE

Walking like giant cranes and
With my x-ray eyes I strip you naked
In a tight little world and are you on the list?
Stepford wives who are we to complain?
Investments and deals investments and deals
Cold wives and mistresses
Cold wives and Sunday papers
City boys in first class
Don't know they're born little
Someone else is gonna come and clean it up
Born and raised for the job
Someone always does
I wish you'd get up get over get up get over
Turn your tape off.

"A Wolf at the Door"
Radiohead

I

I

All I ever wanted was to be just another invisible coward, Max Michels silently grumbled as a drop of blood dribbled down his freshly shaved throat. Almost unconsciously, he'd put off until the very last moment the decision that, once taken, seemed as surprising as it was irrevocable. He was about to break the cardinal rule of Villa Miserias: to stand as a candidate in the elections for the president of the residents' association without the consent of Selon Perdumes.

With the force of a rusty spring unexpectedly uncoiling, the memory of an era before Perdumes' arrival materialized in his mind. Max clearly recalled the principal feature of the day the modernization began: jubilation at the sight of the dust. There was no lack of people who gladly inhaled the first particles of the future. Poor devils, Max now thought. The dust had never cleared: Villa Miserias was a perpetual work in progress.

At that time the residential estate had functioned like clockwork; it still did, although the model was now completely different. Every two years there were elections for the presidency of the estate's board. For eleven days, the residents were bombarded with election leaflets. The most distinguished ladies received chocolates and flowers; those of lower standing had to make do with bags of rice and dried beans. In essence, all the candidates were competing to convince the voters they were the one who would make absolutely no alterations to the established order. There was even a physical prototype for those in charge of running the estate that included, in equal measure, the fat, the short, the dark, and bald: it was a bearing, a gaze, a malleable voice. There was no friction between the election manifestos and the everyday state of affairs.

The foundations of Villa Miserias were conceived on the same basis as Selon Perdumes' fundamental doctrine: Quietism in Motion. Its forty-nine buildings were constructed using an engineering technique designed to allow shaking while avoiding collapse. The smear of city to which it belonged was prone to lethal earthquakes, but the flexible structure of the buildings had prevented catastrophe on more than one occasion.

In the time before the reforms all the apartments had been identical; now they were symmetrically unequal. Each building had ten in total, distributed in inverse proportion to the corresponding floor. In general, the demography was also predictable: in the tiny apartments on the lowest floor, multiple generations of humans and animals lived together. In contrast, the penthouse apartments were usually inhabited by young executives with or without wives and children. In exchange for their privileged position, they had to endure the swaying motion of the building, some of which was caused by the passage of buses on the broad road surrounding the estate. One such resident, who had a panoramic view of the earthquake that reduced the neighboring estate to rubble, defined the spectacle as a waltz danced by flexible concrete colossi.

Perdumes delighted in the improbable equilibrium of successful social engineering. His conversion into Villa Miserias' foremost resident was a gradual process. He'd arrived on the estate as a businessman of mysterious origins and activities. Each person who spoke to him received an explanation as vague as it was different to the others. To give a clearer idea of his character, one only has to say that—so far—it's reasonable to imagine they were all true.

He moved into apartment 4B in Building 10, having offered its owner, the widow Inocencia Roca, a year's rent in advance in exchange for a substantial discount. The inhabitants of Villa Miserias—accustomed to the traditional barter system—weren't prepared for the way Selon Perdumes flashed the greenbacks. Señora Roca was unaware that she would soon be signing over the apartment to him.

Sightings of him were rare: he kept them to the bare minimum. In order to introduce himself to his neighbors, he invited them individually for coffee. He was charming in the most chameleonic sense of the term. His eyes were the shade of gray that can be taken as either blue or green. He was able to guess the most deeply hidden fears of each of his guests and had an amazing talent for giving solidity to fantasies, then offering the finance needed to make them real. The calculated non-payment of a proportion of his creditors was, for him, a great blessing since he practiced a different sort of usury. In exchange for the possibility of being ruined, he sought to acquire loyalties and secrets. Like an expert dentist who extracts a molar without his anaesthetized patient being aware, his magnetism attracted confessions that enabled him to understand people via their weaknesses.

The young couple in 4A became the subjects of one of his first laboratory experiments. After an informal chat, Perdumes noted the tensions inherent in their different origins. The young man had followed in his father's footsteps to become a public accountant; she'd studied literature in a state university thanks to the family Popsicle business. He'd been stagnating in an accountancy firm for two years; she worked as the assistant of an impressively learned academic.

Perdumes explained to them that when it came to making an impression, appearances were everything. Enveloping them in the gleam of his alabaster smile, he told the young man that he should change his old car and buy a new watch. Fine, but that was impossible, they could scarcely cover the mortgage…Eyes downcast, she confessed that her mother helped pay for her painting classes. Marvelous! Don't worry, replied Perdumes' smile. I'll loan you as much as you need and you can pay me back in installments. He was a master of the art of silence. Without moving from his seat, his presence seemed to lose density while the couple made their decision. Of course, they would repay him as soon as possible. It's just a springboard…Great! No problem. Would you like more coffee?

He also happened to know that some women in the building were interested in forming a reading group. Why didn't she organize it? This time the silence was more ephemeral. The girl's eyes lit up with an enthusiasm her husband hadn't seen for a long time. Phenomenal! Don't say another word. Would you excuse me a moment?

Within a few weeks everything was different. The young man was driving a modest new car; he checked the time regularly on his elegant casual watch. Every week, she listened to the heavily made-up ladies who spoke about anything but the books they had briefly skimmed-through. His employers noted the change and began shake his hand when they met. They once asked him to join them for lunch in the small restaurant near the office. She was able to pay for her painting classes for as long as Perdumes' clandestine subsidy to the ladies of the reading group lasted. Every weekend, the couple turned up with radiant smiles to present their repayments.

To explain his theory of secrets, Perdumes used the analogy of the reversible red velvet bags used by magicians. The first step is to show the audience that the bag is empty inside and out. Nothing hidden there. However, the trick consists in inserting a hand in the right place. The commonest secrets are as innocent as white rabbits. Then come the shameful secrets, greasy stains that can be removed with a little effort. As he honed his extraction technique, Perdumes became interested in the secrets that could only be invoked by a black magic ritual. They were barbs that gave pain by their mere existence: the smallest movement lacerated the soul in which they were embedded.

On one occasion, Perdumes noticed that the logo on a young neighbor's sneakers had an A too many and was missing an E. When little Jorge felt the gleam of Perdumes' smile scrutinizing his footwear, he knew the secret was out. He subjected his mother to a weeklong tantrum that only abated with the arrival of a box containing a pair of authentic sneakers. There was also the elderly lady in 4B who used to fill the bottles of holy water she sprinkled on her grandchildren on Sundays from the tap. Or the aged bureaucrat in 2C who boasted of his mistreatment of the Villa Miserias cleaning staff: "Better harness the donkey than carry the load yourself."

Perdumes' prying was sustained by an age-old activity: gossip. Having gained a little of a person's confidence, he was able to access what they knew, suspected or had invented about others. It was an unashamed downward spiral: other people's dirty laundry covered your own to the point where you created a hodgepodge of stinking gibberish, crying out in a muffled voice: "Deep down, we're all disgusting, so there's nothing to worry about." It made no difference that the secret was an invention. What mattered was the perception of that dark thing and its tangled strata. Everyone had something to hide; other people found out about it. The gossip came alive, spreading like a virus that by nature mutated on infecting each new host. Attempts to deny the gossip gave rise to other, more poisonous rumors. Making use of the most innocent gestures, Perdumes would communicate that he *knew* the very thing no other person should know.

Very soon Perdumes had fabricated a network of correspondences woven from founded and unfounded rumors. Whether out of gratitude, respect or fear, the residents in his building adored him: all collective decisions passed through his hands. His indefatigable mind processed the situation until it hit on the two pillars of Quietism in Motion: the theories of the sword and the tea bag.

The former was based on the equilibrium of unequal things, the distinctive characteristic of a good sword. It may be the blade that cuts, but it's the hilt that is in control. When wielding a samurai sword, in order to obtain horizontal equilibrium, the extended finger must be placed on the juncture of the hilt and the blade. If the finger bears down slightly harder toward the blade, the greater weight of the hilt is magnified and wins the day. And from this came the Perdumesian maxim: cannon fodder should respect the rank of the person who holds the weapon. Hence the Quietism.

The motion came from the tea bag. Perdumes would ceremoniously pour the hot water from his antique porcelain jug into a white cup and slowly remove the tea bag from its paper wrapping, allowing his audience to confirm the absolute transparency of the water. The tea bag was then gradually introduced into the cup at an angle of ninety degrees to the surface of the water. Initially, nothing happened. Then, when the tea could no longer bear the scalding water, it exuded a thin, blackish thread that diffused into the water. Perdumes would accentuate the effect by a series of upward jerks. The tea seeped out evenly in all directions until the correct hue was attained. But if one were to move the bag around without rhyme or reason, what would happen, he would ask rhetorically. You might say, exactly the same, he then quickly replied, yet turbid tea is acidic and doesn't have the same flavor. The motion is necessary, in its proper time and place.

After his informal conquest of the building, Perdumes' foot soldiers went out to spread the word. Secondhand samurai swords began to be found everywhere. Others made their own from what looked like sharpened clubs, thus producing an epidemic of three-legged chairs. At times, the tea was replaced by other herbs: toloache, or devil's weed, diffused like a form of plasma, slowly encapsulating the boiling water. In the end, no one could ever give a precise explanation of what Perdumes was talking about; Quietism in Motion had been born. When a couple of disheveled university types knocked on his door to reprove him, Perdumes knew that his spiritual conquest was complete. It was time to move on to action.

2

Why the hell did I shave when she's said she likes me better with a bit of a beard? Max Michels reproached himself without moving away from the mirror. Did she really say that? Shit, I guess so. It's no big deal, it'll grow back in a few days. A few days? As if you've got much time left, you moron. We'll see how much time I've got. Things are going to be different now. Yeah? If you say so. Good luck with what's left.

By this stage, he'd learnt that the best way to escape from the voices of the Many in his head was to seek a zone of consensus. But those barren wastelands offered only a bitter composure, so instead he dived down into a recapitulation of the events that explained his present dilemma.

He went back to the time when the presidency of Villa Miserias was passed on by means of a procedure that was as opaque as everything around it: the outgoing president consulted the most long-standing families. The succession was so automatic it was boring.

When Selon Perdumes became one of the notables with the right to express an opinion, he cooked up a simple strategy for producing a change of tack: first, he gave his blessing to the heir apparent.

It was never certain if he was aided by luck or surgical calculation, but the candidate in question was Epifanio Buenaventura, who was due to inherit Buildings 17 and 19. According to protocol, the election could not take place before the stipulated lapse for registration. However, on the last day an extremely unlikely candidate put her name down: a woman in her early thirties named Orquídea López. After a brush with radical ideas on a steep downward path, the costs of everyday life had transformed her into a public sector employee. Orquídea was the nearest thing to dissidence Villa Miserias had ever seen: everyone assumed her to have been guilty of the wave of hood ornaments stolen from the most elegant cars on the estate. Her revolutionary fervor fizzled out as her comrades swapped the idea of guns for shoulder pads and Friday night Cuba Libres. Orquídea lost her last illusions when the most extreme member of the clan registered for federal taxes: from that moment she changed into a receptacle in search of defining content. Quietism in Motion appealed to her disillusioned side: it seemed to atomize the weight of life in a social setting and deposit it on the individual. Orquídea was tired of moral vestments that didn't match real human dimensions.

The paradox is that she didn't come from that class of people who have a head start in life. And for this reason she tenaciously clung to each new rung of the ladder she managed to ascend to. She didn't miss a single alteration in the world around her: changes of image, the arrival of new furniture, extravagance at quinceañeras, men going off with younger women. Even things that didn't concern her seemed an affront. Why was everything so easy for some people when it had been so hard for her?

Why did everyone pay the same maintenance costs when they didn't get the same level of service? People who lived nearest the security lodge were better protected; in contrast, others suffered more from the stink of trash. Every month she would make variants of these complaints to the administration office.

When the outstanding interest of her downstairs neighbor's debt was waived so he would pay off what he owed, Perdumes had to take her to his apartment and try to calm her. Of course she was right. The most frustrating thing was that everyone else was blinded by sentimental conformity. Had she noticed the gradual deterioration in Villa Miserias? Oh, yes, Don Selon, but that riffraff get what they deserve. Stupendous! Though it's not really their fault, Orquídea. They've never had it any other way. Oh, I know, but what do I do? Sit here twiddling my thumbs? Of course not, Orquídea. But sudden upheavals are bad for everyone. Don't forget that, bad for everyone. Would you excuse me a moment?

Perdumes returned with a sword and a porcelain jug to explain the details of Quietism in Motion. First, we have to accept things as they really are, not how we'd like them to be. If inequality is inevitable, why not accept that as a point of departure? Oh, I don't know, Don Selon. Where does that leave those of us who started at the bottom? Splendid! That's what I'm getting to. It's the reason why I brought my jug. As you well know, those who make the effort get their reward. Unfortunately, they are always in the minority, and it's not fair that the others should get the same, just because. Let's see, I'm going to ask you a question. Don't you find it beneficial to watch your show-off neighbors going on cruises? It's well known that people better off than ourselves help us to try to improve.

If the carrot is too close to the horse, the animal will stop walking. The problem is that some people think we're all thoroughbreds by right.

The dialogue with Orquídea went on for weeks, moving slowly toward more specific issues. Then Perdumes suddenly, with an air of indifference, asked the question: Why don't you put your name down for the election, Orquídea? Jeez, Don Selon! What election? We all know the same old people appoint the next president. Extraordinary! You're right, but only because we've let them, Orquídea. Have you read the regulations of Villa Miserias? I have. If there's more than one candidate, they organize elections. Hmm, so why has it never happened, Don Selon? Brilliant! For the same reasons we've talked about so often, Orquídea, but I believe an increasing number of residents are opening their eyes. Have you seen whose name they've put forward this time? Yes, that halfwit Epifanio Buenaventura, who can't even talk properly. Incredible! Didn't I tell you, Orquídea? You're ready for action. If you don't mind my saying so, more than a choice, I believe it's a duty.

The young assistant in the administration office suspected something was wrong: Orquídea López didn't fling open the glass door. This time she slipped quietly in and stood motionless in front of his desk, regulations in hand, savoring the moment before the assault. After pinning her victim in his seat with her stare, she announced her intention to register as a candidate. Taken unawares, he began to seek a response among the disorganized papers on the desk, but was unable to come up with anything better than noting her details on a blank sheet to gain time while he consulted his superior. Making an enormous effort to contain her laughter, Orquídea demanded the stamped acknowledgement of receipt she still has framed in the living room of her apartment.

Having closed the office early, the young man telephoned his superior to explain what had happened. An emergency meeting was called and Selon Perdumes was in attendance. So much excitement made Epifanio Buenaventura's tongue even clumsier than usual; the scant hair combed across his crown was beaded with sweat. He gave his father a pleading look in the hope of being able to abandon the race. No one knew quite what to say. They racked their brains in search of a strategy to ensure the victory of Epifanio, that representative of the only way of life they knew, but every word he spoke only sunk them deeper into despondency.

"De thing is dat I don't know de firsht thing about campaignsh."

Defeat was a foregone conclusion. Even Perdumes felt sorry for Buenaventura, and attempted to alleviate his suffering. Thus the regulations that would, from then on, be enforced in political contests in Villa Miserias were created.

3

REGULATIONS FOR THE VILLA MISERIAS
PRESIDENTIAL ELECTIONS

I. IN ORDER TO INTRUDE AS LITTLE AS POSSIBLE INTO THE LIVES OF THE RESIDENTS OF OUR COMMUNITY, ELECTORAL CAMPAIGNS WILL LAST A MAXIMUM OF ELEVEN DAYS.

2. TO GUARANTEE A MINIMUM OF FAIRNESS, ALL RESIDENTS WILL BE CHARGED AN EXTRAORDINARY SUM TO BE SHARED BETWEEN THE CANDIDATES.

3. PRIVATE DONATIONS WILL BE ALLOWED UNDER THE FOLLOWING CONDITIONS: THE AMOUNT AND NAME OF THE DONOR MUST BE DULY REGISTERED WITH THE ADMINISTRATION. THIS INFORMATION WILL THEN BE KEPT IN CONDITIONS OF STRICT PRIVACY SO THAT THE VARIOUS DONATIONS CANNOT INFLUENCE THE ELECTORATE'S DECISION.

4. EACH BUILDING WILL ORGANIZE ITS OWN MEETING TO CHOOSE THE CANDIDATE TO BE GIVEN ITS VOTE. TENANTS MAY ONLY ATTEND THIS MEETING BY PREVIOUS WRITTEN AUTHORIZATION OF THE OWNER OF THE APARTMENT.

5. ANY UNFORESEEN DIFFICULTIES AND THE DUE SANCTIONS FOR VIOLATION OF THE RULES STIPULATED IN THIS DOCUMENT WILL BE RESOLVED BY THE BOARD. THE ELECTORAL POWERS OF THIS BOARD WILL BE PUBLISHED AT THE APPROPRIATE MOMENT.

During the period when this document was being drawn up, several objections were raised and were immediately cut short by Selon Perdumes' alabaster smile. Who's going to want to fork out money for an irritating, shallow spectacle? No price can be put on the right to make decisions. Why are people who rent second-class residents? The vision of the owners is more likely to protect what in reality belongs to us all. What will candidates be able to buy with the private donations? The donations are simply to help the transmission of a message. The residents' consciences aren't for sale. When are we going to decide on the regulations for the intervention of the board? Would you excuse me a moment?

The public reading of the document sank all doubts as a stream of water sucks the spider into its eddy. The faces of all present displayed grave satisfaction; they suspected they had created something that was greater than the sum of its parts. No one in his right mind would dare to question it. Epifanio Buenaventura became unusually fearless:

"And we can convinshe dem dat I'm de besht candidate, can't we?"

Selon Perdumes kept his alabaster smile in check. Quietism in Motion had just cut its first tooth.

4

After confirming yet again that there were no tea bags left in the packet, Max Michels wavered between tearing it to pieces for its insolence and ensuring that he was really alone in the apartment. You only got away with it because she was running late, you miserable sod. And what if she finds there's no tea for her breakfast? Better buy another packet before going and committing the supreme idiocy of becoming a candidate. I've got better things to do, she can buy her own fucking tea if she likes it so much. Huh, you're all balls when she's not around. Let's see if it's the same tonight.

At the level temporarily reserved for what he understood as his Himself, Max wondered if he really was about to add his name to the list of previous Epifanio Buenaventuras. Thinking it over, registering for the election was an enormously arrogant act. What did he hope to gain by it? Before being obliged to conclude that what he was searching for was to be found somewhere else, he preferred to finish off his interior monologue. Better to stick with the dreaded Epifanio than see yourself turned into him.

The residents of Villa Miserias reacted to the news of the electoral reforms with indifference. Few of them showed much inclination to follow the spectacle closely, but it soon became apparent that this was an advantage for the candidates. Even Buenaventura and his team realized that hardly anyone had what it took to form a sound opinion: the challenge was to learn to speak the dialect of the guts.

Even though—for obvious reasons—there was no question about the result of the contest, Orquídea floored her opponent with a speech that, if more abstract, also managed to strike the simplest of chords. In contrast to Epifanio, who promised to sort out the plumbing and construct more play areas for the children, Orquídea sketched the porous outlines of a new life: the life they each deserved. She spent a whole night adapting one of her former mantras to fit the occasion. Using the same essential elements, she tweaked them to appeal to the dormant aspirations of her voters:

SINCE NEEDS ARE DICTATED BY ABILITIES, VOTE FOR ORQUÍDEA LÓPEZ

Every apartment in Villa Miserias received Orquídea López's campaign leaflet, which basically asked the residents why their futures should be limited by other people's aspirations. To illustrate her case, she used the example of Chona, the elderly lady in Building 23, whose putrid pension barely met the needs of herself and her beloved canaries. Orquídea's leaflet demonstrated that if she didn't have to to pay the communal water charge, Chona would be able paint the rusty cages in which her only companions lived, and buy special food to make their plumage glossier. And neither was there any reason why she should pay the same for the repairs to the front door of the building when she clearly used it less than the neighboring families.

As Selon Perdumes' outstanding pupil, Orquídea made use of the storytelling tradition to reinforce her message: the reverse side of her leaflet recounted her personal version of a fable clearly demonstrating the benefits of the adage that the whole is never more than the sum of its separate parts. She explained to the residents that the writer of these words was one of the first people to become aware of the serious error of talking to humans about what they should be, instead of what they really are. However, the fable needed updating since hers was not an age in which innocent little bees fitted the bill. The new metaphor had to be omnivorous, must have to fight for its life before going out to face the world, and must even be the enemy of its own siblings. Orquídea was fascinated to learn of a creature that was in the habit of throwing itself to the ground, its tongue hanging out and its eyes turned upwards, so that when its adversary—taking the animal for dead—relaxed its guard, it was able to flee. Without such cunning, the young animal would not even reach maturity as the mother only fed and protected two thirds of each litter, so that the least able were even spared the suffering of going through life, dragging their shortfalls along behind them. Orquídea was overcome by an ecstasy of inspiration and put the finishing touches to her electoral leaflet with a speed that was surprising, even for her.

THE FABLE OF THE OPOSSUMS

IN A POSSUM'S NEST
THERE'S NO PLACE FOR FOWL
THOSE WHO CAN'T GAIN THE BREAST
HAVE TO THROW IN THE TOWEL

THE BEES THAT GIVE HONEY
HAVE GONE UNDERNEATH
STORIES THAT ARE SUNNY
ARE NO USE TO THE THIEF

ENOUGH OF FALSE SERMONS!
CAN'T YOU SEE THERE'S NO BALM?
WHY WISH FOR DELUSIONS?
THEY CAN ONLY DO HARM

WRONG MAKES FOR RIGHT
OH FABLES OF YOUTH!
WRONG BECOMES MIGHT
AND THAT IS THE TRUTH

THE INDIVIDUAL IS KING
THE GROUP IS PURE SCHLOCK
NO COMPETITION WITHOUT SWINDLING
WHY IS THAT A SHOCK?

LAWS PROTECT THE ELITE
IT'S TIME TO TURN ON THE LIGHT
WHY TAKE A BACK SEAT?
JUDGE THE POOR IN THEIR PLIGHT

EACH TO HIS SORORITY
ACCRUING HIS WEALTH
BLESSED BE POVERTY
LET'S DRINK TO ITS HEALTH

IF WE WANT TO KEEP OUR BIRTHRIGHT
LET'S FORGET SAYING THANKS
SQUARE UP FOR THE PRIZE FIGHT
WE'RE BREAKING THE RANKS

VOTE FOR ME: I AM YOU.

The residents agreed: the time had come to leave paternalism behind. Forty-four buildings decided to come of age. By a majority vote, Orquídea López became the first female president-elect. The process gave rise to another local tradition: Juana Mecha had been head of the Villa Miserias cleaning staff for years. The sound of her broom was an unofficial signal for the start of each working day. She was so regular in her habits that mothers knew if they were late dropping the kids off at school by her location when they left the building. She was also given to expressing herself in enigmatic maxims, most of which were ignored by the people to whom they were addressed.

In order to avoid the rush hour on public transport, Orquídea would set out for the office early, so she was always the first to leave. Her automatic "Good morning, Señora Mecha" was returned each day by some snigger-inducing phrase. On one of the days when Orquídea was still hesitating over whether or not to sign up as a candidate, her greeting produced a cryptic barb: "If you put everything in the wash together, the clothes lose their color." Orquídea had spent the whole morning trying to decipher her words. When she decided on an interpretation, she knew what to do next and hurried to inform Perdumes that she accepted his challenge. She was completely unaware she'd inaugurated the strict custom of consulting the beige-uniformed oracle.

5

Looking back on it, Max Michels realized that Orquídea López's historical legacy had been, first, to act as a lever in the destruction of the existing structures, and then to be a slightly inefficient steamroller. She had smoothed the path for Villa Miserias to leave Villa Miserias behind and become Villa Miserias.

Her term in office inaugurated the reign of quantity: the will to count everything. She had promised a form of justice tailored to fit each individual's specific dimensions. This required the residents to provide information that could be statistically represented: the hours of sunlight entering through each window; the number of minutes they spent sitting on the communal benches; their proximity to the green areas that purified the air. A coefficient was created to measure the benefit each individual obtained from the collective services, including such variables as the frequency with which the barrier was raised to let cars through, usage of the entry phone system and even the amount of time the lobby of each building remained dirty due to the order in which they were swept. The residents began to view one other in terms of their numerical values. The premise involved putting a value on the cost-benefit ratio of each and every soul living on the estate.

Orquídea's other great legacy was the transformation of the security force. The guards were used to busting their breeches watching television in the security booth: they didn't even have to shift from their chair to raise the barrier; the rounds they made of the estate were more a matter of stretching their legs. Orquídea started by putting them into uniform: the tight-fitting black suits and berets gave them an air more comical than threatening. There was an attempt to have them armed with pistols, but money was short and, in any case, they didn't know how to use them. Pepper spray became the preferred option. The first week, two guards ended up in the sick bay with their faces burning from the effects of the new security device, one due to a practical joke played by a colleague, and the other from having pointed the can in the wrong direction while testing how far the spray reached.

They had soon caught two petty criminals trying to burgle an apartment in Building 24. The circumstances couldn't have been more compromising: the petty thieves had broken in in broad daylight, armed with a screwdriver, stinking of Resistol glue, and had gotten stuck in the internal wiring duct while making their escape. It was more a rescue attempt than an arrest. They were left sitting for hours, in full view, surrounded by a patrol of the reinvigorated security squad. The verdict was almost unanimous: the residents felt safer after the professionalization of the forces of law and order.

To mark the end of Orquídea's term in office, Perdumes organized a farewell dinner. He gave her a token of appreciation, specially commissioned for the occasion: a bronze sculpture on a marble base, with a gold plaque inscribed with Orquídea's name and the dates. The statue was of an ambiguously sculpted man, leaning forwards, in a position of great strain. With both hands, he was pushing an enormous sphere. The man represented movement. The sphere, impassivity. The New was still far off but Orquídea López had been the piston chosen to set the ball rolling toward it.

6

During the following periods, the outline of Villa Miserias' electoral ritual was more clearly defined. By means of signals and coded language, Perdumes encouraged or frustrated aspirations. He investigated the most intimate affairs of the candidates. It soon became obvious that the least fruitful way to participate was by demonstrating any intention to do so. Those who put themselves forward independently were subtly destroyed. Rumors would begin to circulate about their habits and proclivities: one left his dog's urine lying on the living-room floor for days; another had borrowed money from his mother-in-law to get a hair transplant. The rumors were never completely destructive: they were warnings about what would happen if the person in question didn't desist. He should go about his normal life and simply wait for the appropriate signal.

A dichotomous formula came to be the norm. Its plurality was based on a moving axis, situated more or less halfway between the two candidates. Generally, the contrasts were basic: man/woman, young/old, good-looking/plain. In this way, an impression of difference was transmitted. The reality was that the following two-year periods were almost interchangeable: the same person in a different format. The estate was on a steady course.

At the end of their term, they all received the same statue, with slight updates. The hill on which the figure stood went progressively upward and the sphere advanced a little farther. It was a matter of creating sufficient inertia for it to move unaided, flattening every obstacle that came in its path.

7

The day he decided to stand as a candidate, Max Michels dressed slowly and deliberately. While he was searching every corner of the apartment for his socks, he came across a thick, leather-bound volume on the study table. The night before, he'd been consulting it until the early hours, unable to focus. Irrespective of the content, the shadowy outline of a female figure would begin to form on the paper. Although Max had attempted to quash it by turning the page, each one seemed identical to the last, and the form had gathered new strength to return to torment him.

He aborted his exhaustive search for the socks when he noticed they were in his hand. While he was putting them on, he tried to return to the world of shadows, but a silent voice cut in: Shut up, you moron! Better get a move on before you change your mind. Or don't you have the balls?

It was no moment for confronting the Many, so he opted for taking refuge in continuing his recollection of the situation he'd so often gone through in the past. He was well aware that the beginning of Villa Miserias' contemporary history was marked by the sacrifice of Severo Candelario, the only previous person to register his candidacy without Selon Perdumes' permission. It could even be said everything that had happened before consisted of the construction of a two-level altar. One cosmetic and visible; the other deep and intangible.

The former involved the introduction of the relevant modifications. The majority of buildings already had discussion groups on Quietism in Motion, but the most stalwart had taken things to levels never imagined by its creator, particularly in relation to the degree of scientific precision involved. To differentiate themselves from the many other failed ideologues, they clothed the theory in an almost irrefutable dogma: mathematics. They understood that if one starts from the appropriate assumptions, it is possible to come to the most implacable conclusions. Their minds were like scrap metal balers fed by a particular configuration of reality, and compressing it into a series of theorems that, in essence, proved the same thing: individual destiny can be based on nothing other than a person's abilities. Hypnotized by the demonstrable, they didn't realize that their path transformed the very conception of ability. They were like children who create imaginary friends only to then blindly follow their commands. By means of indecipherable algebraic progressions, they reified the virtue of a lack of scruples. From then onward, those who put their own interests first would be the ones to stand out from the crowd. Mathematics expunged any last vestige of guilt. In fact, they turned it on its head: the greater the determination to excel, the greater the benefit to those others. The new common goal was to ensure the cake continued to grow forever. Talking about sharing it out became a poor-taste anachronism.

The process started with the individualization of the service charges, calculated on the base of the coefficient. The apartments on upper floors paid a higher percentage as it required more energy to pump the water from the cistern up there, the gas had to run through more yards of piping, and they were less afflicted by the racket of the daily bustle down below. The coefficient also addressed the other factors mentioned above, thus condensing the defining characteristics of each person with respect to his peers. Rather than displeasing them, the level of the coefficient became a status symbol. It was not uncommon to see residents open their statements in front of others, arrogantly displaying feigned surprise at the exorbitant rate they were being charged.

The next step was to modify the weighting of each residential unit. If a building contained people of greater value, it was only appropriate that their vote should have more impact. A mathematical model demonstrated that this led to maximization of the well-being of the whole. Despite the fact that lip service was paid to the normal procedure, in reality a handful of buildings made the decisions.

The reforms to the regulations and perception of the estate were in the public domain. Anyone could find out about them. However, another, parallel movement also took place: underground and more expansive. Selon Perdumes called it "poetic mortgaging." With his small initial capital, he was able to get his hands on several apartments, strategically placed throughout the estate. He negotiated directly with the owners. The tenants only discovered what was happening when they received a jubilant letter informing them of two things: first, Perdumes was the new owner of the apartment; second, their lives were about to change. For a modest deposit and absurdly low monthly repayments, they could buy the apartment and not have to go on throwing away money on rent. They didn't have enough for the down payment? They could borrow that too. The letter was a textual version of Selon Perdumes' alabaster smile.

There was a stampede of tenants wanting to take advantage of the opportunity. With the down payments, Perdumes bought more apartments, some of them also on credit. Given the number, he negotiated interest rates that were lower than he charged, and so he was able to pay off his loans with the radiant new owners' monthly contributions. In time, a large portion of Villa Miserias was involved in the scheme. Selon Perdumes gloated. His role as an intermediary multiplied his fortune and, despite not being the outright owner of the apartments, he did possess something more valuable: the dreams of the residents of Villa Miserias.

8

There were two buildings that, for very different reasons, clearly stood out from the others. The reason for the conspicuousness of the first was grounded in the yearning for prosperity, which was producing increasing amounts of garbage. The truck picked it up every morning but, even so, a new accumulation was continuously piling up in the rusty containers. The residents of the building adjoining these containers were convinced they were unsanitary: the smell permeated everywhere, throughout the whole day. Not even the lowest interest rates could persuade anyone to buy those apartments. People considered it beneath their dignity to own something in what became known as Building B, and moved out at the first opportunity. Selon Perdumes decided to change his strategy.

At that time, Villa Miserias' employees tended to live in distant, cheerless communities. They left their houses before the sun had risen and returned under the shelter of the clouded night skies. In addition, the employees often had to work overtime, to the extent that, on occasions, they would get home in time to have dinner, take a nap, and shower before setting out again. This situation was a headache for the administrative department of the estate. The lightest traffic jams caused the employees to arrive late; they were reluctant to work beyond their shift; they were constantly suffering nervous illnesses and their uniforms were always sweaty from being canned up in the public transportation. Selon Perdumes burst into a board meeting with a solution.

Building B was by then almost empty. Perdumes had been gradually rehousing the residents; a few others had moved out of the estate. With the appropriate redesign, he suggested, Villa Miserias' workers could live there. It was a delicate situation; they needed to tread carefully. But also be firm. In order to clearly differentiate Building B, it would be painted light ochre. The fittings would be replaced by ones of poorer quality and taste.

The trickiest problem was yet to be resolved: how would the workers pay to live there? He wasn't thinking of offering his mortgage scheme to more than two of them: Juana Mecha and Joel Taimado, the boss of the Black Paunches, as everyone now called the security squad. Perdumes handed a copy of his proposal to the board, as a mere formality before it was announced.

9

PROPOSAL FOR ACCOMMODATING WORKERS IN BUILDING B

1. OUR ESTATE SUFFERS THE UNDESIRABLE
   CONSEQUENCES OF THE DISTANT HOUSING OF OUR
   WORKERS. FOR THIS REASON, WE ARE OFFERING THEM
   THE CHANCE TO RENT IN THE SO-CALLED BUILDING
   B, AS SOON AS THE APPROPRIATE ADAPTATIONS HAVE
   BEEN MADE, THE COST OF WHICH WILL BE BORNE BY
   THE ADMINISTRATION.

2. OUR COMMUNITY HAS MADE A GREAT EFFORT TO
   BREAK WITH IDEAS THAT HINDER ITS MOVEMENT
   TOWARD THE FUTURE. WE CANNOT EXEMPT THE
   WORKERS FROM THE PRINCIPLES BY WHICH WE NOW
   LIVE, NEITHER FOR THEIR OWN BENEFIT NOR OURS:
   FOR FINANCIAL, ETHICAL, AND MORAL REASONS,
   IT IS IMPERATIVE THAT THEY FULLY COVER THE
   CORRESPONDING COSTS OF THEIR NEW HOUSING.

3. IN RECOGNITION OF THEIR FINANCIAL MEANS, THEY
   WILL BE OFFERED A MIXED SCHEME THAT WILL
   MEET THE NEEDS OF BOTH PARTIES, AND COVER
   THE MONTHLY MORTGAGE PAYMENTS OF THE
   APARTMENTS.

   3.1. THE ADMINISTRATION WILL DIRECTLY RETAIN A
        THIRD OF EACH WAGE. THIS SUM WILL BE PUT
        TOWARD THE MONTHLY PAYMENTS.

   3.2. THE WORKING DAY WILL BE EXTENDED BY TWO

HOURS. THE ENSUING INCREASE IN PRODUCTIVITY WILL ALLOW A NUMBER OF WORKERS TO BE LAID OFF. THE SAVINGS OCCASIONED WILL BE PUT TOWARD THE MONTHLY PAYMENTS.

3.3. IN ORDER TO MAKE SAVINGS IN THE COST OF FOOD, FROM NOW ON RESIDENTS WILL BE ASKED TO TAKE THEIR LEFTOVERS TO THE CANTEEN, TO BE EATEN BY THE EMPLOYEES. THE SAVINGS OCCASIONED WILL BE PUT TOWARD THE MONTHLY PAYMENTS.

3.4. ADDITIONAL ECONOMIES WILL OCCUR IN RELATION TO MEDICAL COSTS AND SICK, LEAVE SINCE LENGTHY TRAVEL TIMES CAUSE A VARIETY OF AILMENTS AMONG OUR EMPLOYEES. THE SAVINGS OCCASIONED WILL BE PUT TOWARD THE MONTHLY PAYMENTS.

4. IN ORDER TO ASSIST THE DOMESTIC ECONOMIES OF OUR WORKERS, IN ANTICIPATION OF POSSIBLE POOR BUDGETING, MECHANISMS FOR REGULATING BASIC SERVICES WILL BE SET UP. IN THIS WAY, THEIR COEFFICIENTS WILL NOT EXCEED A QUARTER OF THEIR INCOME.

5. WHEN THE MORTGAGES HAVE BEEN PAID OFF, THE BOARD WILL DECIDE ON THE RELEVANT PROCEDURE. UNTIL SUCH TIME EACH APARTMENT WILL REMAIN IN THE NAME OF THE ORIGINAL OWNER.

The first person to receive the proposal was Juana Mecha. Broom in hand, she enthusiastically exclaimed, "The mules will get fewer beatings," which escalated to a euphoric "Property will make us free" when Perdumes notified her she was to become a homeowner. In contrast, Joel Taimado's response was the characteristic "Uh-huh" with which he impassively assented to everything from behind the dark glasses covering his face down to his three-whisker mustache.

The workers very soon began to move in. Overflowing boxes wound around with tightly knotted rope, tables with legs that didn't match, and grannies in wheelchairs colonized the ochre building. No one had foreseen the size of the families. In some cases, an apartment was divided between two employees, in a temporary decree that became permanent. The regulated lighting coated every corner with its subdued yellow; the cap on the use of water left more than one person covered in soap mid-shower. In the staff canteen, a certain amount of initial disgust had to be overcome when it came to the banquet of leftovers, which sometimes included half-eaten chicken legs, soup ready-seasoned with lemon and hot sauce, rock-hard beans mixed with rice, and cheese. Some preferred to accustom themselves to cold food as a means of neutralizing the envious glances directed at those who managed to receive protein. To compensate for the drop in wages, several employees moonlighted, doing the odd jobs the owners of the apartments preferred to avoid. The project was pronounced a success. The workers had decent housing and labor relations improved notably. The members of the residential colony got much more for the same money. It was a fine adjustment of the gears that drove Villa Miserias.

10

The other building to escape the omnipresent gray was farthest from Plaza del Orden, the social and geographical center of Villa Miserias. Despite being on the margins, it immediately caught the eye. The two façades visible from within the estate displayed an intervention by a young artist, Pascual Bramsos: a paint-rollered giant composed of hundreds of silhouettes of miniscule men. The figure was in free fall, having received a blow from an abacus thrown by a chameleon brandishing a catapult above its head. Bramsos was intelligent enough to start with the colossus, so the board members thought the allegory of union it transmitted funny. Then, working the whole night, he created the homicidal chameleon. It was well before noon when the order to return the building to its gray normality was issued. Bramsos armed the neighbors, and a hail of eggs rained down on the man charged with the eradication of the work. He only got as far as castrating the giant with a brushstroke to the groin. The author of the work decided to leave it that way as a finishing touch. Perdumes used to amuse himself looking out on it each morning when he got out of bed.

The most eloquent thing that could be said about the estate's residents was that the sum of their parts exceeded, in every sense, their whole. Having pursued imperfect Utopias for some years, they tended to air their bureaucratic frustrations by giving their opinion on anything and everything, just to have something new to spout off about. After Building B, they started on the one with lowest overall coefficient: its influence was close almost non-existent. It was also the only one to have three separate residents' groups with pretensions to legitimacy, but which never sent delegates to the general assembly.

11

Such was, in broad outline, the general panorama of Villa Miserias when the schoolmaster Severo Candelario became the hinge that would close the door to the past and allow in the whirlwind of dust still blowing at the time of Max Michels' decision. Before leaving his apartment, he looked contemptuously at his friend Pascual Bramsos' painting hanging on the wall. For a moment he believed the frame was shaking, that it was trying to detach itself, as if catapulted by some irresistible force. Before this could happen, he took hold of it with both hands and carefully placed it on the floor. For the last time, he stood directly in front of the phrase written on the wall, hidden by the work. The fact was, Max was about to take a quantum leap toward discovering just how big he was.

As he set out, Max weighed up the situation, taking into consideration the reasons that, in their moment, had been behind Severo Candelario's actions. In comparison to Max, who was aware—precisely thanks to Candelario's misfortune—of the insurrection involved in his decision, the teacher had lacked the necessary guile to understand the magnitude of his actions. Candelario had been able to appreciate the texture of the details but not the whole picture. He'd seen the chance to add his voice to something that worked, and so had decided to take an active part in it. His enthusiasm had prevented him from correctly interpreting the obstacles put in his way when he asked for the registration form, or the fact that he was the only male candidate without a mustache in living memory. His campaign had been anything but radical; he helped carry the old ladies' shopping bags, asked the children about their favorite superheroes. At several years' distance, the outcome of the story rested on a single detail, his electoral slogan: "With your constant help we'll get better and better." It was based on pedagogic principles such as the importance of each cell playing its part for the good of the whole and the notion that untiring repetition leads to perfection. Without realizing, he was attacking the very foundations of Quietism in Motion.

Candelario was in the habit of taking things calmly. Years of teaching had taught him that the task of molding souls required perseverance, a quality clearly expressed by his most treasured possession: a growing collection of yearly albums of black and white photos. On each odd-numbered page, a photograph was pasted in exactly the same place. Always the same image, taken every day at 7:19 in the morning, from the same angle. Even when he caught pneumonia, he managed to persuade the doctor to allow him his daily expedition to photograph the tree growing in the green area behind his building.

He had begun to portray the tree when it was still a timid shoot. With the passage of time, it became a proud willow, weeping majestically in all directions. If adjacent photos were compared, it was impossible to see any differences. But then, with an expression of childish glee, Candelario would take the album in his hands and rapidly flick through the pages. The metamorphosis of the willow caused him a spasm of tenderness. With ant-like diligence, Candelario used to say, his camera had captured the unfolding of the tree's soul. After taking his photograph, he would stand, rapturously contemplating the willow, hunting for a tangible difference from that other tree, portrayed the day before. His perpetual failure to find one left him in ecstasy. Then he would set off for school, ready to add a pinch of education to the young minds in his charge.

He was a man of singular ideas. After the years spent studying the great masters, what could he say that was new? It seemed to him blasphemy even to attempt it; the future was set in stone. This was the basis of his decision to join the march of Villa Miserias' progress. It wasn't that he considered that progress to be either appropriate or desirable, but rather it was as definitive as the development of the willow he venerated and he thought it a duty to add his modest abilities to the project. Without any greater pretensions than being a single heartbeat more in the pacemaker determining the pulse of his community, Candelario put down his name for the Villa Miserias presidential election. When he was leaving the administrative office, his candidacy duly registered, Juana Mecha welcomed him to the contest with, "Skinned chickens had feathers once." Candelario took this as an unmistakably good omen.

Neither Perdumes nor the members of the board feared for a moment that Severo Candelario would be able to beat the usual pair of throwaway candidates. They initially took his registration as an act of insolence. However, when they heard his slogan and gauged his potential for causing a breach, they resolved to destroy him without mercy.

"With your constant help, we'll get better and better" constituted a threat on a number of fronts. The word "help" had been exiled from the collective lexicon. It was an anachronism. Time and again, it had been proven how useless it was to pull someone out of the swamp when he was determined to be there. The slime ended by soiling even the rescuer. This couldn't be allowed in a community of high-flying individuals. Moreover, "we'll get better and better" suggested a collective enterprise. The effort needed to get across the message of the individual's responsibility in his destiny had been enormous... It was heresy to allude to their general impact. Candelario was a puppet of himself who could be ignored. But not his slogan. That same night, they asked Joel Taimado to start proceedings in the process of destroying the schoolmaster.

Candelario was so absorbed in his new mission that he didn't notice his neighbors' strange glances or the almost undetectable pauses before they returned his greetings. It was his wife who first made him understand something was wrong. On the second floor of their building, a young insurance salesman shared an apartment with a colleague. Almost every morning, he would take the same minibus as Señora Candelario to the metro station on their way to work. He began to leave a few minutes later, just in time for Clara Candelario to see him get to the main road as she set out through the asphyxiating exhaust fumes of the pedestrian walkway. One day, to clear up her concerns, she decided to wait for him. During their entire walk, the young man spoke on his phone to a client he'd woken up to remind that the policy on his old scooter was due to run out in four months. Once aboard the minibus, he refused to let Señora Candelario pay for them both—something they normally took turns in doing—despite the fact that he was clinging onto an external grab rail with just one foot on the first step. With his free hand, he managed to pass his crumpled bill to the driver, who was annoyed at having to give him change. Each time the bus stopped, he would get off to let new passengers on, without losing his place. When they arrived at the metro, he was the first to disembark and immediately disappeared into the station entrance. His neighbor saw no more of him.

Señora Candelario lost no time in discovering what was going on. The following morning, she planted herself in front of Juana Mecha and asked if she'd heard anything. Without in the least diminishing the trsssh trsssh of her broom, the latter simply responded: "People don't like being reminded they're people." She pointed the handle of her boom to the façade of the building where someone had written the piece of graffiti Candelario would see repeated ad nauseum during the following days: "Candelario, you cunt, who are you going to humiliate next?" Taimado's squad had done its job. The handwritten report detailed an incident the teacher thought had been long forgotten.

The official letter informing him he was to be relocated to a different school had stated that his only sin was naiveté. And possibly overzealousness. Each year a call went out for the Children's Science Olympics, an event the authorities of the state primary school where Candelario worked as a fifth-grade teacher mostly ignored. In the year of the scandal, Candelario had among his students a very bright girl with a great talent for abstract thought. It was she who had brought the competition to Candelario's attention. He began to pay her more attention in class, working with her on specifically designed tasks. As the difficulty of these tasks increased, the girl always rose to the challenge. Candelario put the case before the headmaster, who—after having made sure it wouldn't involve any additional effort on his part—agreed to the teacher's proposal: during the remaining month, the girl could stay behind for a couple of hours each day to prepare for the competition. The next step was to obtain the family's permission.

The best procedure would have been to get this from the mother. The problem was that her job as a secretary prevented her accompanying her two children, so that it was their grandmother who took them to school each morning and collected them afterward. Even though Candelario's proposal would mean taking the boy home and then returning for his elder sister, the grandmother signed the authorization without hesitation. Candelario promised to bring an extra sandwich each day so the child would not go hungry.

The children's father had given up work at a very young age due to an accident in the laundry where he was working: he'd lost an arm in a supersonic rotary dryer while trying to demonstrate to a workmate there was no great risk involved in placing it there. The proprietors of the business had given him a modest payoff in order to avoid a lawsuit that was, in the end, completely groundless. From that time on, he'd spent his days at home, drinking in front of the television. His evenings alternated between episodes of violent behavior and yearning monologues related to the days when he'd been a whole man.

His children did their best to avoid him. Happily, he didn't even notice the eldest wasn't getting home from school until late afternoon. The dispute began during the week before the completion, while she was going over her exercises one night. The father staggered into her room to ask what the hell she was doing at that hour. No point in working hard just to get screwed like him. The child kept her eyes down. She attempted to defend herself from his invective by solving the problem with a trembling hand. The father tore the page from her notebook and left the room muttering incoherent insults. The child's grandmother came out and he pushed her against the wall with his remaining arm. He then sat in the kitchen to finish off his plastic bag of pulque in giant gulps. Later, when the children and the old lady were deep asleep, it was his wife's turn. She tried to control the explosion by explaining that the girl was preparing for a competition. Her teacher had chosen her and no one else. He couldn't give a fuck. What did those frigging old ladies think? That they were better than him because they could ride a bicycle through the park? They were only good for one thing. His daughter wasn't taking part in any competition.

His ban had little weight. First, because, by then, he had no practical authority. For his wife, he was like one of those intoxicated prophets of doom who shout in the streets, under the effects of a solvent-soaked rag. What's more, he wouldn't remember the episode the following day. His mornings were hostage to the hangovers that awaited the eggs his mother-in-law prepared for breakfast.

The tragedy was that the child had heard it all. Her mind paid no attention to the actual words and only processed what was not said: her dad had lost an arm and it was her fault. She stealthily hurried to her closet, being careful not to wake her grandmother or brother—with whom she'd shared a bed her whole life—took a plush turtle out of the plastic bag where it lived, and went back to bed, lying as near the edge as she could. She spent the rest of the night retching up acidic spume into the bag. In the morning, she got up early to rinse the bag out, but no longer had the strength to hide her trembling, the cold sweats and fever. Her grandmother put a damp towel on her head before taking her brother to school. The girl closed her eyes when she heard her father's unsteady steps in the passage. She might as well not have bothered. He did nothing more than grab hold of the doorframe and then continue to the kitchen to sprawl in a chair and await his food.

On the third day of his pupil's absence, Candelario begun to worry. At the close of classes, he asked the grandmother if he could accompany her home to see how the girl was doing. The elderly lady thought that was fine: she was delighted to be able to talk nonstop the whole way and slightly exaggerated her arthritic gait so the teacher would take her arm when they crossed road junctions. As they were nearing the dirt track where the family lived, they saw the girl playing with her dolls outside the house. Her grandmother's shout brought her back to reality. When she realized who was walking beside her, she ran back inside. The schoolmaster picked up her two rag dolls before going into the kitchen.

"Who the hell's this jerk and what's he doing here?" was the father's greeting to his mother-in-law.

"A very good afternoon to you, sir. I'm Severo Candelario, your daughter's teacher. Delighted to meet you. It's just a few days to the Science Olympiad and I wanted to see how…"

"My daughter's not taking part in any competition. Get the fuck out and leave us in peace."

"Sir, forgive the impertinence, but please allow me to tell you your daughter has studied hard and is very excited about the Olympiad."

"Listen, you bastard, no one makes me look small in my own house."

"Would it be asking too much for me to at least say hello to her?"

"Why the hell should you worry about us?"

"Sir, with all respect, it's a good opportunity for your daughter. If she wins the Olympiad she can travel and get a scholarship."

On hearing this last remark, the father lunged at Candelario. The teacher and the dolls leapt to one side and their aggressor tripped on a chair leg. He was unable to put his single arm out in time to save himself and his face smashed into the edge of the kitchen sink. The girl heard the noise and came in to find her teacher attempting to help her father to stand up. Seeing him there, his left eye closed and bloody, she gave such a shriek that the teacher's reflex action was to let the victim fall again to attend to the child, who only stopped screaming long enough to take a breath and start again. The grandmother took her to her bedroom. Candelario attempted again to assist the father, who, in an effort to clean himself, had gotten blood all over his face. He lashed out one last time, with an accompanying stream of insults. The schoolmaster understood that it was time to throw in the towel. He managed to mumble, "I'm extremely sorry," before hurrying out of the family home, consoled by the two sad rag dolls he still keeps as a souvenir of the only stain on his record.

Perdumes planted the story on a few fertile tongues. It immediately put out roots in multiple directions. In one version, Candelario had forced the girl to bring him a steak and cheese sandwich every day. In another, he'd tied the invalid father's remaining arm and one of his legs behind his back. It was the most widely broadcast version that broke Candelario: he'd touched the grandmother and the girl in inappropriate ways, obliging them to carry out the fantasies he mimed with the rag dolls.

The haggard teacher abandoned the campaign without giving formal notification. He was so depressed by the silent disdain of his neighbors that he practically never left his refuge, except to take his daily photo of the tree. And then came the final insult. On the same day as it was announced that the winner of the election was one of the two usual faces—Candelario would go down in history as the only candidate not even to win in his own building—a handwritten circular, without any official signature, was slipped under his front door. It stated that the tree in the green area behind Building 23 was a threat to the safety of the residents and so would be immediately felled. One member of the condominium was required to supervise the team of technicians who would carry out the task. The board was notifying Severo Candelario that he had been assigned this responsibility. He was to present himself in the green area at 7:19 the following morning to undertake this task.

Candelario turned up a few of minutes early to take his farewell photo. Taimado's Black Paunches, dressed up as tree surgeons for the occasion, were ruthlessly punctual. Their electric saws were indistinguishable from their twisted grins. The schoolmaster signed the order unleashing the carnage and they inexpertly began lop the defenseless tree, brutally attacking even the fallen branches, brandishing their saws like obese ninjas finishing off the enemy. The trunk was attacked from several angles. It was hours before they managed to penetrate it, but when the tree was unable to hold out any longer, irregularly shaped chunks began to tumble down. As darkness fell—Candelario had not even moved when the Black Paunches had interrupted their work to eat their usual leftovers—they called it a day, leaving just a few inches of the base, scarred by the teeth of the saws. Candelario didn't notice when the last of the saws was switched off; he could still hear the roar in his head when Clara finally came to take his hand and lead him back to their apartment.

The schoolmaster continued his usual routine. Every morning at 7:19, he would go out to take a photo of the mutilated trunk that would never again grow. He continued to fill albums, continued to flick the pages for visitors. It was now an ode to the decomposition of matter. After his retirement, he would spend hours sitting on his bench, mentally visualizing every detail of his tree. He was never alone; the two tattered rag dolls, by this time without eyes or hair, accompanied him. Severo Candelario became a melancholy statue symbolizing a remote era, almost totally erased from Villa Miserias' collective memory.

12

And what if they heap shit on me too?

Yeah, you bastard. But would it be any worse than this?

Stop talking, you jerk. Just go put your name down. Get it over and fucking done with.

Shit! There she is talking to Perdumes. That great asshole's dazzling her with his smile.

Sure it was really them?

Positive. I'd better get a move on and stop imagining all this trash.

Imagining trash? If you say so. We're always here, ready for any eventuality.

13

It was also a breach for Perdumes, a signal that the time had come to close the polygon, so that all its points led to the same place. The bulldozers arrived and with them the dust. The dust that, from then onward, would so thickly coat the existence of Villa Miserias that the inhabitants only noticed it when it wasn't there. Outside the estate, they found breathing a strange experience, as if something were missing, until they returned to the customary dose of irritation the air administered to their lungs.

His plan to limit the horizon began with territorial expansion: Perdumes acquired an enormous vacant lot adjoining the estate. The founders of Villa Miserias had, in their day, met with a complex ownership regime that had made any form of financial transaction impossible. But Perdumes knew who to talk to and how much to offer. A solemn ceremony was organized to inaugurate the works, during which Perdumes' alabaster smile hit the intervening wall without shaking it, signifying the beginning of the future.

After the demolition of the wall, the present-day limits of Villa Miserias were traced out. With the machinery came the hands needed for the construction of the future. The plot was to be fitted out as a commercial zone with office space. The Villa Miserians would soon be able to realize their most hidden fantasies. Up to that moment, the reach of Quietism in Motion had been limited by the rigidity of its structure, which made it hard to separate the residents by value. From that moment a reverse order process began: Perdumes had traced out the course on which the tide of those with the possibility of grasping a lifejacket would travel.

The already successful financial engineering scheme was set in motion again. In theory, every inhabitant of Villa Miserias had the chance to own his own business: in reality only a few would. The bottleneck was formed by the residents themselves, draped in the material of their specific capabilities and ambitions. Those interested had to put an ear to the chest of the community to learn to hear the pulse of its desires. However, it was good news for everyone: those of limited vision could be employed as assistants, checkout operators, waiters, guards, janitors, and so on. The outside world was no longer beyond the confines of Villa Miserias.

The outer shell was quickly constructed. A concrete monstrosity, hygienic and functional. The interior spaces were also soon occupied by a range of outlets catering for everything from the most essential needs to those no one had ever suspected to exist.

One of the more successful cases catered to the youngest residents. It offered items for the amusement of children, including rattles, soft toys, and construction kits, but also strollers. Each of its articles was adorned with a glowing screen; interspersed between the cartoons and children's movies shown there were commercials made by the store itself. This promoted family harmony since the children could spend hours sitting in front of the screen, their parents frequently watching with them. The children demanded the movie of their favorite bear, which they watched on the belly of a toy bear, along with the commercials in which the bear expressed itself happy to be their friend. Villa Miserias' children would grow up in the shelter of the magical worlds contained in their toys. Their parents gladly forked out the cash in exchange for the free time it bought them.

In addition to the stores, not-for-profit organizations also sprung up. A group of refined ladies launched a cultural center called Leonardo RU, inspired by a new vision: they were tired of the arts being monopolized by a pedantic elite. Their project offered the ordinary person the possibility of buzzing with artistic creativity. A band of experts gave courses in literature, painting, music, and much more, in which they imparted the general principles of a work without the need to read it, see it or listen to it: there was absolutely no reason to expose the members of the center to complex issues. They even offered an express telephone service, something of first importance for social events. With just a single phone call, an overview of the book, movie, or exhibition of the moment could be obtained, including a critique of the weak points of the plot, plus arguments for supporting the notion that it was, in fact, a metaphor for the feeble human condition. There were members who complained because some other dinner guest had come out with the same idea before they could express it, so the experts began to prepare a variety of opinions, in the interests of fomenting plurality and debate.

In relation to creativity, they transferred to the field of the arts the age-old maxim that learning is, in fact, a process of remembering what you already know: the ladies believed that artistic talent was present in everyone, but the snobbism of the elites meant only very few had the right to enjoy it. Numerous artists in the making, assisted by the facilitators, created works of great technical skill.

In painting, the student would give a rough outline of the work. So as not to interfere in the creative process, the facilitator didn't even listen to this. The student would then stand confidently before the canvas, the tutor took his arm and together they would begin to paint. Students were instructed to allow themselves to be carried away by creative ecstasy and to close their eyes during the process. The final product left them feeling so proud that it didn't matter if it was somewhat different to what they had originally conceived. In musical composition, the facilitator would ask the student to say the third note in the scale and then write this down; then the fifth, the first and so on. In the end, without the facilitator having written a single note, a melody existed, written by the student. When it came to instruments, they were taught to play the separate notes or chords and these were recorded. A team of technicians then united them to form a complete song, played by the neophyte. At the end of each course there were exhibitions, dramatized readings, and prerecorded concerts where a new generation of artists were welcomed into the world.

A group of lawyers who believed in the importance of civic unity for eradicating injustice created an organization to help the stray dogs that plagued the streets of Villa Miserias. For a monthly fee, people could adopt a stray from their catalog. The sickly-sweet names beneath the photos would soften even the most hesitant heart. Once the canine had been adopted, the organization took responsibility for bathing and delousing it, administering its vaccinations, and feeding it. As the period of domestication was traumatic for the dog, the adoptive family was not allowed to see it until this had been completed, but they could send it letters and gifts. However, the organization was unwilling to be responsible for outbreaks of violence among the dogs, nor did the owners have time to oversee them. The solution was for the dogs to go on living in the street, receiving food and periodic attention from the association. Once a month, there was a supervised visit in their premises, where the family could meet its new member. The dogs tended to keep their distance; the owners were moved to see the results of the new lease of life they had offered the canines. They would tell it all the family news. Some smuggled in food, in violation of the rules of the organization, which didn't want to have the dogs sniffing around the premises the whole day. Word got around in the doggy underworld, so that the number of strays went on increasing. They were divided between the fortunate that enjoyed the good life, and those left abandoned to their fate. The organization couldn't do everything.

A bar called Alison's also opened and became very popular among the male population of Villa Miserias. They gathered there to yell along with every variety of sporting event, transmitted nonstop, at full volume, on the giant screens covering the walls of the bar. Betting money was prohibited, but clients could make wagers using the trays on which the food and drink were served. The main attraction of Alison's lay in a squadron of good-looking cheerleaders in civilian clothing who chatted with the clients every night. They were perfectly capable of dealing with unsolicited attentions, but the bald gorillas who acted as bouncers still prowled around them just in case. In addition to good looks, another factor was necessary to be employed there: an exceptional head of alcohol. The auditions were brutal. The girls were required to imbibe a succession of different drinks in a limited time, with television screens on and music blaring, to test their resistance in real life conditions. Every time something occurred worthy of an adrenaline rush—a goal, a hole in one, a spectacular crash, or savage knockout—they had to high-five, bonk heads or chests, and scream euphorically. Very few passed the test. The ones left at the end were invincible.

The procedure was for them to go up to tables for a casual chat; soon afterwards, they ordered a drink for which they immediately paid with money from the bar. They would down this in one, amid laughter and sporting banter. The men, however, couldn't allow themselves to be left lagging; a new round quickly appeared with drinks for everyone. It was not infrequent for a visit to Alison's to end in the involuntary use of the bald gorillas' home-delivery service, even if it meant carrying the client. The only memory he would have of the evening was a photo of his group of friends hugging the good-looking girls. He would count the days until he could go back.

Each year, on the evening of the anniversary of the opening of the bar, only the most assiduous clients were allowed in. The festivities included a long-standing tradition: the table that chucked up most didn't pay its check. As the clients sometimes missed the bucket provided for the occasion, by the end of the night the floor would be awash with a slippery, pinkish, lumpy slush. The record—three bucketfuls—was held by a group of middle-aged financial executives, who proudly held up their trophies in the photos displayed on the walls of the most paradisiacal bar ever imagined.

14

The reforms signified the commencement of perpetual change. From then onward, there would always be work in progress. Hence the dust. And also the noise. The transformations were like a loose hosepipe spraying water in all directions. To give them some coherence, Selon Perdumes brought in a man capable of measuring everything. G.B.W. Ponce had acquired great renown in the socio-scientific community for a statistical discovery known as the Ponce Scheme. After years of battling with his algorithms—his beaky condor face lost its glow and his hair started to gray—he'd managed to compress thousands of variables into a method he retained for his personal use, in spite of stratospheric offers to share his secret. Inspired by the philosophical notion that history is just an untiring repetition of itself, he proposed to condense the millions of correlations studied into an accurate predictive method: his aim was to quantify the eternal return. If all thought, every impulse or action is contained in the characteristics that define each individual, he could explain real events without having to wait for them to occur.

He investigated innumerable causal relationships, looking for recurring patterns. Beginning with the most obvious categories—social class, nationality, skin color, religion—he managed to corroborate common suppositions. In general terms, people's thoughts and actions could be blocked out, according to the specific group they belonged to. Ponce concentrated his attention on the remainder, the minuscule deviations within a single group. Why did some millionaires wear denim jeans and jackets? What was the difference between adulterous believers and their chaste counterparts? What did women who lied about their age have in common? Why did hoods indicate a tendency to mindless acts of violence?

He tried out his theory on hundreds of the most elusive variables: the type of music listened to, favorite sexual fetish, being an early morning or night person. Almost all these variables fitted within more general categories, but some stood out for their predictive power. Among people with an average income, those who had had wooden toys were, as a rule, less given to accumulation; those who couldn't dance salsa had a greater tendency for masochistic relationships. He refined and purified until he arrived at the famous Ponce Questionnaire. Seventy-one questions that summarized the narrative of human behavior. With a margin of error of ±3.14%, it could predict political opinions, consumption patterns, movie preferences, the cost of an engagement ring. Armed with his database, Ponce would consult his cyber-seer and note down the answers. It never failed on the outcome of an election, the sales volume of a new model of car, the numbers of demonstrators at a protest march, or the average abortion figures in a particular stratum of women.

It also worked at an individual level. Once a person had allowed him to take an X-ray of his soul, G.B.W. Ponce was the owner of his future. He knew, with terrifying precision, what that person would think or choose given certain alternatives. On one occasion, a progressive colleague had made a virulent attack on his method—the very idea of its implications deeply alarmed him. Ponce announced a public challenge: the colleague should hand him a sealed envelope containing a document outlining his position on various controversial topics, his normal mode of transport, the number of jackets with elbow patches he had in his closet, and other personal peculiarities. He would then complete the Ponce Questionnaire. The computer crunched the data and came up with the right answer on subjects such as his views on homosexuals being able to enlist in the army, the hours of television he allowed his children to watch, whether or not he believed in personal pensions, and his favorite cruise route. The humiliated professor retired in silence. Ponce's flamethrower had melted his waxen autonomy.

Each fresh success gave him greater confidence. He was to be found in the most venerable seats of learning, giving presentations to packed lecture theaters, always dressed in the same way: red canvas tennis shoes, slightly torn jeans, and a white shirt, plus his indispensable dark glasses. He enjoyed seeing the effects of his provocations. Once, he turned up at an ultraconservative university disguised as a robot. He explained to the audience he was going to demonstrate that the only God they should worship was the automaton each and every person has within him, and followed this with barbed statements claiming that fundamentalism could be explained by purely material circumstances. When he stated that 87.3% of evolution deniers treated their subordinates worse than chimpanzees, one young man could take no more and made a lunge for the sound equipment to turn off the microphone. G.B.W. Ponce came down from the stage in a series of jerky, mechanical movements to the sounds of the insults and boos of his devout audience.

What was revolutionary about his method was that it removed the need for studies and surveys. The responses to the questionnaire were sufficient. He updated his databases to keep them fresh and developed parameters for balancing the different variables, including the hedonistic slant inherent in advancing age. Having nothing more to prove to academia, he published a voluminous book of his findings, entitled *God's Dice*. He was careful to keep it beyond the comprehension of non-initiates: the book didn't explain anything. There were thousands of tables with statistical links from which the author could extract at will the conclusions he wanted to develop more explicitly. His authority was such that the arrows of causality began to point in every direction. It was no longer possible to tell what was the origin and what was the outcome.

One man read that self-sufficient women whose partners were addicted to videogames and marijuana tended to break off their relationships. After even the slightest argument, he would accuse his wife of wanting to leave him. He fought against the growing tension by increasing his dose of marijuana, and spending whole days playing videogames. When his wife finally departed, he self-pityingly accepted the fulfillment of the Poncean maxim.

A bureaucrat learned that public servants with double chins, over twelve years of service in the same post, and a predilection for sensationalist magazines, often stole the office staplers. He was enormously relieved to see that statistical absolution of his peccadillo.

A bored housewife read that, in 73% of cases, the first lesbian experience in her stratum occurred with the domestic help. Coming back drunk from a meal with her best friend, she called Josefina into her bedroom and tempered her confusion with imperative commands until she achieved satisfaction. Thanks to *God's Dice*, she ran not the slightest risk of her new secret being discovered.

G.B.W. Ponce was intrigued by the practical reach of his paradigm. When he received Perdumes' invitation, he was certain that Villa Miserias was the ideal laboratory in which to pursue his grand passion: codifying social existence down to the last minor detail. He made it a condition that his questionnaire would be distributed to every resident in the estate. Fabulous! No problem. That's what Taimado and his Black Paunches are here for. He installed himself and his meager belongings in Building 29 and acquired two adjoining spaces in the commercial zone in which to launch his consultancy business, $uperstructure. When the transparent sign on a black background had finally been put up, Juana Mecha exclaimed to anyone who would listen: "If it isn't the same river each time, at least it looks the same now."

15

One of the keys to Quietism in Motion was precisely the fact that it included motion. G.B.W. Ponce had demonstrated that ascent of the social ladder was accompanied by an acceptance of the beliefs of the new rungmates. The members of the former "us" immediately became "them." This in itself was not particularly important. What did matter was ensuring the changes of status were visible: making it clear that the only barrier to excellence was looking back at you in the mirror each morning. Selon Perdumes' favorite example for highlighting the possibilities of social advancement was Mauricio Maso.

Maso arrived in Villa Miserias by accident while still in his puberty. He was living with other children in a sewer, earning a living by entertaining passengers in the metro: on the floor of the subway car he would lay out a T-shirt covered with pieces of broken glass and roll around on then. His skin was like a bloodied sheet of sandpaper, adorned with a maze of raised scars. He withstood the hardships of his profession by inhaling the glue supplied by his boss each night when he reported in. But that irascible tyrant only let the boys keep enough of their earnings for a couple of tacos and a soda.

One time, Mauricio Maso overdid the glue and came out of the metro feeling very disoriented. In search of somewhere to shelter from the rain that was making his wounds burn, he jumped over the wall surrounding Villa Miserias and took refuge among the garbage containers, where he competed with the stray dogs for a share of the leftover leftovers recently discarded there: eating a piece of fat on the bone only left him hungrier than ever. Then he stuck his head into a container in the hope of striking lucky, and found something better than food: a bag of marijuana some parents had found in their teenage daughter's bedroom. He improvised a pipe from an empty water bottle, reactivated his glue-induced stupor with a couple of puffs, then lay down among the trash to gaze into the density of the clouded night sky.

A group of kids passed by on their way to a party and immediately recognized the smell. They followed the scent until they came across Mauricio, sprawled out, absorbed, firmly grasping his bottle in his right hand. He seemed to hear them say something, but the words formed waves in the air that broke before they became comprehensible. The most resolute of the kids opened his fingers one by one to liberate the weed, leaving in his hand a bill equivalent to two weeks' honest toil for Mauricio. He managed to close his fist on it before falling exhausted into a deep sleep.

The following morning Mauricio went on a spree with his unexpected earnings. He went to the public baths to wash for the first time in weeks: the crusts of grime were stubborn, and without his coating of filth, the woman at the cash register didn't recognize the brown-skinned, wily kid who came out. He bought a pirated T-shirt with the circular logo of a famous punk band and spent his last coins on a breakfast consisting of a chocolate-flavored concha soaked in atole.

Maso decided it was time to become independent of his guild and start working on his own, even if it meant renouncing his daily ration of glue. He sought out a stretch of the metro system far from the monopoly of his previous organization and, at night, went back to sleep among the trash in Villa Miserias. With his savings he bought a blanket, which he carefully hid each morning before sneaking out to work

Juana Mecha suspected something was going on when she began to find bloodied T-shirts in the trash. One day she arrived earlier than usual and managed to grab the arm of the frightened Mauricio before he could make a run for it. Vigorously shaking her broom as she walked, she spat out: "Better to eat humble pie than live like this." Maso agreed to work as her assistant. His task consisted of separating out the trash for recycling before the truck arrived to mix it all up again. Mecha lent him a thin mattress and a pillowslip stuffed with a green housecoat; she regularly came by to take him to the leftovers canteen. In the afternoon, before setting out on her long journey home, she would give the kid a pat on the head, saying nothing more than: "Behave yourself."

That was when Mauricio Maso's second shift began. With increasing frequency, the youths began to return to request more supplies. The first time, it took him a few days to find what turned out to be oregano. When the unwary kids smoked it, none of them wanted to be the only one to own up to its lack of effect, so they pretended to be high as kites. Mauricio had kept some back for himself and on realizing he'd been conned, he changed his supplier. His clients congratulated him of the potency of his new crop. They were soon requesting powders and pills. His efficiency produced a rapid expansion of his client base: anorexic models bought amphetamines from him; hangover hippies danced to the beat of the sledgehammers on his acid. As part of his transformation into a businessman, Maso set himself the rule of only consuming his own merchandise.

His appearance was the first thing to change. He smartened up and acquired the first pair of the iguana skin boots that would become his trademark style. He took his rest on a real mattress and bought a portable, battery operated television set. Every night he went to bed in the narrow space between two garbage containers, watching the late-night repeats of primetime cartoons. He got hold of a sheet of acrylic and suspended it like a roof when it rained. He'd never before lived in such comfort.

One night, he was woken by a slight tug on his gray tweed pants. The light of his torch showed a female client kneeling beside his mattress. A few days before, she'd bought supplies from Mauricio for a party her bosses—advertising executives— were throwing to celebrate a lucrative contract for snack commercials. Speaking at full speed, her jaw juddering, she told him they had run out of supplies. And the party was just getting going. Did he have any more? The thing was that they had run out of cash. What could they do? Still sleepy, Mauricio had hardly had time to process the situation when he felt an electric charge rising toward his crotch. The torch went out at the same moment as his zipper came down, liberating his hard-on. He felt a hand skillfully exploring. Then the moistness of a mouth initiating him. Overwhelmed by pleasure, he rummaged in the garbage until he found the sack where he kept his stock. He extracted a few small bags without counting them and the girl left triumphantly. A new method of payment had just been set up.

There was one obstacle in the way of his frenetic business career: Joel Taimado became aware of the activity, at strange hours, around the trash. When he saw Maso going out on an order, Taimado took a look around his territory. He was about to admit defeat when he noticed an anomaly: in one of the overflowing containers there was a slight bulge. He dug around in the bags, smearing his uniform in the thick liquid pouring from them, until he met with a diagonally placed plank, camouflaged to match the color of the receptacle. As soon as he raised it, his jaw dropped with the excitement of his find. Maso's cache contained his merchandise, his savings bound in rubber bands, his television, radio, and torch, his growing wardrobe, and the old photo of Juana Mecha he placed under his pillow each night. All this under the protection of a heavy-duty pickaxe and a Swiss army knife. Taimado closed the lid of the container and treated himself to a first fix right there. As a finishing touch, to leave no doubt about the person responsible for the confiscation, he pissed on the photo of the sweeping woman.

When Maso returned from his chore, he heard singing coming from the room—known informally as the Chamber of Murmurs—where the security squad kept their things. In a melancholy mood, Taimado and his colleagues were singing along, out of tune, to his old radio. The Black Paunches were showing the effects of several hours of drinking cheap liquor, with the addition of the white avenues of cocaine snorted from their truncheons: they were vying to see who could do the whole line in one go. One of them was out for the count in a corner, having attempted to organize a bit of fun. It was a homespun version of those games where the participants hold hands and a machine administers mild electric shocks, causing the muscles to contract, until someone can't bear it any longer and drops out. As he didn't have the appropriate equipment, once the circle had been formed, he asked one of his companions to use his electric prod to administer a shock to the back of his neck, thinking that the effect would be shared equally between them all. This obedient colleague happily let leash the fury of the prod, intending to stop when the chain was broken. The recipient of the shock—his brains nearly burnt to a crisp—writhed to the sound of the guffaws from the others, who were soon able to attest to his body's zero capacity as a conductor of energy. The entertainment came to an end when he stopped moving. The people holding his hands let go and he fell face down on the table, smoke coming from his ears. Between tears and laughter, they slapped his back in appreciation of the show and dragged him to the corner to sleep it off. Every so often Taimado asked them to check he was still breathing. Some pranksters shaved his eyebrows and made up his face, without it even occurring to anyone to wonder why a member of the security squad would have the necessary cosmetics among his personal belongings.

With enviable calm, Maso turned and left to check out what he already suspected. He discovered trash scattered on his bed. When he opened up his cache, he found just a transparent piece of card lying in a pool of multicolored liquid: the image on the photo had washed out. He had no desire to throw it out or replace it with another. Nor even to rinse it to get rid of Taimado's acrid smell. He would continue to put it under his pillow each night.

16

Max Michels had imagined the journey to complete his self-appointed mission would be less protracted. When, for the third time, he passed the security booth where the Black Paunch on duty was sleeping with his feet on the table, he realized that he'd been walking around in circles for some time. The booth and its occupant, the barrier marking the boundary between Villa Miserias and the outside world, the howling of the dogs in the charge of a professional walker about the cross through that boundary, the blaring horn vainly trying to wake the guard, and anything else his eyes and ears were capable of attracting to the attention of his conscious mind, suddenly seemed like incomprehensible elements, completely alien to him. He knew they formed part of a specific configuration, produced by forces—as intangible as they were real—that for centuries had been laughing uproariously at anyone who dedicated his life to explaining them.

"Everything is a dangerous drug to me except reality, which is unendurable," the fat man who signed his book with the name of the mythological navigator had written. How right he was, thought Max Michels, or at least the everyday habits of the majority would seem to attest to its truth. Few people grappled with the unendurable without the temporary escape valve of some form of external assistance, anything capable of extricating them for a few moments from the limitations of the body. Hey, smartass, look at the shitty state your drug's gotten you into: you're blind and you still keep going back for more. Say when you've had enough. We'd be delighted to go on fucking your head.

When the Many were in the right, Max was the first to admit it. But he couldn't turn back now. Not that he wanted to. Better the danger than the pure, simple unendurable reality. Why did he have to be different from the rest? Didn't the moronic Many remember what happened when Taimado had brought about a situation even the authorities didn't, at heart, want?

That was when Mauricio Maso had decided to close the preferred escape valves of the residents of Villa Miserias once and for all. In a single stroke, he cut off the supply of all merchandise, including the pharmaceuticals he supplied without prescription. He pretended not to know his clients. He was, once again, a simple assistant scavenger. His pay was recycled foodstuffs and a place to sleep. At night, he returned to his previous occupation to make a little pocket money. And to not forget where he came from. He threw himself on the broken glass with such vigor that passengers in the metro would give him bills on condition he stopped until they had gotten off. Each new slash was proof that he wouldn't be so naïve again. Juana Mecha offered her support: "They're going to understand what it means to see yourself in the mirror as you really are."

The atmosphere on the estate bristled. The environment creaked. The cart that was Villa Miserias continued to advance at its sluggish pace, but the wheels needed greasing. The principal whiplashes fell on the mules, in particular the potbellied mules in black to blame for the massive, involuntary rehab.

However, the majority of the other employees also suffered from the ill humor of their bosses. Housewives would fly into a temper with the servants if the orange juice was too bitter, if they laddered their pantyhose, if their husbands weren't up to it in bed, or if their lovers asked for a new credit card. They missed the tranquilizers they had been secretly taking.

For a prominent banker and, what's more, member of the administrative board of Villa Miserias, the drying up of his supply of narcotics came at the worst possible moment. His superiors were aware of his unflagging ambition and so assigned him the task of preparing a report that would secure a crucial injection of capital. The deadline was ridiculous. He accepted, confident that his long, cocaine-fueled nights—brought to a close by sleeping pills and a few toots of marijuana to ensure the necessary three hours of rest—would do the trick. Everything was going to plan when Maso took his radical decision. The banker first tried financial inducements to persuade him to change his mind. Then came the threats. And finally the pleas. Nothing worked. His pride prevented him from asking for help: his self-destruction was undignified. On the day of the meeting, he turned up with dark shadows under his eyes; the greasy sheen of the extra layer of gel on his hair accentuated his pallor. The report was unfinished and full of inconsistencies. The investors didn't even waste their time letting him finish his presentation; they politely apologized before leaving the meeting room without even finishing their coffees. His furious bosses also acted quickly. They made him sign his letter of resignation there and then. During the next meeting of Villa Miserias' board, the banker tabled a motion prohibiting employees drinking from the communal water fountains. It was passed unanimously.

To the list of those wronged was added a ballet dancer thrown out of her company for putting on ten ounces; a surly university graduate found himself once again without friends when he stopped bringing ecstasy pills to parties; a couple addicted to amphetamines were unable to bear the crisis caused by the tense tranquility of their nights.

Taimado's boys began to feel the pressure from a number of sides. The people they protected didn't miss a single opportunity to point out the differences that separated them. Their minuscule wages made them dependent on the gratuities they received for almost any action: keeping an eye on the children playing outside, washing cars, helping with shopping bags, repairing broken chairs. The amounts offered didn't decrease, but the guards began to receive them in handfuls of coins of the lowest possible value. During the transaction, these coins would be accidentally dropped, so that the Black Paunch in question would have to get down on all fours to collect them. Some neighbors would enter and exit the estate several times a night just for the pleasure of directing their headlights on the security booth and sounding their horns frenetically to startle the sleeping guard. If the water was temporarily cut off, or there was a power outage, they received peremptory calls demanding they solve the problem immediately; that's what they were paid for. The final humiliation appeared in a circular informing them of the hours they were allowed to watch television in their booth. Apart from these times, it would be locked.

A different threat came from outside; Maso's retreat opened the way for others. Two rival gangs disputed the right to dope the people of Villa Miserias. Since there was a need for substances to make everyday life more bearable, the demand was still there. For the great majority of the residents, the situation was inevitable;

there was nothing to be done. Every so often crusades were organized to warn of the risks but, to tell the truth, this was a ritual
carried out through force of habit with no real consequences. It
often happened that the publicists who organized the campaigns
were under the influence when they thought them up. What
really got on the residents' nerves were the frequent outbreaks of
violence and extortion resulting from the all-out warfare between
the rival gangs. Taimado intervened either too late or too little,
making the situation worse. It was one of the darkest periods in
the history of Villa Miserias.

The initial contacts were carried out discreetly. But the battle
for a larger market meant that boundaries were increasingly trans-
gressed. As in any other business, the bosses demanded ever-higher
sales figures from their dealers. The principal of savage competition
didn't vary; the specific methods of the industry did. The leader
of the first gang to establish itself was a respectable impresario
in the toy business. As part of a training course offered by his
company, he read an article explaining the importance of generating compulsive habits. It was a matter of capturing minds as
early as possible and then never letting then go. Toys appealed to
the childish side of every sort of personality, forming part of a
chain of the perpetual substitution of one artifact for another. The
more he thought it through, the more he was intrigued by the
possibility of transferring these principles to the drug trade. Just
as with toys, the attraction of drugs was universal. It was a case of
capitalizing on the mechanisms of instant gratification. He guessed
that once the habit had been created, the adherence to it would
be lifelong.

The number of habitual users was considerable. Their needs just had to be promptly catered to. The real challenge consisted of widening the client base. The toymaker concluded that the best publicity was the users themselves. In his company's offices, he set up a sort of pilot group composed of kids of various ages, selected by means of a combination of fair complexion, good appearance, tastefully ripped clothing, purchasing power, sociability, and chronic stupidity: the in-crowd of Villa Miserias. They listened to his simple plan. They would receive all the drugs they wanted under the single condition of not revealing they were getting them for free. They were immediately given their first samples. Still under the effects of the euphoria, they asked about the possibility of becoming sales representatives. This was an ideal situation for their boss: When before had a brand image personally sold what he should have been advertising? It wasn't long before some jealous wit nicknamed them the Psychedelic Lolitos; they adored it. All the young dudes wanted to emulate them. The girls clawed for their attention. Teenage consumption soared.

To keep tight control on the workforce, the company created a kind of informal membership badge, a decal designed for the exclusive use of the Psychedelic Lolitos and their ardent followers. It was a voluptuous, mirror-image inverted P barely separated from a stiff, upside down L. The ꟻd brand soon became the emblem of the juvenile class. With an eye on the future, the organization began giving away decals for younger children. Despite the urban myths circulating at the time, they didn't contain any drug; their power lay in a sense of belonging. They were a means of recruiting future customers early.

There was one important niche to attend to: the kids on the margins. They weren't much interested in having fun. The Lolitos had a natural hatred for them. It wasn't that they refused to sell to them—business came before the revulsion of seeing them wearing their insignia—but it was like setting out to grow a desert plant in a tropical climate. They simply had no place in the bacchanalian carousing encouraged by the I'd clan.

A rival gang capitalized on this gap in the market by faithfully copying the profitable scheme with one modification: everything was less brilliant, worse quality, and cheaper. Anemic kids with hair hanging down over their faces and sadistic T-shirts trafficked substances destined to make them even more depressed. Their empty-eyed meetings were punctuated by incoherent bouts of speech; they spent languid hours listening to the instrumental wailing of prog rock groups. To distinguish themselves, the Marginals had an inverted, barbed M tattooed on their forearms. They were such a close-knit group that when a fifteen-year-old died from inhaling what turned out to be detergent, they put it down to his desire to end his suffering. Anything was better than weakening the brotherhood by admitting how harmful the substance was.

Each gang blamed the other for unleashing the war. The I'ds accused the Ws of having cajoled a group of its plastic girls into their den by the use of conceptual maps. Once there, they were given goods that had earlier passed through the dealers' sweaty balls. The Ws didn't deny it. They had been responding to provocation: the I'ds had bribed the avaricious owner of the skate store where the Ws bought their uniform Gore T-shirts and managed to persuade him to stop stocking the gigantic sizes that almost came down to their knees. The Ψs looked ridiculous in tailored T-shirts that didn't even cover their stomachs: a distinguishing feature of the Psychedelic Lolitos. No one was frightened by their death's head logos when they were printed on stretch cotton. The Ψs looked like out-of-work actors. Their most fanatical devotees accused them of selling out to the seduction of appearance.

The inhabitants of Villa Miserias suffered the effects of these confrontations. The price of the laced drugs went up to absorb the increasing costs of arming the combatants with knives, nunchaku, and brass knuckles. Expeditions to avenge insults spiraled. There were no-go areas. The rival groups searched any unwary person who passed through their zone; if someone was wearing the symbol of the enemy gang, they were forced to buy merchandise then and there.

Both gangs made forays into other related activities, such as robbery and extortion. The Lolitos stole imported aftershave lotions from apartments; to impress the girls, they borrowed—without permission—the flashiest cars. Either from carelessness or as a sophisticated form of torture, they would leave tapes of their sickly-sweet romantic ballads in the stereos.

The Ψs, in contrast, developed a telephone extortion network. They would ring repeatedly, at inconvenient hours, and list the names and occupations of the members of the family. In exchange for doing nothing, they asked for pornography to satisfy their onanism. The victims were supposed to leave packages of magazines, movies, erotic photonovelas, papayas—perfect for masturbation—or analgesic sprays to be used in the practice known as the deadhand.

There were also psychological terror tactics. One morning Villa Miserias awoke to a gruesome scene in the Plaza del Orden: blond-haired heads with well-defined features, impaled on posts, surrounded by a wash of red stains and severed limbs. They were the remains of a well-known brand of plastic doll and represented the violent dismemberment of the Гds. The latter responded to this aggression by destroying the Ж's games consoles, tearing up their collectable comics, and leaving them scattered around the green areas. There were warnings to the owners about what would happen next. Confused, hunched under the weight of the gazes trapped in the crossfire, the Black Paunches collected up these messages.

The naked violence exasperated the residents. It wasn't the same as knowing awful things happened in other places where the victims were always far away. The horror was no longer abstract and now it was very close to them all. The routine nature of the violence periodically mobilized those affected into action. When some wealthy member of the community suffered the effects, it was considered more serious than if it happened to the habitual poor wretches. Inflammatory meetings were organized, demanding the resignation of the board, the cleaning up of the Black Paunches, increased security and harsher punishments, the creation of neighborhood groups to oversee the implementation of these demands... The criminal gangs would turn down the heat for a short time. In reality, the excesses that triggered the fury of the moneyed classes didn't suit them either, but it wasn't easy to ask their scorpions not to sting frogs if doing so went against their instincts. The situation would stabilize until the next rocky patch merited a fresh outbreak of the same drama, but with different protagonists.

Joel Taimado felt under pressure to intervene, but the juggling act required was beyond him: in essence, a community with high levels of addiction was asking him to combat the people who were supplying the very thing they didn't want to live without. Even he realized that the demand would be satisfied one way or another. It was a matter of taming the bronco not canceling the rodeo. The provisional solution consisted of a few, very public crackdowns, almost with the agreement of the gangs themselves, as a necessary sacrifice to keep the wheels rolling. This triumph was attributed to a careful intelligence operation. For a couple of nights, people slept more soundly, until the organizational chart of the stricken villains was reconfigured. Taimado was aware that he was just putting temporary caps on molars destroyed by caries. In consultation with Selon Perdumes, they opted for the best of non-solutions: the time had come to talk to Mauricio Maso.

Taimado waited until Maso returned from his night shift. He found him sitting on his mattress between the containers, sucking out pieces of glass from his arms and putting alcohol on his wounds. In his own particular way, Taimado asked Maso to return to his old occupation. In exchange for a cut of the profits, he would turn a blind eye. What's more, since the workers had just been moved to Building B, they could offer him a shared room that would be a haven from the dry winds.

"Sorry my friend, other bastards are taking care of that now," murmured Maso without letting his attention stray from his surgical task.

"Uh-huh. The thing is that the boss is pushing harder and harder for us to do nothing and we're going to end up with sweet FA again."

"The solution's obvious, you son of a fucking bitch. Give me back what you stole and I'll get started with that."

Hearing this demand, Taimado held out the envelope he'd been given in anticipation of just such an eventuality.

"Right. I'm already on the case," said Maso before spitting a gob of blood mixed with alcohol onto Taimado's shoes.

Maso began announcing his return through his appearance. He started washing again, his hair was combed and he had new iguana skin boots. When his old regulars timidly approached him once again with requests, he openly shunned them, sending out a veiled message that something was going to happen.

To clear up any doubts in the communal mind, Juana Mecha repeated to anyone interested: "The speckled cock's about to stretch its wings." Maso was waiting for Taimado to raise the checkered flag.

The first step was to weaken the groups from within, stealthily placing explosives to bring about an implosion. Contact was made with the most corruptible elements: a talent scout in a linen suit promised the Lolitos places on the catwalk of a coming fashion contest, a sure springboard to stardom. They went excitedly home to consult the faithful mirror that never lied. Due to their sinuous ethical principles, the Ws were more difficult to bribe. A handful was persuaded that the group had sold out. The cancerous cells had to die before they contaminated to rest: those who survived could head a new cult. Comparisons with characters from their favorite fantasy sagas were used to convince them. They were commissioned to produce an illustrated book, a compilation of the maxims of their deformed idols called *The Wary Warrior's Manual*. The dissident Ws saw it as a foundational document in the regeneration of the Marginals.

The coopted members of both gangs provided Taimado with precise information on the structure of their organizations. They were also asked to plant rumors about the quality of the goods, already dangerously poor due to the wars. Each gang accused the other of cutting their wares with fertilizer and powdered gelatin. Stories of blindness and other secondary effects were rife. Consumer confidence plummeted.

To assure a simultaneous, two-pronged attack, the turncoat Lolitos were asked to organize a megaparty on a specific day: every year the Ws got together to commemorate the anniversary of the death of a famous guitarist—responsible for uncountable moments of acid-fueled depression—where they spent drugged-out hours listening to his albums under a strict rule of silence. They would gradually fall into a gummy-eyed, drooling trance, before collapsing unconscious. This was the most long-awaited date in the calendar and it was an unmitigated provocation for the Lolitos to play their plastic music on that day.

Taimado had ensured that unusually large orders were placed separately with two of the chief Lolitos, who, to cover the cost, borrowed money from their mothers on some school-related pretext. The mothers failed to note the strangeness of this one-off charge during the school holidays. The Lolito suppliers arrived at the party, walking on air from the weightlessness of the powders stashed in their pre-torn jeans.

When they didn't find their supposed buyers, they attempted to keep cool, but their edginess slowly began to affect earlier clients. Two girls who had a crush on one of them bought a couple of bags from him, only to later flush them down the toilet.

When one Lolito found the other closing a deal, he realized that he'd been set up: his comrade had put in the order just to bring about his ruin. He decided to confront him. They exchanged accusations until one of them lashed out. Biting and hair pulling followed. The struggle reached an impasse: one had an arm around the other's neck and was twisting his nose with his free hand, while the other had four fingers in his opponent's groin, squeezing. They were tangled up in a cloud of groans when the Black Paunches burst in on the party and threw a Cuba Libre in their faces to separate them. The Lolitos were kneading their stinging eyes when they were dragged out.

The Black Paunches gathered the two Lolitos and their mothers in the Chamber of Murmurs. The boys couldn't speak for sobbing. Their mothers had never before seen those pills, powders, herbs, and strips of liquid-smeared paper, much less in such large—albeit diminished, after Taimado's guys had taken their cut—quantities. Amid frenzied anxiety, overflowing love, demented cackles, and visions of two-headed mothers, the Black Paunches looked on as the domestic drama unfolded. The mothers came up with the idea that their sons should work to pay back their debt to the community. The following day, they were handed over to Juana Mecha, who gave them each a baggy beige overall, the uniform they would wear during their temporary membership of Villa Miserias' cleaning squad. They didn't even try to understand her words of welcome: "First they pamper you and then they don't like you being soft." The other Lolitos watched their fallen comrades carrying banana skins between two disgusted fingers: they were thankful not to be in their place. The gang had had its day.

In the case of the Ws, the plan for dismantling them by means of ideological discord functioned to perfection. Perdumes had a new mission for Orquídea López that he would use to check if she had what it took for another project, still in its infancy: the editorship of the first local newspaper, *The Daily Miserias*. For the moment, her task consisted of creating an apocryphal piece of reportage: an invented article, apparently published years before in an influential foreign paper. It would relate a scandal involving the mythical rock musician whose death the Marginals commemorated.

While onstage, during a massive, mud-soaked concert, the musician had produced a product symbolizing the empty consumerism of his native land. It was a pet rock—eyes dangling on a spring and a red rubber mouth—launched onto the market amid a great deal of hype, but which had achieved little success. After questioning the meaning of its existence, the rot it represented, the harm it would do to innocent children, the star had—to the delight of his devoted fans—annihilated the pet rock with blows from his guitar. From then on, they came to his concerts carrying one of the inert pets. During a particular guitar solo of his hit "When Goth Became Pop," they would shatter the stones. As a consequence, sales of pet rocks soared into the millions. So far, the story was true, testified to by hundreds of eyewitnesses, videos, and photographs of fans, forcefully castigating the pacific rocks.

The apocryphal article revealed a secret agreement between the controversial rock musician and the company that had contracted him to express public hatred of its stone pets. The most loyal fans, who went to many of the concerts of what turned out to be his farewell tour, shattered a great number of the stones that—when the star was extinguished with two bottles of barbiturates—were left as a symbol of the social norms that had caged him. The incriminating piece, written under the byline of Stanley Higgins, even claimed that the musician's family continued to receive royalties for many years. The occult nature of the icon was clearly proven: it was one more product of that corporative machine his songs yearned to destroy. Orquídea printed out the article on newsprint and left it in the sun for hours to obtain a tone corresponding to the supposed date of publication. The torn edges were her final touch. Perdumes was amazed by the result. The sham clipping was anonymously left in the mailbox of one of the *W*s who was already questioning the authenticity of the movement.

The high point of the Marginals' annual festivity was the moment when a piece of volcanic rock, with paperclip eyes and Styrofoam lips, was dissolved in strong acid. The *W*s would sing the emblematic song just as the rock was about to completely disappear, with those who were still capable automatically gathering in a circle around the flask of acid. The current leader would raise the container to demonstrate that the solid might vanish but the spirit never. The others would nod to the rhythm of drumbeat, their faces hidden by their flowing locks. This was often the last image some of those present had of the evening.

No one had anticipated the schism that was about to occur. With a true sense of drama, the puppet *W* waited for the climax of the event. Just before the main guitar solo, when the master of ceremonies was already walking to the center of the room, he stopped the music by lifting the arm of the record player. Some of the participants continued to hear the solo in their heads; others spun round, horrified by the sacrilege. The puppet had something important to tell them. They had, for years, been conned by a false prophet. After a long, thorough investigation, he'd found a document by the journalist Stanley Higgins. They were nothing more than pawns in a perverse game of merchandising chess. He went on to read the article aloud in an affected tone.

By the end, he'd triggered a theological debate that would divide the few who could still think into two bands. Those who didn't want to believe him said it was a conspiracy: Why had no one else reported this? It was corporate interests trying to cast a slur on honest resistance. In contrast, their opponents had always known it was true, but hadn't dared to say so because of the prevailing fanaticism. The powers that be had made sure that Higgins was silenced, somehow or other, and that was why the story had been buried. Did they really think a newspaper like that would risk its reputation publishing unverified information?

Doubt continued to gnaw at the fraternity, until the sacrifice of the leader put an end to it. Lost for words, the members would read the article over and over, as if expecting that the next time it would say something different. The arguments put forward by the two sides had reached unbearable levels of abstraction. At that time, they were discussing whether the rock star's outfits were in fact his own or part of the stage set. Only a grand gesture could avoid a confrontation. The leader crumpled up the clipping and put it in his mouth. To help him swallow, he took a swig of the blackish acid that had finished off the stone. A few drops stuck to the paper and charred the evidence; the rest destroyed his vocal cords. His most faithful followers rushed him to hospital, where the internal fire was extinguished by means of a stomach pump. He was close to death. The doctors insisted that the obstruction caused by the paper had saved his life, but, as a lifelong souvenir, he was left with incurable gastritis. Now he spoke in shrill whispers, like a Mafioso past his prime. It was the last time that the Ws met as a group.

17

Mauricio Maso's double life began as had been promised. He moved into a shared room in Building B. At first, claustrophobia kept him awake at nights. But he struck up an almost instant friendship with his roommate, Beni Mascorro, who soon became his right hand man. Additionally, as Maso needed a respectable façade for his activities, he was included on the payroll of the cleaning staff. Sometimes he would forget to pick up his fortnightly pay packet.

He started to surf the wave of efficiency inundating Villa Miserias. If possible, he avoided direct contact with his clients, except in cases involving carnal payment—a number that increased until it became his only addiction. Even then, the merchandise was delivered the same way: first, a message had to be left in his mailbox. Maso assigned each of his clients a codename. He and Mascorro had fun creating labels that hit where it hurt. His order book showed six sprigs of hungry indecisiveness for Stinking

Bedbug, two staples of prickly dandruff for Greasy Playing Card, five encapsulated lonelinesses for Bleeding Wrinkles, two drops of colorblindness for Toxic Baldy, four glassy veins for Big Ears the Whale, twenty spongy domes for Air Injection. Mascorro was in charge of making the deliveries and collecting payment. All packages also included a note containing Mauricio Maso's favorite phrase, deriving from his metro days. On a certain evening, he'd gotten into conversation with a restless, bright-eyed globetrotter on a nonstop journey in search of a piece of a mammoth, lost in his childhood. Before leaving the train, the globetrotter had taken a small notebook from his pocket and written on one page what would become Maso's mantra: "Drugs are vehicles for people who have forgotten how to walk."

As a gesture of reconciliation, Maso offered Taimado free trips for his entire squad. The Black Paunches fell over themselves to scrawl out their orders. Maso and Mascorro prepared them carefully: using spray paint of the appropriate color, they camouflaged significant amounts of the strongest powdered chili habanero they could find. Mascorro had to hold his tongue in ice-cold water for fifteen minutes after sampling a pinch. They made sure all the drugs ordered contained an adequate dose. Maso had a hard time not giving the game away when he delivered the suitcase to Taimado.

No sooner had the avid Black Paunches congregated in the Chamber of Murmurs than they began to feel the effects of Maso's vengeance. Those who inhaled the habanero directly into their brains experienced a reverberation that ripped through their nasal passages to the very back of their skulls. Between shrieks of burning agony, they rubbed their faces in the dry earth of the flowerbeds as if trying to sand them down the bones until the pain was rooted out. The ones who took capsules threw up food, bile, and eventually air, powered by the raging bombs in their stomachs. When the bubbles of love enveloped them, they felt arrows piercing their flesh, as if they were sieves spitting out streams of gastric juices onto the cosmic brotherhood. The acid group was infected by visions of snakes spraying them with flames. Their skin melted and regenerated, only to be charred again by the beasts. The only Black Paunch to inject a substance went into convulsions and drowned in his own spittle. His death was officially put down to a sudden heart attack.

Maso took advantage of the chaos to play his masterstroke. He broke into the Black Paunches' lockers with a picklock and scattered their belongings around the Chamber of Murmurs, leaving a trail of scapulars of the Virgin, music systems, and cologne. Using leftover leftovers, he attracted a dozen stray dogs and locked them in with the food. As the Black Paunches gradually reemerged from their lava nightmares, they found their possessions chewed and covered in piss and shit. They kicked the dogs to death, knowing that they couldn't touch the real culprit. When Taimado passed her with his arms full of stinking clothing, he had to impotently listen to Juana Mecha's satisfied, "That's for soaking my spare mattresses."

18

Maso's business career was on the up and up. There were incalculable advantages to his sector of the market: the initiates always wanted more; they were ready to pay any price, there was no need for publicity, and economic crises made consumption soar. Every night, after giving Taimado his cut, Beni Mascorro would stash yet another briefcase safely away in the apartment. Money was no problem: the difficulties were social acceptance and space. There was a proliferation of anti-drug neighborhood watch groups who received substantial donations to their cause. They organized courses, lectures, and brigades, and produced videos and pamphlets with heartrending stories of ruined lives put back together again. Maso was the enemy, the iron ball attached to the chain of hysteria that linked them all. When the unrest grew, the usual mechanism came into play: one of Maso's delivery boys was captured by a Black Paunch. The neighborhood organizations would record the statistic; the annual report would free up funds for the next exercise. Things went on as normal.

Nevertheless, Maso was still forced to endure the sight of decals showing his face branded with a bleeding cross or the accelerated pace of mothers holding children by the hand when they saw him sweeping up in his beige uniform. His only consolation was one of Mecha's enigmatic, oft-repeated sayings: "Your burden is that they like their guilt so much."

Space began as a practical matter. The briefcases stuffed with cash were squeezed under their beds until not even one more would fit; the other room in the apartment was occupied by a gardener and her grandson. Since none of the owners would rent their properties to Maso, he offered to pay the woman's rent if she moved into the adjoining building. The owner of that apartment gave way when offered a briefcase full of money.

The other residents checked the workers' regulations in search of a rule prohibiting this abuse: the assessed value of their properties had immediately fallen. When the outrage had been carried to its completion, the residents of Building B expressed their repudiation of the event by painting the corresponding part of their façade with an ochre blemish. The workers thought it was a gesture of cohesion. And while the owners came out publicly against the invasion of brooms, cleaning rags, and truncheons, they privately began attempting to rent out their apartments and move to some uncontaminated area. This was the first foray of the divisive stain that would spread throughout Villa Miserias.

Mascorro was the next to be recompensed. It took Maso quite a while to process the separation from him. For a time, they went on sleeping in the same bedroom, using the other room for storage. Before sleeping, Maso enjoyed going into the details of his day, unconcerned by the snores of his roommate, who would wake up at intervals to offer some monosyllable showing he was following his boss's exploits.

It was almost impossible to walk around the apartment without bumping into some piece of imitation mahogany furniture, the huge television set and sound system, the stuffed moose's head fixed to the wall, or Maso's increasingly large collection of clown figures. Mascorro felt intimidated by the clay, porcelain, plastic, plush, and even metal clowns, formed from screws, nuts, keys, pieces of piping, and other odds and ends. However, on Maso's birthday, he turned up with a flesh and blood clown, to the enormous surprise of the birthday boy and Mecha, who, on seeing him, exclaimed: "It's not just with bread that saltwater dams overflow."

The clown entertained them with jokes and party games for two hours, and even gave Maso a balloon carousel. When the function came to a close, Maso began to pull out wads of bills to give the clown as a tip, then closed the briefcase and handed it over to him intact.

Mascorro himself had the second ochre patch painted on the annex of Building B. When he had taken the last packing case from his old apartment, he saw Maso standing firmly in the doorway. Mascorro opened his mouth to speak, but his boss raised a hand; he nodded, gave his subordinate a couple of bone-rattling pats on the back, turned around, and closed the door behind him without another word. While Mascorro was moving his belongings into the new apartment, the neighbors produced a concert of slamming doors.

19

The other tenants in Building B also started to benefit from Mauricio Maso's presence. He had parabolic antennas installed on the roof. These inverted flying saucers were capable of picking up hundreds of channels in incomprehensible languages. But between the linguistic barriers and the hassle of keeping up to date with the new codes for stealing the signal, the end result was that people watched the same programs as before. Even so, several children started to wear baseball caps and T-shirts with the logos of foreign teams; the male members of families blamed each other when the women complained about them having accidentally left the set tuned to porn channels.

Soda and snack vending machines were installed in the lobby. Mascorro was in charge of refilling a basket brimming with coins every morning so that the tenants could buy whatever they liked. They particularly enjoyed the sound of the cans falling. When the captain of the cleaning staff soccer team asked for help in buying new gear, Maso didn't hesitate. They agreed to order the same color that already distinguished them.

The maximum cohesive element was a small altar—also in the lobby—surrounded by black candles, kept alight day and night. They illuminated the image of a religious icon that was particularly characteristic of a certain sector of Villa Miserias. Although the protectress had been born into a different social caste, her mercy was great enough to find a place for those brown skinned sons. Maso and his men repaid her with complete devotion.

The artist Pascual Bramsos' paternal relations were deeply religious. In spite of the protests from his historian mother, his grandmother had taken on the task of indoctrinating her small grandson with her beliefs during the regular outings when the parents left him in her care. The child's bed was underneath a shelf, on which rested an image of the Virgin, surrounded by candles to ward off evil spirits. On the evening of the accident, an electrical transformer exploded, shaking the whole apartment. The candles tipped over and a stream of hot wax fell directly onto the boy's ear. Despite numerous operations—paid for by the grandmother—instead of an ear, he was left with what looked like a pink, processed-cheese cauliflower with a hole in the center. Bramsos' childhood was a form of medical torture. Nevertheless, it was not his grandmother he blamed, but the Virgin who had decided to mutilate him.

When he was old enough, he honed his technical skills in art school. He was in training to respond to the aggression.

The first thing he gave form to was an impeccable clay Virgin. Then he intervened in the figure until he attained a syncretism of traditions, affinities, phobias, and hatreds. He allowed her to retain the long habit covering her legs, but undressed the upper half of the torso, leaving uncovered a pair of intentionally augmented breasts. Her proud head was draped in a tunic, hiding her hair. On her face, he placed a black mask with a long, pointed nose. The reddened lips were slightly parted. When he showed the piece in an exhibition at the art school, it had to be kept under guard because of the anonymous threats to destroy it.

Maso heard of its existence from an employee who supplemented her earnings washing clothes for a number of residents, including the Bramsos family. The description appealed to both his love of bright color and his violent hatred of organized religion. When he was still a child and working in his subterranean slash show, strong rains had one night flooded the sewer he lived in and he'd sought sanctuary in a church. The following morning, he woke to find the face of the priest smiling into his delicate features. He invited Maso to his rooms, offered him a shower, food, and clean clothes. He requested that, before leaving, Maso come to the confessional for purification. As Mauricio Maso had never been in a church before, he thought it normal to find himself in the narrow cubicle, on his knees before the seated parish priest. He closed his eyes, as he'd been taught, and listened to a passionate prayer in a strange language. The rising crescendo of the voice frequently faltered. The boy felt a slight tug at his head as the priest said: "Now I'm going to pardon your sins." When he opened his eyes, Maso understood what that absolution involved. He managed to push the man away from him and crashed backwards through the fragile wooden door. Priestly threats of God's revenge and eternal hellfire followed him as he left.

Mascorro communicated his boss's interest in the piece to Bramsos. The budding artist already had radical ideas about selling his work, but his fondness for the products of the prospective client eased the exchange. Maso reified the representation; his neighbors followed his example. Taimado ordered his men to make offerings of some piece of their personal armory. The altar was littered with knives, ninja stars, truncheons, spiked rings, and sharpened screwdrivers. Other employees showered her with their cleaning rags, bottles of bleach, gardening gloves, toilet brushes. Juana Mecha welcomed her with: "Dispossession can only be covered up by dispossession."

20

And just to fucking cap it all, she has to be a journalist, thought Max Michels as he picked up a copy of the free newspaper in which there would surely be an article written by her, secretly directed at him. While he was aware of how arrogant his paranoia was, it didn't make it any less probable that he was right. Expecting an attack from the Many, he considered the possibility that the threat lay in her professional intelligence, which openly defied Max's stereotype of his sort of woman. Confronted with this strategy, the Many decided to attack on another flank: As if you were bothered about that, you sod. What you're really afraid of is anyone knowing. Don't trouble your head, you're already dead meat. The others will find out sooner or later. That's a cert. But then, who knows? Her interests have got nothing to do with mine. Think so? That's your problem, smartass.

Feverishly leafing through that day's issue, Max had the impression of having read it a hundred times before. The news items, headlines, advertisements, and trivia were decidedly secondary. What mattered was the statement of intent: Selon Perdumes had been convinced that transparent information was a well-calibrated thermometer for measuring the development of a community. As people became masters of their own destinies, the responsibility to know what was going on and offer justifiable opinions increased: the residents had to stop being mere spectators of what concerned them. The reforms had offered an opportunity to crystalize needs: it was the moment to create a newspaper, *The Daily Miserias*. Perdumes had a clear idea of the appropriate format. Based on a study by G.B.W. Ponce, he knew that Villa Miserians spent 6.8 minutes a day informing themselves of their reality. He had statistical evidence of graphic preferences, type of language, topics of interest, and the ideal length of articles. There had been no time to lose or gaudiness to be stinted.

The result was a concise newspaper, in which illustrations, photos, and boxes with huge arrows predominated. The house style manual specified rules and proportions: after a given number of words, there should be a box recapping the main points, a smaller box summarizing the larger one, yet another that would continue the compression, and so on until it was condensed into the keyword that was the focus of the entire text. Ponce had demonstrated that this optimized the retention of information because it allowed each individual to go into the text as deep or shallow as he pleased. At first sight, the articles looked like those charts representing the stages of a competition, in which the winning words advanced to the next heat, until the supreme word had beaten the rest. The language was colloquial; the reporters were trained not to insult the intelligence of their readers: they should refrain from using vocabulary not in the daily lexicon of the majority.

The aim was to attain a delicate balance: gathering the opinions of people so as to then mold them. Perdumes explained it using the allegory of a fountain that feeds on the water of a river, only to then return it, transformed, to the stream before feeding once again on that slightly modified source, in a patient reiteration that eventually modifies the raw material through its own elements.

The articles should utilize the time-honored inductive technique of representing a general idea by a few individual testimonies. It was prohibited for reporters to explicitly reveal their beliefs. Every case required the support of an impartial witness. In this respect, *The Daily Miserias* also introduced an innovation: it made absolutely no difference whether or not the witness to an event actually existed. This wasn't a con or some arbitrary decision. Ponce explained to Perdumes that, from a statistical viewpoint, one person's opinion in a population consisting of anything over 878 was already irrelevant when it came to representing the feelings of the majority. He'd demonstrated this in practice with a simple exercise: comparing the reportage of four newspapers, each with a different political tendency, on an antiwar march in a distant country. In every case, the testimonies offered to illustrate the mood of those present coincided with the editorial line of the paper in relation to the war. The most progressive reproduced the words of a father, heartbroken at the death of his son—a medical student specializing in epidemiology—who planned to go to a poverty-stricken region to fight a pandemic. The most conservative, in contrast, interviewed an elderly lady waving a placard with a picture of a hippie wiping his ass with a national flag. She'd lost a grandson, but was proud of her "hero who gave his life to protect our freedom." The two newspapers holding the center ground offered the opinions of people who were against war but understood that it was sometimes necessary, or who supported this war but demanded transparent information in relation to its cost and duration. If this was correlated with the papers' estimations of the number of marchers, his point was proven.

What's the difference, asked G.B.W. Ponce, between looking for someone who expresses the viewpoint you want to transmit and a sensible journalist who captures the atmosphere through the words of a person who doesn't exist, but is more representative of the collective feeling? Why always use a tangible witness? In statistical terms, it's the same thing to be one in a million as to be zero in five thousand. Used correctly, the new technique was, in fact, more objective than its predecessor. But it couldn't be employed lightly: it had to be carefully introduced until there was no longer any noticeable difference.

Readers were also given a voice. Subscribers were offered the privilege of entering a raffle for the right to compose their own columns in the section called Para-Doxa. The topic could be chosen at will since the idea was to discover the views of the common or garden resident, whose voice was not generally heard. Feedback was important, so the contribution was accompanied by a comment in the leader column. This wasn't to intimidate the amateur writer; it simply pointed out issues that had been omitted, clarified myths not in keeping with the new times, or cited eminent experts who had demonstrated a particular phenomenon. Gradually, the tone changed. The veiled message slowly permeated the invited contributors. Para-Doxa was a reflection of the change in the pulse of the average Villa Miserian.

The Daily Miserias became the main media organ on the estate. Its readership was so varied that the editorial staff even organized a competition for the most successful publicity campaign. Talented young creative producers came up with highly ingenious ideas. In the end, a designer rocking chair shop with an abundance of exotic letters in its name won the prize with a strategy based on insulting its customers. The central image showed a young couple relaxing in their stylized rocking chairs; the expression on their faces was one of vacant surprise, as if they had been caught at a blank moment. The caption above them read: "The Espumas were dumb enough to fork out three months' salary to experience our exclusive brand of comfort. Are you going to be left behind?" The unpronounceable rocking chairs became the emblem of homes with aspirations to respectability in Villa Miserias.

Orquídea López had been appointed editor-in-chief of the newspaper. Her combative style fitted perfectly with the braggadocio journalism of *The Daily Miserias*. Even the first issue had exposed a scandal: embezzlement perpetrated by the estate's treasurer. As part of the maintenance of the buildings, the board had to arrange for greasing the hinges of doors, cleaning external windows, carpeting halls and stairways, and putting fertilizer on the green areas, among other tasks. It was the treasurer who supplied the necessary products, and the residential estate had an informal arrangement with a hardware store that offered its principal client discounts.

Disaster loomed when the unfortunate treasurer started dating a much younger girl whose needs exceeded his income. In collusion with the hardware store, he began to buy poorer quality products and used the savings to give her the rubber charm bracelets all her girlfriends were wearing. And there were also dinners at the best taco bars. Orquídea López undertook a thorough investigation to expose this crime to the community.

The eight-column headline announced: DUSTSTORM OF EMBEZZLEMENT. Based on anonymous sources, the article gave details of the operation, the amounts involved, and the items the corrupt official squandered them on. There was a sketch representing those involved with plump figures and tracing the embezzled funds from the hardware store to the girlfriend. The box summarizing the main points of the story gradually tapered down to the word "rat." One resident corroborated the report: "I knew something was going on. The doors were more squeaky than usual, even though they were regularly greased. My kids said I was crazy." This first revelation of a filthy scandal had established the credibility of the newspaper as an organ working in the defense of civic truth.

2 1

Before ringing Pascual Bramsos' doorbell, Max Michels fixed his
eyes on his own apartment, just visible in the distance. Had she
come back from her morning's tasks? How could you say you were
the owner of a concrete structure hanging in midair? Leaving him
the apartment had been his defunct father's most generous and
perverse deed. Where would he be living with her now otherwise?
Since he was by then closer to completing his registration as a
candidate, he allowed himself a small provocation of the Many:
Going to let this pass without even a "Fuck you," are you? Nothing. Well I'll be damned! Their silence maddened him more than
their aggression. Just the thought of blowing up the apartment
with all of us in it...

The works he now felt so ashamed of had commenced with the
commercial expansion, but the truth was that the dust was never
going away. The T&R construction company had taken on the
task of transforming of the structures of Villa Miserias; its hydraulic
equipment demolished the nostalgia standing in the way of an
inflexible future. The task consisted of transferring, as faithfully as
possible, the inequalities of the new order to the external reflection
that would give them visible form. T&R had to ensure that the
environment adapted to the proprietor and not the proprietor
to the environment. Incentives to be different had to be created.

Through a new twist in the financing scheme, the residents were
given the chance to locate themselves in their corresponding realities. The original concept of Villa Miserias had involved two apartments per floor. At Perdumes' request, T&R suggested a new design.

The apartments on the first floor and one of those on the second were divided in two; the third floor remained as it was and the top floor would become a single, spacious penthouse.

The assessed value of the properties increased and with it the rent, so that a number of families had no choice but to move to the smaller apartments. The prices of the most luxurious properties ensured that they were out of the reach of the great majority. The resettlement was a protracted act of violence. Despite a natural resistance to change on the part of the residents, in general the mechanism itself was allowed to assign each to his appropriate place. The subtle manner in which the elderly couple, Don Feli, and Doña Bere—long-term owners of apartment 4A in Building 6—were crushed served as a warning that sentimentality wouldn't stand in the way of the advance of the estate.

As a young woman, Doña Bere had inherited the property in which she resided with her two sons, living frugally on her husband's wages as a hydraulic engineer. After the children had left home, they got by on their pensions. When a brusque T&R executive presented them with the opportunity to spend their last years in an apartment double the size, they both knew this was nothing more than a formal procedure required by protocol. The couple had neither the means nor the desire to accept the offer. It was then suggested that they consider moving to one of the redesigned apartments on the lower floors. They'd be more comfortable with less space to worry about; and with the price difference, they would have sufficient savings for any of the eventualities associated with their age. Don Feli showed the executive the door: he left without responding to the hand held out to him.

The power of the new times sprung from the patience of its mechanisms. The elderly couple were no rivals for the ravenous breach that opened up between those who had most and those with least. As the upper floors filled with the beneficiaries of the merchandising lottery, these same people defended their right to employ sweepers to brush away the rest. The first blow fell when the coefficient of the service charge was raised in proportion to the size of the apartment. At the same time, T&R began making the alterations to the building, so that the rebellious elderly couple found themselves regularly without such basics as water and electricity. When they submitted a complaint to the board, it was explained that they would have to put up with it in the name of progress.

T&R then started remodeling the adjoining apartment to form a single living space, leaving the demolition of the thin dividing wall until the end. When Don Feli saw the outdoor Jacuzzi arrive, he knew there was no way to prevent the inevitable. The construction company finally defeated them by attacking their sleep: they paid the workers overtime to drill through the night. Their nerves shattered, the couple submitted another complaint. They again came up against icy bureaucracy. With no desire to discover what the next measure would involve, the couple went straight to T&R's offices to negotiate their property transfer. There, they were met by the same side-parted executive with his superior air. They were lucky. One of the apartments on a lower floor of the same building was still available. Their relocation wouldn't be too traumatic. Unfortunately, the market had fallen a little since his initial offer, so they wouldn't get as much for their money. The elderly couple didn't haggle.

Resignedly, they accustomed themselves to their new confines. Don Feli's long years in hydraulic engineering told him that no dam could contain the impersonal tidal bore they were swept up in.

23

Villa Miserias' public spaces had for years been bogged in functional insipidity. The board had no desire to do anything more than was strictly necessary. When consulted on the matter by Perdumes, G.B.W. Ponce explained that if people took their total lack of responsibility for granted, what was normal became a no man's land. They had to stop treating the residents as if they were invalids. The board decreed that each unit had to be responsible for its own immediate environment. Those buildings with more proactive checking accounts gave their green areas such a face-lift that they looked like something from an architecture magazine; new, more elegant buzzer systems were installed, watched over by private doormen, who also washed the residents' cars; the potholes were filled. The revaluation of the buildings contributed to giving the residential estate a smarter appearance as it encouraged the sluggards to keep up with their neighbors. Perdumes was gratified to see the effects of this break with the arbitrary tyranny of the board.

There was one outstanding issue: what could be done about the public spaces that didn't benefit any specific person? The communal funds wouldn't stretch that far; and these spaces were considered to be unfair, as they didn't benefit everyone equally.

While the solution generated complaints from those who were mired in the past, the overwhelming majority welcomed it with tacit approval, particularly when they began to see the tangible results: the concessions for the improvements were spread around. The high wall surrounding Villa Miserias was spruced up by courtesy of a paint company. The trash containers were exchanged for larger ones, with an automatic recycling system that separated the garbage according to consistency, thanks to the generosity of a household appliance firm. The rusty swings were transformed into a small city for children, with a pirate ship, outdoor trampolines, climbing frames with rope bridges, and electric cars. The flat-screen TV store donated pieces of their equipment with a message from the owner wishing the children a happy playtime. The new barrier giving access to the estate carried the logo of a soft drink. Even the uniforms of the cleaning staff and the Black Paunches were changed for a more fashionable, flirtatious brand.

24

The resettlement was like an hourglass that was, from time to time, gradually turned over; it had the particularity that the most privileged stratum of grains formed a pressure block against the walls so as not to fall through the opening like the others. The result was a mass of grains, densely packed at the base, distantly observed by a superior compact layer. Apart from a few disoriented grains that somehow remained in the intermediate space, the greater part of the glass was empty, so forming a tension between the opposing poles.

But there were two sides to the magic of Quietism in Motion: if one of the privileged grains lost its guile, it would suddenly slide and fall to the bottom with the rest. On certain inexplicable occasions, one of the grains from the inferior heap would rise up until it was rubbing shoulders with those above. The image of the whole varied little, although gravity ensured that growth tended to be greater in the lower half of the hourglass. Adaptation to a new stratum was always more laborious when it involved descent. Those who fell never ceased to look upwards to the sky and recall with nostalgia the good times when they were fortunate grains. Alternatively, the grains that made it to the top mingled with the others so that only a trained eye could tell the difference. It was to Perdumes' great relief that the hourglass had become so fixed in the consciousness of the estate that a new upending was now unthinkable.

The commercial expansion created the need for cheap labor. In addition, the increased consumption generated more trash, in both its literal and metaphorical senses: once the taboo that had confined the workers on the estate to Building B had been broken, they began to occupy the tiny apartments T&R had redesigned. Each relocation involved an application of the ochre paint signaling the condition of the occupant; the rectangles spread progressively until the mixture became more vertical than geographic. In a good percentage of the buildings, realities so disparate that they seemed to correspond to completely different species coexisted. Only the weight of the daily bustle of the estate and a vague presumption of just deserts stopped the sparks rising upward.

Just in case they did rise, the process of reinforcing the security forces in terms of both manpower and equipment continued.

There was also a proliferation of private mercenary groups to protect the right to ostentation of the most prominent residents. They moved around in a popular make of tank, disguised as an ordinary car. When Juana Mecha saw a motorcade of wry-necked bodyguards pass by, she exclaimed: "Reality's just got more real."

This phenomenon was a direct corollary of Quietism in Motion. The rules were perfectly clear: they allowed for struggle that was harsh, merciless, unequal, abusive, cruel, deceitful, stark, implacable, traitorous—and other such derivatives—just so long as it occurred in the financial sphere. The barbaric times when physical force assured a place in the hierarchy were fortunately a quaint memory. Now a pudgy administrator, trained to teach the secrets of the market, could, in the event, crush a squadron armed with military hardware. There were no two ways of looking at it. Endorsing the use of physical force to defend oneself from financial issues was as absurd as allowing an illiterate person to use a dictionary in a spelling quiz. Competition was the static motor of the times, as long as it was understood on the basis of a set of norms designed to prioritize certain characteristics, backed up by a monopoly on public and private violence, in order for that monopoly to preserve its growing possessions.

The productive transformation had its political counterpart: the residents of Villa Miserias were ready to choose for themselves. As access to the struggle was through a locked door, it was always the same person—broken down into such aspects as a greater of lesser degree of charisma, articulacy, and physical presence—who competed. The living legend of Severo Candelario served to dissuade naïve enthusiasts. Perdumes filtered out undesirable candidates and set others on the stage. Once there, they were free to tear one another to pieces. Their policies were interchangeable, and they articulated them like parrots repeating dogma. They were unimportant: a study by G.B.W. Ponce revealed that 88% of residents neither remembered nor understood the platforms of their future authority figures. It never occurred to anyone to question the direction of their plans. The generally held belief was that this was the best of alternatives. Debate centered on the outer shell.

Radical policies went no further than to propose the quota of leftover food per household be proportional to the coefficient, or that the board offer free vouchers for tai chi classes. Perdumes made sure that the form the root took was never mentioned. To do so would be as fruitless as proposing a modification of the climate. The electoral debate must not attack the beliefs that had formed reality in this particular way. As was his custom, Perdumes made use of an image: a dog doesn't abstain from biting its master because of a calculation of the negative consequences this would involve; the nature of the relationship meant that the act would not even occur to the animal.

With the sphere of ideas duly anaesthetized, the fight was centered on rumor and scandal. The elections were a test of a candidate's ability to sling mud at his rival in the appropriate style, and at the proper moment. The residents gave themselves up without reservations to the swing of the pendulum of indignation-forgetting-indignation-forgetting-indignation-forgetting offered by the revelations and accusations of the campaigns.

The Daily Miserias reported it all with sensational impartiality. If the scandal was of a sexual nature, they automatically doubled the print run for that day. Orquídea López had a strict ethical conscience: the readers had a right to know everything. Private life became a thing of the past with the decision to enter the public sphere. Sometimes she had to use indecorous methods to obtain information, but Orquídea justified this with the notion that every journalist is a paid detective and you can't go into the sewers without getting your shoes dirty.

Each day, there would be a front-page opinion poll carried out by G.B.W. Ponce—all the candidates used the services of $uperstructure. Ponce would analyze what his database had already told him: the quantitative effects of the electorate's opinions. He had never fallen outside his ±3.14% in his prediction of the results.

25

By the time Max Michels came to his decision, a fair number of managers of the winds of change blowing through Villa Miserias had already come and gone. Perdumes continued to present them with a statue to commemorate the end of their terms of office; it was still the same man with a sphere, but with one variation: the man was now upright, his arms akimbo. Standing at one side of the sphere, he now had no direct contact with it: he simply supervised its correct course.

Max left his apartment and knocked on his friend Pascual Bramsos' door. He found him working on an installation, soon to be exhibited, that had involved cutting dozens of egg shells in half and then—after cleaning them—filling a number with plaster to strengthen them. The exteriors of the shells were painted with an imperceptible layer of varnish. The piece was designed to be shown on a single occasion. The eggs would be glued very close together on a concrete base measuring nine feet by three, with the solid shells randomly placed, so that a volunteer could attempt to walk over the work without breaking any of the others.

Max took Bramsos' arm and asked if he would accompany him on an important mission. As they entered the administration office, Bramsos still had no idea of Max's intention. When the latter said, "I've come to register as a candidate in the election," his friend and the assistant exchanged wide-eyed glances of surprise. A pencil rolled from the desk onto the floor under the impulse of the gentle current of fresh air entering through the window.

II

I

The succession of millions of instants, memories, smells, voices, joys, sadness, and all the other elementary particles constituting that thing he called his life seemed to Max Michels completely contingent and necessary. Everything was so fragile; the least variation would have ruined his present configuration. He wouldn't be that Max, but another. At the same time, not even the most irrelevant things could be questioned. That's how it had been, period; on a gilt plaque on the wall of the apartment his father's familiar axiom was written: "The measure of each man lies in the dose of truth he can withstand."

Shortly before dying, his decrepit father had asked for a moment alone with his only son. True to the meticulous judicial principles that ruled his existence, he first explained the plan for ending it: Max was about to come of age; he was leaving him the apartment and a trust fund to cover his expenses until he finished his education. He wasn't going to spoil his son by willing him the rest of his patrimony: it was going to the private institution of rigid freethinking in which he'd once studied to become the eminent member of the legal profession he now was. In return, the institution promised to place an effigy of him at the entrance to the library.

"Maximiliano, at this crucial moment, I am about to inform you of your true inheritance," he said with solemn magnanimity. "You must exercise extreme care in relation to the specious reasoning of the weaker sex. Keep women at a prudent distance from family and friends, both of which are sacred treasures in the attainment earthly joy. And last but not least, show yourself to be powerful with those of humble origins and humble with the powerful. A tendency to equalize either of those extremes will diminish you."

Max had narrowed his eyes as he scanned every self-satisfied furrow of his father's face, as if deliberately searching for something he knew he wouldn't find. Was it his turn to say something? His father had reached out a hand to seal the moment with a firm clasp, just as Max had been taught to do since his childhood.

"The serum that breathes the last ounce of energy into my veins is on the point of running out. Be so good as to leave me and call the nurse."

"Goodbye Dad," Max had said, hurrying out of the room.

Minutes later, the last thing Dr. Michels' elderly heart did was to obey the order to stop, and Max entered adulthood three weeks before the date marked on the calendar.

2

The burial service and the various eulogies stressed Dr. Michels' honesty and rectitude, but principally his healthy obsession with the concept of truth. He'd debated with the ancient theoreticians on the concepts of natural vs. positive truth, and had regretfully admitted that, even in terms of revealed truth, it was a man-made concept. This conclusion made him implacable: he offered up the meaning of his existence to finding ways to avoid the temptation of diverging from the truth. What he found was deeply unappealing. Outside of vague moral notions and Manichean fables, truth was, in reality, no use at all. It maintained its status as a shared ideal only because of a tacit acceptance of its unlimited non-observance. Without lies, we would be constantly getting snagged: co-existence would be unviable, especially with oneself. He carried out a careful experiment, and realized that he lied no less than fifty times a day: how he was feeling, a person's appearance, his liking for the family of a loved one, his social viewpoints. The consequences of always telling the truth would be, in fact, unpleasant.

He also came to the conclusion that, without self-deception, we would never get out of bed. The ability to work at a mechanical task for no other reason than to receive a paltry wage with which to educate our children to work at a mechanical task for no other reason than to receive a paltry wage, accompanied by a partner absorbed in her own repetition, increasingly distanced by the layers of routine and resentment waiting to rise to the surface, with only such occasional palliatives as holidays that only throw more light on everyday uselessness, or alcohol-fueled outpourings to friends that end in our babbling theories so stupid we are ashamed to recall them, spurred on by the possibility of experiencing the pleasure of guilt produced by sleeping with one of their wives, escaping from our crushing personal horizons to the peaks represented by a son's first tooth, the possibility of seeing him compete with other children of his age to see which of them is most loved by his parents, or by the professional recognition of a boss with rotting teeth, pleased by the increase in efficiency of the gear mechanism we grease, or the lows caused by the death of someone close, or the eruptions of frustration against some public figure stupid enough to transgress society's lax codes of corruption and tolerance of his excesses. If we didn't find, every day, hundreds of lies to silence the many who inhabit us, if we didn't get even with our bodies by an injection of thickness into our arteries, if we didn't put up with our envy of others in order to envy someone else, if we didn't fool ourselves into thinking that the worst has passed, we couldn't play out the daily comedy. The dilemma of existence reminded him of an actor trained to get inside his character until he actually becomes him, but who hasn't been shown the method for getting back out. What alternative had the madman with the bushy mustache offered him? Art. It was a viable solution for a few; for the immense majority—including Dr. Michels—it was unattainable, unthinkable.

He consciously encapsulated all his objections and stored them in a remote corner of his mind. From meditation, he borrowed the technique of automatically abandoning any notion related to what one did not want to think about. Every time some current appeared, threatening to drag him into the whirlpool of TRUTH, he would take refuge in the dirty pool of *his* truth. He understood that it was a matter of ambition. He ought to renounce the immaculate concept and focus on a fenced-in, pragmatic, realizable version: completeness is not human. Conversely, one had to be intransigent in relation to agreed truths. Only that way can chaos be tamed. He would not allow young Max to be seduced into falling into that pit of shining truths that was poetry.

Centuries before, someone had warned of the danger to society involved in its metamorphoses. Dr. Michels had a clear understanding of this: how can a better future be constructed if things change in relation to the names they are given? If a chair was not only an object for sitting on, it might occur to one person to crash it down on another's head. Only an objectified language could kill the thing and put it at the service of human development. His son would live in a certain, solid world, far from the phantasmagoric abstractions that had been the downfall of so many.

Max had displayed a lively intelligence from an early age. When he was five, his father had tried reading him a classic treatise on the truth, but it had been too hard for him. Dr. Michels, therefore, changed tack: every night he would take up a thick, leather-bound volume and open it at random to tell Max a story. It was the moment when the two of them were closest. If during the day Dr. Michels was absorbed in his own occupations and the nature of the person whose task it was to attend to them, in that intimate rite with his son he shed a number of the prejudices that ruled his acts, and became simply a slave to the stories he rigorously recounted to his son. Max listened with a mixture of nervousness—he didn't want to disappoint his father by not understanding—and desire to hear the variations that sprung each night from what seemed to him the same book.

The most frequently repeated story was entitled "The Land of Things with Multiple Names." As soon as it began, Max would shut his eyes especially tight, trusting in the pressure of his eyelids to ensure he wasn't overcome by sleep before the ending.

3

"Once upon a time, there were two children who lived happily in the forest with their parents. Everything in their simple, honest life was in harmony; every element of their surroundings was the result of pleasant familiarity. Their father had warned them never to cross the clearing in the forest: on the other side was The Land of Things with Multiple Names. Nothing there was what it seemed. Even the most inoffensive thing might drive them crazy: words were in command there and every day they decided to name things differently. For example, the word 'tree' suddenly tired of its leaves and wood; it wanted to expand its domain, briefly spread its roots, so it lay in wait and, when a jaguar passed by, it seized its name. Now it was no longer 'jaguar,' and everyone knew it as 'tree.' Its spots began to show knots of bark and branches sprouted from its legs. Its gait became increasingly ponderous; it could no longer pounce. In time, it took root and became anchored to the earth. Its jaguar memory slowly dwindled. It would watch the other wild beasts hunting swiftly, remembering that it had something in common with them, but it no longer knew what. Eventually, it lost any trace of its former name.

"The names lived in a constant state of war, attempting to convert others to their meaning. Not one of them was sure what anything was called. An anarchy of forms reigned and what today was one thing might not be tomorrow.

"The ruler of that country, Princess M, was in constant search of new names to enrich her realm. She used to trick them by offering a fun-filled world in which everything played at being everything else and nothing was ever boring. They were free to recover their names and leave when they wished, but they never did. Once they had discovered the pleasures of escaping from the tyranny of fixity and understood that her magic allowed them to be everything and nothing at the same time, none of them wanted to quit her kingdom. It was like an endless masked ball, liberated from the crushing responsibility of being always the same before others.

"One day the children's football accidentally went beyond the confines of the forest. On other such occasions, they had turned around and returned home, but this time the little boy was determined to enter the forbidden land, so he crossed the threshold with a firm stride. His sister waited to see what would happen. She watched as her brother attempted to pick up the ball and saw how it bounced away from him, reaching ever-greater heights. The boy allowed the ball to move away and then ran at it, kicking with all his might. The ball gave a whimper and flew off like a shot. It soon unfolded a pair of majestic wings: 'eagle' had stolen its meaning. For a while, it played a sort of aerial soccer with the boy, but as it was every moment more 'eagle' and less 'ball,' feathers began to cover its surface and the outlines of a beak and talons appeared. As the boy ran to kick it one more time, it took flight at the last minute—pretending to be reacting to the impact of his foot—and carried out a series of swoops that filled the boy with excitement; he had never before managed to kick the ball in that way. When the former ball was completely 'eagle,' it masterfully took to the air, thanking the boy for the chance to free itself from its fixed leathery existence.

"The girl crossed over to join in the fun. They ran happily around finding unexpected properties in each thing. 'Rabbit' lost its solidity and color, floating hither and thither like multiform cotton wool: it wanted to be 'cloud.' The little girl picked a clover plant that then spitefully sprayed her face with a repugnant smell: it was beginning to transform into 'skunk.' They went along, marveling at it all, not thinking of the road home, until they came to Princess M's castle.

"They had never seen anything so miraculous. The princess had such control over words that she had constructed her castle of an infinite number of them, arranged in such a way that it appeared to each observer in the form he wanted to imagine. The two children saw the castle of their respective dreams, which changed as they conceived some new element: they saw a file of immense towers, waterfalls of chocolate, nonexistent animals composed of fantastic combinations, wild hanging gardens. Colors seemed to have been exclusively created to be displayed in that kingdom. Princess M was awaiting them inside her castle.

"Everything felt comfortingly familiar. With unaffected warmth, Princess M showed the children her rooms and looked on in satisfaction as they made use of the possibilities of language to manipulate things at their will. The princess was excited to think that she had found lasting companions. Finally, she could demolish the walls of her terrible loneliness. Perhaps these children would evade the fatal destiny of so many others who had come before them.

"The children were enchanted by the metamorphosis of their surroundings. Their family home seemed a distant memory; they were thankful for their escape from the predictable world where everything was always the same. It was fine for simple people like their parents, happy with their tranquil routine, but they were made for something different. The princess taught them increasingly sophisticated techniques for manipulating words. They were prodigies, easily meeting each new challenge. Princess M played with them for hours, making and unmaking unimaginable worlds. Even the words were amazed by the fluidity with which they changed: the meanings would last seconds and then they were a different brick in the construction of another madcap reality.

"The Land of Things with Multiple Names was not exempt from terrible dangers. The children had to be on their guard against attacks from words wanting to impose their meanings. The simplest defense was to make oneself invisible. The princess told them that if they did not attempt to hold onto their own meanings, no one could force another onto them. The words that lost their identities were those so stubbornly vain about meaning just one thing that they were easy targets for the envy of weak-spirited concepts, affirming their identities by taking possession of others'.

"In demonstration, she called 'pig' and ordered it to attempt to steal her meaning. Although aware it was destined to fail, 'pig' automatically obeyed. At first the princess resisted, concentrating on the features that defined her as the beautiful and powerful M. The children watched incredulously as she began to grow a hoof and her well-modulated voice was replaced by high-pitched squeals. 'Pig' thought it perceived a possible victory: no other word had gotten so far in an attempt to steal Princess M's meaning. With her last glimmer of thought, the princess imperceptibly changed tack: she forgot all her defining features, put up no resistance to being something different, stopped trying to appear in her accustomed form. Instead, she concentrated on breathing deeply so she would seem like the air that entered and was expelled from her lungs, without struggling to be anything but her being, renouncing the pursuit of adjectives that originated in external mirrors. 'Pig' was thrown back against the wall. It made its painful way out in search of a victim more inclined to give up its meaning. It seemed to the children that Princess M was more beautiful than ever.

"The boy and girl mastered invisibility. They delighted in walking around with an air of vulnerability, easy prey for any word hoping to extend its meaning. They would keep a sly watch on the onslaught and, at the last moment, withdraw behind a cape of transparency, leaving the confused word in search of a new target. Nevertheless, just as with all their predecessors, the children became ever less satisfied with the game of changing forms. The obedience of the concepts was not enough, they longed for total incorporation, to eliminate the boundaries that separated them from language and take on its properties in a permanent way. If in their distant past livese they had used words to name and order the world, they now wished to *be* the names and *create* a new order each day, to carry within themselves all possibilities. The challenge was to convert themselves into people of their own design, with capabilities only limited by the confines of language. They wanted to cut any connection with external reality, inhabit the worlds produced by their own minds.

"One day 'firefly' accidentally flew into the girl's mouth; instead of spitting it out, she swallowed it. She felt light, aglow. She tried a similar experiment with 'iron' and, although she found it difficult to digest, she felt more solid. She tempted 'moderation' to take possession of her and rather than making herself invisible, she did nothing. The word attempted to penetrate her from all sides without success. From that moment on, 'moderation' refused to have anything to do with that soul: she became insatiable, devouring whatever she could. Her aim was to retain every characteristic of the other, to be all things at once. She buried her essence under fatty layers of the foreign attributes she accumulated as she tore the words apart to incorporate their properties. Her addiction distanced her from her brother and the princess. It had stopped being a game. She gobbled sacks of words without even noticing their meaning. Each day, she had to make herself a new dress, as she would have burst the seams of the previous one.

"The time came when she was no longer recognizable. She couldn't even move: she was a sphere capable of conjuring up any form, color, texture, past and future, dream or nightmare. It was as easy for her to evoke a tropical form as a glacial one. She relived nonexistent moments when she saved lives, won prizes, was a river, or visited distant planets. No one else existed for her. Eventually, she no longer fitted on the page, so she stopped being part of the story. She existed in an eternal limbo, where she only had herself to satisfy the holes, monsters, and specters her imagination constantly created and filled.

"Her brother had not come out of his room for a long time. He seduced words to stay with him in his refuge by telling them the plans he had for them: he would use them to reach a place no one had ever been before. His skill in arranging them would completely erase the distance between a thing and its name.

At first, they proudly lined up to be part of the worlds he dictated. They were conscious of participating in something beautiful and enduring. But then he began to demand more of them; poor 'anguish' made a great effort to disperse its mists and become pure negative emotion: nothing it did was ever enough. The boy flogged it with a whip of terrifying, incomprehensible phrases. With each lash, he demanded greater effort and drama. It was no good. There was always a residue between the emotion and the meanings. As a punishment, the boy loaded it with sophisticated adjectives. 'Anguish' became increasingly more artificial and lost all its effect. It then received more lashes, until it could no longer even stand on its own two feet.

"The density of the accumulated words was immense. It was impossible to walk around his room without bumping into some weary, famished concept. Then the foreseeable happened: the words rebelled and turned on their master. They had had enough of being used to originate tangled, insubstantial environments. Their plan worked perfectly. The boy was so entranced by what he considered to be his poetic talents that he no longer paid attention to the effects of his arrangements of the words. While he thought he was creating complex abstract worlds revealing the depths of the soul, the words silently regrouped to form an unbreakable cage.

"When the boy tried to go outside for some fresh air, he realized what had happened. His flowery constructions were nothing more than thick bars. He started to unmake them, subjugating one word at a time: terrified, they gave in to his will. 'Guile' had seen this coming, so it gave the signal to move to the next phase: the words began to swell until they ruptured their boundaries.

The cage became a lump of spongy concepts. The boy panicked. He didn't understand the meanings. He could see tightly packed letters impeding his escape, without knowing what they referred to. The words had swollen to the point where they were empty. The boy crashed his head into one of the bars. The impact shattered 'greed' and left the aggressor with his face splattered with its ink. With the boy now confused, 'waters' gave the order for all the words to force down until they expelled their waste matter. The floor of the cage was flooded with the dots of 'i's, accents, the feet of 'm's, even whole letters the most coquettish words wanted to replace with others. 'Broom' bustled up to order the boy to sweep up the fetid waste. When the boy had finished, the words covered the floor in waste matter again. He was trapped in an interminable cleanup operation of the residues of language, expelled by words that had absolutely no meaning.

"Princess M was left alone once more in her interminable wait for someone capable of playing with the words without being destroyed by his own pretension. Others came, but with decreasing frequency. 'Applause' took command of her realm, boasting of all the traps into which so many naïve people had fallen while attempting to seek her favor by dominating the words.

"The children's parents searched for many days without finding them. They had already lost all hope when the two children suddenly returned as if nothing had happened. The parents smothered them in kisses, hugged them tightly. Although they felt something important was missing from the children, they were so relieved to have them back that they preferred to let the matter go.

"During the children's stay in The Land of Things with Multiple

Names, 'simulation' had carefully studied their appearance and bearing. When it heard of their respective downfalls, it split in two and adopted their forms. It was tired of being a shadow of the real thing and wanted to experience the solidity of reality. After meeting its new parents, it felt at ease in its welcoming surroundings and they all lived happily ever after."

4

"My son, as you travel the path of life, littered with innumerable joys and setbacks, you should proceed with extreme caution. Pleasing lies are among the most addictive of temptations: you should avoid them at all costs," his father would say, giving him three pats on the head before turning out the light and leaving the room.

Young Max would see forms dancing in the darkness. As he fell asleep, he would visualize flowers gobbling mules that became men wearing top hats and smoking cigars through their luxuriant beards. He didn't want to let his father down: with all his might, he would try to deny the magical attraction of Princess M's realm. His head spun. He was used to creating a mental image of his black, long-eared dog, fast asleep under the window looking out onto the green area. Whenever it saw a cat prowling along the wall outside, it would start barking wildly and bound to the window, crashing into the glass in its fury. On one particular occasion, the cat seemed to be taunting the sleeping dog. It moved its head up and down, making its enemy appear insignificant. Max's first impulse was to wake the dog and point out the cat: it seemed a betrayal of his pet's pride to let the provocation go unpunished. But when he was overcome by fondness at seeing it breathing so peacefully, he changed his mind. In the end, if it didn't know of the cat's presence, it was as if it didn't exist. Max would then fall asleep on the frontier between the two kingdoms, thinking about how to keep a foot on either side.

The father had methods of persuasion. Axioms and stories were an important element of a correct upbringing, free of illusions. There was just one thing missing. Dr. Michels was a firm believer in the notion that the flesh only remembers if it is branded with iron. Punishment had a spiritual value. The forbidden remained abstract until pain made it concrete. If taking a bite of a simple piece of fruit had opened the way to thousands of years of disastrous suffering, the importance of what was forbidden could not be underestimated. His son would some day be grateful for the small burn marks that would prevent his later expulsion from the paradise of just men.

The doctor's idea was an adaptation of a classic children's story: every time Max told an untruth, he would paint his nose with gentian violet. The objective was to mark him with that purple liquid so often that Max would interiorize the stain and his mind would be fortified against lies.

The problem was that Max didn't tell lies. He never attempted to cross the limits set by his father. The doctor would listen, discouraged, to his son's voluntary confessions of naughty acts: he had secretly given the dog a chicken bone; instead of doing his homework at the set time, he had spent thirteen extra minutes coloring in a picture in his pirate book; he'd considered drowning a cockroach in the toilet, but had finally put it in a box and taken it to the garden. Max's confessions removed the doctor's weapon; they took all the pleasure and meaning from punishment. The unopened bottle of gentian violet was his greatest failure. Max didn't understand the harm his natural transparency, unmolded by castigation, could do him. For the doctor, it was like building a house of straw and spending the rest of one's life hoping the wind never blew. He decided Max would have to learn the hard way: he would make his son tell an untruth whether he liked it or not. The end justified any means.

The doctor showed himself to be in possession of a sadistic form of creativity. He elaborated situations that would place Max at a crossroads where, whichever direction he took, it would lead him away from any possible truth. He set traps in the areas where Max was most vulnerable. He knew, for example, of his son's adoration of his old nanny, who had, for as long as he could remember, filled the gaps left by his mother's many absences. The nanny was used to involuntary austerity; for her, it was enough to eat stale tortillas smeared with refried beans and a little diced cheese. But she loved the iced buns that could be bought by the packet and would carefully hoard her loose change to treat herself once every two weeks. The first time the doctor succeeded in painting Max's nose, he bought a whole box of buns and asked that no one touch them. The nanny watched in desperation as the sell-by date approached; it seemed unpardonable that they couldn't be eaten. When she'd almost saved enough to buy a packet for herself, she decided to open one of her master's, hoping to replace it before he noticed. When the doctor confronted her with the absence, she admitted her guilt, offering to pay for the buns immediately. He told her not to worry, said she could eat as many as she wanted. It was a cheap price for what he would get in exchange.

"Maximiliano, would you be good enough to come here for a moment?" he called as his son was getting ready for school.

"What is it, Dad?" asked Max, not suspecting the trap.

"Do you by any chance know who ate the buns I expressly asked not to be touched?"

His words fell on Max like a hammer blow to the neck. He knew it must surely have been his nanny. Any answer he gave would incriminate her. If he accused her, it would not only be a betrayal, but also a lie, since he was not completely certain she had done it. Trembling, he looked at his father, who already had in his hand the purple punishment he was anxious to administer.

"It was me, Dad," he said in self-sacrifice, his head bent.

His father took his arm and marched him to the kitchen. The nanny was dunking a bun in atole while listening to the news on her old radio. She suspected something was going on when she saw young Max's tearful eyes and tried to shield him by asking if he wanted quesadillas for breakfast. Max shook his head, proud of his ineffective attempt to protect her.

Max's father took him to the bathroom and sat him on the toilet seat. As he soaked a piece of cotton wool in the purple liquid, he consoled his son with his exquisite affection:

"My boy, when your understanding is sufficiently mature, you will realize that your father is your best friend. Other people with whom you form emotional relationships will come and go; your father, in contrast, will always be there for you." He then meticulously covered every inch of Max's long straight nose in gentian violet.

In the beginning, he invented slight variations of the same scheme on a daily basis. Threatened with his dog being given away, Max took the blame for an act of destruction instigated by his father, and the same happened when the neighbors complained that some hyperactive kid had been ringing bells and running away and when Max's trousers were found to be inexplicably covered in mud. It was just a matter of provoking a situation that would end in an admission of guilt. His father would then conduct an investigation that exonerated Max, punish him for lying and send him to school with a purple nose. The first time the young cleaning woman, Juana Mecha, saw him coming out of the building looking like a clown who'd just received a scolding, she gave him a candy and prophesized: "Your invisible rays will eventually dazzle them."

As the father's addiction took hold, his methods became more absurd. He once handed Max an article to read on the fluctuations in the stock market:

"Maximiliano, would you be good enough to tell me which company experienced the greatest fall in its share price yesterday?" From his tone of voice, Max knew that there was no way of knowing even the nature of his fault.

"I didn't understand the article, Dad," he replied, bored by the pantomime about to unfold. He would have preferred to move directly to the punishment without the need for so many formalities.

"Let's examine the case more carefully. You surely remember that the article mentioned a case related to sausages?"

"The brand we buy. It said something about rat meat." Max watched as his father's features closed ranks around his disproportionally long front teeth. Who would have imagined there were rats with tortoiseshell spectacles?

"Making use of your faculties of reasoning, would you say this referred to something good or bad?" the rat-detective tenaciously countered.

"Very bad." Max longed to drown out the inquisitorial voice in a stream of purple water.

"So, if we follow this reasoning through, based on our faithful friend logic, would you be inclined to say that the situation of the sausage factory improved or became worse?"

"Worse." Submerge it until not even the rat could hear its cries.

"Do you see that you did in fact have all the necessary information for answering my question? Notwithstanding, you looked your father in the eyes and said in all confidence that you didn't know. Come with me to the bathroom this instant."

On another occasion, he maliciously asked, "Maximiliano, if you were to search your heart to find who you have more affection for, would you choose me, or would it be perhaps your mother?"

"I love you both equally."

"My son, what you say is impossible. First, because emotions cannot be scientifically measured. Moreover, without conceding your assertion, the possibility of your loving us equally is practically zero. I am sorry to have to tell you that you are, once again, lying."

By the final semester of his last year at elementary school, the ritual was wearing thin. However, the doctor's determination to conclude his educational cycle wasn't going to weaken when he was so close to completing his mission. Each morning, without even getting out of his bed, Dr. Michels asked his son if he'd lied the day before. If Max replied that he hadn't, he would—by use of twisted syllogisms—demonstrate the opposite. In the case that he admitted his fault, the doctor would ask for an explanation. When Max came up with something, his father would send him to the bathroom to paint his own nose with gentian violet. It often happened that his nervousness would stop him thinking of any specific untruth; in that case, he'd lied in saying that he had lied. He only told the truth at weekends and on public holidays.

At the request of a kindly teacher called Severo Candelario, the school authorities interrogated the child about the matter. He explained that the gentian violet was just to keep at bay the germs produced by a strange allergy. (His lie to the school director led to the next day's punishment.) Their duty done, the topic was never mentioned again.

His classmates weren't so indulgent: they insulted him and invented cruel nicknames; he wasn't allowed to take part in any of their games; they filled his backpack with rotting giant radishes encrusted with potato noses; they threw erasers at him and slapped his head when they passed him. Max understood this was all a consequence of the discipline imposed on him by his father, so he generally forced himself to put up with it until one day, during recess, a boy tipped purple jelly onto his hair. In what was almost a reflex action, Max wiped off the offending dessert and flung himself at his aggressor. He pulled him down by the hair and after banging his face into the ground a few times, forced him to lick up every last bit of jelly. The child cried loudly as he spat out pieces of gritty purple jelly. Severo Candelario had witnessed the entire scene. When he thought things had gone far enough, he ran up to pull the furious Max away, then carried him to his classroom to calm down and sent the nurse to look after the other child. In his report on the event, he stated that the boys were wrestling when the injured party accidentally hit his head. That was the last time anyone bothered Max; from then on they just ignored him.

5

In addition to a stronger character, Max gained something more valuable during his purple year: the close friendship of two other, obviously different children. Nothing could now break that initial pact of mutual protection between Max's nose, Pascual Bramsos' burned ear, and the almond-shaped eyes of his desk-mate Sao Bac-Do. She came from a distant land with swarms of bicycles and pointed hats; her parents had arrived by chance in that foreign country, seeking refuge from the rain that burned their children. While they were learning the language, they worked industriously in their small laundry. Even at that early age, all the other children had been taught to make judgments based on similarity. Rather than perceiving the seed of extraordinary beauty, they saw in Sao a girl with a prominent forehead and slit eyes who couldn't pronounce her 'r's. When she'd transformed into a teenager with a mystical attraction, she would laugh as she spurned the gallantries of those same boys who had enclosed her in a circle, uttering guttural sounds, and stretching out the corners of eyes with their fingers.

Sao, Max, and Pascual formed an order with rules that were incomprehensible to others. They used to meet during the recess in the musty tunnel connecting the two schoolyards to take their revenge—via marbles—for that day's insults. The marbles were given warped versions of the names of their principal tormentors, and then, in fine, black felt-tip pen, Pascual would draw some feature on them, making them objects of fun. The three were also the masters of a secret Head World, where everything was the opposite of the reality that besieged them outside the tunnel. In Head World, you walked on the ceiling, and the ground protected you from the whims of the subsoil. It was inhabited by beings with half-molten ears, multicolored noses, and eyes like lines that stretched to the horizon. The three monarchs had a circus in which they kept scary caged creatures that provided a contrast to themselves, reminding them of how lucky they were; contemplating those symmetrical appearances, the lunch boxes with designs of robots with missiles for arms, listening to the smooth chatter made them dizzy. Those beings reproduced automatically on contact, producing a shower of raindrops made in the image of the hundreds of thousands of others; they communicated by a song of elongated vowels, puckering their open lips to show their teeth. Sao, Max, and Pascual used to act out their favorite part of life in their own world: they would enter the circus ring, performing a dance only they knew—learning its steps meant escape from the cages for the interchangeable creatures—and move about under the spell of the beat of imaginary drums, while the freaks of normality looked on in perplexity. Some began to imitate them and so others would join in too. By the end of the recess, everyone in

Head World would be contorting themselves to the rhythm of its three creators. When the school bell rang, they all immediately disappeared, incapable of accompanying them to the real world where they each had to take up their respective roles. Hand in hand, they would run back to the classroom, still glowing with the acquired powers their classmates would never experience.

6

Dr. Michels worked in a cyclical way. To be precise, he considered that the cult of luxury that was beginning to spread through the air of the age to be the result of a lack of boundaries, the capricious desire both to have and be everything at once. For this reason, it was his duty to train Max to see beyond the falsities of immediate pleasure and penetrate into the gauntest regions, however hard it might be. He went back to the beginning to verify if the paint on his son's nose had seeped into his bones.

"Maximiliano, be so good as to come here for a moment."

"What is it Dad?" Max came toward him calmly, uninterested in the new means of turning his nose purple.

"Given the perceptiveness you have inherited from me, have you by chance noticed the clothing your nanny wears on the days when she rests from her work-life duties?"

The doctor challenged his son to meet and hold his gaze. Max was slow in responding, hoping to anticipate the landmines.

"She wears the same pink uniform every day."

"You are surely aware of the reasons why she behaves in that way."

"So she doesn't wear out her other clothes."

"In that case, do you not find certain contradictions in the fact that she possesses a number of articles of cheap clothing, but decides not to wear them?" Without giving Max time to reply, he inserted another bar into the construction of his character, "And answer me another question. Have you noticed that even on those occasions when we offer her a portion of our food, she chooses to enjoy her plate of slightly rancid refried beans?"

"She doesn't like to take advantage."

"If your words are true, how do you explain that we have repeatedly caught her secretly sampling our bacalao during the Christmas festivities?" Before Max could draw breath, he continued, "Hold your tongue while your father is speaking. I will finally ask you to reflect on the following. Have you noticed the smell in the kitchen when your nanny has spent a considerable time there?"

Max felt the cold sweat emitted by every pore in his body become a torrent. Normally, when his father had him on the ropes, he would go immediately to the bathroom, without saying a word, and paint his nose. Now, on the point of disobedience, his knees began to buckle; he found it difficult to breathe.

"Please reply, Maximiliano."

"The food sometimes contains strong-smelling ingredients."

"And what about the evenings she spends watching television without cooking?"

"The smell clings to her. Some days she doesn't have time for shower."

"And how would you respond if I mentioned the rank scent of the perfume she puts on to go to mass?"

Max ran to the bathroom and picked up the bottle of gentian violet. Dr. Michels followed him as quickly as he could. Before the liquid could soak into the cotton wool, he thundered, "Maximiliano, do not even consider disobeying your father in this way!" That moment was fixed in Max's memory as the passage from a hard but cushioned world to a complex one, constructed from thorns. He thought of all the boring classical plays his father had taken him to. Beneath the bizarre costumes, the innocent cardboard scenery, the inviolable honor of damsels, and gentlemen who would choose death rather than stain that honor, beneath all that was a true lie: bald actors and actresses with sagging flesh—their miserable lives plagued by trivial cares—who their own characters would have roundly despised. Soaking the cotton wool would mean a prolongation of his sojourn in the phase from which his father's expectant gaze wanted to expel him. They stood quietly, like two gunslingers, each waiting for the other to make the first move. After a few moments, Max threw the piece of cotton wool into the bin and put the cap back on the bottle of gentian violet. He lowered his arms and whispered, "We're not all equal. They are different."

"I couldn't hear what you said, my son."

"I said we're not all equal, they are different!" shouted Max in a rush of relief.

"But…?" The doctor was unwilling to trust his own joy.

"But they can be happy in their own way."

"Maximiliano, at last. Let us seal this happy moment with a fatherly embrace. You can throw away that bottle; it will no longer be necessary."

Max fantasized of kicking his father in the balls before running to beg his nanny to forgive him. He saw his mustache suspended in the air, like the smile of the ubiquitous cat he so hated, and gave him a stiff embrace, which his father interpreted as effusive. The sacrifice had been worth the effort. Max had become a man. After Max had finished getting dressed, he moved quickly through the living room, without the courage to say goodbye to his nanny. Before shutting the front door, on his way to Bramsos' apartment, he turned to look at his mother, listening to music, encapsulated in her usual chair. Max waved and turned away quickly, with no desire to find that, once again, she hadn't returned his greeting.

7

Max was as used to his mother's unchanging character as he was to any other piece of furniture in the apartment. Since leaving her job as a cataloger at the natural history museum, she spent her days in a space closed off by the books on insects in which she would bury herself for hours, only ever moving to make a cup of tea to accompany her cheese and biscuits. Max's mother felt the same affection for him as for the rarest bug in her collection: entomology had taught her not to get attached to the handful of those insects whose transitory lives crossed with those of equally insignificant species. Even the most spectacular examples, with demented forms, sensual colors, and fascinating behavior patterns were just bugs. Perishable, forgettable. While some of her colleagues anthropomorphized insect behavior, she believed otherwise: it's not that bees organize themselves like workers, or that grasshoppers display similar courtship rituals to those of humans; rather that man shares all that is most voracious, abject, and primitive with other species. If mankind were considered utilizing the same parameters used for insects, it all made sense. She called it anthropoentomology; for years she'd been starting to write a scientific treatise explaining her theory.

When Dr. Michels had crossed the threshold into his sixties, he began to worry about the matter of descendants. Before that age, he'd had no time to let his attention stray from his career: a couple of marriages—for the look of things—but nothing more. At this stage, what he wanted was not a wife, but a young uterus. He was an honorary member of a committee that awarded grants in the arts and sciences, so when a timid entomologist came before him in obvious need of support for her nonsensical project, he didn't let the opportunity pass. To the discomfort of the other members of the panel, he attacked her virulently.

"Young lady, with all respect for a distinguished member of the weaker sex, how can you suggest that we behave like insects, that we are motivated by the same basic impulses? Have you not visited the great ruins, museums, and monuments? Have you not read the most sublime poetry, listened spellbound to the immortal operas, cried with pity for your fellow man? Insects do nothing but sting, eat each other, suck blood, and reproduce. How do you dare waste the time of these busy, distinguished people?"

"What Dr. Michels is trying to say is that your project is somewhat unorthodox. But don't worry, leave your documentation with us and we'll review it in accordance with our canons of equality and transparency. Thank you for your interest," cut in a colleague to put an end to the interview on both sides.

A few days later the girl received a phone call from Dr. Michels' secretary, inviting her to have breakfast with him. He dressed carefully for the date and arrived twenty minutes early; she, in contrast, appeared wearing denim dungarees, her hair combed with her fingers, and sat down without saying a word. The doctor went through the usual courtesies, asking if she had had any difficulty in getting there, commenting on the weather, recommending the blueberry and nopal cactus juice, and expressing his envy of her casual clothing. The young woman answered in monosyllables. Dr. Michels got straight to the point:

"Young lady, you must surely have noted how brusquely I behaved during the committee session. I ask you most sincerely not to be alarmed. To tell the truth, I'm intrigued by your project. I too have dedicated my life to the investigation of the truths that define us as human beings. Gifted, as I am, with an agile and consequently, curious mind, I am always open to filling it with novel ideas. Your concept of anthropoentomology fascinates me." He paused to give his words greater weight. The girl looked at him impassively through her conscientious-student spectacles. "The fact is that the committee is composed of honorable people who take their mission seriously. However, our funds are limited and we are obliged to support projects that offer the greatest benefit to society. Those of us who have the privilege of donating want to obtain the greatest yield from every penny we invest. For this reason, it is necessary to ensure that the projects, in turn, generate funds, a patent that can be exploited, or a piece of new information that can be capitalized upon. Without wishing to question in any way the validity of your undertaking, I have to confess that it is an unfruitful project, of limited accessibility. In addition, given the potential unpopularity of your conclusions, I find it extremely unlikely that the committee will decide to offer you financial support."

The young woman started to rise, her eggs scrambled with broccoli untouched. Ignoring her movement, the doctor continued, "My dear young lady, I earnestly beg you not to be hasty. It is my principal desire to help you. Much against my most gentlemanly instincts, I felt myself obliged to attack your project, since that was the only way of ensuring the committee gave it due attention. I am not only one of the founding members, but am also among the most active. Be so kind as to place your invaluable confidence in me. I know the best route to advance our project."

The doctor arranged a number of other appointments with the girl to notify her of further developments. He described acrid discussions during which he reduced her project to ashes. On each successive occasion, the other members of the committee were more enthusiastic; they were close to the point where they would decide to approve it. In fact, the committee hadn't mentioned the project again. Dr. Michels had the power to authorize the funding with a simple signature, but first he wanted to be certain of obtaining the desired trade-off. Time was running out. During one of their meetings in the usual place, he decided to take the next step.

"My dear young lady, you know that I feel a great affection for you. My admiration for you goes beyond the physical, since it finds more attraction in the intellectual sphere. Throughout my life I have been a man of strong convictions. Based on this certainty, I would like to ask you to do me the honor of agreeing to marry me."

The engagement was sealed with a firm handclasp. The doctor had learned that it was ineffective to launch a battle too soon; everything could be won at its given moment. What was essential was to secure the uterus; then he would find a way to fertilize it.

As a wedding gift, he announced that—to the applause of the rest of the committee—she had been awarded a sum that would comfortably cover the costs of her research. His fiancée was unperturbed by the announcement. She coldly observed every detail of the social rite designed to celebrate her change in status within the hierarchy of her species.

Uncertain of what to expect of her companion's sexual habits, she decided to protect herself by using condoms during the wedding trip. When she had further information, she would decide what form of contraception was appropriate.

On their return, the doctor claimed to have a rash caused by the latex. After persuading her to have an intrauterine device fitted, he arranged an appointment for his wife with an old family's regular gynecologist. At the same time, he also asked the secretary to schedule an advance meeting between himself and the physician.

Once they were alone, Dr. Michels explained his problem with dramatic sincerity:

"Dr. Jerski, if I can talk to you man to man, allow me to point out that, as males of the species, we know every woman's fulfillment lies in motherhood. However, I have, by chance, fallen in love with a deeply confused female. My wife suffers from the delusion that she does not want children. I'm sure that if we give her the opportunity, she will change her mind."

"I see," said Dr. Jerski thoughtfully, struggling between his loyalty to professional ethics, his firm conviction in the right to life and this unexpected contribution toward a comfortable retirement. "There is one possibility. We can put the decision in the hands of God."

Dr. Jerski was careful to explain to Señora Michels that although the device had a very good track record, it was not infallible. He then placed it with surgical precision at an angle that did not completely close off all possibilities. Eleven weeks later, she was back in his office and he confirmed her suspicions. Despite the human effort to impede it, God had blessed her with the gift of life.

"I warned you right from the start. This child will be your responsibility," she told her husband.

Dr. Michels was bursting with restrained joy. He had not the least doubt about the gender of the child. Maximiliano was on his way.

The future mother approached her pregnancy with scientific devotion: she registered every event and compared it with manuals stipulating optimum times. The doctor was obliged to wear gloves if he wanted to feel the embryo's tiny legs. Her curiosity came to an end when she gave birth to a boy like any other. After that, she shut herself up in her nest to observe her insects. The anthropoentomological treatise never got any further than a little disorganized research. She vegetated for some years in her cataloging work at the museum until, one day, she simply didn't turn up.

The doctor handed over the basic care of his son to the nanny. She was in charge of bathing, dressing, feeding, and playing with him.

His father, for his part, instilled the principles that would form his character. Instead of the usual, phonetically simple phrases, Max learned to read by the inscription on the living-room wall:

"Now then Maximiliano, be so good as to repeat with me, 'The measure.'"

"The measure."

"…of each man…"

"…of each man…"

"…lies in…"

"…lie sin…"

"…the dose…"

"…the dows…"

"…of truth…"

"…of tru…"

"…he can withstand."

"…pecan with stan."

The mother treated her son with cordiality. When Max came running, proud to show her his drawings of flying whales that had drunk all the water in the sea, she would comment:

"Interesting. The ability to represent cetaceans with fantastic characteristics suggests above-average creative-cognitive development for your age."

On the day Max's first tooth fell out, his nanny followed the custom of placing it under his pillow and then exchanging it for a coin. Full of his achievement, Max was going to school to spend his riches on candy when his mother intercepted him:

"Max, it's absurd to believe that a mythical being trades dead teeth for pieces of metal with an exchange value for humans.

The sooner you rid yourself of these silly expressions of the collective consciousness, the better it will be for your evolution as an outstanding member of the species."

8

Not long after the end of Max's purple torment, the elementary-school graduation ceremony took place. His contribution consisted of dancing with his classmates, dressed as a skeleton. Before the festivities, his nanny spent several evenings sewing white bones onto the black suit. When Max went to his mother so she could see him in his costume before he left—Dr. Michels had a meeting that couldn't be put off, but would end it as soon as possible to see his son—she stood inspecting the physiognomy of the bones. Closing her eyes, she pressed two fingers to the bridge of her nose to maintain control until something snapped:

"I'm fed up with so much stupidity! Is that a femur? Don't they even know how many frigging ribs there are? Do you really want to know the truth, Max? Why all those filthy stories with veiled messages? And that damned phrase, castigating us every day! Did your dad believe he was making you a man when he indoctrinated you with all his idiocy? Come on, I want you to see something!"

Although it was some time since she'd been in it, she darted off to his father's room, pulled a chair across to the closet, put two telephone directories on it, and climbed up to reach the leather-bound volume containing the hundreds of stories that Max religiously listened to each night. His father had promised that he would show him the book some day; Max was burning with the desire to see what the lettering was like, if there were illustrations. He longed to finally understand what sort of structure could combine so many different beginnings and endings. The characters moved freely through the various stories: sometimes they were good, sometimes bad. If a story began on the last pages of the book, his father would suddenly open it again at random to finish the tale. The nanny stood between Max and his mother, trying to prevent her inopportune revelation of the contents of the book. His mother slapped her face and advanced toward her son.

"See for yourself the lie behind your father's truths." She handed Max the book and went to her own room to pack her things.

Max rested the book on his bony knees and contemplated it for an instant, laying inner bets about its precise contents before opening the cover. He began leafing feverishly through the pages. The book was shattering his most improbable suppositions. Just as his father did, he jumped from one page to another and was stunned by what he saw. He examined every inch of the fantastic worlds that had been his bedtime stories each night and was finally able to see what the mountains, princesses, animals, and other creatures that had guided him so many times to the land of sleep were like. Devastated, he closed the tome. The hundreds of pages of the book were blank; there was not a single letter written there. It had all, all, all been a lie told by his father.

Max lost any desire to attend the graduation party. Between sobs, his nanny attempted to comfort him by the means she had at hand: she offered him cake, said she would prepare chilaquiles. Max added four books to the tower of telephone directories and returned the leather-bound book to its place. He made his nanny swear that she would say nothing to his father.

Dr. Michels arrived at the graduation ceremony very late and sat at the back of the auditorium. When it came to the sixth grade class, his eyes played a trick on him He easily recognized Max's friends among the dancing skeletons and convinced himself that Max was the boy behind Sao and Pascual. He proudly followed his movements and applauded loudly after a series of reverse steps that seemed to defy gravity. When the piece had finished, he went to give his son a pat on the back and discovered his mistake. Max was not to be found anywhere. He hadn't taken part in the dance. Furious, Dr. Michels went home to demand an explanation.

The first thing he saw on entering the apartment was a note stuck over the inscription on the wall:

THERE IS NO SUPERIOR BEING CAPABLE OF DICTATING QUANTUM LEAPS IN THE EVOLUTION OF ANY SPECIES. THE MALE HORSEFLY CANNOT FEED ON BLOOD; THAT IS NOT IN ITS NATURE. EVEN IF THEY ARE REPEATED AN INFINITE NUMBER OF TIMES, LIES ARE LIES. I'M LEAVING HIM THE ONLY THING THAT HAS MATTERED TO HIM DURING ALL THIS TIME. THE APPARATUS IS HIS AND HIS ALONE. DON'T ATROPHY IT IN THE ATTEMPT TO MAKE IT YOUR OWN. GOODBYE.

E.

"She said she'd only take what she needed to live," finished the nanny.

"Where is Maximiliano now?"

"Sleeping in his skeleton costume. He wouldn't take it off."

"This unforeseen event will necessarily bring tranquility to our home. With the passage of time, it will become clear that we now have one less ghost to fight," said Dr. Michels aloud—but to himself—as he served himself a whisky with mineral water.

9

Dr. Michels' only allusion to his wife's departure was to order the nanny to throw the few remaining traces of Max's mother into the trash. He didn't even need her presence to dissolve the marriage. From that moment on, she simply stopped existing.

Max, for his part, dealt with his abandonment by taking refuge in Head World, where the three children took turns to reign in their world. Their scepter was a hammer Pascual had borrowed from his father's metal workshop. Whoever carried it had the prerogative to decide such things as the rules for that day, the scope of the games, the flavor of the ice cream they ate. At the end of each session, when they had to go home for dinner, the monarch would grant the other two a wish with a touch of the scepter. In this way, they would all make it safely through to the following day's meeting. Although they could ask to be changed into any creature or character, they almost always requested the power to fly or to create an invisible force field to protect them and their world forever.

On the last day of the summer vacation they played with melancholic intensity. As the sky reddened in the late afternoon, Sao began the closing ceremony.

"Sir Max, due to your position as an honored member of Head World, I grant you a wish. What would you like today?"

"To be what you hold in your hands," said Max, pointing to the scepter.

"I can't do that. I'm the queen today."

"I don't want to usurp your reign, Your Majesty."

"But I can't give you the scepter. How can I be a queen without it?"

"I'm not asking you to give me the scepter. I just want you to change me into it. From now on, I want to be known as Sir Max Hammer."

"I, Sao, Queen of Head World, employing the powers invested in me by the brotherhood of Head World, change you into a hammer. Welcome Sir Max Hammer."

Draped in his new investiture, Max bumped into Juana Mecha on his way home and stood in front of her to see if she would notice any difference. After a moment of complicit silence, the sweeper finally said, "Now you know. The Supreme Being is the biggest egomaniac of all."

10

So many precepts, punishments, stories, and frustrations were not going to simply disappear. Max had suffered an overdose of truth, but it didn't frighten him now; quite the opposite: he'd learned to explore its limits by prodding with a pointed stick, and the softness of the flesh didn't bother him. Things continued the same, but everything was different. His only option was to see them as they were.

In his building, there was a little boy who looked on in admiration at the games invented by his elders. He used to do tricky maneuvers with his yo-yo to impress them. They, in turn, would sometimes allow him to accompany them to the store to buy candy. The boy repeated every word uttered by Max he could manage to remember.

His parents still encouraged the boy and his sister to believe in Santa Claus. They would sit with their children to write letters to him, ensuring they didn't ask for anything unviable, making them see reason with the argument that there were many poor children with no toys, so it was unfair to ask for too much: one request per child, preferably something that could be paid off in installments over the following twelve months. That year, they had negotiated with their son until he was persuaded to ask for the maw-shaped castle of his favorite cartoon hero: a muscular righter-of-wrongs with bright red underpants and plush boots.

On Christmas Eve, Max invited Pascual to sleep over and they took turns to keep watch at the window looking onto the parking lot. When the moment arrived, Max gave the signal. The young parents were excitedly walking to their car to fetch the presents they would leave at the foot of the crib. Pascual carefully focused the powerful lens of his camera and caught the scene to perfection. They had conclusive evidence that would destroy their little neighbor's superstitious belief in Santa Claus.

They let a few days go by. The child came out each afternoon to play with his castle and Bramsos photographed his earnest enjoyment of his gift. One afternoon, Max asked if he could borrow the boy's plastic superman, promising to give it back the following day. The doll then underwent an extravagant photo shoot and was returned intact to its owner.

The friends developed the film in Señor Bramsos' darkroom and made the prints that Pascual would work on.

The first anonymous envelope the harassed parents received contained a shot of them taking the presents from the trunk of the car. They had no idea who could have sent them such a thing. They always kept themselves to themselves. The photographs that arrived later terrified them.

One showed their son kneeling by his castle. Using black felt-tip pen, Pascual had covered the walls in mold. He drew the muscular hero, in his underpants, standing proudly on top of the left-hand tower, brandishing a bloodstained sword that looked recently used. Suspended in the air in front of him was the decapitated head of Santa Claus; below, his hands still stubbornly clasped the presents they were carrying. The head with its dripping strands appeared to be falling directly toward the unwary, smiling boy.

Next came the photos of the doll posing in extreme situations. Pascual had organized several suicides for him: the superhero blew his brains out with a shotgun, threw himself from a cliff into a crocodile-infested river, tied himself to the railroad tracks where a train severed his legs. Another series showed him in a skintight, black leather suit practicing fellatio on his age-old archenemy— a mummy with unwinding bandages—or masturbating in front of the mirror, excited by his own physique. The doll had been posed before the camera in basic postures and Pascual's pen had done the rest.

All the prints had the same message written on the back: "If you don't want your son to know the truth...don't tell him it."

Their nerves in tatters, the parents asked the head of security, Señor Joel Taimado, for help. Each photo caused him a new snigger he made no attempt to suppress.

"Why are you laughing, Señor Taimado? It's your job to make sure we live a peaceful life! We'll complain to your superiors."

"Uh-huh. Umm. I mean, the thing is, I'll report an F25-14 to headquarters. And while we're waiting for instructions, you tell me how much you're willing to shell out to get the preliminary inquiry started."

The investigation didn't uncover any conclusive evidence. It must have been someone on the estate; someone with a camera; someone with a black felt-tip pen. The nightmare came to an abrupt end. The little boy's parents never knew why. The fact was Max and Pascual had gotten bored: they were looking for a new challenge.

11

In early adolescence, the friends had had a class teacher whom several generations of pupils had nicknamed Chucky. On one cheek she had a prominent scar left by failed rejuvenation surgery; the tightly stretched skin of her face seemed to be gathered together in a clump by a brooch at the back of her head; her raised eyelids and slightly parted lips gave her an expression of permanent surprise. The surgeon who had operated on her had been unable to explain the cause of the cleft that furrowed her left cheek like a narrow strip of stagnant water. Chucky's tolerance of her nickname was limited.

During one of their first classes with her, Sao raised her hand to ask a question about the exercise they were doing. When she noticed her, Chucky returned her attention to the teachers' edition of the textbook, without which she never stirred. Despite years of teaching history, she still failed each and every pedagogic assessment, but her answer book—and her distant relationship to the head of the union—allowed her to go on taking out her frustrations on her pupils year after year. When her arm was tired, Sao put her hand down and the teacher then allowed her to speak. Trying to remember what her question had been, she unwittingly said:

"Señorita Chucky, I wanted to ask if…"

The entire classroom broke into a guffaw composed of the accumulation of stifled giggles.

"Now, child, come and stand here in front of me this very moment," the teacher counterattacked. "I want you to clasp your hands behind your back. Raise your left knee. Very good, that's it, right up to your chest. And will you now tilt your head to the same side. Put out you tongue and hop on the other leg until I tell you to stop."

Sao calmly obeyed. Max and Pascual looked at each other in fury. They were already planning their revenge.

The school carried out periodic earthquake evacuation drills in which the pupils would line up and walk to the yard in an orderly fashion, happy to miss class. The authorities timed the exercise and made a headcount in accordance with the stipulated procedure.

Despite these mechanical simulations, the last earthquake had produced a stampede of pupils, as well as teachers suffering panic attacks.

Max patiently awaited his chance. The day he heard the wailing of the alarm, he put his things down slowly and joined the end of the line. Their teacher led them through the door. As he passed, Max picked up the answer book and put it under his T-shirt. Before they reached the schoolyard, he briefly broke file to throw the book into one of the trashcans.

Chucky realized what had happened the moment they returned. She searched every child's backpack down to the last pencil: the book wasn't in the room; some vandal from another grade had taken advantage of the confusion to steal it. The replacement copy would take weeks to arrive. To cover its absence, she divided her class into groups and assigned each a topic to explain to the others.

At the end of the day, Pascual extracted the book from the trash and slipped it into his backpack. They had to act fast; if the new book arrived too soon, their plan would be ruined.

The scheme involved selecting certain pages from the book and reproducing them, with slight modifications. The result was impeccable. This done, Pascual utilized a common technique for correcting errors in books that have already been bound; he sliced off pages, leaving only a thin strip on which to paste the replacements. He took great pains over every detail, including the type of paper; the most exigent editor would have approved the amendment. They planted their landmines throughout the book, leaving the most powerful explosive device for their final act of vengeance.

Within a few days, the book had been anonymously returned.

The schoolteacher inspected it and verified it was intact. Her vandal theory was immeasurably reinforced. She once again took up her classes, with blind faith in whatever the teachers' edition of the textbook said.

The pupils' schooldays generally passed between boredom and fear of authority. They didn't question even the most ridiculous errors. When Señorita Chucky began to swerve off course in directions that didn't correspond with their own books, they resignedly noted down the rewriting of history in case the new version appeared in a test.

At Max's express request, the pupils learned of the all-out warfare between cavemen and the dinosaurs. The teacher gazed in astonishment at the illustration of primitive men, clothed in animal skins, being devoured by tyrannosaurs, or lifted like ragdolls by pterodactyls. Another scene showed a rock shot from a catapult knocking out a placid diplodocus. The accompanying text box explained that the dinosaurs had become extinct during the ice age, but humans had survived by taking refuge in their igloos. Señorita Chucky attributed her pupils' surprised faces to the spookiness of the information she was imparting.

During the rest of the year, they learned that: the conquistadores had arrived in steamships, loaded with hydraulic excavators to loot the indigenous people's precious metals; popular revolutions were spontaneous uprisings aimed at defending financial freedoms from the beardies who wanted to go back to bartering fruit; a top-secret military base existed, where beleaguered individuals could take lifelong refuge from the harassment of the masses—a fact which explained several disappearances or supposed assassinations.

That gilded cage was home to stuck-up musicians, outlaws with thick wrists and delicate hands, fallen extraterrestrials, presidents who defied the military-industrial complex, mustachioed dictators, and sombreroed peasants whose ghosts crossed mountains lashed by solitude. The schoolmistress was fascinated by these historical events she didn't remember from previous years. The information she was transmitting to these young minds seemed nobler than ever.

At the end of the academic year, the pupils took part in the production of a short, contemporary adaptation of a historical play that, as a form of social service, was performed for some nearby community. On that occasion, it was the turn of the Villa Miserias residential estate, where a good many of the pupils and teachers in the school lived. As the script of the play was in the teachers' edition, Chucky had responsibility for the casting and direction of the contraband work, written by Sao. The pupils put a great deal of effort into learning their parts.

On the day of the performance, Plaza del Orden was packed. The front rows had been reserved for the school authorities and distinguished members of the community: Dr. Michels, Selon Perdumes, Orquídea López—ex-president of the residents' association—the directors of the T&R construction company and the entrepreneur Mauricio Maso were all there. Everyone, in fact, except for Severo Candelario, who didn't have it in him to go and applaud his former pupils. Chucky had to take a few drops of a tranquilizing liquid to calm the nerves caused by the packed house.

In the first scene, Sao appeared dressed as a one-legged president, hopping over the frontier to attend a summit meeting, hosted by a leader with a deformed ear, played by Pascual. She found him sitting in his chair, incessantly banging his right fist on the top of his desk. The other arm was attached to a drip, fed by a holy water font containing beer. Not even the entrance of the president could halt the beat of the desk-banging fist, which only stopped when forcibly subdued by an assistant who, during the rest of the scene, struggled with the arm that refused to lie quietly.

"Good morning Emperor of the Cosmos. How are you?"

"What? Quiet! Am watching domination on my screen. Far planet not accepting freedom even with a gun pointing at its head."

"I've come to make you an offer: I want you to buy our territory. It's rich in bronze."

"What? Why I want cacti and prickly pears? Not interested in territory. Interested in minds. Television series, action pictures, and sports do dirty work."

"If you don't buy it, we'll paint it red or yellow."

"What? Okay. Buy half, no more. Not another word. Out of here!"

The second of the two acts showed a massive invasion of President Sao's land. In flagrant violation of her promise to say no more, she had instigated her compatriots to rise up and insist on the colonization of the whole country. The neighboring president considered it necessary to send in troops to protect his borders.

The stage was stormed by an army of casually elegant university professors, their hair ruffled by the winds of their native city. They were armed to the teeth with machine guns firing 10,000 supply-and-demand curves per second, grenades that blew social work programs to pieces, knives that burst illusory bubbles of collective well-being, bulldozers of any distortion of the market that came in their path. The rear was covered by a battalion of corporate lawyers equipped with the specialized codes they used to defend themselves from their clients' right to excess.

A fierce battle broke out between the invaders and the local army—then making a stand in a convent—led by a general who responded to the codename of Hummingbird. They defended themselves against the onslaught with cannons firing thick tomes of a great treatise on the subject of capital, catapults from which they slung guerrilla manuals, and by digging pits that, unfortunately, closed up before the enemy troops fell into them. They succeeded in momentarily holding back the assault with the help of a handful of deserters from the other side—distinguished by the fact that they had giant four-leaf clovers on their helmets—who had rebelled on discovering that the army provisions didn't include the dark beer they drunk by the gallon. Their contribution waned when the local hard liquor put them out of action for the rest of the battle.

General Hummingbird was taken prisoner and, standing before the leader of the occupying forces—Commander Milton—pronounced his famous words of surrender: "If your women didn't have such big tits, you wouldn't be here."

In the final scene, Cadet Max was chased by an elite commando unit of foreign professors. Their aim was to tie him down and hold his eyelids open with tweezers, so he would be forced to study graphs, models, and data—with their corresponding theories—until his only means of thought was through the repetition of their dogmas. Struggling for breath, Max climbed a hill, only to find himself surrounded by the enemy on the highest point of a castle. Rather than surrender, he wound a reel of a forgotten surrealist movie around his body and threw himself to his death. The body lay unbroken on the ground.

In the meantime, the professors were training his compatriots: some, threatened with whips, were solving differential equations on a chalkboard; others were passing through arcs of fire as a test for obtaining interviews with transnational companies. Yet others were attempting to balance on a rubber ball, their hands tied behind their backs, while trying to reach with their teeth for the acceptance letters from the university where the respected professors taught. The members of a last group were dressed as clowns; their aim was to stand for public office, where they would be able to implement what they had learned. The curtain fell as President Sao gave a sigh of satisfaction: the ideas of the invading circus were being correctly implanted.

Not a single person applauded. The only sounds were those of incomprehension and outrage. Juana Mecha broke the silence with a general comment: "If the comedy is to be repeated, it shouldn't be played as a tragedy." The next day's edition of *The Daily Miserias* stressed the dreadful acting skills of the youths; it was a boring play, of no interest to the audience.

Chucky was hauled before the school authorities: the Villa Miserias board had threatened to withdraw their annual donation if she was not disciplined. She turned up to prove her innocence with her teachers' edition of the textbook in hand. The school director confirmed his suspicions: it contained the traditional version of the play; the whole thing had been a subversive invention of the teacher.

Unaware that Max and Pascual had exchanged the apocryphal book for the normal version, Chucky lost her cool. Her incoherent behavior left the director no other choice: as a requirement for remaining in her post, her dose of antipsychotic medication was tripled. Inhabiting a pain-free limbo, the schoolmistress continued to teach class for years, faithfully following every line of her book. And just in case, she would even take it to the bathroom with her.

12

Max broke the spell of the leather-bound book that had told him so many lies by learning to use it to his own advantage. He noted the differences between the effects of oral histories and those issuing from a book: the written word perhaps clung to the permanency it had gained on leaving behind the changeable uncertainty of orality. To assert the supremacy of the oral over the written seemed by now as absurd as claiming it was the tail that chased the dog, which was, in fact, running away to avoid biting that tail. Whatever the case, it was enough for Max that it sometimes worked.

Dr. Michels never came back until late and the nanny regularly settled down to watching that evening's telenovelas, so Max was in the habit of making the most of this situation by inviting girls from his class to spend the evening in the apartment. He employed a variety of approaches to ask if they would like to hear one of the stories from his magic book. Whether it was from curiosity, affection, or embarrassment at refusing, the girls almost always accepted.

Max would fetch the book, get the girl in question to sit on the bed, leaning against the headrest, and then close the door to avoid being bothered by the overacted wailing coming from the television set in the kitchen. He'd ask her to close her eyes so she could immerse herself in the story.

"Remember not to open them until the end. Right?

"Once upon a time there was a very beautiful princess called Tama. From the moment of her birth the king and queen loved her so much that they set out to ensure she would always be very happy and know nothing of the evils of the world. Their daughter deserved only the best. She slept on a mattress with springs of gold, her head resting on pillows stuffed with peacock feathers and covered by a counterpane of the finest silk, freshly woven each day to ensure she slept sweetly. The king and queen had the designers of the most expensive brands, the chefs of the most luxurious restaurants, brought from distant lands. Princess Tama had never worn the same outfit or enjoyed the same dish twice.

"So as not to expose her to the dangers of life, they kept her shut up in an immense palace. Award-winning architects designed gardens of enviable ingenuity for her. Her favorite was the vertical garden that adorned the façade of the most exclusive nightclub in the world; the princess adored the horizontal palm trees. Her retinue of friends—hired from strictest model agencies—watched out each night to ensure that no coconut fell on her head as she entered the club. The king and queen packed the venue with celebrities, who would arrive, radiant, in streamlined sports cars; the most sought-after DJs played dance music for the beautiful people of the species, brought there each day to Princess Tama's complete satisfaction; the walls were decorated with photo after photo of the princess being hugged by the rich and famous. She knew nothing of ugliness.

"In the mornings her servants applied face packs made from the purest avocados and cucumbers. A sumo wrestler gave her relaxing massages to eliminate accumulated fat. The king and queen acquired a team of the best cosmetic surgeons in existence to remove any imperfections on the princess's body.

"Travel could be long and dangerous. What's more it was a bore. Why go all the way to some place to see what the princess could have at home? She only had to name a place for her parents to reproduce it in the palace. There were artificial beaches and snow, scale replicas of the emblematic monuments of a diverse range of countries, whose natives were even hired so she could sample their customs. Princess Tama got to know an infinite number of places without the need to leave the palace.

"Her life passed like a permanent vacation in the most desirable locations, to which only the crème de la crème went. Their pride at being able to give their daughter such happiness moved the king and queen to tears.

"One day, when the princess was passing the quarters of her favorite maidservant, she heard moaning coming from the bedroom. Alarmed, she knocked repeatedly. After a pause, the maidservant breathlessly opened the door, wearing her blouse back to front. The princess asked if she was feeling all right and noticed something strange in the flat tone of the reply; she decided to verify what was going on.

"She ordered a servant to give her a duplicate key to her paid friends' doors. Then, one afternoon, during the siesta, she went quietly to their quarters and heard similar moans. Silently, she opened the door. The princess had no idea what was happening: a girl was sucking the penis of one of the male models, while another penetrated her from behind. Three more, entwined with yet another male in a chair, were provoking mutual spasms and whimpers. The princess let out a scream that froze the scene. No one knew what to do. They all feared the worst punishment in the realm: to have their names removed from the guest list of the nightclub. In despair, two girls sinuously approached the princess. While one kissed her, the other guided over her nude body. The princess didn't stop them. She too was soon naked. Although it was all new to her, she was a natural.

"Her encounter with one of the boys became more intense. They gradually distanced themselves from the rest until they were alone in the adjoining room. The princess made it clear that she was ready, but the young man decided that, as it was her first time, he would take her carefully; he lay her gently down and slid on top of her. When he met with the first difficulty, he attributed it to the usual virginal narrowness. He pushed more forcefully, but there was no way to break through the barrier. The princess was panting with anticipation. The model gathered a little momentum for another assault on her hips: the result was the same. The princess stamped her feet in the air in desperation.

"The youth then asked a friend to take over from him. Under the expectant gazes of the other members of the party, the princess and the replacement slowly aroused each other. The princess felt her legs opening in response. With his penis in his hand to gain greater force, the nervous boy attempted to break through and satisfy her. Nothing. It was no good. Just as with his friend, the obstinate barrier began to cause him pain, to the point where he gave up.

"There was a generalized sense of panic. A mulatto girl tried with her tongue. Then with two fingers. Impossible. Nor did it work using the tip of one finger to ease the passage. The princess was, quite simply, impenetrable. In the funereal atmosphere, they dressed and attempted to console her; said that's how it was at first. The princess left in a flood of tears. The others stood in mourning for fifteen minutes before starting all over again.

"The princess burst into her parents' bedroom: 'Mother, father, why is that no one can penetrate my vagina when they can my friends'?'

"The king and queen had expected this moment. The king kissed his daughter on the forehead before leaving the royal chamber, closing the door behind him. The queen sat the princess on her lap and began a patient explanation.

"'My child, you're not just any maiden. You are Princess Tama, heiress to everything you see around you. Haven't we done enough to please you?'

"'Yes mother, but I want to experience the thing that makes everyone else cry out.'

"'I understand, child. Don't worry, the day will come. But there's something you should know: when you were on the way, your father and I made a vow to dedicate our lives to making you happy. Absolutely nothing would get in our way. While we were planning every detail, your father had a dark thought: What if some opportunist were to come along, wanting to take advantage of your dowry? Just the thought kept him awake for nights. He consulted the wise men of our realm in search of a solution. No one knew how to protect you until a mysterious stranger appeared a little before your birth. He offered a costly way out of our dilemma. We were willing to give him whatever he asked, but he didn't want money: he asked for your father's dignity. He gave it up without hesitation in exchange for protecting your happiness.

"'The stranger handed us a potion and told us to give it to give you on your birth. It was an age-old formula for detecting the deepest intentions. Whenever a person attempted to make you his own for the wrong reasons, it would form an icy barrier inside you that would prevent this happening. Only the penis of the chosen one could break through it to join with you in eternal happiness.'

"The princess became calm on hearing her fate. From then on she would dedicate herself to finding the prince capable of breaking the spell. She spent hours imagining him: only someone who united the best of everything would be worthy of her. She felt more special than ever.

"Candidates destined to failure began to file past. Naturally, the princess first concentrated on those of greatest worth: actors, rock musicians, communications magnates, politicians, textile manufacturers, yoga teachers. The rumor of her search spread, so that aspirants came to shower her with gifts. They would relate daring exploits, hoping for the opportunity to put their penises to the test, then go home under a black cloud of shame, swearing never to return.

"The number of suitors diminished; the palace was emptier by the day. The princess lived between frenzies of excited anticipation and disillusion. The last suitor to make an attempt was the bloated presenter of a celebrity gossip program. After that, the palace was deserted. The princess passed her days in her room, lamenting her lot and looking back with nostalgia on the innocent euphoria of days gone by.

"The king and queen were desolate. They once again consulted the wise men of their realm to try to remove the curse. Hundreds of inefficacious remedies were tried, until an old man with a luxuriant white beard and small round spectacles appeared. He analyzed the problem while puffing away on his unlit pipe: when the king heard his suggestion, his first thought was decapitation. But the old man was not afraid. Love of the princess would overcome all: the preparations were made to put his theory into practice.

"The best artisan in the castle devoted himself to the commission, making very careful note of the size, curvature, and consistency. He worked the piece with a mixture of the finest materials: a combination of hardness and ductility was required. The artisan locked himself away until the task was completed, then he handed it to the king and queen, exhausted but satisfied. Now it was just a matter of waiting to see how it fared.

"The queen entered the princess's chamber and gave her a mahogany box, then left without saying a word. The box contained a small penis with a close resemblance to the royal member she had once accidentally glimpsed.

"She stroked it slowly, holding it between her two hands. The penis began to swell. The princess let her fantasies run wild. When she'd helped it grow to full size, she decided to carry out an experiment: she pressed lightly and heard the barrier break. The penis had passed through the wall of ice and slipped smoothly inside. Between tears and howls, the princess manipulated it. Finally, she knew what carnal love was. She climaxed with a shriek of jubilation, releasing years of frustration. The sorcerer had been as good as his word. "From then on, so the legend goes, on nights of a lunar eclipse, the princess can be seen masturbating on the surface of the moon, in eternal union with the royal penis she never again forsook. The subjects were inconsolable. Nothing mattered any more. The royalty had gotten a liking for cloistered opulence. And they lived happily enslaved ever after."

Max would close the book noisily, as if to startle the girl from her trance, before deciding on the next step.

The reactions varied widely. Some of his guests thought that the story was an affected cliché, of no interest at all; these girls would ask Max if they could turn on the television. Then came the ones who felt deeply uncomfortable; they would hurriedly gather up their belongings and leave, hardly bothering to say goodbye. A third group captured, with flattering perspicacity, the underlying meaning of the story; the most direct of these took the initiative. Max's favorite reaction was when the girl got so wrapped up in the story that she forgot where she was. The most aroused began to touch themselves up or even masturbate. Max would look on delightedly before joining his companion.

Each of them had her own threshold and Max respected these limits. Sometimes too much: even in the cases of the least inhibited, he would stop just short of the final step. It wasn't that he had prejudices. Or felt remorse. In fact, he didn't know the exact reason; it was as if he refused to leave the confines of those worlds where one could do whatever one wanted. His life had passed among malleable parabolas, based on concrete reality, but unconstrained by its rough surface. While he might be able to use tricks to seduce minds, he was paralyzed by the honesty of naked bodies. At that point, all his constructions served no purpose; from that moment on he was reduced to being nothing more than Max. The girls would acquire presence just as he began to vanish. His rhetorical structure crumbled as if afflicted by an acute case of leprosy. Max was left vulnerable. He would brusquely leave the room and not return until sufficient time had passed to find that evening's girl dressed—in the case that she'd waited around for him.

On one occasion, he tried out his technique on a willfully precocious subject of somewhat complicated lucidity, the daughter of a pair of therapists from a country known for its hermetic complexity. She calmly accepted Max's invitation, ready for anything.

The girl listened to the fairy tale with a slightly bored expression; she was more interested in its object than the wrapping. Lost as she was in her own fantasies, Max had to lightly shake her leg to indicate that the story had finished, at which point she threw herself on him. Max made an effort to follow her lead while the girl guided him with unhurried mastery until they were on the verge of the point of no return. She interpreted Max's hesitation as a typical case of repression, requiring a slight nudge. With an agile movement, she placed herself at Max's back, lying on one side. As if ensuring it wouldn't be stolen, a hand took hold of Max's penis; the other moved downwards until the phalange of an index finger had been inserted in his anus. The hand holding the penis sensed its growing hardness, thus corroborating the girl's theory.

Max allowed her to go a little further, more fearful than excited. The girl judged that she had done enough: it was her turn to enjoy. When she was already on top of him, Max pushed her away to make his escape from the room, staying away longer than usual so as not to have to see her on his return. The girl came out of the bedroom, screaming his name; Max made certain that the bathroom door was locked and tried to breathe quietly. His nanny watched the girl in her panties, her breasts hanging loose, pass through the living room. Before banging the apartment door, she shouted in farewell:

"Know what you are? A fucking cunt-tease!"

13

The nanny had laid the table with the best cutlery and crockery. Dr. Michels was giving an important dinner that night: he'd invited a client and his family to celebrate a favorable outcome in a family dispute over the control of a waste pipe company. On the doctor's advice, the client had carried out a meticulous operation involving buying up the shares of minority stockholders. He'd cooked the figures to show a bleak outlook: in fact, he was doing them a favor because of the responsibility he felt to them as long term investors in a family business. To avoid unnecessary problems with his brother, he failed to mention these private arrangements until he had majority control of the company. His first act as chairman of the board was to order an audit of his brother's management. Then, without showing him the results, he asked for him to either resign or face the consequences. The brother had gone to court to fight for his right to continue manufacturing the pipes through which passed the shit of the city they lived in.

Dr. Michels made use of all the judicial resources at his disposal: he hired a private detective to uncover every extravagant habit of the belligerent brother; he had the proceedings postponed by means of the disappearance of the case file, a maneuver known in the professional argot as a judicial review; he pulled the necessary strings so that the case would be heard by a judge with whom he occasionally went on drinking sprees. After years during which Dr. Michels had deployed an ingenious range of delaying tactics, the judge ruled against the bankrupt brother, the sentence being based on an obscure legal technicality.

The dinner was to celebrate the verdict.

Max had been holed up in his bedroom for hours, looking for answers in the blank pages of the storybook, unable to understand why he was a prisoner to that nothingness. He felt like a mime artist who can't find the way out of the enclosing walls his own hands had created. Having inhabited a world of representations for so long, its objects showed themselves to him as phantasmagoric compositions, unified by a trick of perception. For an instant, the girls in his room would change from attractive women, panting with the desire Max had aroused, to strange beings composed of a heap of bones and viscera, draped in a façade of treacherous tits, asses and pubes. The function of those body parts was to lead him into a state of rapture in which, in exchange for a few moments of pleasure, he shed the invulnerable armor plating he had, with so much effort, forged. His guts decreed a break on reminding

Max that he hadn't eaten anything all afternoon. He went to the kitchen to make a ham and cheese quesadilla.

"Maximiliano, what a pleasure to see you! I'd like you to have the honor of meeting my friends the Sierras, who have been my most valued clients for some years now. We are here together to celebrate a piece of wonderful news. Sit down for a moment and join the festivities."

Without turning round to look at him, Señor Sierra held out a flaccid hand to Max. The young wife stood to give him a kiss on the cheek and rested her hand on Max's shoulder as Dr. Michels outlined the most outstanding features of his son's life. She expressed her pleasure in these achievements by gently massaging his collarbone. The couple's small child was kneeling on the floor, playing with a toy gas truck that went flying into the air when he crashed it into the dinner table.

Max sat for some time in complete silence. Without any movement on his part, he felt the scene before him retreating a level, leaving him outside its frame, so he could watch it with detachment. The texture of movements, objects, and voices seemed to blur; images went into slow motion, the conversation was more diffuse. In contrast, Max was gaining a sort of outlying vision from the interior of each element of the scene. The most subtle gestures and phrases, their hairstyles and clothes, and the voraciousness with which they attacked the pâté and olives, spoke directly to him in code. He understood things he couldn't have explained if asked. His father and the client were two hunters of silences, lying in wait for the least break in the conversation to grab control and display a mixture of wit and encyclopedic knowledge, making incisive pronouncements on some pressing topical issue. The wife listened to it all without hearing. Suddenly, she'd join the conversation with expressions of agreement, admiration, surprise, shared reproach, and other manifestations of inanimate life. She took a circular compact from her large purse, opened the mirror to add a layer of blush to her makeup, freshened the red of her lips, and corrected the angle of her long wispy bangs until she was once again ready to pass unnoticed. The toy gas truck continued to crash into the dinner table.

"Maximiliano has an outstanding talent for telling stories. When I allow myself the luxury of considering his future options, I see him as a sports commentator or news anchorman. I don't have to tell you, my boy, of the huge salaries earned by those who excel in those areas."

"What are you talking about, Dad?"

"Now, now, Max. At your age, I too was a rascal. I'm aware of the tactics you use with your little girlfriends and I'm proud you know the secrets of the leather-bound book." His father gave him a wink of complicity.

"At your age, I liked watching Westerns," Señor Sierra unexpectedly put in. "They helped me a lot in understanding the mentality of the underclasses. These people never, in fact, want to move up the ladder, but they need us to make them victims. The only way to help them is to be like the sheriffs of the old West: you have to show them the line and whip them before they cross it. It's for their own good. That's why our pipes have given a living to so many people. It's the same with family. I only have to give my wife and my son a look to keep them under control, and they are grateful because they know I do it from love. I sacrifice myself every day for them to live the way they do. We need structure and stability. Don't forget, Max, discipline and an iron glove."

The rush of blows was too much for Max. His kidneys were spinning from the one-two-three-four-five-six...Bile flowed to his eyes. Like an echo, he heard their coarse laughter, bathed in the tequila that was loosening their tongues. The kitchen door opened and the nanny came in carrying a dish of roast pork loin with mushrooms, surrounded by halved chambray potatoes. While she was serving the guests, Max broke the silence:

"Señor Sierra, I must say you're a very valiant man."

"Thank you, my boy. But why?"

"It can't be easy to find the courage to say so many stupid things so calmly and in such a short time. Only someone very sure of himself can wear his imbecility on his sleeve like that. I don't know how you do it, but it's worthy of admiration."

"Maximiliano! Apologize to my friend Sierra this instant! As the boy's father, I ask you to forgive his insolence. His words were unacceptable, but I hope you will understand that my son is going through an extremely confusing stage."

"Your friend, Dad? And all those times you've said your clients are like cows in the East, as sacred as they are dumb? Said you sell them your name at a high price for something any second-year student could do? Told me you amuse yourself waiting to see what new ways they can find to roll in the mud you've just cleaned off them? And you call that man your friend, Dad? Couldn't you do with a bit of gentian violet?"

"Sure, son. Your father and I share certain codes you don't

comprehend. Friendships are based on these sorts of tacit under-standings. You think that out of the whole world, you've found the people most like you? Don't delude yourself. If you didn't share a social class, you wouldn't even know them. You think that within the miniscule group of people you have the possibility of knowing, you get on better with other weirdoes like yourself? Sure. Well, you'll see just how strong those friendships are. It's enough for one of you to have a little bit more than the others and it'll be all over.

"Unlike you, I don't fool myself and neither does your father. I know the day I stop paying his monthly retainer he won't be available to answer my calls. He knows the same would happen if he didn't help me make three times that retainer. It doesn't mean we're not friends enough to go out whoring together. Forget the sentimentality. It's a win-win situation."

"Maximiliano, what my friend Sierra has just expounded with his accustomed eloquence also means that when a man reaches maturity, things…"

"Is my hair real spongy? That's why I hate it. I can't keep it either bouncy or a bit…" Coming out of her self-absorption, the young wife accidentally interrupted Dr. Michels.

The only sound to be heard was of knives and forks cutting pork loin before it was processed by teeth. The doctor fanned his face with his linen serviette. Señor Sierra took a drink of his tequila, placed his glass on the table, but before he could retract his hand it had picked up the glass again to take another swig. The woman touched up the compacted mass covering her forehead and nose. Max's lower lip trembled. The toy gas truck continued crashing into the dinner table.

"Don't take it badly, son. That insolence of yours can be channeled to good use. You might even become a useful man. Chin up!"

"Thank you Señor Sierra. You're right. A useful man. Like you and my dad. Codes. Life as it really is. Not as we'd like it to be. Excuse me please, I've got a lot to learn."

"No problem, son. Don't forget, discipline and an iron glove."

"Just one question, Señor Sierra. If I follow your advice, will I get to be like you?"

"Well, son, things aren't that simple. You need determination, vision, talent. If you make sacrifices and work hard, maybe, one day."

"That's what I'll do, sir. I know it's tough but I want the reward. I'm going to dream of a brainless life. Be just like everyone else except for the odd quaint obsession, like collecting glass holders from exotic places or reciting from memory the line-up of some famous team. I'm going to study to join a profession that gives me the chance to sell things in order to buy other things. I'm dying to spend my days in an office wearing designer clothes I don't even know how to appreciate, competing to prove to my boss I've just the right mixture of obedience and guile. Before I'm thirty my manboobs will be sagging and I'll have a triple chin, but I'm sure to find a modest woman who's interested in other frivolities. I'll fulfill my duty to accumulate, and we'll be able to afford the latest music system, dine in the best restaurants, and rub shoulders with some friend of a friend of an important person. And she will always dress impeccably, make me look good at dinners like this, spicing them up with innocent jokes about how disorganized I am. With luck, we'll have very pretty children and we'll be able to video every single thing they do. I'll go on, like you, padding myself with the fat of pleasures that distance me from any real contact with myself. None of that matters because I'll have learned to value my friends as my father does. We'll be able to boast of having young lovers we shower with gifts. When I'm old, I'll have reproduced myself in various clones of my mediocrity who will come to my funeral to cry without asking why. You've opened my eyes, Señor Sierra. I owe you." Max rose from the table before his father could even recover from his shock.

"What a wonderful dinner party! Let's get drunk!" the wife interposed as she put on a CD with a dizzying beat to dance with Dr. Michels, who was unable to decline her invitation. He swung his hips almost automatically while watching what his son was doing. Señor Sierra quickly knocked back two double tequilas. The toy gas truck went on crashing into the table.

Even the music seemed shocked when Max came out of the bathroom. Señor Sierra demanded an explanation of the doctor, without daring to speak it. His wife was swaying with her arms in the air, her palms open outwards. Max had, for the last time, taken the bottle of gentian violet and painted his whole face, with the exception of his nose. He looked like a burns victim who has just been prescribed a protective bandage. He went up to his father, raised his arm to gather momentum, and when he dramatically brought it down, held out his hand. "Goodbye, Dad," he said before going out, completely ignoring the guests. As the door slammed shut, he heard the toy gas truck crash one final time.

He strode firmly out of the building into the shelter of the night. He had only one place in his mind: Sao's parents' laundry. With any luck she would be on the late shift, before they closed.

As he was on his way there, Juana Mecha pushed her broom into his path. On noticing the clean triangular island in the mass of purple, she pronounced:

"Some people say purgatory is a place rather than a time."

14

Despite the fact that the laundry was closed, light still filtered under the metal roller shutter. Sao would be putting away the last of the equipment. Max knocked, using the code he shared with his two friends; the private door was soon opened. The expression in Sao's almond-shaped eyes changed from their habitual smile to stupefaction: it was years since she'd seen the purple stain and it had never before been so extensive. He gave her a hug, brushing his face against her right cheek, and then repeated the action when he saw the purple mark of solidarity on his friend's dark skin.

"What happened?" asked Sao as she locked the door behind her.

"Another overdose of truth."

"Come on. Let me clean you up."

Sao took an olive green and purple striped duvet from its cover, folded it in two, and lay it down in a space near the ironing area. She told Max to take off his shoes and left him sitting there while she went to fetch alcohol, cotton wool balls, and a damp towel. She knelt down in front of him, resting the full weight of her buttocks on her bare heels, naturally holding her back straight, as if she were suspended by a taut cable attached to the center of her head. Then she patiently began to uncover Max's face. Each cotton wool ball removed a layer of purple that seemed to be grateful for finally reposing in the trash. Max was thinking of all those oasis mirages that forced him to keep walking without fixed direction, his legs heavy with dejection. Although he could repeat her words, he wasn't listening to her; he felt Sao's breath as a residue of the events of the day she was recounting to him. As she leaned forward, the low neckline of her blouse allowed him a glimpse of the nipples crowning small breasts. After the waist, her thin torso broadened again at the hips, before passing on to a pair of legs accustomed to walking. Max had never considered her in that way before.

When Sao had finished rubbing his face with the damp towel, a different Max sat before her. His forehead was more creased, giving him a melancholy air, as if he'd discovered that, underneath the surface of things, there are other, hidden surfaces.

The closeness of their bodies quashed the barrier of childish fraternity. Following an improvised script, they came together in a kiss that incorporated all the abuses suffered by Max and Sao on their way to the one-way street they had just found themselves on. They lay down on the folded duvet, giving themselves up to their caresses. Sao noted Max's erection, contained by his pants, and hurriedly eliminated obstacles until they were both nude.

Max felt his habitual shudder. He tried to gain time by positioning himself over Sao, his head toward her feet, so they could explore each other with their mouths. When her moistness was uncontainable, Sao rotated her body to be in tune with his. For once Max wasn't thinking. He scarcely noticed when Sao took hold of his penis to gently break her hymen. There was neither too much nor too little space. Max felt as if the step that had, on every other occasion, cooled his ardor had now been made just for him. Sao held tightly to his back to synchronize their movements, but also to ensure they didn't lose themselves until they had finished what they had started. There was a single spasm, a single cry, and then spent calm. With his head resting on Sao's shoulder, Max very slowly separated himself from her. A deep, lingering kiss sealed the moment. Sao stood and went to the bathroom, waddling like a duck; nostalgically, she wiped away the blood. After thinking it over for a few seconds, she returned and sat next to Max. Stroking the thick chestnut hair that reached his shoulders, she spoke a private thought aloud.

"We can't do it again, Max. We'll end up making a shitty mess of it."

"No worries. We'll find another way."

15

After the episode with the Sierra family, Max's cardboard relationship with his father became even more corrugated. On the surface, everything seemed the same: the majority of the time his father ignored him with distracted cordiality. They had breakfast at the same table without exchanging a word, the doctor reading the newspaper and tapping his spoon four times on his cup to indicate to the nanny when he needed more coffee. Max was about to finish high school; in a few months he'd have to decide the direction his future life would take. Whatever his decision, he'd already disappointed his father.

The problem wasn't his scruffy appearance. The doctor was confidant that, when the moment came, Max would cut his hair, gel down his side parting, and exchange his Baja hoodies for something more appropriate. And neither was he concerned about his son's friends. That likeable oriental girl was no threat and life would take care of giving the one with the mutilated ear a thrashing. Max would discover the people who he should, in the real world, one day become. He'd learn that the only lasting friendships are based on mutual social benefit, would soon acquire the prejudices indispensable for accessing the most appropriate circles.

His son's professional future wasn't worth worrying about. And it was the conviction that Max would never surpass his own achievements that made that lack of concern possible. Conscious of his proximity to his final sunset, the doctor trusted his pact with his organism: in exchange for only moderate mistreatment, his body promised not to cling to life when its condition became deplorable. That time was not far off. And as the doctor wouldn't now see Max become somebody, why waste his thoughts on something that didn't involve him? It was a matter that occupied him on a remote, abstract plane, situated far enough away to allow for fatalism.

Whenever he looked at his son, what he couldn't bear were all those wasted precepts. Max had so thoroughly assimilated them that he'd crossed the boundaries of disillusion. He'd converted the noble, upright truth, designed to protect us from ourselves, and by extension from others, into an uncomfortable lantern, shining straight in the face, blinding with its excess of light. His case was like that of elite fighters, trained in the most lethal techniques, programed to inflict maximum pain without the capacity to feel it, who one day decide to change sides, and use all they have learned against those who trained them. It's almost impossible to bring them down as they anticipate the movements of the master-executioner. The doctor considered this bitter irony: he'd succeeded in perpetuating himself in his son, but in a version he found repulsive.

16

Pascual Bramsos was determined to go to art school. He wanted to free himself from parental patronage, which meant he needed an income that would allow him to live independently. One day, he heard his aunt complaining about the cost of living as she was paying back some money she'd borrowed from his mother. Before handing over the bill, he saw her look with hatred at the national hero adorning it. Pascual ran to his bedroom.

He took a bill of the same denomination and carefully excised the portrait of the hero and pasted it onto a sketchpad; the remainder, he cut into thin strips and composed the image of a hill topped by a scaffold, from which hung the head. He drew a tongue protruding downward from the mouth, and a pair of uplifted eyes, signifying strangulation. With fine pen strokes, he provided the fallen hero with a limp body, swinging in the air. He was surrounded by four thickset men in frockcoats and top hats, smoking cigars. They were each holding an unusual bell, larger than the potbellied men ringing them. Sharply pointed vibrations emanated from the bells and stuck like thorns into the statesman's body.

It was a tortured death without any possibility of peace since the body swayed chaotically in all directions under the ferocious attack of the bells. On the edge of the sheet, Bramsos drew a frame formed of thousands of money signs, packed together as closely as possible without quite touching. A few hours later—after he'd lined up a squadron of mighty soldiers with bent heads, pierced by mortal thrusts—he decided the piece was finished.

When he gave the artwork to his aunt, she and her sister stared at it in astonishment. Señora Bramsos was aware of her son's talent for drawing, but she'd never seen one of his original designs. Moved, his aunt pressed the work to her breast.

"Sorry, Aunt Hilda. I can't make a gift of it. But I'll sell it to you cheap," said Pascual, breaking the spell with his avarice.

"What do you mean, sell it to me cheap? How much?"

"Twice the value of the bill. It's just that I need to save for my education."

The aunt's offense transmuted into understanding. The amount was reasonable, and it was a noble cause. Pascual had discovered the only possible way he could accept payment in exchange for his art.

Bramsos established the rules: the first was that the client would decide how much he wanted to spend on the work; he would then hand over the cash value of the materials needed to produce it, plus an equal amount for the purchase. The other rule was that the client had to respond in writing to the question "What use is money?"

His first clients were from members of his extended family, moved by either envy of the unsettling works others had acquired, or the desire to help the young student. Bramsos made trial versions to understand the properties of this new material, continuing at the same time to explore the technique of collage with super-imposed drawing. He also slid bills across the canvas to paint tenuous opaque tones, or ground them up and whisked the resulting powder with egg white and other materials to obtain a form of paste, with which he painted curved and static figures, whose veins seemed to be corroded by the very material that gave them life. Some people offered him coins rather than paper money: when he had enough, he produced sculptures from the molten metal.

His favorite piece was commissioned by a university professor of social theory. While the deal had been agreed and the professor was writing his note stating that money was a diabolical invention designed to alienate the masses, his driver walked back and forth from the car, carrying a heavy sack containing thousands of one-peso pieces.

"Young comrade, I'm giving you the only treasure the people can afford. Let's see if you can tune in to its hidden essence."

To consolidate his idea, Bramsos accompanied the professor to his car. He observed him standing by the back door as the driver hurried to open it. The professor got in without giving him a glance. Once the driver was ready, his employer raised his hand in a signal to depart. He made his farewells to Bramsos, forming a V-for-victory with his fingers.

Bramsos created a plaster mold—to be filled with the molten coins—for a scene in an outdoor market. The stallholders were selling offal, herbs, and serapes to passersby. One trader had left his pea stall to walk to an adjoining space, where the scene underwent a drastic change. An old man with a goat-like beard and sloping shoulders was standing almost directly in front of a number of closed doors.

The pea seller appeared behind him and, with one hand, held open a door, inviting the cornered old man to enter. The other was raised, on the point of bringing down an icepick to relieve his victim's suffering with a lethal blow to the head. Behind the open door some kneeling monks, their heads bent and hands held high, were waiting to adore him as soon as he crossed the threshold.

He poured the liquid metal into the mold and, when it had hardened, broke the plaster shell revealing the tragedy. The smoothness of the metal surface gave the figures an ambiguous anonymity. When the professor saw the work, he observed the scene for some minutes before saying:

"Young comrade, I don't know if you're being insolent or profound. Help Fernando to put it in my car."

This time the professor went to the front door of the car and got in, clearly disgusted to have to travel next to the driver. He didn't give Bramsos the victory sign, but pointed a single finger at him, wagging it up and down.

He placed the sculpture in the garden of his house, explaining to visitors that he had commissioned it from a young, undiscovered artist, who had simply given his idea material form. The professor would them embark on grandiloquent explanations of its meaning. His audience would be instantly lost in in an intellectualized thicket: twilight, idols, false consciousness, the dance of commodities, permanent revolution, woolen serapes, interpretation, hegemony, immortality, goat stew, social engagement, artisanal mescal, deconstruction, past elegance, and various other concepts surfaced for air before returning to dive into the solemnity of the orator.

Growing fame and the earnings from what he called his green

period allowed Bramsos to become financially independent. Remaining in the same residential estate, he moved into a unit that—in honor of the oddballs that inhabited it—soon began to be known as the Others' Building, and converted the entire apartment into a studio. He was, however, scarcely able to make ends meet until, one day, Beni Mascorro, the inseparable friend of the wealthy scavenger Mauricio Maso, turned up with four suitcases filled with paper money from a variety of countries. Mascorro wasted no time in explaining the purpose of his visit, adding: "My boss has clients all over the place. If you need a bit more, just tell us."

Bramsos counted his share incredulously: it was enough to enable him to live comfortably until he finished art school. If he put special effort into the piece, he could negotiate a life pension of marijuana when it was done.

He laid a large canvas on the floor of his studio and, using the bills at his disposition, created over ten different hues of paint. He forcibly reduced the paper to a pulp in oiled mortars. He then put the mixture into metal cans containing paint of opaque tones: bright yellows, reds, and oranges. It was as if the dominant ashen green of the money infected the bills of other colors with its desolation.

He dipped his paintbrush at random into the various pots, splattered paint in all directions, and covered the diagonal axes of a canvas in figurative shapes. Next, he perforated the bottoms of various cans, and left paths of dripped paint on the surface. He borrowed a neighbor's ferret and had it run over the multicolored pool; the pet contributed to the painting by leaving a confusion of small pawmarks flanking the wake left by its belly and tail. Bramsos then used a fan to spray centrifuged paint on another part of the work: the medley of different techniques was focused on texture rather than form. He laid layer over layer until he'd squeezed out the last drop of paint, then stood on the table to view the result from above. He was satisfied with his motley ode to multinational extravagance.

Bramsos let Mascorro know that the work was ready, and his client requested a home delivery so he could meet the artist. Once the painting had been hung, covering a whole wall, Maso came in to view it, wearing his cleaner's uniform.

"Hey, you bastard! What the fuck is this meant to mean?"

"Nothing in particular. You see, I usually ask my clients to comment on what money means for them first. In this case, I had to guess."

"Yeah? So, 'cording to you, what's money mean for me?"

"Splattered shit we accumulate so we can swallow it, and so the others can't swallow it."

Maso laughed quietly as he gave Bramsos a pat on the back.

"Frigging artist, you don't know the first thing. But I like it. I want another, double the material this time. But words aren't my thing. I'll draw something so you'll get it."

Maso made a quick scrawl, folded the sheet of paper and handed it to Bramsos. On his way back home, the artist threw it in the first trashcan without even unfolding it.

Mascorro came by the next day with twice as many suitcases. Bramsos separated his supplies from his pay and shut himself up to work. This time he emptied the contents of the bags on the floor and mixed the bills as thoroughly as he could. He created children like small angels flapping their wings in snow, swept them from side to side, threw them at the ceiling so he was showered in the acid rain.

When he'd eliminated all trace of discrimination in terms of value, point of origin, color, and graphic style, he began taking bills one by one, sticking them precisely onto a canvas, the same size as the first. After completing a first mosaic, he immediately began to apply another layer, and continued this ant-like task until the last bill had been pasted on. On inspection he had the impression of a heterogeneous battalion of mercenaries, awaiting the order to earn their pay in blood, and decided to get in first: he used his strongest steel-blade Stanley knife to break their ranks with firm incisions; he made a circular cut, as large as, the canvas could bear; with a spatula, he took the skin off the damaged surface, leaving an expanse of injured bills. This done, he traced out a new, concentric circle with his knife and again scraped it with his spatula until it was lower than the previous one. This operation was repeated with increasingly smaller diameters, deepening the scraped area each time. The culmination was a small orifice, through which the white of the canvas could just be seen. The piece was a kind of inverted circular pyramid, like an eddy, incrusted in the block of pasted bills.

"And what's in the frigging hole?" asked Maso when he saw the piece.

"If you look carefully, you'll see that at the very bottom is everything that exists in our world. After so, so many turns, we arrive back at the infinite, but by a different route. A very different route."

"No way, you bastard! Look frigging Beni, come see my present for your new home. Give my friend here another suitcase as a bonus."

"I'm sorry, but I can only accept the amount stipulated in the contract."

Before leaving, Bramsos shook hands on the deal that assured him an unlimited supply of free drugs.

17

After a while, Sao and Max suggested that their friend hold a retrospective exhibition of his wealth-work in the gallery belonging to a group of ladies who organized art classes in the newly inaugurated commercial zone of the residential estate. They were certain of obtaining permission from the owners: the name of each piece was the amount employed to create it. The owners were credited for the loan of their works: it was an elegant way of announcing their acquisitive power. Sao and Max curated the exhibition, saying they were surrounding wealth with poverty without fear of friction. The opulent pieces stood proud, looking down on the expanding belts of misery of other realities with the minimum of necessary goods.

Part of Bramsos' artistic policy was never to refuse a request. An enlightened beggar had commissioned a piece to remind him of his much-loved years as a poverty-stricken student. With the six one-peso coins he received, Bramsos decided to make a series representing the man's descent in the world. All of them showed an identical coin, placed on the sill of a window, looking on to a building with eight windows. Even the first coin had a squalid, if serene integrity. It contemplated the windows opposite, occupied by scenes of everyday grayness, scattered with various white fantasies. There was a family having dinner in silence; a man alone, watching television with a beer in his hand; a boy playing piano, and, naturally, the scene of a woman undressing. The next in the series showed the same coin—a little tarnished, and slimmed down in terms of both thickness and width by Bramsos—looking from the window at the same building, but now with one pair of curtains closed. The tone of the scenes was slightly different: two children were fighting over a toy; a couple was arguing about bills; a little boy was memorizing the dialogue from a gangster film. As the series progressed, the coins became increasingly tarnished and meager. Their view was reduced by the number of closed curtains. The paintings became increasingly sordid; injection marks on arms; battered women being dragged by the hair; gamblers losing everything they had on a single hand; teenage girls hiding in bathrooms, taking abortion-inducing remedies. In the last painting, the coin was only recognizable as such because the viewer already knew what it was. It was almost a smooth, curved piece of wire, with barely the strength needed to look out its window. The figures it saw seemed condemned: a wino in rags, reeling and throwing up while rooting in the trash for something to eat; a woman being stabbed in the abdomen as muggers stole her purse; a pervert sodomizing a hen in front of his eight children, with hardened snot around all their noses and mouths; a domestic employee throwing a pan of boiling water in her boss's face. The other windows were dark with desolate hermeticism.

The vagabond agreed to allow the series to be shown in the exhibition on condition that his name was omitted—it was the only anonymous loan—and the curators arranged the six pieces around Maso's miniature infinite, too absorbed in its abundance to realize what was happening.

Visitors were given salon notes for the exhibition, written by Sao and Max.

Ladies and gentlemen,

Welcome to this first retrospective of the work of the well-known artist Pascual Bramsos, whose green period has caused a stir among art lovers and specialist critics. We hope that it will also be to your taste.

Some relevant data to help you appreciate the collection:

—5% of the pieces represent 84% of the total value of the exhibition.

—The sum of the three most expensive works would be enough to buy a folding bicycle for every resident of the estate.

—Pieces of medium value make up only 14% of the total.

—The most marginal works have been the subject of numerous academic studies. Critics highlight the social conscience of an artist engaged with his community, with no trace of elitist frivolity.

"Bramsos inverts and juxtaposes the bifrontal values of an obtuse representation that both attracts and repels the viewer toward the oblong abyss of his own ethereal identity, blurred by the most recondite interstices of the omnipresent panic of contemporary society."

The Happy Seal Magazine

"A load of filthy shit."

I've Got the Talent, art supplement

"With the skill and originality of the great masters and the unashamed freshness of every deconstructive avant-garde movement, Pascual Bramsos has opened a channel through which future generations, condemned to live in his dazzling shadow, will pass."

Information Bulletin of the Foundation
for the Friends of Falconry

The exhibition was a success, although Sao and Max had to bite their lips to stop themselves bursting into laughter at the sight of the solemn reading of the salon notes. Bramsos took the liberty of selling the vagabond's series at a thousand times its original value. When he handed over the bulging envelope with the proceeds, the former owner calmly counted the bills, divided it in two in accordance with the artist's work code, and returned the whole intact so Bramsos could create a new piece for him.

18

Since she was a small child, Sao had defended herself from the pus of scars with an instant smile. It was the only thing she'd been able to bring with her from her native jungles. She'd forgotten her mother tongue to the point of learning to pronounce her r's normally. When her father celebrated the anniversary of the horror by getting drunk on rice liquor, Sao didn't understand a word of his pent-up ravings. The alarm bell for helping him to bed was the shrieking produced when the burning powder fell from the sky. Señor Bac-Do would wave his hands in the air, attempting to brush off the string of incandescent ticks buried in his skin.

It was as if Sao never lost the hope of healing her own open wound by trying to provide what others lacked: she volunteered to bathe infants in an orphanage; she took hot food to the estate's security guards; she lent money she never asked to be returned to ex-boyfriends. Max would laugh when reminding her of the time she burst into tears on being shown a cartoon of a spider hanging from its own web, in which it had woven its farewell message.

Now that she was able to formulate what she'd felt as long as she could remember, gratitude expanded her inner black holes. It sucked in with a voracity that shrunk her spirit. She had become a walking pincushion enclosed in her skin. The tension invariably materialized into the two questions she had never been able to answer: Who? Why?

She wanted to discover the mechanisms behind the complex planning of uniform discipline. Millions of people linked in a common mission, ready to destroy life for abstractions based on other abstractions. Like a mechanic dismantling a machine in search of the principle generating its movement, Sao wanted to learn to take apart the rhetoric guiding the people possessed by the abstractions. What was hidden behind the feverish squandering of energy? What was the cause of so much expense, so much sacrifice, for the sole purpose of reaching into others' way of being in the world? She would imagine a chessboard with irregular squares.

They had indentations and hills, thick vegetation and sandy deserts. They were ruled by armies using diverse tactics. The objective was the same in all cases: to impose a way of life on the other colonists before the colonists imposed theirs on them. The crudest battalions attempted to assert their supremacy by force; they doled out beatings, dressed the wounds, and readied their victims to be instilled with their customs. Others carried exotic products whose novelty enchanted the locals to the point where they were very soon doing somersaults just to acquire them, and began to resemble the suppliers as they merged with their merchandise.

The most astute battalions were the ones impossible to resist. They didn't have to do anything; they just existed. Period. They exuded an aura of such charm, such enviable candor, that people would beg to imitate them. Whatever their age, character, appearance or level of physical coordination, they all appeared young, kindly, handsome, and expert dancers. They played a flute that, instead of sounds, emitted images. The followers would see examples of their most memorable moments: a dramatic soliloquy, some sporting feat, a million-dollar deal, or a disinterested aide during a famine. They obtained the surrender of entire territories without firing a single shot. They were the vanguard: the promise of terrestrial glamor without cares.

The scene would dissolve in Sao's mind when the whole chessboard descended into pitched battle. She was dazed by the anarchic flight of grenades, juicers, designer shoes, speeches to the oppressed, missiles, insipid comedies, torture chambers, tax exemptions, patent medicines, killer drones, and electronic music. Each band utilized its finest weapons. They overran territories in search of beings to colonize, classifying them according to the basic dichotomy of friend-enemy. Both received the same treatment. The only difference was that they made a favor of forcing the friends to obey; the enemies were first raped, and then afterward had the usual orders barked at them. All the graphic, sonorous, commercial, or ideological violence was concentrated in a few knotted lines that sent Sao's teeth over the edge. In the end, nothing was new. The same old turbulent enigma: Who? Why?

She decided to study the history of regimented aggression. Perhaps if she understood the different ages, forms, wrappings, and justifications for broadening the range of fear by transferring it to others, she could calm her caffeine-fueled melancholy. Sao easily passed the exam to study international relations.

19

Max was experiencing his own personal future dilemma. His father had for years encouraged him to follow in his footsteps, but along a different path. The doctor finally hammered in the nail during a family dinner. Taking care that Max would overhear, he commented to a distant relation:

"Quite true, dear cousin, at the level of the law on which I practice, there is no place for anything but genius, and I very much fear I have so successfully taken my place on the pedestal that Max will have to carve his name in some other sphere. He's not a bad boy, just a little soft. Maybe if life hardens him, he'll become a competent administrator. Though it remains to be seen what he might learn to administer."

Max put great care into planning his revenge. Where would his defiance hurt his father most? What he needed was something vague, subjective, useless: a profession disdained by society. The greater the possibility of financial failure the better. Against the diminutive might of the law—his father dreamed of a world in which every single possibility had been foreseen, codified, and sanctioned—he had to pose the ungraspable; some anarchic, subjective sphere. For hours he searched for the answer in the book so often used to indoctrinate him with lies, staring at pages, awaiting certainty. One sheet of white muteness hurled him to the next until he arrived at the end of the book and firmly banged it shut. At last, he had it: literature.

Not long afterward, Max arrived home, exuding rebellion and waving the form for enrollment in the university admission examination before his nanny's eyes. He knew something was going on when she didn't share his excitement:

"Little Max, your father's had a very bad turn. He's been taken to hospital."

"The frigging bastard. Even in death, he's found a way fuck me up."

The doctor and his body were respecting their gentleman's agreement.

Not long afterward, fearful of wasting the munitions he'd stockpiled, Max communicated his professional decision to his dying father. Without saying a word, Dr. Michels put two fingers to his son's cheek, he gave it a couple of affectionate pats—followed by a third that bordered on a slap—before resting his head back on the pillow. His eyes fixed on Max, with unbearable slowness, he relaxed every one of his nerves and fell asleep.

Between the related formalities and his ambivalent mourning, Max didn't take the exam. He was devastated by another nascent loss: in strict accordance with labor law, the doctor had left instructions to pay off the nanny for her long years of service. Her invisibility and tough weathered skin camouflaged the proximity between her and the doctor's ages. And that was the cause of her serenity in the face of the stingy acknowledgement she received: she knew she didn't have long to live either. Her exclusion from any public health program had lead her to deal with the blows, illnesses, and habitual wear and tear of being on her feet for fifteen hours a day by visits to bonesetters, herbalists, and other specialists in patching up ailments. Her body understood the limitations of her caste, so it didn't demand first-class maintenance. The nanny felt that the cracks were about to join up, and she wanted to undergo that generalized collapse in the shelter of the tin roof and dirt floor of the shack where she'd grown up, and return to the starving hens and metal-eating goats of her hometown. Luckily, baby Max was already a man: she didn't have the strength to protect him any further.

Max helped her to pack her belongings into a cardboard box. Not even some thirty years of service were enough to fill it. As a farewell present, he brought her a shining new transistor radio. Her old one lacked several buttons; the dial had faded from use, so she had to tune it by trial and error.

He accompanied her to the bus that would take her to the station, noting for the first time her hunched back and laborious gait; her furrowed face; the chipped teeth; her leathery flab; her poorly graduated spectacles; the darned dress; her swollen feet;

her smiling silent tears. The nanny was crying for the only thing all those years had left her: the memories of a life that had made it possible for the Michels family to live its own.

Max broke down at the sight of the packed bus that would swallow up his nanny forever. He felt as if every one of his organs would make him pay for the years of his family's miserliness. He desperately tried to think of some formula for returning her life to her, for turning back the clock on the thousands of small acts involved in feeding him, washing and ironing his clothes, tidying his bedroom, and taking and collecting him from school... When he saw her crying, it was as if the step of a staircase were disconsolately lamenting being close to the point when no one would tread on it again. The nanny's thick lips parted to say:

"Goodbye, Max my child. I'll be looking out for you from the Valley of Skulls."

"Don't say that Nanny. I promise that as soon as I've gotten everything organized, I'll come visit you."

Limping, she boarded the bus, tightly clutching her box. As soon as she was gone, Max had a numbing sense of foreboding. He ran back to his building, falling flat on his face on the stairs in his hurry. He kicked open the kitchen door to confirm his fears: the transistor radio was still there. He attacked it viciously until it was unrecognizable. Several plates and glasses suffered a similar fate. Still panting, Max flopped onto the kitchen floor among the debris. He cleared a space on the icy tiles to rest his head, and that was how he passed the first night of his future life.

20

Around that time, Max was having difficulty distinguishing between his own and external upheavals. Since the residential estate had first set out on its ambitious expansion project, Dr. Michels had often advised him to prepare himself for the new challenges; only real men, men with balls, would triumph. All types of business opportunities were now opening up. And also opportunities to mold the collective destiny through the only solid nucleus of social life: the individual. The sciences of the public sphere focused on dissolving the dangerous sentimentalism that produced so many calamities. Anything that couldn't be quantified was ideology, and ideology was equivalent to the absence of freedom. The notion of a total identity only leads to servitude; it had to be eradicated. The way forward lay in boosting the sum of accumulation. Egoism was the most infallible defense against the repetition of barbarity; charity allowed failures to fail. The no-opportunity whiners would be the first great burden to be shed. Better to follow the example of the poor boy who overcame unspeakable hardship to achieve his dream of becoming the fire chief.

Max put his name down for the second round of admission exams. This time his choice of subject was different. Sao and Pascual came round to his apartment to hear his decision. Once they were drowsy on the baked dough and the bubbles in their sodas, he came out with it:

"I wanted to tell you both that I'm not going to do literature. I've thought it through, and times are changing. I don't want to study a completely useless subject."

"How do you mean?" interrupted Pascual

"Shit, you know what I'm talking about," replied Max brusquely.

"Forget it, Max. Those aren't your own words," insisted his friend.

"It's easy for you to say that. You threw yourself off the cliff and landed on your feet. I don't want to end up giving classes to frigging lazy fatties. I've been reading about the new opportunities for participation in the public sphere. It's amazing, nowadays you can even measure your soul and reeducate it to turn around, move forward."

"Hell, Max, you've forgotten about our pact quickly."

"What pact, shithead?"

"You really don't remember? The one about digging in our heels and not toeing the expected line. I just hope you don't turn into one of them too quickly." Pascual left hurriedly without saying good night.

"I don't know what's wrong with that moron. What do you think?" said Max, turning to Sao.

Sao was unwilling to say anything until she was sure how serious Max was. She sat beside him and hugged him closely, ran her hand down his back as if wanting to ask his shoulder blades what she already knew at heart. Max shielded himself by kissing her, and they started off down a path already trodden. This time Sao was prepared. Before things went too far she took a sheet of paper from the back pocket of her unbuttoned jeans. She lay with her head on Max's legs, slid her hand down her own belly to her expectant pubes. She then handed him a piece of paper on which was written a poem by one of her favorite writers, a man who had decided to blow his brains out when he was scarcely past twenty, before he could enter an empty world of pure rhetoric. Without having to be asked, Max began to read:

If walking, I walk alone
through deserted, abandoned countryside
if I speak with friends, of drunken
laughter, and of life,

The words organized themselves to form a private enclosure that excluded Max. His voice came from a nearby dimension, located on an inaccessible plane.

If I study, or dream, if I labor or laugh
or if a gust of art transports me
or if I gaze on nature fresh risen
with new life,

Sao began to gently stroke her skin with a fingertip, stopping at every pore of the soft textured surface, moving the finger slowly up and down, down and up.

You alone rule my heart
of you alone I think, for you every fiber quivers
for you alone my thoughts thrill
for you, beloved.

Unhurried, she sought out the right fold, the elongated fibrous point that would initiate the flow of moisture. She was a little disappointed on finding it, as that marked the end of her search, so she moved her hand away to purposely lose it and start over again.

I am drawn to you with growing passion
with a force I've never before know,
without you, life is empty,
sad and dark.

When the flood was irreversible, she carefully allowed it to spread more widely, including in her generosity her pubis and crotch. Her finger was a convulsed serpent, thrusting in search of more.

If all latent energy in me is awakened
to the powerful appeal of love,
I long to see that burning flame
enter my heart.

Sao's disengaged hand came in to play, strategically moving in the opposite direction. It passed over the small mounds of her breasts and moved on to her skull, against the grain of her hair, until it reached Max's jaw, squeezing with mild sadism. She introduced a finger into his mouth, allowed it to be caressed by the tongue before returning it toward her nipple. Then she sketched circles around the nipple until it was thoroughly aroused.

I long to rise toward the infinite ether
and shout my passion to it
I long to communicate rebellion
to the universe.

The moans were like a shrill chorus; they crashed into the boundaries of the invisible field, augmenting in tone with each rebound. Impossible to tell if they came from Sao, or if she were a creation of the moans.

I long for nature to throb
with the pulse the spirit stirs in me
I long for splendorous love
to shine in your unmoving eyes.

The hand alternating between her breasts allowed itself a new flight: it steadily approached Max until his lips were murmuring in her ear. The finger deferred the explosion. Sao's entire body was beating to the rhythm of his uneven breathing.

Tell me, why do you evade my gaze
my love? Or do you still not understand
the burning ardor that consumes me?
The flame you ignite.

Time and space canceled each other out. Colors merged into one. One luminous hue. There was no longer Max. Nor non-Max. Just a cry, a liberated shudder. A suspended tremor. The restraining hand attempted to prolong it. Just a little. The bow tensed in an instant previous to the firing of the arrow that would release a cascade of exhalations, returning to diffuse normality.

I have no peace if you are not near:
I long to follow you everywhere
to drink the air moving around you
and never abandon you.

Sao resurfaced to satisfied calm, her breathing separated from Max's. He stroked her forehead tenderly, proud of his role in their meshing. She drowsed for a few seconds then opened her eyes. "We shouldn't underestimate complexity," she said before standing to help him gather their things.

21

The beginning of the academic year distanced the three friends on certain levels. There were obvious, practical reasons for this: they were each absorbed in their new obligations and friendships. Pascual formed a rock group called Eidola, specializing in livening up events, playing stylized cover versions of classic songs. Sao divided her time between her studies and the laundry, while Max widely expanded his curriculum both to the left and right, in theory and in practice. He was determined to take a good look at the truths his father had venerated. By now, he was now aware of the farce: it was a cult founded on a lie; his father had used preaching about truth as a means of avoiding having to confront that. Who was soft now? Was it manly to hide behind grandiloquent axioms, designed to enforce formulaic thinking?

At the same time, the link between the friends weakened in the realm of excuses. Their spontaneous meetings were a thing of the past. Trying to coordinate free periods became a tedious exercise. Sao and Max made a solemn pact: every so often they would get together for their secret poetry recital. The sheet of paper became so creased from use as to be illegible. But it was no longer needed: Max knew the poem by heart. They both played their part in jealously guarding this point of resistance against the latent threat that making their individual ways in life would definitively separate them.

22

Max began studying political science at a moment of transition in the paradigm: the intention was to distance the area of study from social anthropology, now seen as an ideology-driven pseudoscience. Based on false foundations, its scaffolding was increasingly skewed. Its vision of the historical progress of societies was reduced to the absurd pronunciations of hypocritical egomaniacs. First they had constructed horrific utopias, and only later elaborated rigged laws to demonstrate the inevitability of that future without chains imposed by the few.

The counterattack of liberty was based on the opposite premise: the only chains were those that attempted to see man as anything but a small creature, with small yearnings and a narrow mind. Man's principal desire was for an absence of obstacles to achieving his small, utilitarian satisfactions. The crucial pirouette consisted of a new definition of the object of study: human beings passed from being a species determined by the weight of its habits and natural and social structures—most of which it neither knew or understood—to a rational consumer trying to maximize his desires and frustrations. He appropriates as much as possible for his personal use, but also for the pleasure derived from depriving others of what he has. If the earlier paradigm committed the sin of investing man with responsibilities exceeding his stature, the new one tore off all his necessary epidermal layers, until he was reduced to a purely egoistic being who, even in altruism, only desires to satisfy his own vanity.

Differential calculus showed that such a situation was optimal for the whole. The citizen-consumer model was not restricted to the goods and services markets. It also applied to the only relevant political action: voting. That simple act became the common coinage for expressing dissatisfaction with product-candidates who would become entertainer-governors. The political future was determined by the maxim: "The customer is always right." Rational selection had no limits: it allowed for the construction of models for contemplating works of art; determined the most appropriate time to marry by means of curves representing the inverse relationship between unfettered fun and the stability of commitment; measured the proportional utility—in terms of benefits and obligations—of having pets or children; founded a new mathematical system of ethics for deciding whether or not to commit corporate fraud, taking into account the possibility of being caught. In short, it was an anti-utopian utopia. All that was needed was for thousands of millions of people to learn to behave in the way stipulated by the models. They had to be educated to reasonably channel—fighting any form of radicalism or eccentricity—the unlimited torrent of alternatives that defined them. It was simply a matter of burying the collective ghosts that had, in the past, roamed whole mental continents. Luckily, these were now nothing more than a bitter memory.

Max thrashed as best he could to keep afloat in a pool with no bank to cling on to. The mask with pretensions of not being a mask was warmly welcomed by the majority of the teaching staff and students. In theory. As with any conversion to a new liturgy, it required certain leaps of faith that short-circuited their predecessors. The academic community felt itself besieged by a cybernetic principle: no hardware, no software. Without a certain amount of mental capacity, the transplant was a complex—sometimes impossible—operation. Emptying the brain of its previous contents was easy; the promise of a free future was enough to win hearts. The problem arose in then filling the mind with an ideology that attempted to define itself by pure absence. This soft rigidity posed dichotomies that confused many of the new devotees.

And none so much as the issue of limits. While differential calculus inelegantly resolved the matter from the viewpoint of logic, its sociological disciples were condemned, before they even started, to babble. Mathematics solved the metaphysical-infinitesimal problem of whether or not limits exist by coming down roundly on the side of existence. Although all previous developments suggested the contrary, limits could be defined and enunciated. The proposition that even the closest conceivable point was always separated from the limit by various infinites didn't stand in the way of proceeding with a firm step. "As if" became the skeleton in the closet that was never mentioned. Limits went from being a theoretical impossibility to solid rock that could be built on. The system functioned impeccably. And that buried any conceptual contradiction in the premise.

The dimensions of the dichotomy exploded when it was transferred to the field of social organization, where the concept of the limit was even more resistant to aligning itself with some coherent flank. It was a pariah for both hawks and doves. No one could silence its uncomfortable questions: What should free consumers do about those who insisted on not enjoying that freedom? How far could fundamentalist practices and ideas be allowed to threaten the capacity to consume? Was it legitimate to use force to oblige others to be ruled by the ideals of guilt-free consumption? And if not, should the ideology of free consumption sacrifice itself, allow its own destruction before limiting those insisting on not consuming freely?

Innumerable variants on those themes were debated in the international symposia speakers attended in order to be put up in luxury hotels—all expenses paid—and vigorously outline the new theoretical principles of political action. The flow of scholarships, residencies, and research grants was constant. Important newspapers and magazines reproduced learned articles crammed with quotations proving something or other. The aim was not so much to arrive at certainties that would threaten the objectives of the academic industry—that would be opposed to the principles of the new perspective—as to imperceptibly mark out the sphere of discussion. No more debates on oppression, property, injustice, alienation, worldly pleasures, cages, liberation theologies, political kidnapping, or anarchist bombings. Given a fanatical acceptance of certain unquestionable principles on which the rest of the apparatus rested, civilized attack could be encouraged, just so long as it adhered to the monolithic plurality of the cause.

They were unsettled times, with great confusion and hilarious syncretisms. There was, for instance, one lecturer with upper-arms bulging with fat who attempted to impart the new divinatory sciences: she was supposed to teach the students to construct probable scenarios and project equilibriums. It was a matter of classifying reality into viable alternatives so that it didn't veer toward the undesirable ones. A tool of deceptive simplicity existed that simulated games in a four-block diagram. The participants made decisions based on their own situation, taking into account their assumptions on the behavior of the others. The basic dilemma used was that of two prisoners who had to decide, without consulting each other, whether or not to confess to a joint crime. The lecturer had to demonstrate that although the optimal decision was not to confess—in which case there was no proven crime—the ultimate equilibrium was for both to confess, and thus equally fuck each other up. The key to the theorem was a blind faith in the fact that the other would seek personal salvation.

The lecturer spent the first class attempting to explain the diagram and its functioning. After remembering so many letters and numbers, she had to sit down to rest for fifteen minutes, while a student fanned her to waft away her flushed embarrassment. The criminals escaped from their square prison each time she tried to explain her thought processes to her students.

"If number two doesn't confess and one does, there's no equilibrium because, given what they know, added to what they know the other knows, there's no incentive to reach a point of equilibrium."

The students gazed at her, uncomfortable and embarrassed.

"Listen, it's not my fault. That's roughly what the book says. It isn't that easy to translate.

"But get it into your heads that the important thing is that it depends. If hegemony sutures the imaginary reconstruction, the two criminals could fraternize and not give way to the repressive intimidation."

"Why?"

"It says here that's not the right question. Now it's 'Why not?'; remember, not why but why not."

Even paid agitators had to reconfigure their proposals in relation to the new geometric politics. Their efforts to harangue the student body in the language of the new times left Max with a sense of sympathy for the absurd. A leaflet posted on the faculty walls captured the effectiveness of the virus in the jargon of the day:

COMRADES:

THE AUTHORITIES CONTINUE THEIR POLICY OF APPEASING
THE OWNERS OF THE FREE MARKET.

THEY OPPRESS THE PEOPLE BY KEEPING INFLATION LOW

THROUGH RAISING PRICES.

SAY NO TO THE PRIVATIZATION OF THE TAMAL SANDWICH
STAND!

FREE ATOLE FOR ALL UNIONIZED WORKERS AND STUDENTS!

NOT ONE STEP FURTHER!

COME TO THE RALLY AND DROP A SLIP OF RECYCLED
PAPER IN THE SUGGESTION BOX.

THE STUDENT ANTI-IMPERIALIST STRUGGLE COMMITTEE
FOR INCLUSIVE DEMOCRACY.

23

Max's study plan also included a synopsis of the history of political thought. Based on academic readers summarizing classic texts, he seemed to perceive a movement that was the antithesis of the tone of the contemporary panorama. Classical thought was presented with a sort of veneration of the obsolete: the great philosophers had served as a transition to the present evolutionary stage; they were like highly gifted children who managed to get a glimpse of something, but always within the framework of superstition. They functioned as pearls to adorn, with some erudite reference, contemporary debate; were relics testifying to the passing of other times, now distant from the universality of science.

What Max noted was the inverse: despite its hyper-realistic pretensions, political narrative was acquiring an increasingly fictitious character. The point of departure and the end met to close a circle that no longer even bothered to take into account some of the most manifest features of any attempt to explain the social sphere. In years gone by, the graybeard who signaled the disenchantment of the world proposed setting out from "what is" as it presents itself, even as a point of departure for those who wanted to transform reality. In present times, the reverse process was followed: to set out from a list of indisputably good desires, and to assume that—with sufficient will on the part of those with power—one could reach a just Utopia where everyone would stay in the place corresponding to him.

Everything could be justified in the name of the transformation of the inert masses into proud, participative citizens, conscious of their rights and obligations. What did it matter that "what is" was widespread hunger, violence, ignorance, rage, banalization, morbid curiosity, and snobbism? There was no way that the poor taste of gatecrashing the institutional-perfection party would be allowed: the ballot box will make us free... handsome, smart, good, and better. Anything not in tune with the choir of new ideals was punished with the most absolute segregation: it would be banned from mention at conferences, in cultural magazines, and on boring television programs in which regulated cruelty was extolled. The simple fact that people would periodically turn up in their millions to scratch a determined mark on a piece of paper—without having any real idea of the implications of the alternatives—was sufficient to legitimize any state of affairs. Brutality became a leftover concept to be corrected little by little. Gradually. In installments. Of course plurality involved self-criticism: it wasn't a perfect system, but it was the best ever invented. That was enough to make it impossible to question.

There was in the university one muscular provocateur who enjoyed quoting a melancholy, heteronymic author: even the most avant-garde were indignant about the proposition that the distance between a cultured man and the average worker is greater than that between the worker and a monkey. Fascist! Reactionary! Think again, buddy! Did you know he spends the whole day eating tuna, lifting weights, and watching videos of gory fights? I've heard he has more than one girlfriend at the same time! He's a pervert!

The council of notable academics—always the same people— decided to expel him from Eden: unlike them, he would never have life tenure ensuring a comfortable existence. He wouldn't attain the paradise of thirty years reciting the same books to generation after generation of naïve students. It was one thing to be tolerant, but quite another to allow the teaching of inappropriate thought. Young minds were not yet ready to be corrupted.

This man was the only member of the staff willing to oversee Max's thesis. The original title, "Have You Ever Seen a Democrat Without Shoes?" was rejected by the course coordinators. Anxious to get around the red tape, Max opted for *The Construction of the Imperfect: The remaining challenges for participative theology.* The committee was thrown off track by the agglutination of terms from the dominant canon, so didn't notice the actual meaning until the thesis had been printed out.

Max concentrated on a simple exercise. He made an exhaustive review of those theoreticians who postulated the existence of society as a communal pact. Without exception, he found that in exchange for the renunciation of natural freedom and individual power, the collective yoke always offered something else:

protection, well-being, respect for private property etc. He examined the texts line by line and came to two conclusions:

1. Rights are created and conceived by man himself. Not being, in themselves, either universal or evident, their validity was subordinate to their efficacy. If they were not observed during any given event, they had no purpose. Rhetorical rights are equivalent to nothing.

2. The shell of the pact has absolutely no value as such. Without the promised benefits, it is an empty form with no justification in itself. If institutions don't respond to its specific aims, the dissolution of the pact becomes legitimate through the same line of reasoning that brought it into existence.

As the requirements of the thesis included some form of numerical analysis, Max added an appendix with three graphs. The first was entitled "Liberty." To draw it, Max got hold of historical data on the percentage of the population in prison in industrialized nations and calculated the ratio, weighted by population size. His coefficient of prisoners demonstrated an unequivocal tendency to rise: increasing numbers of citizens in affluent countries enjoyed the benefits of development from behind bars.

The second was called "Equality." It was very similar to the first, except that in this case what was charted was the coefficient measuring the distribution of wealth. Here again, there was a pronounced tendency toward a concentrated high-income group on a planetary scale, greatly increasing the gap between haves and have-nots.

He named the last graph "Fraternity"; this simply showed the number of armed conflicts per year, weighted by the number of deaths and the costs of war damage. Even if a couple of historical peaks that went off the graph were omitted, once more, there was an indisputable rise.

He rounded off his thesis with a single-page conclusion, left completely blank. After a less than exciting viva, marked by unease and latent tension, Max was awarded a university degree. Sao and Pascual invited him to dine on their favorite mushroom quesadillas in celebration.

24

After his graduation, Max thought over his options for setting out on the path of social rhetoric. The trust fund left by his father was very clear: he would only receive money for three months following the completion of his studies.

He regularly checked the classified ads of *The Daily Miserias*, but the same job opportunities appeared again and again: plumbers, bathroom maids, watchmen, cellar men, weekend child-minders. One day, almost by accident, before turning the page, he saw the following announcement:

WANTED: SOCIAL SCIENTIST NOT GIVEN TO STUPID
AFFECTATION. THOSE INTERESTED SHOULD
CONTACT $UPERSTRUCTURE ON 55 73 93 94.
NUMBSKULLS NEED NOT APPLY.

He'd heard talk about the wizard of social-trends analysis who had recently arrived in Villa Miserias. It was said that his equipment for dissecting the collective spirit was so powerful that it could dispense with the soul itself; it was capable of publicly denuding it without even the need to look.

After a call so succinct it left Max wondering if it had actually taken place, he was invited to a meeting with G.B.W. Ponce, the messiah of $uperstructure, at Alison's. The same day. Twelve minutes later. Ponce's identifying features: graying hair and an undone tie.

Max was there a minute early. Ponce was already waiting with two beers. Before giving any sign of having noticed Max's presence, he finished his own off at full speed.

"So you're interested in sticking your head in the gutter, are you?" he asked by way of introduction.

Max hesitated before responding to this unexpected question. He considered asking his potential employer to repeat it, but that didn't seem to fit with the etiquette of the occasion. Instead, he remembered that arrogance was prescribed.

"Pleased to meet you, Señor Ponce. I'd just like you to know that shit doesn't frighten me. I've spent my whole life escaping from fairy stories. Even when they are well-intentioned, they do a lot of harm."

This was enough to confirm G.B.W. Ponce's intuition. The boy was hired.

"Let's just get one thing very clear, er…Max? You're called Max, right? I'm not offering you anything more than my vision. It looks a whole lot like the one people think they have. The difference is that I can show you what to do so that they can't tell their vision from mine."

"That's enough for me. And I offer not to look away, no matter how crude the spectacle is."

"Come in tomorrow and we'll arrange the details. Welcome."

Welcome. Welcome. Welcome… The sounds echoed in staccato, unsuccessfully trying to catch Max's attention. He was already at another table. Without his body. He was urgently fantasizing about how to get to know the woman he couldn't take his eyes off: Nelly López, Orquídea's niece. For Max, her black eyes tinted the entire place. He stood up, following a silent command, halting on his way every few steps to inhale composure. At her table—unaware of Nelly's scribbling in her notebook—he stopped to check, for the last time, just what he was contemplating.

"Hi, I'm Max Michels. I think I've just fallen in love."

The first answer came from a nearby table, where a group of youths were downing beers to celebrate their grades. In imitation of the celebration on the screen, the most euphoric were splattering the floor with what remained of their drinks. The empty glass crashed to the ground, looking something like a shuttlecock spewing beer. The last rebellious drops traced a perfect parabola before hitting the floor, awaiting the cloth that would soak up their identity, without any possibility of return.

III

1

"Exactly who are you?"

"Who else would I be? Nelly López."

"And what are you doing here?"

"Well, you asked me in."

"Do you sleep with everyone who asks you in?"

"The ones I like, yes."

"Just curious."

"Ugh. Don't tell me you feel more at home with the usual stuff?"

"No way. This is very dark. I need to see you."

"Ah, no. Leave it be. You have to get used to it."

2

When Max woke there was no trace of his guest. Even the sheets had been straightened in the half where she'd slept. Although he hadn't drunk much the night before, his mouth felt furry, his head heavy; home to a constellation of fugitive stars, twinkling moments in the life of Nelly, as recounted by herself. In his mind's eye, he could even see the moment when they went to his bedroom.

After that everything was a solid wall of darkness. His skin remembered the shudders, but however hard he tried, there was no image associated with them.

Some inner sense was warning him not to get involved with a presence capable of destroying him: their respective strengths were just not comparable. He fantasized about throwing every insult he knew at her, saying the most wounding things he could think of. It wasn't that he wanted to cause her pain, but simply to make her refuse to see him again. But at the same time, he was consumed by the desire to sink back into that incandescent darkness. It was a matter of instinct. Of pride. Never before had his body cried out with such shuddering delight. His cells went into hyper at the very thought of it happening again. But the absence of self-congratulatory images was unbearable; he was almost uncertain that the events had actually occurred.

It was all an extension of the impenetrable blackness of Nelly's eyes: voracious irises that unwillingly ceded a little ground to the snow of the eyeball. Even before they had left the bar, he had been determined to find some nuance, patchiness, wrinkle, some chink of difference within that black cavern. Zilch. Nelly gave nothing away. The very notion that she possessed pupils was an act of faith. Max got as close as he could; they had to be somewhere. Nelly's amused smile breathed laughter at him. After that failure, he consoled himself by trying to demonstrate that a more intense black existed in the world outside her eyes. First he compared them with the glass of bitter, sugary liquid on the table; the ease of their victory made him want to throw the fluid in her face. He found a black lighter that, for an instant, seemed to aspire to a comparison.

After that Nelly gave him the clip that restrained her cascade of waist-long hair; its prongs paled in comparison with her eyes. Max next tore off a piece of the black cloth surrounding the autographed photo of a sporting legend hanging on the wall. He was immediately surrounded by bald gorillas, and had to give a little something to soothe their itchy palms. When that final adversary was defeated, Nelly asked him to stop. All this—with the added frustration of not being allowed to pay the whole check before moving on to his apartment—left Max with an awareness of the inevitability of his future:

"What's the point? Your eyes are blacker than the deepest melancholy."

The next flashback had them in Max's living room, each holding a glass of wine, sitting on the old sofa that had been reupholstered so many times; at this particular moment, it was covered in the faded, apricot-colored material Max hadn't changed since his father's death. Behind them hung the familiar axiom: "The measure of each man lies in the dose of truth he can withstand." Incapable of destroying the plaque, Max had muffled its message beneath a work by Pascual Bramsos, an unsolicited gift from the artist not long after he'd started university. At first it had seemed a celebration of a new cycle, but, after all the hours of contemplation, Max now understood it had more to do with the end of an era.

The painting showed three small, upended, paper sailboats. The boat on the right was decorated with a purple nose; the one in the center had a pair of almond-shaped eyes along its whole length; the left-hand boat was distinguished by a scorched ear, dripping globs of flesh. All three rested on dog-eared toothpicks covered in tiny splinters—somehow resembling peculiar, pockmarked men—and were plowing through the sinuously textured sea. The toothpicks, in turn, hung from the crests of three deep waves, blue arcs—surging inexplicably from the upper edge of the painting—impeding their upward descent. As a frame, Pascual had covered the four shores of the canvas with a single, long strand of red yarn, glued in studied disorder, so that it was impossible to follow its garbled path. The continuity of the frame was unquestionable: it had no visible beginning or end.

"What does it mean?" asked Nelly after frowning at the artwork for several minutes.

"According to Pascual Bramsos, the moment before the destruction of a world."

"So you really do know him?"

"Yeah, I think I still do."

For the following few hours, Max had alternated between wondering if his anxious desire was going to be satisfied, and continuing to feign a genuine interest in the story of that apparition. With respect to the latter, his lack of autonomy was calming: Nelly was like an orchestral conductor directing the entrances and exits of an evening's music, and for the moment she wanted to talk. Even so, Max had the impression that the words she spoke—issuing spontaneously from some other place—were laboring under the obligation to match up with her metallic voice. As soon as they were out of her mouth, they were free again. At times, Max allowed a number of them to pile up unheard so as to snatch instants of contemplation. Then, when he was on the point of losing their meaning, the threads of the narrative meshed together. Despite this distraction, the various passages of Nelly's tale rammed into him like concrete blocks, leaving him in a pleasurable state of bewilderment. With maddening assurance, she was building to a climax.

3

"It's like I grew up on a small farm, where the six children were seen as just one more species of the badly treated animals we made a living from. My dad was always saying he didn't make any profit on us. Can you believe it? Saying we were too delicate to eat the pigswill; that it would be at least ten years of outgoings before we started to be useful; that the village doctor charged more than the veterinarian and did a worse job. And then, just to top it all off, he'd complain that the law said he had to send us walking two hours to school to waste our time with learning those letters that didn't even help balance the books.

"And the thing is, my dad didn't believe in God either, he was just afraid of him. Like, in his way of thinking, just doing the religious stuff was enough to get God's approval. That's why he regularly attended mass, took communion, went to confession, gave small change to beggars, had his children baptized, and didn't curse or anything. But in return, he was free to commit any other kind of cruelty that wasn't actually prohibited. His main punching bag was my mom. He was always going on about how she'd given him four bitches but only two dog pups. Where was he going to find the money to pay four different punks to take them off his hands?

Like, for years, it disgusted him to see her with a kid hanging from her boob the whole day. And that's not all. The bastard used to rape her every night, and there was my mother, letting it happen, just giving a few sighs while she waited for him to finish. And the rest of us, listening to him bellowing and the bed creaking. The only good thing was that Dad was quick about it. It was only when Mom had a vaginal hemorrhage that he stopped knocking her up. Can you imagine how it would have been if he hadn't? But the thing is that without a womb, she was hardly human for him. Even though she went on cleaning, sweeping, ironing, cooking, and putting up with his badmouthing, he didn't see her as a woman any longer. And—what do you think of this?—he used to torment her, saying that God hadn't made a mistake; that there was a reason why he'd sterilized her with that red flood. But the stupid cow kept her mouth shut. I never heard her complain or answer him back. Every time I go to visit, she's just the same. Only more sickly, looking worse. Her face more worn and haggard.

"You city folk always imagine you find out about sex when you're pretty young, but I'd say the opposite, that we learn about it earlier on the farm; and not because they teach us about it in school with little diagrams. My brothers snicker about their first time, saying it was with some she-goats and a can of condensed milk. Does that sound like a joke to you? It does to me. Just from listening to the mules, I knew what my dad was doing to my mom every night. And then—you won't believe this—when I was nine, some frigging farmer stood there gaping, just imagining what my boobs would be like in the future. Instead of saying something, my dad gave him a friendly slap on the shoulder and they went off to play cards.

"But, like, I already knew I was different. Even as a child, I could see that with a body like mine I was going to be different from my mom and my sisters. Take it from me, we stopped going to school as soon as we were old enough to milk a cow and carry a pail of milk. It's a miracle we even learned to write our own names. My sisters were already well and truly over the hill before they were even grown up.

"Dad used to get together the money to give them quinceañera parties, and then let everyone know he had a head of cattle for sale. You can't imagine how pathetic it was. Now, I think it was like auctioning off a worn broom—they were like skin and bone from malnutrition. Take it from me. They hardly had eyes, just two dead marbles crying out to be owned by someone else. When the oldest got pregnant by a drunken skirt-chaser, he put her out there in some hovel to starve in the cold. The other two went on drudging away for Dad. Nice job that; busting their guts to serve him and getting paid with insults.

"So that's how it was, but in my case, something took pity on me and made me different. I don't know why, because we all came from the same place, but I was made of more solid stuff, and so I was sharper. It's just that thanks to the flesh between my skin and bones, I could see the world didn't begin and end at our farm. When I was around thirteen, I started noticing a kid a bit older than me—one of his jobs was to collect the dung we used as fertilizer, and even his once-weekly wash couldn't get rid of the sour smell. He was the first person to be hypnotized by my black eyes. I thought about him back there in the bar, because he was just like you, getting real close, trying to see if there was some trick.

No way. Anyway, I wasn't a kid anymore, so I let him do whatever he liked. One day, somewhere between riled and horny, he picked me up and threw me onto the straw in the stable. Can you believe it? He didn't just want to fuck me; he looked at me as if he wanted his eyes to get inside mine. When he'd finished, he sunk his head into my shoulder and cried. To tell the truth, I didn't even enjoy it, but it didn't bother me either. I cleaned myself up a bit and helped him to feed the pigs.

"Ugh, you've no idea how it was. Whenever we could, we escaped to the stable and got down to it. I even started liking the way he smelled. Gloomy though that farm was, there were contraband tastes and smells there in the hay we rolled around in. But the day my dad saw me looking happy, he knew something was up. Even though he's the stupidest man I've ever known, the old fool is sure good at spotting any attempt to get out of the cage—if you'd seen the number of dolls and toy cars he stamped into the dust, just because he saw us playing with them—and by that time, he was keeping a close watch on me. He wanted to know why I didn't just play possum like the others. He checked my hands and my clothes. He knew something was going on and he was convinced he could find out what.

"On the farm, everyone got on with his own thing. Imagine, we'd walk past each other without saying a word. The others were like part of the landscape, especially my sisters with their blank expressions. That's why we didn't bother much about hiding ourselves away, but now I come to think of it, me and that boy were pretty stupid. We only ever waited till Dad was asleep or had gone to the store. One day he snuck up on us at just the wrong moment.

Jeez, if you'd seen the beating he gave that poor kid. He went on hitting him with a shovel until two of the farm hands stopped him. Then he told Mom he didn't talk to prostitutes. And you know what? After that I was even more invisible to him.

"You see, that's when I really found out what it was like to become one of them. All the long years to come suddenly weighed down on me. In a mirror in my head, I saw myself deformed. I used to lie in the stable and try to masturbate, but when I finally managed it, I felt even sadder. What I think now is that it wasn't pleasure I was looking for, just to escape for a moment.

"And that's how it was. Like, I was used to living as if I had a layer of paste numbing me to outside contact. My dad was right, we were just another species of animal he struggled to raise on the farm. And the worst was when the kid snuck back one day. At first, I didn't even recognize him. He told me a bonesetter had pummeled him all over—and him howling with pain—trying to heal the damage my father had caused. He was lame in both legs, and on his head he had a bald patch from the blows to his skull. He stood looking at me with something like hate and just told me to grab my stuff, that we were going to the city on the tomato truck that left in the early morning.

"I watched him walking off with his new limp. Then, without even giving it a second thought, I packed my few clothes into a bag and waited nervously for the hours to pass. At the time we'd agreed, I went to the kitchen—walking on tiptoe for fear my dad would hear—like I was crossing a minefield. I heard the sound of the truck waiting for me on the dirt road. When I was about to go out the door, the light came on. Jeez, I can't describe the frigging panic. My whole life was going down the fucking drain. Thinking there was nothing for it, I turned round to face him and saw my mother with a shawl over her head, like she was a spy trying to hide her identity because of what she was about to do.

"'Hurry up, my girl, he might wake up. I've written my cousin Orquídea's number on this envelope. God bless you and care for you. If anything goes wrong, call my cousin.'

"I can't tell you just how surprised I was. She handed over the money she'd been secretly saving, together with a pretty empty hug. My knight in shining armor was waiting for me in the tomato truck. The great idiot didn't even get out to help me in. I'd never left the farm before. I was like under a spell, watching that whole dry landscape pass by. For the first time, after all that nothingness, there was something.

"We came to a market that looked to me like the biggest one in the whole world. I gave the envelope with the money to my new boss; he gave the driver a couple of bills and we left. He already knew the city a little. With my money, he paid a month's rent on a small room in some poor neighborhood. The door was hardly shut before he was good and horny, and started stripping my clothes off to celebrate our new life.

"The next morning, we went out, looking for work for him. As he was ambitious, he wanted to try his luck first in a department store. Boy, you should have seen it! When he wouldn't give up, the assistant threatened to call the store security team if he didn't leave. As for me, it was the usual, you know: Would I like to meet him for a coffee when his shift was over? So we spent the whole day walking. We felt like the frigging city had already calculated just how many ants it needed to do its drudgery. It was like other people didn't even move to one side if they wanted to pass where we were standing. "One night, he told me he wanted to take a walk round the block on his own. And what do you know? He never came back. With my last few coins, I phoned my aunt, Orquídea. What with all the crying and confusion, I felt like every car, building, policeman, street seller, tram, and beggar was part of a machine trying to tear me to pieces. Luckily, I spotted the plaque on an old palace and my aunt was able to locate me. She came hanging on the arm of a bearded guy with a beret and hugged me like we'd known each other all our lives. She took me home, making me feel like it was no big deal. And that's how she started looking out for me. What do you think of my arrival in Villa Miserias?"

4

Max dressed hurriedly so as not to be late for his first day at work. He hesitated a little on seeing his long hair in the mirror: Ponce hadn't mentioned anything about appearance. As he jogged down the stairs from the third floor, Max considered the two possibilities related to his change of status to a proprietor of a prestigious apartment: upward, on his own steam, or downward with someone else's help. Without having done a thing, he was now worth more than the residents below him. Even the apartment on the second floor that hadn't been split had degraded through contagion: the owner couldn't charge the same rent because of the washing hanging in the neighboring windows.

Max was aware there was no way of stopping the leap into nothingness. His only doubt was whether, when he pulled the ripcord, a parachute would appear or an iron block. Juana Mecha saw him leave with his air of radiant misfortune.

"Watch out for the holes with another hole in the bottom," she said with genuine concern.

"Don't worry, Juanita. I'm not afraid of the end of the world."

He crossed Plaza del Orden and went into Villa Miserias' commercial zone. There, the dominant aesthetic was functionality: each of the individual premises had its own particular lack of personality. Taken as a whole, they were like a giant piece of discolored bait, designed to attract short-sighted fish. In *The Daily Miserias*, Max had read an article by his new boss on the factors determining the behavior of regular customers. He was surprised to find they were the opposite of what he'd expected: nowadays, the stores were using negative emotions like anxiety and inadequacy as hooks. In the past, they had promised a cosmeticized form of happiness, a better life brought about by the product in question. Things had changed: the prevalent mood was more like putting on your best finery to go to a funeral. No brand now offered paradise. Rather, they communicated the idea that their non-essential products lightened the burden. Max stopped to breathe in the atmosphere. It didn't even smell clean. G.B.W. Ponce had rounded off the article with his usual figures: 87% of purchases generated greater unease; 91% of customers made themselves unhappy imagining there was a better, cheaper version of the thing they had just bought; 79% suffered heartburn on seeing new residents laden with bags of who knew what; the cleaning staff collected a weekly average of a cubic foot of fallen hair from below the ATMs; 98% dreamed of their next spending spree before having finished the present one. Max meandered until he came across the arrogant, slime-green sign, commissioned from Pascual Bramsos. The words were formed by a fine layer of bills glued on a white background:

$UPERSTRUCTURE

WE TELL YOU WHAT YOU DIDN'T EVEN KNOW YOU
THOUGHT

He also noted a small metal plaque assigning the design of the internal space to the architect Horacio Rorka. Inside, the employees moved freely between plasterboard cubicles with comatose workstations. An artificial plant flourished in each corner; Rorka had explained to Ponce that they saved water, avoided termites, and, anyway, the air conditioning system made up for photosynthesis by recycling the air they all breathed. It had also been shown that plastic plants contributed to lowering levels of labor unrest. G.B.W. Ponce reigned over an accountant, a secretary, and a team of six young economists who their boss affectionately called the Crushed Humps. They spent the twelve hours of each working day performing regression analyses on their computers until the lenses of their glasses had tripled in thickness. Panic fueled their search for infallible causalities.

Only the director of the company had an individual space: a circular abomination, assembled from tinted glass panels, situated in the heart of the $uperstructure offices. It contained only a desk and two slender chairs with backs curving slightly forward: a technique for keeping the spine alert and reducing the proclivity for wasting time on mental strolls. Ponce didn't even need to oversee his employees; the level of paranoia on its own was enough to meet his aims.

Max entered warily and stood by the disciplinary chair marked out for him. He found Ponce in the stage prior to making a new rip in the veil: after having interrogated his tables for hours, he lent an ear to the numbers, waiting for them to whisper a new maxim to him. Then he entered into dialogue with them, expressing his level of agreement or incomprehension. Max listened to the low monologue.

"So they're ready to accept the naked truth? Yes, yes, I see. But they've been inoculated against nausea. Great. We'll go with it then." Ponce raised his head and scrutinized Max through his dark glasses, as if wondering who the hell he was and what he was doing there.

"I'm Max Michels. Yesterday, you told me to turn up for the job."

"Tell me about yourself. I'll order a coffee. Your place is out there with the others. I'll explain what I want you for. I need you to start today."

"May I sit down?"

"The list of candidates for the presidency of the colony closes in two weeks. They've all contracted us. First we give them an edited version of this document. Read it. Apart from the last part— that's internal and confidential—everything else is a report on how things stand. It functions as an equitable starting point. Then, depending on the style of each of the candidates, we give personalized advice. We track the changing opinions of the voters during the campaign: they only tell us what we've known from the start.

There's rarely any great difference between the photos at the starting and finishing lines. The ballot box simply reflects the pre-existing irrationality. It's to do with charisma, physical appearance, or what people think will happen if the candidate wins. But you shouldn't underestimate the relevance of the process: it distracts the residents for a while and legitimizes authority.

"The last time round, I came across a kid crying with rage because he didn't come of age for three weeks, and so, couldn't vote. I tried to console him by explaining that no individual vote mattered, but he answered with the commonplaces his parents had instilled in him. The same old argument that if we all thought the same way, no one would vote, and then you couldn't complain, and all the rest of it. Did you hear about that girl's suicide last week? I asked him. Of course he had; she was a classmate. Do you realize that if we all thought like her, and all committed suicide at the same time, Villa Miserias would cease to exist? He told me to fuck off and left even more furious than before, though calmer too, because he had a specific target for his frustrations.

"Max, I want you to understand the psychological importance of the vote. The crucial point is that each and everyone feels he decided. Or that he lost because the boneheads didn't listen to him. Because they didn't understand the things he did. It's a unique mechanism. The whole is condensed in each consciousness. The illusion of having an effect is key. It's the basis of the system. Without it, the whole thing would collapse. Or maybe not. Could be it's the last annoying foothold. That's exactly what we want to verify."

"We want to?"

"You'll get it later on."

"And what do you expect me to do?"

"Be my lantern. My method can extract any information, but it has to be pointed in the right direction. Read the document. This community has evolved in the only possible direction. Each individual has to be free to triumph or fail according to his own abilities. It's even immoral to help people who don't deserve it. A waste. From the point of view of the species, it's to do with maximizing pleasure. What matters is the absolute value, not how it's distributed."

"But then, does your theory of absolute value mean people whose lives are fucked up don't suffer? Don't you think, in that case, you have to subtract their level of misery from the well-being?"

"They suffer because they haven't learned to accept themselves. Because they're still duped by the promise of a better world for everyone. If they understood that everyone has what they deserve—opportunity or otherwise—they'd live in the unworried calm of resignation. Ugly people understand their limitation: that's why they interbreed. Unless they're rich or famous, they generally don't rub shoulders with the good looking. It's the same with the have-nots. They need to understand there are forces with a life of their own, forces as arbitrary as genes that determine the direction their existence takes. In fact, they know and accept it. All that's needed is a last turn of the screw. Calling things by their proper names. It's time to see if they're ready for the words to match the reality. I can't overemphasize that, deep down, they know it. Now we're going to find out if they can tolerate hearing it."

"How do you plan on doing that?"

"Go home and study the document. We'll continue tomorrow."

5

THE ART OF BLOWING GLASS WITHOUT BREAKING IT
BY ORQUÍDEA LÓPEZ

A GLASSBLOWER HAD A DILEMMA: HE WANTED TO CREATE A RECEPTACLE FOR HIS COLLECTION OF STONES. THE FEW MOST BRILLIANT STONES NEEDED THE ORDINARY ONES TO SUPPORT THEM AND ALLOW THEM TO SHINE. THE GLASSBLOWER TOLD HIMSELF THEY WERE ALL EQUAL. IT WAS JUST THAT SOME WERE MORE EQUAL THAN OTHERS. HE TRIED MAKING A CYLINDRICAL RECEPTACLE: THE STONES MIXED ANY OLD HOW, THE MOST PRECIOUS WITH THE COMMON HERD. THE GLASSBLOWER WONDERED HOW COULD HE ARRANGE IT SO THAT EACH STONE STAYED IN ITS PLACE. HE INCREASED THE WIDTH OF THE BASE, BUT THAT DID NO GOOD. THE BEST STONES STILL TUMBLED DOWN AMONG THE MASS OF OTHERS. WHAT HE NEEDED WAS A RECEPTACLE WITH A WIDE BASE FOR THE POOREST STONES, A NARROW NECK FOR THE MEDIOCRE ONES, AND ABOVE THAT A FUNNEL SUPPORTING THE MOST VALUABLE.

THE EUREKA MOMENT CAME WHEN HE REALIZED EACH STONE WANTED TO FEEL IT WAS ACTIVELY PARTICIPATING IN THE PROJECT. AT THAT, HE TRIED PUTTING THE GLASS PASTE INTO THE KILN WITH ALL THE STONES, CAREFULLY CONTROLLING THE TEMPERATURE. FROM EXPERIENCE HE KNEW THE MOST DANGEROUS MOMENT WAS WHEN THE HEAT MADE THEM GLOW RED. THE ANGRIEST MIGHT TAKE

CONTROL OF THE SITUATION AND DECIDE ON THE SHAPE OF THE RECEPTACLE. THE GLASSBLOWER HAD HEARD SOME AWFUL STORIES. THE STONES WERE VERY RESENTFUL AND SUSPICIOUS OF ANYTHING AND EVERYTHING. THEY SPENT THE WHOLE TIME SNITCHING TO THEIR SUPERIORS. THAT'S WHY HE HEATED THE GLASS VERY CAREFULLY.

FIRST, HE BLEW THE BUBBLE FOR THE BRILLIANT STONES. THEY WERE THE ONES THAT WOULD BE REMEMBERED. WHEN HE SAW THEM IN THE MUSHROOM-SHAPED CYLINDER, HE WAS DEEPLY MOVED. AMONG THEM WERE SOME THAT STOOD OUT, BUT THE GLASSBLOWER HAD SELECTED THEM CAREFULLY SO THAT EVEN THE LEAST HANDSOME REPAID HIS EFFORTS TO SOME EXTENT.

THE NEXT STEP WAS THE MOST DELICATE. THE GLASSBLOWER FORMED A NARROW TUBE THAT WOULD PERMANENTLY SEP-ARATE THE DESTINIES OF THE TWO RACES OF STONES. HE BLEW THE GLASS, FEARFUL OF DISRUPTING THE NEW ORDER: THE NECK WAS SO NARROW THAT A SNAP OF THE FINGERS MIGHT BREAK IT. THE TRICK WAS THAT THE STONES WERE BY THEN SO CLEARLY SEPARATED THAT IT DIDN'T EVEN OCCUR TO THEM MAKE A FUSS. IN THE END, THE RECEPTACLE LOOKED LIKE AN INVERTED WINE GLASS WITH AN OSTRICH NECK.

THE FINAL PHASE WAS TO MAKE THE BASE SINK DOWN-WARD TO CREATE A HOME FOR THE MASS OF STONES. THE GLASSBLOWER MADE IT AS SHALLOW AS POSSIBLE SO THAT THEY WOULD FILL THE ENTIRE SPACE. ALTHOUGH THEY DIDN'T KNOW IT, THESE STONES SUPPORTED THE ONES LIVING ON THE PEDESTAL ABOVE THEM.

THE GLASSBLOWER WAS TIRED BUT SATISFIED. HE HAD FINALLY FOUND AN ARRANGEMENT THAT DID JUSTICE TO EACH GROUP OF STONES, AND, THEREFORE, TO THE COL-LECTION AS A WHOLE.

WHAT LESSON DOES THE GLASSBLOWER'S STORY TEACH US? WE ALL KNOW THAT FOR MANY YEARS VILLA MISERIAS HAS PUT A LOT OF EFFORT INTO TRANSFORMING ITSELF. THE OLD STRUCTURES DID THEIR JOB, BUT THEY HAVE RESISTED THE NECESSARY ADJUSTMENTS WITH ALL THEIR MIGHT. THEY ARE LIKE THE MOST STUBBORN STONES THAT WANT TO HAMPER THE ASCENT OF THE BEST. LUCKILY, WE HAVE QUIETISM IN MOTION. IT'S LIKE A GLASSBLOWER THAT DOESN'T IMPOSE PREFABRICATED MOLDS ON ANYONE, BUT PUTS US ALL IN THE KILN SO WE FALL INTO OUR COR-RESPONDING PLACES. THAT'S WHY IT'S THE BEST MOLD, BECAUSE IT DOESN'T ALLOW ANY OTHER TO SHAPE IT.

IN ALL THESE YEARS, OUR COMMUNITY HAS............, AND TODAY WE CAN SAY THAT WE HAVE FOUND............ TO CONSOLIDATE THE GROUND WE HAVE CONQUERED WITH SO MUCH EFFORT............

6

Nelly's metallic voice began to sound in Max's head. Despite the onslaught, he managed to go on reading a few more lines of Orquídea's pamphlet, until it annexed the last of his attention. Max wasn't even conscious of the transition; he was simply there in his apartment once more, listening to her, spellbound. After that, he didn't even make an effort to resist.

"So, like I was telling you, my aunt Orquídea took charge of my education. She sent me to school and helped me with my homework in the evenings. Ah, I can't tell you how patient she was, because my dad had made sure we were as ignorant as sin. I can still remember how I felt when she gave me a map of the world to hang on the wall. Can you imagine? Me, who'd never even left the farm, and now I had the whole world in my bedroom. She used to spend hours there with me, just looking at it. I drew a knife where the farm was and used a ruler to measure how many inches it was from the places I imagined to be so incredible.

"Well, when I was fifteen, the first part of my life came to an end. My aunt Orquídea knew how it was when my dad set up those cow-walk shows on the farm. She was really kind, and organized almost the exact opposite, a private party where I had all her attention. The beardie with the beret was there too. And like she'd read my mind, she took me to my favorite hamburger joint. The waiters put a paper hat on my head and sang happy birthday, and—you'll never guess—they pushed my face in the cake. I was so happy I didn't want them to clean off the cream. I've still got a photo from that day stuck on my wall. My eyes are like black jaws nibbling at the white cream.

"But then, you know, the way it always is, there has to be something bad. So, what happened was that—I'm not sure how to put this—well, the thing is that the beardie started being very affectionate with me. If you get my meaning. Imagine. He was giving me the same looks as that farmer I told you about, only that my body was in better shape to receive them by then. The pig used to whisper secrets right in my ear, or sit me on his lap while I did my homework. When we were in the car, he'd lean close over me, supposedly to fasten my seatbelt. If my aunt went out and he stayed to look after me, he used to read me revolutionary poems about free love with no restrictions, and talk about the feast of naked bodies floating in clouds of ecstasy. What an idiot. And so cheesy, right?

"But you see, I was still pretty innocent and I started having fantasies. I used to dream that we went off together somewhere, anywhere, the farther away the better. And I couldn't even look my aunt in the eyes for the guilt. But the worst wasn't even feeling like a traitor. I got that out of my head, thinking I hadn't responded to any of his advances. What tormented me was that I liked it a lot, that I was pleased with those advances. I'm even ashamed talking about it, but, like, the truth is, right then, I could have spat in the face of my aunt, the only person who'd ever been kind to me.

"So then, one morning when my aunt was making me a sandwich for school, I couldn't stand it any longer and told her everything. I was sure she'd put me on the next bus back to the farm, but, anyway, it was a great relief.

"You won't believe it, but that was when my aunt became almost a goddess for me. You can't imagine how well she reacted. She hugged me so hard it made me cry. Yeah, she told me off, but not for what had happened. She was mad that I was having to put up with that good-for-nothing's stupidity. She was already fed up with him—the beardie spent the whole day going on about his theories and proclamations, but the one who paid the bills was my aunt—and now she'd found out about the other…Well, I don't have to tell you. I'm sure she only did it to make me feel better, but she said she was grateful to me for giving her a reason to send him packing. Then she said something that stuck in my mind like it was chiseled in marble. She asked me to listen carefully, because she was going to tell me the only thing I needed to know to stop me ever again being a victim of sly, abusive hicks. That is, men in general.

"'Every woman is sitting on her most lethal weapon. If you learn to disguise it with the fantasy men need, they won't be able to fuck with you.'"

7

THE DUST WE INHALE HELPS TO REMIND US OF THE PAST WE'VE THANKFULLY LEFT BEHIND. THE PERPETUAL CON-STRUCTION WORK MEANS WE REMEMBER THAT ALL THE TIME. VILLA MISERIAS WON'T BE STOPPED, WHETHER THEY LIKE IT OR NOT. THOSE WHO CAN JOIN THE TRAIN WILL ENJOY THE BENEFITS, AND NO ONE'S GOING TO SHED A TEAR FOR THOSE WHO CAN'T.

THIS IDEA TOUCHES ON ONE OF OUR MAIN ACHIEVE-MENTS IN RELATION TO EVERYDAY LIFE: CREDIT. WE'RE VERY LUCKY THAT ALMOST EVERY HOUSEHOLD IS IN DEBT IN ONE WAY OR ANOTHER. THE MAJORITY OF PEOPLE BUY THEIR BRICKS AND MORTAR IN INSTALLMENTS, ENSUR-ING THEY ALONE ARE THE OWNERS OF WHAT IS THEIRS.

THEY HAVE ADVANCE EXPERIENCE OF THE HORN OF PLENTY THAT IS PROPERTY. THEY ALSO TAKE ADVANTAGE OF THE POSSIBILITIES OFFERED BY THE PRODUCTS IN OUR COMMERCIAL ZONE. RESIDENTS OF THE COMMUNITY ANSWER WITH THEIR WALLETS THE FUNDAMENTAL QUESTION OF OUR AGE: WHY WAIT A MINUTE LONGER TO HAVE WHAT CAN NEVER FULLY SATISFY ME ANYWAY?

THE PILLARS OF THE COMMUNITY STAND OUT FROM THE PARASITES IN THAT THEY ALMOST ALWAYS TRY TO LIVE BEYOND THEIR MEANS. THOSE WHO ARE CONTENT WITH WHAT THEY HAVE NEVER CATCH UP. THAT'S WHY QUIET-ISM IN MOTION LAYS SO MUCH STRESS ON LACK, BECAUSE ONLY IN THAT WAY CAN THE COMMUNITY CONTINUE TO ADVANCE. THE EMBITTERED PHILOSPHER EXPLAINED IT VERY WELL WHEN HE SAID THAT THE IMPORTANT THING IS THAT WE KEEP MOVING OUR LEGS AS WE GO DOWN THE SLOPE, BECAUSE IF WE STOP, THE INERTIA WILL HIT US.

THAT'S WHY CREDIT ALSO WORKS IN ANOTHER WAY. IT FORCES THE RESIDENTS TO BE DISCIPLINED AND STAY IN THEIR ALLOTTED PLACE. THE DEBT COLLECTORS DRESSED UP AS YELLOW JESTERS WITH THEIR JINGLING CAPS SHOW THE ENTIRE COMMUNITY THAT THOSE WHO DON'T PAY UP HAVE NO SAY. AS SOON AS THEY HEAR THE JINGLE, THEY BREAK INTO A SWEAT AND RUN OFF TO FIND THE MONEY TO COVER THEIR DEBT.

IN THIS LAST PHASE OF THE HISTORIC DEVELOPMENT OF VILLA MISERIAS, TO FINALLY GET WHERE WE WANT TO BE WE NEED TO CALL THINGS BY THEIR PROPER NAMES,

JUST THE WAY THEY ARE. WE HAVE TO DO AWAY WITH ADJECTIVES THAT SOFTEN REALITY, SO EVERY RESIDENT CAN TELL HIS DREAMS FROM HIS NIGHTMARES.

FOR THOSE WHO SAY THIS ISN'T TRUE, HERE'S THE EXAMPLE OF OUR EMPLOYEES. WHY ELSE DO THEY STAY WHERE THEY ARE IF IT ISN'T BECAUSE THEY LIKE STAGNATION? NOT ONE OF THEM HAS COMPLAINED ABOUT NOT BEING ALLOWED TO BUY THEIR APARTMENTS. THEY EAT THE LEFTOVERS WE GIVE THEM WITHOUT COMPLAINT. THAT'S THE CHARITABLE SIDE OF OUR PROJECT. WE WANT TO HELP THEM SEE IT'S NO ONE'S FAULT, IT'S JUST THEIR PLACE TO BE ON THE WRONG SIDE OF AMBITION. I'M SURE WHEN THEY UNDERSTAND THAT, THEY'LL FEEL LESS INFERIOR. THEY'LL UNDERSTAND THEY'RE JUST DIFFERENT. IT'S TIME FOR THEM TO ACCEPT THEY WANT WHAT THEY HAVE. WITH THAT MINOR CHANGE, THEY'LL BE ABLE TO ENJOY THEIR VULGARITIES, AND NOT STAND AROUND STARING, WITH THAT VICTIM LOOK, AT PEOPLE WHO REALLY DO SET OUT, EVERY MORNING, TO GET EVEN A LITTLE BIT MORE.

8

"And you won't believe it, but it took me a long time to understand my aunt Orquídea's words. The thing is, I thought, with all the education I was getting, I'd lose that rustic farm-girl air, and then I wouldn't be always feeling like an overflowing drain. But that wasn't how it was at all. The more I learned, the more confused I felt. Complexes are really sly, and they came out of corners I didn't even know existed. I felt like a fraud the whole time, a fraud anyone who got close enough could show up. It was as if I had a stamp on my forehead I had to hide any way I could.

"The boys in my class at high school started bothering me the whole time. Overnight, I'd become the one they were all after. And the truth is, I can't tell a lie, getting to fuck me wasn't exactly difficult. Just a bit of a come on, and you were almost there. It was like the worse they treated me, the quicker I gave in. And as my reputation spread, more of them wanted a slice of the cake. And the stories they told about me. Some were true, there's no denying it, but they got exaggerated a lot in the telling. The other girls hated me. And none of my girlfriends were exactly good looking, so things got worse. We were always talking about my tangled love life. And even if their boyfriends were less handsome than mine, I couldn't stand it. I used to play the innocent until the boys felt I'd got my eye on them, and then they couldn't resist. I lost several friends that way. But don't go thinking those affairs lasted long. No way.

"The few who didn't notice me paid dear. I made sure they fell for me, behaving as if I was drooling over them. Like I was ready to be their slave, be whatever they wanted. And they were clueless, but once they'd swallowed the hook, I sent them packing. I'm not trying to boast, but some of them were obsessed with me for years.

"When I masturbated, I almost always used the same fantasy. I imagined a rough man had me in a corner, trying to rape me. I'd run as fast as I could, beg for help, scream, scratch, hit, and bite him. I'd resist as long as I could, then he'd overpower me and tear off my clothes, sometimes with his teeth. When the inevitable was about to occur, I'd surrender, saying 'Enjoy me,' and we'd be bumping and grinding in the ultimate fuck.

"All the guys who jumped on my carousel were crazy with jealousy, but, like, you might not believe it, usually I hadn't done anything to cause it. The truth is, it was always the same accusation, that I loved getting a reaction out of men anywhere I went. To avoid problems, if we went to a bar, I'd stick to them like a limpet, kiss them every so often so they'd feel safe. I wouldn't even turn my head to look at someone who wasn't sitting in our group. But it was no use, things always went wrong. I'd go to the bathroom and someone would try to chat me up, or they'd send a drink to my table and then the boyfriend would feel insecure. One of them—he was really crazy—kicked me in the ass because he was sure I was flirting with the waiter right in front of him.

"The quarrels could be bad or not so bad, depending on how drunk they were at that moment. But when they got mad, they all felt the same hatred of my beauty. When we went into a bar, they were real proud to have me on their arm, but that same vanity made them imagine I was always wanting to throw myself at someone else, anyone. Like, you should have seen it, they'd go from doing absolutely anything to please me to telling me I was an out and out slut. They'd say I only wanted to be with them until something better came along. I can't tell you how many times we left places screaming and crying.

"I'd get home really terrified and go over every detail of the evening, trying to understand what I'd done wrong, why they'd got so aggressive. I'd feel bad about things I hadn't done. It'd take me hours to get to sleep, going round in circles, feeling

I'd done something awful. The next day, it would be the same old routine; the call to say sorry, dying of shame but acting like nothing had happened. The excuse was always that they were drunk and couldn't remember anything. Sometimes they'd make themselves believe their own paranoid fantasies, and got even more highhanded. They were so sure I spent my whole life planning who to fuck next. But the joke is it was never them who ended it. With the exception of one boy, who really regretted it later, it was always me who called the whole thing off, and, I have to admit, it was almost always because I'd got someone else lined up.

"But look, it's like they say: if you can't beat 'em... Gradually, I began to think the men, my aunt, and nature were right. That's when I decided to really let my instincts have free rein. If they wanted me to be the slut everyone could enjoy but nobody owned, hey, I wasn't going to put myself out to show them I wasn't. The more I told them about my promiscuity, the more they wanted to be with me. I warned them from the start I was extroverted, and wasn't going to change just for them. I spent the whole time talking about my previous experience. I acted like a vamp, even with their brothers, but stopped just before the point when anyone could complain. Now that I think of it, what I was doing was taking revenge for all the harassment I'd suffered before, and not even really going with other guys, because, up to then, I hadn't cheated that much. I was just shooting off fantasies that tortured their imaginations.

"My life began to center around finding new guys to swallow up, see what they tasted of, and then spit them out. And however cold I was about breaking up with one, I'd start on the next with real passion. I had such convincing ways of letting them know

I liked them. I took an interest in what they were interested in and—this is going to sound weird—it was like I adopted some of their characteristics too. If they liked baseball, I went happily along to the stadium to watch their team. With the TV addicts, I'd stay up till dawn, watching anything. If they were those hippies with money, we'd go on vacation to unspoiled beaches. But when they were like dummies with gel, it was designer hotels with only a few rooms, like the ones film stars go to. Their friends became mine. The truth is, I've been so afraid of being alone, for a long time I've been everything without really being anything. But I'd discovered that having them always on their guard, afraid I'd throw them over for someone else, was infallible. I'm sorry, but that's the way it's been.

"My aunt was ultra-proud of me, more than for any good grade or school stuff. She didn't say so, but she'd seen I'd finally understood her maxim. Imagine, she even did up the maid's room on the roof so I could use it when I wanted, without bothering her. She knew she didn't have either my age or looks any longer, so in some way she was toying with them too, but through me. I think I kind of healed her wounds too."

9

A BETTER LIFE FOR THOSE WITH THE ABILITY TO ENJOY IT
SHOULD BE REDUCED TO THE LEVEL OF THE INDIVIDUAL,
THE ONLY ORGANIZATIONAL PRINCIPAL BASED ON EGOISM.
IN VILLA MISERIAS WE WANT TO REPLACE THE CHAINS

TYING US TO OTHERS, SO WE CAN BECOME A COMMUNITY
COMPOSED OF LOOSE LINKS WITH NO MUTUAL OBLIGATIONS.
THE BEST WAY TO KNOW A PERSON ISN'T BY ALL THAT
ROT ABOUT THE SOUL, BUT BY HIS THINGS AND HIS APPEAR-
ANCE. HOUSES, CARS, TELEPHONES, CLOTHES, WATCHES, BALD
PATCHES, PAUNCHES, MAKEUP, COSMETIC SURGERY, BOTOX
INJECTIONS, DOMESTIC SERVANTS, AND OTHER ACCESSO-
RIES, DON'T JUST GIVE US EASE AND COMFORT. PEOPLE
WHO THINK THAT ARE WRONG. NOWADAYS, LUXURY IS
THE GREAT STRATIFIER OF OUR TIMES. IT TELLS US MORE
THAN ANYTHING ELSE ABOUT THE ASPIRATIONS OF OTHERS.
POSSESSIONS ARE LIKE A PROSTHESIS THAT COMPLETES
OUR BEING. THEY COMMUNICATE WITH EACH OTHER TO
UNITE THE PEOPLE WHO SHOULD BE TOGETHER. G.B.W.
PONCE HAS SHOWN THAT MEMBERS OF SOCIAL CIRCLES
TEND TO BE SIMILAR. AMONG THE DIFFERENT STRATA, THERE
ARE ALMOST NO DIFFERENCES IN GOOD LOOKS, ACQUISITIVE
POWER, POLITICAL IDEAS AND THE REJECTION OF COMPLEX-
ITY. THE MASTERMIND'S EXPERIMENTS HAVE ACCURATELY
PREDICTED FRIENDSHIPS AND ENGAGEMENTS IN PILOT
GROUPS OF OVER TWO HUNDRED PEOPLE. BEING WHAT HE
POSSESSES ALLOWS A PERSON TO MIX WITH PEOPLE LIKE
HIM, SO HE DOESN'T HAVE TO DISILLUSION THEM WHEN
THEY FIND OUT TOO LATE HE'S IN THE WRONG PLACE.
THE RECONSTRUCTION WORK DONE BY T&R HAS MADE
US STRATIFY FROM THE BOTTOM UP. THE INTENTION IS FOR
OUR BUILDINGS TO REFLECT THE DISTRIBUTION OF ABILITIES
IN THE COMMUNITY. G.B.W. PONCE HAS DEMONSTRATED

THE RELATIONSHIP BETWEEN LIVING SPACE AND MENTAL-
ITY. JUST BY KNOWING THAT IN THE LARGEST APARTMENTS
THERE ARE, ON AVERAGE, TWO AND A HALF BATHROOMS,
AND IN THE SMALLEST, ONLY ONE, CAN GIVE US AN IDEA
OF THE ASPIRATIONS OF THE INHABITANTS. IF NOT, HOW
CAN WE EXPLAIN THE FACT THAT WE LIVE TOGETHER WITH-
OUT FRICTION. THE PEOPLE AT THE BOTTOM RESPECTFULLY
GREET THE "PALEFACES" UP AT THE TOP, AND OFTEN CARRY
OUT THE TASKS THOSE PEOPLE DISLIKE FOR A SMALL GRA-
TUITY. AND NOT JUST THAT: THEY DEFEND THEIR RICH
NEIGHBORS AGAINST PEOPLE THEY HAVE MORE IN COMMON
WITH. NOTHING GIVES A CLEARER DEMONSTRATION OF
THEIR BELIEF IN QUIETISM IN MOTION. ON THE ONE HAND
THEY ACCEPT WITHOUT COMPLAINT THE DESTINY THEY
HAVE ASSIGNED THEMSELVES; ON THE OTHER, THEY ASPIRE
TO ONE DAY BE LIKE THOSE WHO COULD CHOSE SOMETHING
DIFFERENT. THEY ACCEPT THEIR PLACE AMONG THEIR PEERS,
BUT DON'T RELINQUISH SEEING THEMSELVES REFLECTED IN
THE SHINING POOL ABOVE.

IF WE ACCEPT THAT MATERIAL STRUCTURES ARE A
FAIR INDICATOR OF THE VALUE OF SOULS, WHY CAN'T
WE RECOGNIZE THE SAME AT A POLITICAL LEVEL? IN THIS
SENSE, AS A COMMUNITY, VILLA MISERIAS IS ALSO IN THE
VANGUARD. WHILE OTHERS HYPOCRITICALLY DEFEND
EQUAL PARTICIPATION, WE SIMPLY CLARIFY WHAT WOULD
HAPPEN ANYWAY.

THROUGH OUR ADVANCED ELECTORAL ENGINEERING,
WHICH GIVES MORE POLITICAL WEIGHT TO THOSE WHO

HAVE MORE REAL POWER, WE SHRUG OFF THE CONTRADIC-
TIONS OF ELECTORAL SYSTEMS. ON THE ONE HAND, IT'S
OFTEN SAID WE ARE FREE TO VOTE ACCORDING TO OUR
CONSCIENCES: THEY SAY A RATIONAL VOTER CAN REWARD
OR PUNISH PERFORMANCE WITH HIS VOTE. BUT AT THE
SAME TIME, LIMITS ARE PLACED ON DONATIONS AND ELEC-
TORAL PROPAGANDA IS REGULATED.

SO, WHERE DO WE STAND? IF CONSCIENCES ARE SUPREME,
WHY IMAGINE MONEY CAN BUY THEM? AN INFORMED VOTER
WOULDN'T RUN THE RISK OF BEING INFLUENCED BY LIES
THAT GO AGAINST HIS OWN GOOD JUDGEMENT. THE SAT-
URATION OF MESSAGES SHOULDN'T AFFECT HIS RATIONAL-
ITY EITHER. AND THE SAME GOES FOR SLOGANS. IF VOTERS
ARE SO INTELLIGENT, WHY ENDLESSLY REPEAT SLOGANS
DESIGNED FOR IDIOTS?

WELL NOW, IF INSTEAD WE ADMIT THAT VOTERS CAN BE
MANIPULATED AND ARE UNINTERESTED AND LAZY, THERE'S
NOTHING FOR IT BUT TO RECOGNIZE THAT THE COLLECTIVE
DESTINY RESTS ON THE MASSES WHO MAKE THEIR DECISION
BASED ON POPULARITY, PREJUDICE, AND BANAL SLOGANS.
EVEN THE MOST FANATICAL DEFENDERS OF THE PRESENT
SYSTEMS ACCEPT THAT THE PERSON WHO INVESTS TIME AND
MONEY IN SUPPORTING A CAMPAIGN EXPECTS SOMETHING
IN RETURN, AND THAT THE BARRAGE OF ADVERTISING SWAYS
THE ELECTORATE. VILLA MISERIAS, NO LESS, HAS TAKEN THE
LOGICAL LEAP FORWARD IMPLIED BY ALL THIS. WE NO LONGER
NEED THE FARCE OF EACH CITIZEN HAVING EQUAL WORTH.
GIVING MORE WEIGHT TO THE RICHEST BUILDINGS MEANS

ACCEPTING WHAT WE ALREADY KNOW. IN THIS SENSE, THE
FORMAL RECOGNITION THAT, IN PRACTICE, SOME PEOPLE
ARE MORE IMORTANT THAN OTHERS MAKES US MORE DEM-
OCRATIC, NOT LESS.

SOME PEOPLE HAVE ASKED US WHY WE DON'T JUST
FORGET THE HERD. WOULDN'T IT BE MORE HONEST TO
LIMIT THE VOTE TO THOSE WHO REALLY MAKE THE DECI-
SIONS? BUT THAT VISION DOESN'T TAKE INTO ACCOUNT
THE ROLE OF THE MASSES IN KEEPING A WATCH ON EXCESS.
IN THE PRESENT DAY, THEY ARE ESSENTIAL FOR EXPRESS-
ING RAGE AT THE PERIODICAL POLITICAL SCANDALS. THE
SHORT MEMORY OF THE RABBLE MAKES IT A BULL READY
TO CHARGE AS OFTEN AS NEEDED. IN THE SAME WAY,
ALTHOUGH IT'S KNOWN THAT A MINORITY DECIDES, IT'S
IMPORTANT THAT THE REST FEEL THEY PARTICIPATE IN
SOMETHING HIGHER. EVEN IF THEY ARE COVERED IN DIF-
FERENT SKINS, THE FLOCK KEEPS ALIVE THE ILLUSION OF
PARTICIPATING IN THE SELECTION OF THEIR SHEPHERD.

•

10

"You see, people always think just because I have a chaotic love
life, it means I'm irresponsible, but it's nothing like that. If I learned
anything on that frigging farm, it's that you have to earn your living
day after day. Do you remember I told you I've known I was different from a very young age? Well, it's a bit like that. Since I was small,
I've had it very clear I wasn't going to rely on any man to keep me.

"And thanks to aunt Orquídea helping me to catch up, I became a very good student. I wasn't the kind that needs to be watched to make sure they do their homework or revise for exams. What happened was that, as I was growing up, I managed to separate my private life from my duties. People say it's impossible, but in my case, open sexuality sits easily with my pretty methodical discipline.

"When I went back to school, I used to help my aunt with things for her newspaper. My favorite part was when she let me go with her to do interviews. Do you know who impressed me most? Well, Selon Perdumes. Like everyone else here, I'd heard so much about him from so many different sources, I didn't know what to expect. His smile bounced and echoed around the whole room. When he spoke, the words came out somehow really resolute, but also really slow and deliberate. Every time he said something, I had the feeling the words had been on the tip of my tongue an instant before. I remember it was not long after that day that I decided to study journalism. Amazing, huh?

"The thing is, I've made a really big effort with my studies, but, in the end, doors keep opening for me because of my looks. Though I try to act dumb and pretend that's not the way it is, at heart even I know it's true. My classmates, teachers, sources for getting interviews, even the interviewees, all change their tone when they see me. You know, one time I even interviewed a female shaman—can you imagine?—for a university newspaper. She had a white streak in her black hair. Anyway, they'd told me she was frigging pompous, but as she was so nice to me, afterwards I told her that her reputation seemed to me very unfair.

"You'll never guess what she replied. She began saying it was true what they said about her, but the difference with me was because she was obsessed with physical beauty. And while she was trotting that out like it was a biological law, she was stroking my hair. I was so nervous I couldn't even smile. But things didn't end there. She grabbed my face between her two hands and moved hers very close to my lips. I'd resigned myself to the worst, when she said, 'Don't worry, child. I'm too old to have illusions. Just let me look at you for a while longer. You make an impact on either sex.' See, I'd done all the research and stuff for the interview, and the woman comes out with that. You can't imagine how I felt, I was on the point of changing professions.

"I suppose you think I'm exaggerating, but, like, it's a bore to be always struggling against labels. Because don't go thinking everything's a bed of roses. Lots of times, the ease they welcome me with turns to hostility when they see I'm trying to behave professionally. I swear, it's the same thing, again and again. They tell me I'm wasting my life doing this job, that chicks like me shouldn't have anything to do with real life stuff, that I should find myself someone to set me up in a house and keep me…Nowadays, I think a good part of my vocation has to do with showing them they're wrong. I don't know, but maybe if I learn to write well about what's behind appearances, they might stop seeing me as pure appearance.

"And it's true, my aunt has been an angel. A few months back, she offered me a job on *The Daily Miserias*, so I'm working formally for the paper now. She needs help reporting the campaigns for the presidency of the residents' association. I don't know why, but she says it's historic, very important, that every angle has to be covered. Right now, she's involved in negotiating the advertising and headlines, so, the thing is, she wants me to write most of the articles. Panic stations, right? It's my first big break. I want to prove to myself I'm not just a satellite orbiting around the man of the moment. Who knows, maybe someone will be really interested in taking a look at what's behind the eyes that frighten them so much."

II

SO, THERE'S NO TWO WAYS ABOUT IT. VILLA MISERIAS HAS THE CHANCE TO MAKE HISTORY. AND MORE THAN THAT, WE HAVE THE CHANCE TO DO AWAY WITH HISTORY. WE CAN REACH THE PEAK OF OUR DEVELOPMENT, NO LONGER JUST HERE, FOREVER MOVING IN THE SAME DIRECTION. TO MAKE OURSELVES UNDERSTOOD, WE TELL IT LIKE IT IS. SINCE POL-ITICS IS APPARENTLY NO LONGER RELIGIOUS, THE CONTEST HAS BEEN DIVIDED INTO TWO LARGE CAMPS. THERE ARE DIFFERENT NAMES FOR THEM IN DIFFERENT PLACES, BUT HERE WE'LL CALL THEM THE DREAMERS AND THE VILLAINS.

THE DREAMERS ENJOY THE GOOD LIFE WHILE WHINING ABOUT INJUSTICE, AND THEY WANT TO SHOW SOLIDAR-ITY WITH THOSE WHO HAVE NOTHING. THEY BLAME THE SITUATION ON THE VILLAINS, BECAUSE THEY STAND BY THE PRIVILEGES THAT, IN FACT, BOTH GROUPS ENJOY. THE DREAMERS WANT MORE PUBLIC SPENDING, BUT IT'S LIKE

THEY'RE TRYING TO STAUNCH A HEMORRHAGE WITH A BAND-AID. AS IF THEY DIDN'T KNOW THAT, BY DEFINITION, YOU CAN'T LIVE ON MORE THAN YOU HAVE FOREVER. THEN DISASTER STRIKES, AND THERE'S A CYCLICAL CRISIS. THAT'S WHEN THE ELECTORATE VOTES FOR THE VILLAINS WHO TALK ABOUT TIGHTENING BELTS.

THE VILLAINS EXPLAIN THAT POVERTY IS THE RESULT OF THE DREAMERS' IRRESPONSIBILITY. THE VILLAINS LIVE THE HIGH LIFE WHILE MAKING ADJUSTMENTS AND CUTS THAT ALWAYS HAVE MOST EFFECT ON THE SAME PEOPLE. THEY DON'T WORRY ABOUT LETTING THE WATER RISE UP TO THE NECKS OF THE MAJORITY. THEY KNOW PEOPLE PUT UP WITH IT, GET USED TO THE RAPID WORSENING OF THE SITUATION. WHEN THINGS ARE ABOUT TO GO UP IN SMOKE, A CHARISMATIC DREAMER APPEARS AND TALKS ABOUT SAVING SOCIETY FROM THE VILLAINS. THEN THERE'S A CHANGEOVER, AND THE WHOLE GAME STARTS AGAIN, WITH ALMOST THE SAME PEOPLE WINNING AND LOSING.

THIS PIECE OF THEATER COVERS UP THE LIE UNITING THE DREAMERS AND VILLAINS. ALTHOUGH IN PUBLIC THEY SAY THEY HATE EACH OTHER, THEY IN FACT NEED ONE ANOTHER TO CONTINUE AS THE TWO FACES OF A PRIVILEGED CASTE. ALTHOUGH THEY GIVE POMPOUS SPEECHES, AT HEART THEY ARE THE SAME AS THE REST OF US: SIMPLE LITTLE MEN, DRIVEN BY THE SAME EGOISTIC CONCERNS. YOU THINK THE DREAMERS AREN'T SO GIVEN TO ACCUMULATING PROPERTY, YOUNG LOVERS, AND HONORARY DOCTORATES? BUT IT'S THE SAME WITH THE VILLAINS. DO YOU THINK THEY

WOULD THROW LOVED ONES ONTO THE STREET OR LEAVE THEM WITHOUT A HOSPITAL? FOR ALL THEY ACT AS IF IT WEREN'T SO, THEIR FLESH IS AS WEAK AND HUMAN AS ANYONE ELSE'S.

FOR THESE REASONS, WE IN VILLA MISERIAS ARE PREPARED FOR THE FINAL SYNTHESIS. FORGET THE EUPHEMISMS. NO MORE LIES. WE WANT A DISCOURSE THAT EXPRESSES WHAT WE ALL KNOW, BUT NEVER SAY. FOR YEARS WE'VE BEEN TEACHING THAT EACH PERSON HAS TO TAKE CHARGE OF HIS OWN FUTURE. THE RESIDENTS ACCEPT THIS IN PRACTICE. IF NOT, HOW CAN THEIR PASSIVITY BE EXPLAINED? YES, THE BLACK PAUNCHES ARE BETTER EQUIPPED NOW, AND IT'S TRUE THAT MANY NOW HAVE THEIR OWN PRIVATE SECURITY, BUT WE KNOW THAT THERE ISN'T AN ARMY IN EXISTENCE THAT CAN OPPRESS A WHOLE POPULATION, BECAUSE THEY DON'T EVEN NEED VIOLENCE TO SET LAW AND ORDER ON ITS HEAD. LET'S IMAGINE THAT PEOPLE IN OUR COMMUNITY STOPPED PAYING THE SERVICE CHARGE. OR THAT NO ONE VOTED IN AN ELECTION. THAT PEOPLE LEFT THE TAPS RUNNING ALL DAY. WENT OUT INTO THE STREET NAKED. THERE ARE AS MANY WAYS TO PARALYZE A SOCIETY AS THERE ARE PEOPLE IN IT. A GENERAL ADHER- ENCE TO CUSTOM IS A SILENT VOTE IN FAVOR OF KEEPING THINGS AS THEY ARE. THE KEY IS THAT EACH PERSON THINKS THAT, WITH A LITTLE EFFORT AND LUCK, WHO KNOWS, HE MIGHT BE THE ONE TO LOOK DOWN FROM THE SUMMIT.

DEEP DOWN, THE LIBERALS WHO WANT THINGS TO BE DIFFERENT AND THE CONSERVATIVES WHO DON'T WANT

CHANGE ARE FIGHTING FOR THE SAME THING. THEY BOTH WANT TO IMPOSE THEIR TRADITIONAL VISION OF HOW TO ORGANIZE THE ESSENTIAL HIERARCHIES OF OUR SPECIES. ONE SIDE GOBBLES RED MEAT AND GUZZLES FINE WINES, THINKING HOW TO MANAGE IT SO THAT NO ONE IS EXCLUDED FROM THE TABLE, BUT AT HEART THEY KNOW THERE ISN'T ENOUGH FOR EVERYONE TO LIVE THE WAY THEY DO. THE OTHER GOBBLES RED MEAT AND GUZZLES FINE WINES, CONVINCED THAT IF THE IDLERS WANTED, THEY COULD HAVE THE SAME AS THEM.

THAT IS WHY WE NEED A CANDIDATE WITH THE COURAGE TO STATE THE OBVIOUS: WE ARE NOT EQUAL; WE DON'T WANT TO BE EQUAL; WE PREFER TO ATTEND TO OUR SMALL PLEASURES THAN FILL SOMEONE ELSE'S BELLY. G.B.W. PONCE HAS CALCULATED THAT A SMALL EXTRA CONTRIBUTION WOULD REMOVE THE NEED FOR THE WORKERS TO EAT LEFTOVERS. A SURVEY HAS REVEALED THAT THE VAST MAJORITY OF RESIDENTS APPROVES THIS MEASURE, BUT WHEN THE ADDITIONAL CHARGE WAS PROPOSED, ALMOST ALL THE RESIDENTS' ASSEMBLIES VOTED AGAINST IT.

WE WANT TO GIVE THE PAUPER BACK HIS DIGNITY. WE NO LONGER NEED TO PROMISE HIM WE ARE WORKING TO ASSURE THAT, ONE DAY, HE CAN GIVE UP BEGGING. THINGS ARE THE WAY THEY ARE, NOT THE WAY WE SAY WE WOULD LIKE THEM TO BE. THE TIME IS RIGHT. WE ARE READY TO LEAVE BEHIND THE MENTAL AGE OF THE MINOR. VILLA MISERIAS IS CAPABLE OF BECOMING THE MOST TRULY HUMAN COMMUNITY EVER. WE MUSTN'T MISS OUR APPOINTMENT WITH

HISTORY. WE ARE LOOKING FOR THE PERFECT CANDIDATE TO
TAKE US WHERE WE HAVE WANTED TO BE FOR A LONG TIME.

12

Max finished reading the document through for the first time.
He had the sensation that his body was extending a few inches
beyond his skin; minute, sharply pointed darts were piercing it by
the million. A last memory from before the lava of darkness filed
through his head:

"Arc you dating anyone?" That was the first thing that occurred
to him to break through the density of Nelly's narrative.

"Oh, well, I mean, more or less. Yes, I've been like with the
same guy for over a year. But the truth is, he's really boring, and
I'm fed up with him," replied Nelly, now on her feet, impatient
to end that stage of the conversation.

"Look, Nelly, don't be so hard on yourself. You haven't had it
easy, but the important thing is you don't have to repeat the same
old mistakes."

"Oh no, hey… Max. You haven't understood the first thing! See?
I explained it all so carefully, and you come out with this. Well, no
way, come on, let's go to bed. I'm ready for the night to begin."

13

Sao and Pascual filled the gap Max was leaving in the triumvirate by fully occupying themselves with other things. For Bramsos, in addition to the time spent in his studio, his group, Eidola, was hired to provide the entertainment for such celebrations as Mauricio Maso's forthcoming birthday. On one of the days when Beni Mascorro appeared to give him his weekly free packets, he also handed him a list of what seemed to be song titles. Bramsos didn't know a single one.

"Wait a minute. Don't go yet. What's this?"

"They're the numbers the boss wants you to play at his party next week."

Sao, who had finished her undergraduate dissertation, was still doing a few shifts at the laundry, which was where Pascual sought her out to ask for help in creating a visual spectacle to accompany the set. He had neither the time nor the inclination to learn the party requests: although Eidola used plenty of creative license in their cover versions, this was too weird. As he didn't have an accordion—an essential element of his patron's preferred music— Bramsos was thinking of using the event to inaugurate an instrument he'd mainly designed to play a version of his own favorite piece.

At first sight, Bramsos' instrument looked like a normal electric guitar, with a crack along its full length. The innovation was in the materials: it was a polystyrene guitar with plastic strings. Bramsos had worked away tenaciously until he found the right mold: the polystyrene beads gathered up the vibration generated by the ambient white noise in the strings. Each note silenced some of the innumerable particles of discreet shrillness that formed it. The music was composed of varying tones of silence, harmoniously snatched from the imperceptible din his guitar channeled.

He had yet to play the guitar in public. The song he intended to interpret had caused its original creator enormous problems. The audience had stormed out of the auditorium, feeling its collective leg was being pulled. That's what made Bramsos think of a more tangible complement to calm the stir.

14

It was the night of the celebration on the terrace of Maso's penthouse. A pig, hanging head down, bleeding to death, and a lamb skewered over the burning coals were waiting to fête the aristocracy of Villa Miserias. Maso had decided to give the party an Eskimo theme. The guests had to knock back a Siberian Husky before being allowed to enter. The bar was crammed with glasses, ashtrays, lighters, and ice cubes, all shaped like igloos, plus igloo-shaped containers full to the brim with other substances. Beni Mascorro had been put in charge of handpicking a selection of escorts from a high-class agency. They were distinguished by their short, figure-hugging dresses, made from artificial sealskin, finished off at the neckline with a strip of daring pale fluff, the origin of which no one was interested in checking. Maso had arranged for them to mix with the crowd to raise the tone of his party, and offer his male guests the possibility of something more later on.

A contingent of Black Paunches was chatting together while looking out for any act of illegality. Taimado had arrived early to check everything was in place, and when, half way through the evening, he noticed he'd had too much tequila, he began to top up with periodic snorts of cocaine to stay upright. From between the lenses of his inseparable sunglasses poked a jaw crowned by the pencil mustache encrusted on his top lip.

Juana Mecha had donned a flowered dress for the occasion; her thick lips were shining with a fine coating of pink lipstick. She didn't usually drink, but had allowed herself a few glasses of wine, served from the transparent acrylic igloos. Although Maso had set Mascorro the task of entertaining her, his help wasn't needed. Every time he looked, Mecha was accompanied by someone different: the high society of Villa Miserias was in constant search for new ways to contact their inner selves. A few days before, during the most exclusive Canasta game in the estate, a woman who masked her thinning hair with a permanent wave emotionally recounted an epiphany she had experienced on hearing one of Mecha's pronouncements: she was coming home from the gym at noon—exhausted and distressed because she didn't know what to tell the maid to prepare for lunch—when her driver carelessly dropped the case containing her makeup bag. Juana Mecha had hurriedly appeared on hearing the repeated shouts of, "Eufemio, why have you done this to me? It's not fair! I don't deserve it!" His nerves making him even clumsier, Eufemio made a mess of gathering up the tubes of mascara and lipstick so they could continue on their way. His mistress was already on the verge of a panic attack when Mecha simply said:

"Don't take it out on him, señora. The ground's really clean. Nothing can dirty your twinkling lights."

The woman was instantly overwhelmed by an avalanche of revelations: it wasn't poor Eufemio's fault he was so clumsy, one had to have compassion for him. She went up and pointed to the cosmetics he had missed in an attempt to help him pick them up more quickly. She was moved to think that even someone like the sweeper could appreciate the purity of her soul at just a glimpse. And particularly in those clothes! She suddenly understood how trivial some of her worries were. What did it matter what the maid prepared for lunch? As long as she did it with love, it would be a delicacy. She rewarded Juana Mecha with a resounding red kiss on the forehead, and stood breathing in the dusty air while Eufemio hurriedly closed the case. She walked away, marveling at the great lessons to be learned from insignificant acts.

The word soon spread. The guests at Mauricio Maso's party included all the important ladies in Villa Miserias, and it was the ideal opportunity for them to undergo their own mystical experiences by consulting Juana Mecha. Moreover, the unrefined features of the be-broomed seer increased their desire to decipher their personal enigmas. While they were near her, the ladies were pleased by their absolute lack of prejudice. They were so open to the world, they were capable of receiving something from anyone at all. Quivering with excitement, they didn't notice the wine had had its effect on Juana Mecha. One by one, they took her hand and tried to look spiritual, so as to be imbued by her wisdom.

"I feel like pissing on you."

"Oh! Any time. Receiving your golden shower would connect us on a cosmic plane. What an honor for you to have chosen me!"

"Your husband's got an asshole stamped on his face."

"Did you hear that, darling? I knew! The company's going to promote you to the toilet department! That's one in the eye for those people who didn't believe in your dreams!"

"You're like she-wolves in heat. You don't even give off a scent anymore."

"Ladies, take a minute to think of how many men silently admire us."

"Water, earth, and fire will seal your plastic pact, all barefoot, wearing colored tunics."

"It's happening. It's happening!"

When she was tired of exchanging honeyed words for insults, Juana Mecha staggered over to say goodnight to Mauricio Maso. The grateful ladies watched her with pursed lips and sucked-in cheeks. That night, the foundations of her reputation as a Play-Doh oracle were laid: she was so wise that each person heard exactly what they wanted to hear.

In one corner of the terrace, keen to avoid his presence causing any unease among the guests, was the retired teacher Severo Candelario. As if following the decree of a chronometer, he was taking small sips of some unknown bitter drink. For the entire night, he stood there, humming quietly along to the background music, stopping whenever anyone came within a prudent distance. Taimado, still gloating over the massacre of the tree, didn't miss the chance to take the piss.

"Uh-huh. Didn't I tell you? Give it a break, Prof. If you're going to do that mummy act all night, you'd have been better off sitting like a frigging stiff on your bench."

15

Sao and Pascal were sorting out the final technical details behind the curtain Mascorro had improvised from a sheet. Eidola were going to perform a dozen or so songs before the tougher stuff Bramsos was saving for the finale. Sao was checking the equipment they needed to project a short film during that number.

Max was very tense when he arrived at the party, apparently looking for something he didn't want to find. He greeted his busy friends with the nostalgia of the excluded. As the concert was about to begin, he positioned himself to one side of the stage, his skin prickling with annoyance. His eyes swept the terrace one last time, stopping irritably on each person, annoyed and grateful that it was that person and not the other one. Even completely different women became her for a moment, then no, then maybe, and finally no again. Could that be her over there?

Bramsos opened the set with a jocular version of a rock standard played in an exuberant tone to attract the attention of his audience. Eidola's style was so flexible that, at times, the title of the song was the only way of recognizing the original. Maso's guests listened distractedly to the native adaptation of the classic. In Bramsos' fatalistic delivery, the black, illiterate hick who defies destiny to play guitar like no one else in the world, was replaced by a handsome youth—also illiterate—who couldn't sing or play any instrument. For food, he used a knife to scrape jam out of the bottom of an empty jar, while watching TV on his stolen cable channel. A talent scout took him to audition to be the next manufactured pop star. The agent convinced the record company executives they had before them the new heartthrob of empty-headed teenagers. Fame and money followed, with skin-tight jeans and a potato stuck in his throat. Bramsos was about to launch into the tragic ending when Mascorro disconnected the amps. The intimidating iguana skin boots were marching toward Eidola's lead vocalist.

"My friend, don't fuck with me. What the hell are you playing?"

"One of the best rock songs in all history according to Roll…"

"The fuck you are. Didn't Beni give you the list?"

"It's not our style…"

"Look, you frigging artist, don't go giving me that."

"What do you want, then?"

"What do you mean, what do I want? I always want more."

"I mean right now."

"Ah. I want you to stop wasting my time when you already know what I want."

"Just give us a moment to regroup."

"That's the fucking way."

Max was so absorbed in what was going on in his head that he didn't hear the music stop. When he felt the stab of a familiar scent, almost by coincidence, his two eyes closed at the same moment. With one, he was begging that it wasn't, with the other that it was.

He opened them, resigned to what he had already surmised: a few yards from the on-stage argument stood Nelly, her arms crossed, thoroughly enjoying the clash of musical tastes. Max managed to restrain his first impulse when a rationalization took pity on him: she must be covering the event for the society section of *The Daily Miserias*. Of course, he would go up to say hello, but there was no need to be obvious about it. He'd wait until she'd finished work. Was that idiot behind her the boyfriend?

Bramsos explained the dilemma to the other members of the band while making long work of connecting up the amps to gain time. The only solution was to change rhythm and intention. Give every note more cadences, a more colorful tone. His voice had to be directed at hips, not necks. He had to interpret the same songs, more or less in the styles requested by the boss. And wait to see what happened. He started with the jaunty requinto they'd just played, slowing down the tempo, letting the percussion take the lead. The change of direction was clear. Maso felt he was on familiar turf: his guests were now dancing horizontally instead of vertically; they were swinging their hips, not their hair. In the middle of the number, he grabbed Bramsos in a neck-pull to bang foreheads: he was giving his blessing; they could go on playing.

Max tried to pretend he hadn't noticed that Nelly had spotted him. Or that, without a word to her boyfriend, she was walking toward him. He exaggerated his indifference to the point of turning to the bar to nod at some nonexistent person. Nelly touched his shoulder lightly and greeted him with a kiss very close to his lips. Now it was the boyfriend who was watching the scene, feigning immersion in Eidola's lively dramas.

Nothing better occurred to Max than the obvious icebreaker questions. Nelly, in contrast, communicated on two different levels. On the most superficial, she chatted with amused sympathy; she was aware of Max's inner turmoil, knew that it was possible for her to alleviate it, but felt it was too flattering to allow it die out altogether. She replied to his questions with sardonic courtesy, letting him know just how predictable his repertoire was. He needed to do better than that with her, though she would let it pass just for once. As if in compensation for her mild cruelty, she unleashed on Max her full range of smiles, shoulder massages, vaporous giggles, tugs of the hand and other signals to remind him of the dark ardor she possessed.

Max's initial nervousness mutated into a permanent state of alert. He felt as if he'd sprouted a rigid consciousness of every word and gesture. Another state of consciousness then observed what the first had registered, only to be critically inspected by another that judged the preceding judgment, and so on successively. Pulled in all directions by this whirlwind, Max—or whomever it was who could still call himself that—was crammed in his own head among the competing ghostly screams. Each voice was sure it knew the only way to fight the earthquake of black eyes playing innocently with his hair.

When the polite trivialities ran out, a new fear raised its hand to be heard: the fear of paralysis. Max regrouped his loyal forces and decided on his strategy: conclusive action. The Many could demand whatever they liked; they could insult and humiliate him any way they pleased. Max would bear the lethal blows bravely. They wouldn't divert him from the collision with the thing he most wanted in life:

"Nelly, I know this is going to sound ridiculous, but there's something very powerful about you. I can see infinite forms in that darkness."

"Oh, yes, Max. And you make me feel some very strange things in my guts."

"Don't worry. I know there are still some obstacles in the way."

"Maybe not. I've already started to shake him off. But don't come out with that stuff about being drunk and not remembering a thing afterward. Ring me tomorrow?" This time the kiss hit the mark, watched by the resigned boyfriend, who did nothing more than follow Nelly to the door, grateful that the public phase of his humiliation was over.

16

Eidola finished playing their list to riotous applause. Maso's terrace resounded with demands for more as the curtain closed. Then, while Bramsos was sending the musicians off with a hug, Sao set up the projector. They had rehearsed the strict synchronization needed during the 4 minutes 33 seconds of the piece.

The curtain opened again to show Bramsos seated on a bench wrapped in the halo of a reflector, his polystyrene guitar exuding a dull glow. The audience stopped clapping, sensing something strange was about to happen. Bramsos waited for the silence to spread. When he saw expectation frozen on the faces in front of him, he gave the agreed signal.

The screen showed "4:33" in black letters. Pascual withdrew

the hand muffling the strings and closed his eyes tightly for maximum concentration. The piece was extremely demanding emotionally. His left hand held the neck of the guitar, while the other supported it from below. The instrument was free to deploy its essence: each string began to vibrate in response to the white ambient noise.

Normally Bramsos dominated the instrument, willing it to tread the practiced chords. His guitar broke down the white noise into an archipelago of anorexic tones; melodies navigated the sea of thorns captured by the instrument and returned amplified. Bramsos had spent hours analyzing the components on the seven basic chords, liberating infinite combinations. On the floor in front of him, was the scrap of paper on which he'd written his guide:

C	REPRESSED FRUSTRATION
D	RAMPANT GREED
E	IMPOVERISHED PLEASURE
F	REASONED HIGH-HANDEDNESS
G	CLOYING FRIVOLITY
A	NUMBED VANITY
B	HEDONISTIC INDIFFERENCE

The particular feature of "4:33" was that it didn't impose any restraint whatsoever on the elements channeled by the polystyrene guitar. Bramsos' arduous task was to remain completely still throughout the whole piece, resisting the impulse to tackle the fleshless white noise, and guide it along bearable paths.

His ears were splitting, begging him to intervene; they were begging for some sort of progression of melodious silences to confront each of the various registers separately, rather than piled one on top of the other. The uninterrupted knot they formed seemed desolate to Bramsos. Breathing regularly and deeply, he clenched every muscle, wondering when the ordeal would be over. Feeling pity for his audience, he repented the torture he was inflicting on them: they had come to have a good time, not to be reflected in the mirror of the environment they moved in. Bramsos opened his eyes in shame, ready to stop if the anguished crowd demanded he do so. Their reaction was beyond his worst fears: except for a couple of confused individuals who had their hands pressed to their ears, no one else had heard anything at all.

Behind him, a man with a thick beard, and the appearance of a lunatic appeared on the screen, shouting randomly. He was driving a motorbike at high speed, without any fixed direction, and was wearing a cotton sweatshirt, onto which he'd sewn additional material to lengthen the original arms. Despite his great speed, he took time to assimilate his surroundings: physical objects seemed to be placed on a tray for his mind to break down.

Every so often, he came to a wall that impeded his progress. He then got off the motorbike, took out his tools, and began to take the bike apart to repair it and make improvements before putting it together again. As in a silent movie, the images were interspersed with his thoughts:

"The motorbike doesn't in fact exist."

He continued repairing the parts that still worked until the hooded figure that had been slowly pursuing him appeared. There seemed to be something evil in his expression. The madman calmly continued to reassemble his motorbike, then started off again, just before the shadow could capture him.

His body language suggested he was flagging: he was taking less notice of the objects around him; it was more difficult for him to tighten the screws. The hooded figure was getting closer. The motorbike seemed on the point of falling over, and in fact soon did.

His efforts to raise the bike were futile: it seemed to weigh tons. The hooded figure slowed his pace, wanting to calmly savor the process of capture. The madman had no option but to confront him. His nemesis removed his cloak, finally revealing his identity. He was a more conventional version of the madman himself: closely shaven, his hair gelled in a perfect side parting, his initials embroidered on the pocket of his sweatshirt. The madman directed his thoughts to a very distant point, in some remote corner of his inner self. It was not that he lacked the courage to face his pursuer, he was just uninterested in doing so.

The other effortlessly lifted the motorbike, took a handkerchief from the pocket of his pants, and cleaned a mud stain from his brightly polished shoes. He gave his unkempt double one last bewildered glance, started up the motorbike, and rode off without looking back: nothing besides the goal inscribed on the horizon existed for him.

The madman picked up the garment lying bundled on the ground and wrapped it around him. Now it was he who set out in slow pursuit. As the piece came to an end, the screen showed a final idea, fading with the last wails of Bramsos' guitar:

"They can change the system as often as they like. But so long as they don't change the thought structures, everything will be just another version of the same."

The audience awoke from its stupor to hail boos down on the performers, their yells pushing against the crowd at the front nearest the stage. The hatred, the possibility of someone doing something, were palpable. Maso ordered the Black Paunches to intervene. Very unwillingly, they surrounded Sao and Bramsos so they could gather up their equipment. The DJ broke the tension by playing a hit by a spacesuit-clad boy band. The crowd immediately forgot the unpleasant episode and began to dance.

Max broke through the faltering barrier of Black Paunches to stand in solidarity with his friends. Bramsos kept his attention fixed on the cables he was stowing away and refused the invitation to have a drink in Max's apartment: he had to get up early the following morning to work on an installation.

"I'll come for a while, Max," cut in Sao, dismayed for her friend.

"Fine. I'll just say goodnight to my boss and then I'll be ready to go."

"See you later, Max. And I'll call you tomorrow Sao," Pascual said, before hurriedly quitting the party.

17

G.B.W. Ponce had been making notes for hours without moving from the bar. For him, these occasions were like a vast laboratory; he couldn't waste his time interacting with people. Even so, he wasn't too interested. He'd understood the setup from the start and had made his arrangements. At the right moment, he'd leave, without thanking his host, accompanied by one of the Eskimo girls he'd haggled with until they had come to an agreement. It was almost time. He sought her out in the shadows deepened by his dark glasses. But instead of the girl, Max appeared on his radar:

"What's up? Enjoying yourself? Good party, right? Have you read the document? What do you think?"

"I thought it was, in one sense, interesting."

"That word is meaningless. Do you understand your task?"

"Yes. I've got to find a candidate."

"Right. The chief said he was coming along tonight, which means he isn't. He has to approve the proposal. We need to get moving. There are only a few days to go."

Ponce located the Eskimo and went up to nudge her gently toward the door. Before he began to wonder what he'd gotten himself into, Max took refuge in Sao. The two friends left arm in arm. It wasn't clear who was hanging on to whom.

18

In his apartment, Max contemplated the artwork covering the plaque. He fetched glasses in metal holders and wine, put on some lounge music, and sat on the armrest of the sofa, his bare feet on the apricot upholstery, straightening his back as if he were trying to achieve an angle of exactly ninety degrees.

"This is all so weird, Max," said Sao. "You've never used glass holders before. And that music! And you don't usually sit like that." Max was horrified to realize that she was right: he'd precisely recreated a scene from a few days before. In that same place, he'd patiently waited to see what Nelly's next step would be. The smile in Sao's almond-shaped eyes made him feel ashamed: she understood him, without making judgments.

He went to his desk for the worn piece of paper, and returned, waving it uncertainly. Sao wasn't sure either. She felt that there was no going back to the past now. She had to make a choice between hurting her friend's feelings and protecting herself. She lay back as usual, her jeans unbuttoned, calming her instinctive uncertainty by telling herself they were her ideas, that the scene had never turned out badly.

> If walking, I walk alone
> through deserted, abandoned countryside
> if I speak with friends, of drunken
> laughter, and of life,

She was thinking too much...had to let herself go...otherwise she couldn't...why hadn't she said no?...poor Max needed it now...touch yourself slowly...carefully...little by little...don't rush it...it wasn't a matter of getting there...again...start from the beginning...don't do this to Max...not now...he could go under.

If I study, or dream, if I labor or laugh
or if a gust of art transports me
or if I gaze on nature fresh risen
with new life,

Would he realize if I faked it?…at least a bit more…so it won't
be so obvious…there's no way out…more cruel to trick him…I
think he already knows…concentrate…you like it too…nothing's
happened…or maybe, deep down, it has.

You alone rule my heart
of you alone I think, for you every fiber quivers
for you alone my thoughts thrill
for you, belov…

"Max. Please. I'm really sorry, but I can't tonight. Forgive me. I
don't know what's happening."

"Don't worry. I completely understand. I'm really frightened,
Sao. I don't want to stop now."

"Me neither, Max. Me neither. Let's just hold each other a little
longer. Then I'll go home."

19

Max didn't know where to start. How was he going to find a
candidate? How could he spot the signals? He recalled the pact
not to toe the expected line, come what may. The difficulty was

in guessing where the pitfalls might be. His father had been a pretty obvious villain; it was simple to not follow his example in any way. Max had even thought of the rule of opposites: if at each alternative, he placed himself in his father's shoes and made the contrary choice, he could ward off the danger of becoming him. It concerned him that this might be a trap, that fate's strategy might be to use what Max didn't want to be as a lure for eventually converting him into what Max didn't want to be. Or maybe he did? Which of them all was Max? Were there differences between some of the scenarios?

Perhaps the two enigmas were just one. No one was being tricked. Nelly made no bones about it: all those who had preceded him had failed the test. How arrogant to suppose that he was any different. Sao and Pascual could see it all clearly, but they preferred not to watch the fall at close quarters. Sao sadly admitted to herself that her generous compassion had its limits: Max had made a conscious decision. But not even he had any idea of the tone of that consciousness. It only served to point out the direction things were taking. He had no idea why he was so anxious to put himself in a place that wasn't his. Who was he revenging himself on? Why punish himself? Did revenge or punishment even exist?

Orquídea López's document was brutal. The transformation of Villa Miserias was indisputable. They'd spent years subtracting part of the sum, always in the name of everyone's right to be no more than a part, never again the sum: what belongs to everyone belongs to no one. The new creed demanded the move from being a community of nobodies to a plague of somebodies in motion. That somebodiness wasn't for the weak. Max had a precise image of it: thousands of self-sufficient islands separated by the icy, black waters of egoistic calculation. The best thing would be to remain alienated on your own island, but it was only human nature to go to another, take what you needed, and return to your own to guard what you'd amassed. Once again: no one was being tricked. There were even a larger proportion of accomplices than victims. Exonerating those who didn't have the threshold of basics covered, the remainder had the sentencing judge in their pocket.

Max's internal judge allowed him to act any way he wanted—it wasn't the castrating sort—but, in exchange, he was condemned to be conscious of it at every moment. He could silence his vanity attempting to satisfy Nelly's. He could take an active role in the delivery of the hammer blow: eliminate the residue of some aim that wasn't small sensual pleasures. He knew the new Villa Miserian Leviathan would no longer justify its authority with an appeal to a common higher good. Now its reason for existence would be to guarantee the right to tread and be trodden on. The law enforcement bodies would be used to protect the victors in a war waged under other different categorizations. Max had the right to be a chain linked to other chains—some above, others below—but he would carry the prison with him wherever he went. This was his non-election: he locked the barred door from outside, opened his mouth wide, and swallowed the only key that would allow him back into a world from which, even in this first moment, he felt almost completely excluded.

20

Early the next morning, he rang the doorbell of the López family's apartment: he had decided to get as close as possible to the original source. As the regulations allowed for non-consecutive reelection, Orquídea might be the ideal candidate for implementing the plan. But Max had to be cautious; a theoretical instrument didn't always function in practice.

"Oh, what a surprise! Good morning, Max. Please, come in. Hey, but the thing is, Nelly's taking a shower. Will you have something while you're waiting?"

Max didn't remember ever having met her, so couldn't imagine why she was addressing him in such a familiar tone. He shook his head and then immediately regretted refusing her offer. Orquídea had no trouble reading his vacillation; she brought him a cup of coffee, exactly the way he liked it, with plenty of milk and one sugar. She found him inspecting the bookshelves, looking at a number of leather-bound, dusty volumes, bearing the name of his hostess, and organized by the Roman numerals stamped on the spine: Works, I, II, III, to XVIII.

"Hey, that's everything I've written since the paper was founded," she said proudly. "I sometimes pick out a volume at random and read a couple of articles. You wouldn't believe how much it impresses me to see that those people who were personalities in their day aren't even remembered now. That's why I like my job. Maybe I don't make decisions that affect a lot of lives, and the powerful people of the moment look down on me for not being in the loop, but I'm still here and most of them aren't."

Max got straight to the point.

"I've read your latest unpublished pamphlet."

"Oh, yes. I'm so pleased. G told me. What did you think?"

"It seems a little risky. You yourself say that the neck separating the winners from the losers is very delicate. I'm not sure they'll want to hear that. But I'm not employed to have opinions."

"Ugh, Max. Just one thing. You think that way because you're a sentimentalist, I know from what Nelly says. I'm not the sort who imagines you're doing anybody a favor by hiding their reality. A belief in victimhood is the main barrier standing in the way of the rabble. The system, the rich, the lack of shoes, always someone else's fault. Me, I'm convinced the indispensable requirement for deserving something different is recognizing that you deserve what you've got now. Some people can, others can't. It's that simple."

"Why don't you want to be a candidate?"

"Oh, no. Not that again. I already told you. I get anything I want for free, I'm invited to the important parties; with just a phone call I can keep them awake at night. And the best is that none of that has a sell-by date. Just the opposite. Like, you can't imagine. When we started the paper, I'd be kept hanging around hours until someone told me the interview had been canceled. But now it's me who makes the conditions.

"Well, Max, I'm pleased to have met you. I have a feeling we're going to see each other again very soon. I'll see if Nelly's out of the shower."

Nelly appeared with her hair frizzy from the damp. Her white blouse followed the contours of her body with compact voluptuousness. At each meeting, Max had the sensation he was seeing a different woman, even more disturbing than the previous one. Nelly, however, greeted him with the same kiss as the night before. Without saying a word, or moving from where he was, Max suddenly found himself sitting at the table with her, both of them drinking coffee, laughing over the events of the extravagant party.

After she'd finished her coffee, Nelly adopted a more serious air. "Crazy, eh, Max? Listen, my aunt told me about your job. And what do you think? She suggested doing a profile of possible candidates for the newspaper. Like, I can't mention the characteristics they're looking for, but I can insinuate. And then I thought we could do it together. How about it?"

"Brilliant. It's ideal for me. I'll just have to check it with my boss. I'm not sure he'll like the idea."

"Really? Heck, don't say you're already regretting going with me? That's exactly why my aunt spoke to G. Well, and him so happy to have a written testimony of the process. You know how his charts are always telling him pretty strange things. Now he says you never know what might happen, so you have to be prepared. Anyhow, you do have to remember there's only a week left before registration closes."

"Yeah, I know. Your aunt was my first failed interviewee. Even if it's just a matter of protocol, I was thinking of going to see Severo Candelario next."

"Oh, yeah. Perfect! Like, just let me make a few notes first. I'll meet you at his bench in a couple of hours. The prof's sure to be there, all crushed as usual." She stood at Max's side, stroked the back of his neck, her nails running through his distinctive hair. After checking one more time how he was looking at her, she added, "See? You're already more handsome than before. But I'm sure you'd look even better with short hair. Jeez Max, you really would be irresistible then."

Max left, more confused than ever. On paper, things were going the way he wanted. He was spellbound. She was suggesting they spend their days together. She was even making his job easier: Nelly's report was the perfect cover for his mission. Max had to probe how ruthless they could be without them being aware of it. This way he could pass himself off as the journalist's escort.

His self-absorption shattered at the entrance to the barber's shop. Well, he'd been meaning to get his hair cut for a while. It was so uncomfortable. He was too old. And if Nelly liked it, all the better. No. He was going too fast. He didn't have long before the next appointment. She might think he'd do anything to please her. All the better. He went to the $uperstructure offices to kill time, and rooted about in the company's newspaper archive to go over once again the Candelario debacle.

21

In a special supplement celebrating the tenth anniversary of the beginning of the reforms, Orquídea López had dedicated a long article to Severo Candelario's fall from grace. She had even persuaded the schoolmaster, whose good manners prevented him from refusing, to contribute his collection of photos of the tree for the front cover.

Orquídea then commissioned one of those photo-collages in

which hundreds of small images form a larger figure standing out from the background. Skillful manipulation produced the image of a bulldozer flattening a faithful representation of the tree in all its splendor, composed of an infinite number of tiny photos of itself. Superimposed at the bottom was a real photo of Candelario, witnessing the scene from his bench. In an arrogant typeface, the headline of the supplement read:

SENTIMENTALITY CAN'T STOP VILLA MISERIAS!

The article fixed for posterity a sensationalist version of the episode with the young girl and laid particular stress on Candelario's spectacular defeat as the only candidate in history not to win in even his own building. In this way, it was a demonstration of the coming of age of the Villa Miserians: they were ready to watch out for themselves, to crush any pervert with a shady past in their quest for power.

Max felt as if he were reading a text on paleontology: Candelario had been punished for being a man of his time, at just the moment when his time passed into the hands a different type of person. And now Max had to choose the ideal candidate to tear off another layer of the skin enveloping reality: the age of the death of stories was approaching. People had no time for well-meant nonsense that inevitably turned out to have been a bad idea. The new era needed its first spokesperson to announce that it had arrived with no intention of departing.

"What are you doing here?" G.B.W. Ponce's shaded voice wanted to know what his money was being spent on.

"Hi, boss. Just killing a bit of time. I'm going to interview Severo Candelario in a while, and I wanted to go back over his story."

"Okay. Better make your own mind up than have someone do it for you." Ponce left the room, only to return a few moments later. "Shame you're going. The chief's due here any minute."

22

When he arrived at the green area where Candelario passed his days, Max found Nelly sitting beside him. She was laughing openly at one of the schoolmaster's anecdotes, her knee brushing his thigh. Max hesitated as he noticed the schoolmaster's reddened eyes fixed on the imaginary outline of the tree. He was able to overhear enough to understand that he was telling Nelly how he'd been slowly led to the slaughter.

"Now so many years have passed, I'm almost glad for my dear tree. It wouldn't have liked the courtesy care of that soda company." While pointing one finger toward the sign overlooking the green area, Candelario showed Max his old camera. "My friends look at the albums with their empty landscapes and think I'm senile. They don't realize that my camera captures much more than what can be seen at first sight."

"Oh, Don Severo, don't be like that. Please, chill out. Look how prettily the flowers are growing. Daisies are fascinating," interrupted Nelly. "Look, instead of getting all nostalgic, why not answer me something? With all your experience, what would you like to say to the readers of *The Daily Miserias*?

What can they expect from the next election for the presidency of the colony?"

"I'm sorry, young lady. I don't have anything interesting to say. Those things are outside my jurisdiction now."

Nelly settled herself more comfortably on the bench. As if accidentally, her leg was now brushing the nervous schoolmaster's thigh a little more closely. Max decided to ignore it: don't be a fool, leave her alone, don't say anything, she's more spontaneous than you.

"My only recommendation is this," said Candelario with prophetic dejection. "Don't imagine what went before was better. It was just different. The spirit renews itself in ways only it understands. The fact that I like the times less doesn't make them worse. In the end, it's a process of transformation."

"And if the spirit was to finally announce its new form under your name, Don Severo?" countered Max.

"What do you mean, young man?"

"You could run as a candidate again. This time say things the way you've learned they really are."

"Children, I have to go now. My wife is expecting me for dinner. I've already had my fill of all that. It's someone else's turn to grease the garbage grinder. At my age, I'm no longer under the illusion that it matters who's in charge of it."

23

They dined on Nelly's favorite dish: prawns in sweet and sour sauce. Then they took a stroll around the mall and had an ice cream at a place not far from Max's office. Max finished his off in three spoonfuls, afraid of running into G.B.W. Ponce, but anxious that Nelly didn't notice his fear. The avalanche of adrenaline had left him feeling emptied out. He wanted to go home in the hope that the tornado tearing through his mind would lose strength there. The voices, headlines, bulldozers, guitars, drills, faceless bosses, and exclamation marks were all swirling around. In the central void was a blob-like shudder. Max lacked the words to name it, but he knew perfectly well what it was.

"Hey, Max, I don't know, but you seem very quiet. You're getting bored with me, right? Is that it?"

"No way. It's not that. Just the opposite. But I'm worried about finding the candidate in such a short time. Is your ice cream good?"

"Really good. But don't worry. Like, I'm sure my articles will turn out well. Trust me, you'll see." Nelly offered the palm of her hand for Max to stroke with his fingertips. She teased him by fixing her black eyes on his until he was incapable of holding her gaze, at which point Max turned as if something else had caught his attention or uttered some oblique remark as a means of escape. Nelly rewarded him with an embrace, rubbing her nose against his, her heaving breasts mocking him as she giggled.

"What are you laughing at?" he asked tensely.

"Oh, Max. Nothing," replied Nelly, suddenly indifferent.

"Well, whatever, but I have to go back home. There's a report to be written. Plans to be made," Max replied in an offended tone. Nelly didn't take the hint.

"You know what? I've had an idea. I'll go fetch my things while you get your hair cut just over there. Ring me when you get back and I'll come round to your place. It's so exciting! You're going to look so handsome." This time she kissed him in a way that made any reply ridiculous.

Max decided to rebel: if that's the way things were, he'd have his head shaved to set a precedent. The sacrifice of his long hair had to be some use: her repentance for having asked me to do it. Let's see if she likes how it turns out.

When he returned to his apartment, he immediately rang her to say he was ready. In a rush before she arrived, he ran into the bathroom, where he'd so often painted his nose with gentian violet. That mirror had cried in sympathy with him during so many episodes of mute frustration. In addition to the obvious reaction—shit, I didn't know my hairline was receding so much, why the fuck did I have it cut so short—Max was startled by his reflection. He implored the face in the mirror to help him find the solution to the problem, but the realization that the individual on the other side was as lost as he was left a bad taste in his mouth. He thought of his nanny. Where was she now when he needed her? He turned to see all the different sides of the reflection, someone had to be able to answer the question burning inside him: Who the hell is this imbecile that won't stop staring at me?

24

When the bell rang, Max jumped to open the door. Different again. He could just look at her for the rest of his life. Get out of the way, you moron, let her in. Shit, I've got nothing in to offer her. Is there any sushi left over?

Nelly attempted to suppress the mocking expression prompted by the sight of Max's incipient baldness. She didn't quite manage. Not wanting to make matters worse, she opted for withholding her opinion of his new look, and beached up for a few minutes on Bramsos' painting. Max stood motionless, not knowing where to go. When Nelly seemed to be getting bored, he offered anything that came into his head, and soon discovered that all Nelly wanted was to relax and watch television. Could they go to the bedroom?

Max took off his shoes and arranged the pillows against the headboard of the bed. He sat down, his legs outstretched, with the air of a scolded child awaiting his fate: Nelly appeared in a pair of flimsy pajamas that left her navel bare. He searched for a program that might amuse her, then quickly changed it before they even had time to see what the program was. He did two runs through the channels in that way, until Nelly's sigh of dissatisfaction told him she'd had enough.

He decided to leave on a documentary about the defensive strategies of insects. The presenter gave details of their astonishing variety: they changed color until they merged with their surroundings; secreted repulsive or toxic substances that repelled or paralyzed their predators, or reared up in intimidating postures. Among this vast repertoire, the most effective technique was always flight. Nelly was riveted.

Taking great care not to make any noise, Max wriggled out of his pants, lay back on one side and began to timidly stroke Nelly's belly.

He then immediately repented his clumsy come-on—Should I stop? No, that would be even more obvious: it wasn't doing any harm. He lingered on the very edge of prohibited zones, sneaking a look to see if there was any reaction. Zilch. A sense of the ridiculousness of it all bubbled up inside Max. His fingers stopped moving. He gave her a defeated kiss on the cheek to add a tinge of affection to his failure. Then he rested his head on Nelly's shoulder; he envied the stick insect that was avoiding being eaten alive by a tarantula with its perfect disguise. He soon fell asleep.

Shortly afterwards, he was woken by a hand guiding his own inside Nelly's pajamas. This gentle ruse offered him a clue about how to behave. Nelly didn't want to take risks: she explored her body, guiding Max's fingers as if they were a copy of her own. Obedient to her will, those fingers soon felt the moist effects of the guided contact. With short-lived calm, Nelly found her breasts and led Max's mouth toward them: No, not like that, slowly, ugh, no, just brush them with the tip of your tongue, not so hard, oh, not so slow, a bit more, now bite. Bite me! Yes, that's it, go on, go on.

Such was Max's concentration on the task at hand that he had no energy to spare for personal pleasure. He attempted to depart from the script and suck an ear, but a tug at his neck brought him back to his assigned place. And so they continued until their breathing was completely synchronized. Nelly stood up to undress; Max did the same. She touched his shoulder to push him backward and straddled him.

Max closed his eyes to focus his senses onto a single point. Nelly was moving in coordinates that Max had never even imagined existed. It was worth anything to experience this. He opened his

eyes again to confirm that this was really happening to him, to
Max Michels. A blow paralyzed his nervous system: all he could
see was absolute darkness. His other senses corroborated that many
things were moving. His sight was brazenly lying: it showed him
only a black surface, pierced by sharp points of light. He closed his
eyes again to reconnect the blocked channel, but it was no use: he
was completely blind. Nelly continued along her own path, with
increasingly violent shudders. In the hope of finding something
to anchor himself on, Max clung to her hips with both hands. He
felt sweat bursting out, smelled the explosion, tasted Nelly's breasts
again, heard her shout curses directed at no one, but he couldn't
see anything. Detached from the rest of his body, he accompanied
Nelly in a simultaneous climax. She yielded control and flopped,
satisfied, onto his body. Max blinked in silence. Groping about,
he was lucky enough to find the remote control and switch off
the television, extinguishing the only source of light, a source he
could not see.

Only the hope that this was a temporary phenomenon, that he
would recover his sight, allowed Max to stay lying there, swamped
in a gushing spring of cold sweat. Nelly gave him one last lick of
her tongue before falling into a deep sleep, leaving Max alone,
trapped in himself. The Many stampeded in: you're fucked now,
what's happening to me? Why me? Let her go you don't dare this
is what you wanted you wimp you don't have the balls other men
do. Max managed to escape the onslaught when the night outside
considered it was enough. A last thought tortured him before he
surrendered to unconsciousness: you can sleep if you want, but
you'll have to wake up sooner or later. And we'll still be here.

In the morning, it was the same old Max who awoke. What had happened to him? He didn't understand the first thing. I think it must have been the excitement. They say the intensity can blind you. Where's Nelly? Best not to say anything to her. Why worry her?

He put on a T-shirt and went to find her. She was in the kitchen, wrapped in a white bathrobe, holding a mug of tea, and waiting for it to cool. Three used tea bags lay on the table. Her nose seemed annoyed. Her slightly parted lips were covered in a layer of fresh saliva. Her wide-open eyes seemed to want to bore through the tiles of the kitchen floor. Her breasts were rising and falling in an uneven rhythm: she must have been sobbing for quite a while. She looks more beautiful than ever, thought Max. And suddenly he felt he was abominable. This wasn't the moment to bother her. Poor Nelly.

He attempted to put an arm around her, but she moved away and blew her nose. It was nothing, some days she woke up feeling hypersensitive. It'd pass. Max's consternation was not quieted. Had she realized what had happened? Perhaps she thought it was her fault. He begged her to tell him what was wrong.

"Oh Max, it's like you don't understand me, but the thing is I'm a fraud. I've always known that people say things that aren't true about me. And, I don't know, I'm afraid they'll find me out. And then…I don't want what we've got to be just a passing thing," Nelly attempted to reply, in so far as her sobs would allow.

"But why do you think that? Don't be silly. Everyone admires you so much." Max was trying to gain time in order to say something, anything, more intelligent.

"Really? But I've never written anything serious. You know, it's all just society pieces. Oh Max, be honest, please. What if I'm not up to it?" Nelly was searching for answers to her rhetorical questions in the bottom of her mug of tea.

"Come on, first try to calm down. I'll help you as much as I can. You have to learn to look at things from the right angle."

"Jeez, it's just that last night was really intense. Do you know something? I like knowing I'm not alone, that I've got you with me. Things are different now that I've got to think for the two of us. And, well, I owe everything to my aunt, but the truth is, living with her doesn't leave me enough space now."

"Nelly, listen carefully. You can stay here as long as you want. This is your home too."

"But, it's just I don't know if you want me. Look, don't be shocked, but what if you're saying things you don't even believe because I'm crying? Oh Max, I want to care if you leave me."

The memory of the blackness returned to Max with a vengeance: better face up to it now, while there's still time. What is the blindness saying to me? A benevolent member of the Many attempted to explain there was only one beginning to everything and that's why it was so important. It would also decide which of all the possible Nellies would appear before him. Max cut the voice in his head off short: I couldn't give a fuck. I'm not missing this.

"There's nothing to think about. We're in this together. My friends don't understand it. They're stuck in their adolescence. They think I'm still the idiotic boy who used to play Head World. What they don't know is I'm not looking for a girlfriend any more. What I want is a companion in life." Max squeezed the four fingers Nelly had placed in the palm of the hand he held out to her. The intention was twofold: not only to convince her, but, more importantly, himself. "I've lost the spare key, but I promise I'll get a copy made today."

Nelly rubbed the tears from her eyes and drank down half her tea in one go. She put the dirty cup on the kitchen table, stood up, and walked past Max as if there were no perplexed person standing there. She soon returned, dressed in her usual protective covering.

"Well, Max, thanks for everything. Sorry, but I have to get some writing done. Will you let me know what we've got on today?"

She gave him a quick hug and, before Max's excitement began to bubble up again, sealed their pact with a light bang of the door.

25

While reading Orquídea López's secret document, Max hadn't fixed on what suddenly seemed a glaring detail. Although there had been several years between them, they had both studied in the same department. When he had been asked to read the pessimistic metaphysician, Max had photocopied the only copy in the library. Among the various layers of underlinings, marginal notes, and even expressions of despairing love left by previous readers, Max's attention was caught by an aphorism marked by arrows pointing in both directions. More than arrows, they gave the impression of being fishhooks.

The philosopher described the hustle and bustle of human exis-tence by the use of a potent image: if a man is descending a slope, inertia makes him pick up speed at a consistent rate. If the vertigo produced by this acceleration makes him try to brake, the man will receive a sharp jolt. His best bet, therefore, is to keep moving his legs and continue downward at the rhythm dictated by the slope. The aphorism had impressed Max strongly. He'd used it on several occasions since then as an excuse for doing something that would later be judged stupid, giving in to any impulse that posited him as a defenseless victim: better let oneself be carried down the slope than try to stop the career toward impact.

He was now convinced that the hooks had been drawn by Orquídea. It was no coincidence that she had cited just that passage in her document: she too had once been equally impressed by it. Was it possible that all this time Max had been acting under the influence of an outside force?

In the refuge of the $uperstructure archive, he read on automatic pilot the administrative feats of the recent presidents of the residents' committee. Rather than articles, he had the impression of reading one of those formulaic texts found on sale in any stationery store. In the blank spaces, the reporter could insert insignificant details such as the name of the official in question, the particular announcement, the benefits it would offer our children, the information used to discredit its detractors. Beyond that, the articles were interchangeable.

He even found homogeneity in the scandals! They were either financial or sexual, and leaked to the press. General indignation! How can he still look us in the eye? Citizens demand justice! Blood! The complex excuses: Yes, it's my telephone, my voice, my bank account, my signature, but it's not me. It's a smear campaign. Resignation. Public condemnation. Low profile. Oblivion.

He had scheduled interviews with various former presidents during the day. After that, he had no idea what to do. Nelly would arrive with her suitcase in the evening: she would surely expect some intimate moment of welcome. Or would she be very tired? And if she noticed something odd? Maybe that's really why she was crying this morning. The other guys would have had her shouting out until dawn. Was his night blindness an accident, or the start of a cycle?

He was interrupted by shaded footsteps. G.B.W. Ponce was making his mid-morning rounds to stretch his legs.

"I didn't realize you were here. What a shame! The chief's just left. He wanted to know how things were going. There are only a few days to go."

"Yes, I know, that's why I'm seeing the most recent past presidents today. Though, in fact, I think they're all the same person."

"Exactly. That's the problem."

"Yeah. I don't know where to look after that."

"Perhaps we're getting ahead of ourselves. It's possible that the future era hasn't been born yet."

"And in that case, what do we do?"

"That's your job. To find him. Invent him. I don't care which. Give us a candidate who has the courage to connect the real reality with the visible reality."

26

The flesh and blood versions turned out to be just as insipid as those featured in *The Daily Miserias*. Max and Nelly were like repentant spirits, obliged to undergo the penance of meeting them because of some sin committed in another life. The ex-presidents of the residents' association were like members of a sect who had stopped believing in their God. They repeated the same empty dogmas they didn't even appear to understand:

"That's right, democracy is a day-by-day practice. Look at those children playing on their luxury pirate ship. That wouldn't be possible without the generous donation of the company. And it's a good thing they know someone has to pay. Things that come free have no value. When they're older, they'll understand how to exercise their rights and responsibilities.

"The unions are a cancer that kills the aspirational worker. Instead of letting him shine, they pull him down to "the level of the mediocrities." When I lowered the compensation payments in the collective contract, they called a strike. But the truth is their hearts weren't in it. It was protest for the sake of it. The usual rabble rousers were there, with their outdated placards. Then what happened? Nothing. Everything went back to normal. They'll never be free until they get rid of their corrupt leaders.

"The important thing is to listen to the residents. It's the only way to empower them. I used to read the Para-Doxa section every morning, everyone knows it's written by ordinary people. That was key to understanding what the ones that can write and think. We're here to serve them. You call the shots. You have to be informed so you can keep an eye on us. But if you don't vote, you can't complain. We should all be equally committed.

"You're young, and you don't remember what it was like not to be free. We had to put up with revolting traditional cakes, boring wooden toys, movies with moral messages starring wrinkled divas, and soccer games between fifth-rate teams. Now, in contrast, you can exercise more freedom in a single day's shopping than in a year before. People won't appreciate what they've got until they lose it.

"Quietism in Motion did away with the big bosses. Before, they could do whatever they liked. They owned our lives. Now even the president of the colony has to answer to the investors. The day they close their little businesses and move somewhere more prosperous, Villa Miserias will be finished. The best thing is that you never know just who they are or what they want. Constant fear helps stop from people thinking outside the box.

"My wife studied art history. She says it's right that the artists like that one with the burnt ear don't have go begging permission from the board to exhibit their work any more. Or ask them to contribute paintbrushes, or plaster, or all the other stuff they use. Now they can live off purchases by private collectors. If you knew how much they're paid for those things! And no one understands them. Even I could do what he does."

27

Aware of the futility of commenting on their experience, they walked in silence. Max told himself the only reasonable thing to do was to resign. But what about the money? He needed his wages more than ever now. She wasn't moving house in the strict sense, but even so...He'd be spending for two now. I don't care about the money. I'll get it one way or another. My father was a fucking idiot. And Pascual is just the same.

There initially seemed to be no one home at Nelly's apartment, but a sleep-deprived light coming from the study said otherwise—"Hey, Max," whispered Nelly, "we'd better leave without making any noise. My aunt's putting the edition to bed."—Max stood intrigued, looking toward the study. Nelly tapped her foot impatiently.

"What's up now?"

"Nothing. Let's go." Max picked up her bag and they snuck out like two thieves unsure of the authenticity of the booty they have swiped.

Outside the door to his apartment, Max took Nelly's set of keys from his pocket. While looking for an original key ring to hold them, he'd found a shop selling tiny dolls in the form of legendary writers. The tag didn't say who they were, and Max was unable to identify most of them. He'd finally chosen one with the air of a majestic magus. He had a bushy white beard, a round straw hat rested on his head, and he had the air of peaceful wisdom of the man who has seen everything. Everything that was given him to see. Now he neither liked nor disliked anything. Age had freed him from those categorizations. Is the figure really saying that, or is it just me thinking it? Max wondered as he paid at the cash desk.

He flourished the key ring, holding the writer by his hat. Like a teenager surprised to receive the over-the-top gift she'd asked for just in case she was actually given it, Nelly was bubbling over with excitement. She snatched the keys from him with a kiss, then proffered her purse for Max to hold for a moment: she didn't want anything to get in the way of her triumphal entrance. The first key wouldn't go in: it must be the one for the hall. The other fit into the lock but wouldn't move. Every effort her slender fingers made to turn it deflated Max's rosy fantasy a little further. A broken fingernail put an end to her struggle.

Max stepped forward to demonstrate that it was a matter of applying force. Or there was a knack to it. Or neither of the two: the key didn't open that door. Now it was stuck in the lock. Max held it with both hands and put his whole weight into tugging. Nelly tried to reattach the piece of broken nail. When the key finally came out, Max stumbled backward and, in his attempt to keep his balance, kicked Nelly's suitcase, which then dramatically tumbled down to the landing below. He hurried to bring the suitcase back up, hugging and blowing on it as if this might alleviate its pain.

When he examined the keys, he understood what had happened.

"Forgive me, Nelly. I'm an idiot. I've had copies of my office keys cut. I can't understand how it happened. I'm really sorry. You'll have the right set first thing tomorrow."

He offered her his own keys so that at least it would be she who crossed the threshold first, but Nelly dragged him forward: Max opened the door and stood to one side to let her enter. As he followed her, the suitcase he held under one arm and her purse hanging from the other weighed down his shoulders. He closed the door and silently interrogated the effigy of the writer magus.

His situation pierced the sage to the quick, but he could not help Max. He simply offered the same distant gaze.

28

Nelly walked straight past the table set for two. Max went to the kitchen to warm up the rice and duck in the microwave. When he came out carrying a tray, she was floundering among Bramsos' inverted boats.

"Jeez, I can't tell you how much I'd like to meet him. Can you imagine the things that must go through his head? I don't think the rest of us can have any idea."

"I don't see him that way. He's not really all that different to me. Or anyone else. We grew up doing everything together, and he got lucky. Sao, on the other hand, is very special."

"Hey, Max. Who's this Sao person?"

"She's my dearest friend."

"Ah, she must be incredible. Listen, what do you think? Shall we invite Bramsos round? My aunt has a recipe for meatballs in chipotle sauce that I'd love to make for him."

"Okay. I'll ask them both if they can come around one of these days."

"Cool! Give me plenty of notice so I can get everything ready."

Nelly went off on a spiel about the respective talents of her exes. The range of their abilities was extraordinary, but not because any one of them was outstanding in terms of virtue, or even enviable in any way. The main thing that drilled into Max's brain during what seemed an endless reflection was the way Nelly pronounced the words, which, for different reasons, were always tinged with lack. Her numerous exes had almost done this or become that. But never succeeded. A real shame. So much talent wasted on organizing events for rich bankers, making advertisements, selling wine and hors d'oeuvres, presenting television programs for slovenly old ladies, swapping bureaucratic jobs, training the tennis teams of private universities, working in brand and patent law, importing jet skis, advising companies on tax evasion, serving at craft stalls in bazaars, managing a fleet of cabs, photographing models on exotic islands, putting bars and restaurants out of business, or doing masters degrees in finance. Were there really so many? What can I do against all of them? The Many took the lady's side: don't be such a macho jerk let her finish it's none of my business there must be a reason why she chose me this time. Had she enjoyed the dinner? I'll open another bottle, maybe not, she'll think I want to get drunk.

"So Max? Do you agree?"

"Yes."

"You don't even know what I'm asking."

"You're right that talent is the greatest possible gift. It separates the sheep from the goats."

It was that belly laugh of Nelly's that melted his heart most. In an instant she was sitting astride him, her back turned, molding herself to his body. The pressure of his hands running over her quickened her breathing, as if she was short of breath and could only get it back through the next stimulation.

In a slick maneuver, Max lowered her to the carpeted floor.

He raised her skirt and removed her panties. Nelly unbuckled his belt and pushed his corduroy pants down to his knees. Max checked he could see her: everything was in order. The black eyes were blazing. He lowered his briefs, determined to remove the bitter taste of the previous night. In parallel, his internal cinema began projecting disjointed scenes: Nelly's half-veiled expression was shown to him in dribs and drabs; spaces were prolonged; then prolonged a little more. When they were ready to move in unison, the screen went black.

Nelly didn't notice Max's eyes opening wide, like plates about to shatter. Or that his movements became almost robotic. Even the friction was silent. Nelly's hands on his buttocks kept up the rhythm alone. It was lucky for Max that she would climax very soon. But this time he couldn't go there with her. He jumped up like a dog dowsed in water to cool it down and ran jerkily to the bathroom. Once there, he locked the door to seal his black enclosure.

He shattered the mirror with a thump, demanding it showed him something, if only the imbecile he couldn't bear to see. But now that lifelong ally was turning its back on him. Max couldn't even see the hand he was frenetically waving before his eyes. He sensed the assault of the Many, returning to carry out their threat and slumped down onto the toilet seat. His panic was so complete that he didn't even remember to close his eyes: you knew it, you frigging asshole. Why bother? you're just not up to it, you're out of your element, you're a piece of shit, bet you think the others couldn't either, you're obsessed with them, your father was still fucking whores at almost eighty, ask Pascual to take over, you keep on with your faggy poem, this isn't going to stop, every time she goes...

"Max, what's wrong? You're frightening me."

"Just give me a moment, Nelly."

"Hey, don't do this to me. Open up."

Without raising his head, Max stretched out an arm to open the door. He might as well face the music. Nelly felt around for the switch, and when the light came on, she appeared in all her perfection before him. He could see her studying him, a frown on her brow. She seemed to be reading his mind: this is impossible, I don't understand anything. What the fuck is happening to me?

"Hey Max, are you sure you're okay? Why did you run off that way? That's never happened to me with anyone else."

"Take no notice. Even I don't understand it."

"Oh Max, come here, take it easy, just chill out here with me."

Nelly knelt down and put his penis in her mouth. The effect was immediate. Max shuddered inwardly, expecting to lose his sight again. Nelly used all her skills to please him, looking at him from time to time with her dark tenderness. While continuing to fear the worst, Max gave himself up to the pleasure on another plane: what was happening was the most beautiful thing he'd ever seen.

"See, it's no big deal," said Nelly as she stood to press Max against her belly. "Come on. Let's go to bed. We've got some important days ahead of us."

29

Although Nelly fell asleep at once, Max remained alert to the threat of a new onslaught. The Many, however, were resting.

For the moment. He took advantage of this breathing space to focus on his other great source of anguish. In two days he had to hand over the name of the candidate: he was more confused than ever. He remembered a technique used by firing squads: a rifle was loaded with blanks, so that one of the executioners didn't in fact shoot the condemned man. As no one knew which rifle held the blanks, each member of the squad was able to believe it was his, that everyone but him had killed the prisoner. In this way, last minute crises of conscience, guilt, and other such problems were avoided. He checked Nelly, and thought what he liked most was seeing her asleep at his side.

That morning he had come across Juana Mecha while he was trying to get into the building, carrying the takeaway food he'd just bought. The sweeper had hurried to hold the door open for Max, but he'd stood in silence before her. When he was finally ascending the stairs, he heard her fleeting comment:

"It doesn't matter how you play the game, zero is always zero."

When he turned to ask her what she meant, he had to settle for the lulling trsssh, trsssh of her broom.

Was he searching in a place where there was nothing more than nothing? Although he thought he had an inkling of the nature of the trick, whenever he tried to uncover it, it vanished into thin air. There was no doubt that the principle feature of the new times was individual freedom. Its anonymity allowed for unthinkable atrocities: as there was now no one to blame, these atrocities became part of the scenery, just as natural as anything else. Hadn't Maso sponsored a young photographer to produce a series of photographs of children rolling on broken glass in the metro?

The opening of the exhibition had been a grand affair, with sparkling wine and sophisticated canapés. Everyone was dressed to impress. The cheapest of the photographs cost more than any of the subjects with their open wounds could earn in years. Something had to be done for those children without a future. Statistics showed they soon became delinquents. Awful. Could you get me another glass of wine, please?

The answer was only just out of reach: all Max had to do was hold the flame closer. The problem was, to whom. To himself? As he tossed and turned in bed, the paradoxes filed past him: How was it possible that, at the cusp of the individual's freedom to choose anything at all, everyone wanted exactly the same thing? History was plagued with sorcerers' apprentices who unleashed forces no one could then control. Did they want the naked truth? Fine. The next step would be to consult the most real power of the moment. Tomorrow he would consult Mauricio Maso.

30

On previous visits, it had been accepted that Nelly was accompanying Max. This time it was different: taking Nelly was a prerequisite for being admitted to Maso's presence. They rang at Beni Mascorro's door to pass on their request; the latter ogled Nelly while Max was speaking. He then picked up the phone and dialed his boss's number, making no secret of the reasons why he should see her.

Maso's corporation occupied itself with a wide range of activities: they rented premises in the commercial zone, were partners in the most harebrained business schemes, received requests for donations from civil society groups, met with members of the Villa Miserias board, organized taco parties with mariachis. In addition to costing him a fortune, this respectable façade formed a distraction from the stress of Maso's more lucrative business. There, he had to deal with pushers with mutilated faces, organize beat-downs, suffer the scorn of furiously pious people, accept the loss of whole harvests due to adverse weather conditions. Something unexpected turned up every day. It was a thankless task that Maso fantasized of abandoning to start up a clown academy. He knew that would never happen. He'd opted for a whole-life profession.

Max and Nelly arrived at the prearranged hour and were received in Maso's office with all the courtesy of the educated businessman he prided himself on being. He invited them to sit in a couple of chairs on the other side of his mahogany desk. Max's line of sight was obstructed by a rhinoceros horn posing as an ornament: he had to lean to one side to speak to his host.

Nelly started by asking about his business activities. They had decided to proceed with caution; if they didn't find an open-ing to broach the subject, without actually having to name it, they wouldn't force the issue. Maso stressed the many souls who depended on him for a living. He unbuttoned his shirt to show the scars crisscrossing his chest. He told them he prayed before his personal Virgin every morning so as not to ever forget where he came from.

Max's attention wandered for an instant. He was traveling in a hot air balloon from where he couldn't make out what was below, on the surface of the Earth. It was ridiculous to consider Maso as a candidate. Really? Why? How were the hidden and the visible to be brought closer together? Could some doctor cure me? The oculist would brand me a liar. This idiot is smitten with her. He thinks she doesn't look at anyone else that way. Now's the moment.

"Don Mauricio, how do you feel about the brain damage some of your products cause your clients?"

"I think they're old enough to decide whether to take 'em or not."

"And when it's minors who are consuming them?"

"I think they're old enough to decide whether to take 'em or not."

"They say you have a special relationship with the authorities."

"My friend, that's the way life is, you cut your coat according to your cloth. The suits are hypocrites. Just how many of those top guys would pass a lab test do you think? They all love getting wasted. And Taimado and his grimy paunches have been in my black book for years. But I know, on their wages, they can't even afford a drink. How do you spect them to protect your little lady here? Ask Ponce if there's ever been a white security guard."

"So you think ends justify means?"

"Don't give me that stuff, my friend. Your naive notions don't fit my reality."

"And the violence?"

Given the lack of serious argument on the part of the reporters, the businessman continued his diatribe:

"Say, you frigging skinhead, why don't you take a good look at who generates that violence? I'm going to tell you something I've told your boss's boss plenty of times: I'll leave any time they want. You don't remember what happened when they couldn't get hold of the stuff. The residents voted with their noses.

Just how do you think I get my money? It's very simple, my friend. So long as they go on liking getting smashed, and liking it more every day, someone will do my job. Don't you think it's better to just get on with the party in peace? That's the way they do it in white countries, and no one says a word.

"When the whole thing got too big, I hired an assistant with some education. He manages all the admin. He's always saying I have to use his business principles to run even the main trade. Do you really think those respectable entrepreneurs are any less filthy? Even the priest asks me to play golf with him now.

"And have you noticed that not one of those palefaces knows who my colleagues are? Pure starving to death selling in the street for three centavos. Why do you think we all have nicknames here? Señor Cerdo, El Huevon, El Jisus, La Canal, La Majesty, El Hermano Campana, El Pellejo, La Bestia, El Osmo, La Kivek, El Kavi, Los Tocinos, La Cana, El Cuki, El Pachi, El Lupercio, El Agallas, La Claya, you know, no one gets away without one. The buyers need us as the bad guys in their movie. The ones who get hooked are the same ones who rage about the fact we exist. In a few years, when the whites say it's not illegal any more, it really will look profitable to them. That's what happened with alcohol."

"Aren't you afraid of being locked up?"

"Look, my friend, if I go, I'll take them with me. Everyone's got something to hide. But I'll tell you another thing. No one's going to take the good days from me. Every year, on the Virgin's birthday, I walk on my knees to the metro, with my glass on my back, and I ply my trade for the whole day, just like before. That's how I give thanks for the chance of getting out of there."

"One last question, Don Mauricio. The election for the presidency of the residents' association is coming up. Do you have any preference?"

"I prefer the ones who aren't sanctimonious, but in truth I don't really care. They know if they leave me to do my work, I don't make trouble, and even help out when I can. I give them one of my boys and some stuff every so often so they can brag about it. That's the way it's been done for a long time in rich countries, and everyone's happy. Only a moron would come along trying to change the way things work here. If that's what you want, it's your problem."

31

Thanks to Sao's diplomatic maneuvering, the two friends were having dinner at Max's. Nelly spent the afternoon preparing her aunt's meatball dish, and when Max returned from doing the shopping, he found the table laid for four. The smell of chipotle peppers stung Max to the core: she's never cooked anything for me.

Nelly let him take care of the final details. Jeez, it was so late, she'd still had to get ready. Would this miniskirt be all right? What time's he coming? It's so exciting. I hope he's not the sort to keep me waiting. The sound of the bell coincided with the final sip of Max's first whisky of the night.

He was on his way to open the door when the beautiful whirlwind caught him up. He never ceased to be amazed by each of Nelly's new inventions of herself. This time she'd outdone herself.

I'm so lucky! Anyone would give anything to be in my place. Including Pascual.

Nelly welcomed the guests using two different forms of body language. She politely offered her cheek to Sao. Bramsos she took by the arm, and led to the painting, explaining her abstract interpretation of it. The artist had time to corroborate that his friend had not in any way been exaggerating in his description of his new girlfriend. Sao hugged Max, giving him the wide smile he had so often found a comfort. He clung to her shoulders as if wanting to disseminate the effect. When this didn't work, he freed himself, his body limp.

Right from the beginning of the evening the two groups remained separate, except for Max's disguised attempts to intercept his enemy's advances. Nelly wanted to get Bramsos' secrets from him. Where did his inspiration come from? How did it feel to have that talent? Had he enjoyed the meatballs? How had the injury to his ear—Could she, like, see it close?—influenced his work? Had he read her articles? —Really, I have to do a profile on you.—When was he going to play his plastic guitar again? Would he like more tequila?

"I'll get it. I'm going to serve myself another whisky. Anyone else?" As his initial impulse was insufficient to get him up, Max teetered over his chair. Pascual cackled on seeing how drunk his friend was. With a frown, Sao suggested he'd had enough. Nelly paused, and then continued explaining to Bramsos that life without art wasn't worth the effort.

As he stirred his whisky with a finger, Max noted that the Many were preparing for an incursion. He decided to combat them with the only weapon at his disposal. They wouldn't be able to fuck with him if he drowned them out with whisky.

He heard Nelly's questions about Bramsos' studio. It must be like going into the guts of his work. She'd love to visit it one day. "Why don't we go there now?" asked Max in a slurred voice. Nelly's face silently lit up. Sao and Pascual looked lazily at one another. It seemed there was no way out. Sao began to gather up the dishes, but Nelly, already in her jacket, told her not to bother. Still impregnated by the acrid smell of chipotle, the two scrambled couples walked arm in arm toward the disaster area that was the studio where Pascual also lived.

32

A few yards before what was known as the Others' Building, Max stopped to inspect the chameleon spray-painted onto the façade. He'd often seen the image, but this time it was different. Gravity seemed to have gone into reverse to throw the figures upward and change the direction of Bramsos' work. Max no longer saw a chameleon brandishing a catapult, after having brought down the giant with a blow from an abacus. He could now clearly appreciate that the tightly knit mesh of tiny men were reaching up to crash, of their own free will, into the weapon. The artifice consisted of the catapult being in full view. Then the chameleon simply waited for the herd to hurl itself to its destruction on the abacus. It wasn't a descent but a leap upward. Almost everything was clear to Max now: he just needed, urgently, to check one detail.

"I don't feel so good. You all go ahead. I'll walk Sao home and then go to bed."

Bramsos was perplexed by the trap his friend was laying for him. Nelly offered Sao a hug as warm as the one she gave her boyfriend. One pair entered the artist's warren, the other set out along a well-trodden path. Sao had never seen Max in such a bad way before. She loosed the shackles and allowed herself to be led wherever she was required.

33

They quietly raised the metal roller shutter of the laundry. Although several years had passed, Sao and Max still had a vivid memory of all the details of that past scene. Sao recreated it with minimum of natural variations: on this occasion, it was a duvet with gray diamonds she spread on the floor.

She would have preferred to start by wiping away the gentian violet with her innocence. But there was now no place for euphemisms. The sheets of creased paper were a thing of the past: the compromise solution had run its course. It was her or Max. She gently lay him down and merged onto him with a sad kiss.

Max kept his eyes fixed on her. He needed confirmation that he could see her before doing what had to be done. He already felt himself on the edge of the abyss; now he just had to blow up the road back.

What followed was defined by the mutual desire for its conclusion. It was so impersonal that it seemed to involve isolated organs, accidentally linked in one body, entwined—without really knowing why—with another, also composed of randomly assembled parts. Not even the sounds belonged to either of them. When the moment arrived, both Sao and Max felt enormous relief: she because her affectionate sacrifice was over; he for having retained his sight during the entire procedure. His intuition was confirmed: everything would go back to normal now.

The decision was almost made. One breath of wind would be enough. He dressed hurriedly. The sun was already up. Sao said goodbye without her lopsided smile. She would stay there to open up in a few hours.

34

On his way home, Max was gloating over his victory: that dumb bitch needed to watch her step. He thought I wouldn't get involved in her game. From now on things were going to be different.

He hadn't, however, counted on the wisdom of the broom bringing him back down to the dusty earth. As she did every morning, Juana was sweeping the sidewalk to clear it for the residents. Max wasn't sure if his ears were deceiving him or if the sweeper's aged voice trembled:

"You can't run away from what's been broken any more, only the repairman can get you out of this mess now."

35

Nelly was still awake when he got back. She'd already zapped through the television channels a number of times. Where had he gone? She'd been so worried.

"You didn't seem too worried when you went off with Pascual."

"Oh, Max! What are you talking about?" Her incredulity appeared genuine. "Like, don't make up stories. It was you who suggested going to the studio. You who left me alone with him. I can't tell you how awkward it was. Then I got home and you weren't here."

Max desperately searched for objections but didn't find any. She was right. I'm a moron. What was I trying to prove?

"Forgive me, Nelly. I was drunk. I can't remember a thing. I'm sorry if I behaved badly."

"Oh, Max, come here. Lie down with me. Just don't doubt me again. Cuddle up close. We need to sleep for a while."

36

There would be time later to reflect on everything. The registration period ended that afternoon: he either had to give G.B.W. Ponce a name or never return to the office. Why go to see the repairman? But then he didn't have any better ideas. The absence of the Many felt very strange. They had more ammunition than ever to fuck him up now. They were up to something. Maybe they were just as hungover as he was. Nelly, fortunately, was having breakfast with her aunt. That gives me time. Time for what?

Max went to the workshop of the eccentric character he had heard was named Schuler, who specialized in mending a bit of everything. The first step was diagnosis. Sometimes his task was limited to pointing out that the object in question was functioning as it was meant to. The trick was to accept it as it was.

For instance, a customer might bring him a broken blender and, after a brief inspection, Schuler would return it intact. Of course he could repair it, but his advice was that it was better not to mix things. Or it might happen that another person would bring him a tennis racket to be restrung. On examination, he would find that the head of the racket was warped. Any clumsy handling might cause it to break. The repairman would reinforce the head with an invisible ceramic coating and the new strings would be set into a firm structure, leaving it ready to deal with the most arduous of matches.

As the norm was to take an object with you, Max dusted off the old bound book belonging to his father. The repairman examined it on both sides. As he leafed through, he carefully stopped at certain pages, then scrawled something incomprehensible in his notebook.

"Tell me, what brought you here?" he asked Max, getting straight to the point.

"My book isn't working any more. It used to tell hundreds of stories. Now the pages have gone blank."

"Hmm. Let's see."

With deep concentration, the repairman tore out a number of selected pages and inserted them into a paper shredder.

He returned the book to Max together with the tangle of paper strips.

"Done. Put them somewhere safe, so you never forget them. Now, my fee, please."

"You're going to charge me for tearing out some pages?"

"The skill isn't in tearing out the pages. It's a matter of knowing which to choose."

37

When he left the workshop, Max knew what he had to do. He felt as if he had a panoramic vision of Villa Miserias and as he took in the estate from a greater distance, what was lost in terms of detail was gained in clarity. Finally, Villa Miserias was a small speck of dust within an interconnected constellation. Max had traveled a concentric spiral that was exploding in all directions at once. There was only one road open to him: he was going to register as a candidate for the presidency of the Villa Miserias residents' association.

PART TWO

There is no truth without fools.
White Noise
Don DeLillo

DAY I

LET THERE BE LIGHT: THE CONTEST BEGINS
Nelly López

Dear readers of *The Daily Miserias*, today our coverage of the elections for the presidency of the Villa Miserias residents' association begins. As you know, our only loyalty is, as usual, to you, and this time is no different. And it makes no difference to us who is competing in the election. For your benefit we are going to dig around in the dirt whenever necessary. What's important is that you have all the information needed to make an informed decision, because you are the basis of a community that wants to be free and democratic like ours.

At the last moment, we finally learned the name of the second candidate. It was a big surprise to discover that fellow resident Max Michels had registered for the election. The downside is that he's never held any public office, so we don't know if he'll be able to win over voters. The residents have matured a lot in the last years, and they have no patience with time-wasters. Let's hope candidate Michels understands that from the start.

The other candidate, Modesto González, welcomed his opponent by saying, "I hope this young man, with his slightly strange friends, is up to our appointment with history. The voters always win and only they know the best alternative. I have no doubt that

I will gain the support of the majority of my fellow members of the residential estate."

We're going to keep a very close eye on what could be a very exciting campaign. For a start, there's candidate Michels' logo, which looks like it was made for a conceptual art prize. His campaign slogan sounds more like a riddle than a proposal. It's not that we think it's a bad thing to have a bit of creativity in the campaigns, but we haven't come this far just to have someone questioning our efforts. The residents already know what they want. The candidates have to understand that their only function is to remind them.

What truth am I supposed to communicate to them? What's underneath all those layers of comforting lies? I don't know, but apparently that's what my bosses want to find out. They think sadism becomes something else the moment it comes out of the closet and openly accepts responsibility. It's the law of the weakest installed as the strongest. The one who manages to accumulate the largest amount of others' guilt wins. Wins what? The game depends on acting as if you didn't know the only certainty is everyone loses in the end. Loses what? It's curious that a poor moron like my father should chose such a powerful phrase for our family axiom.

I'm not sure that Ponce's ire was genuine. It was somehow studied. As if he'd already considered the possibility and wasn't completely displeased. Am I going to be a prediction in his questionnaire? But he immediately called the chief to tell him the news. They wanted to hold an emergency meeting, and the chief said he was on his way. I imagine they'll warn me off. How far back does my dossier go? They can't know everything. Unless... No, that's unthinkable. Anyway, I couldn't wait. I'd arranged to meet Nelly at Alison's. She doesn't like to be kept waiting. She's said so several times.

She got horny when she heard the news. Offered me a solemn pact. Respectful enemies during the day, and at night... Not sure about that. I'd considered telling her what was going on, to see if together we could unravel the enigma, but her eyes were spitting out black lava. Only a wimp would let the moment pass. Better not say anything. I have to keep my focus until the election is over.

*She hardly gave me time to close the door of the apartment.
From the first touch I was on the alert for the coming of darkness.
I had to keep reminding myself not to close my eyes. To see as
much as possible. And then a little more. Perhaps it was a tactic
she used to avoid showing herself lost, vulnerable as one is, as we
all are. That's fool's talk... Even if she knew how, she wouldn't
do it, no one could want that for anyone else. Or could they?*

*Well, I got through the first round. Nelly was already in her
underwear, more perfect than ever. The Many began with their
usual stuff. Why me? I haven't done anything wrong. Really?
Don't act the moron fag, and so on. I took a backseat. And in
the meanwhile, I had my eyes peeled to steal more Nelly from
the night to come. When she got to her feet, I thought the last
part was beginning, the part where I'd be present without being
there. And that's how it was. But she gave me a great excuse.
She mustn't know what's going on. No way. Not until the
campaign's over. Maybe that will cure me. Yes. Just get through
the eleven-day circus. What doesn't kill you doesn't kill you.
Nelly ran out of the room and came back with some sort of
plastic sheet in her hand. "Put it on. That way I won't feel
I'm throwing myself onto the enemy before the show starts."
Then I heard that priceless laugh. It was a pig mask. Hugely
relieved, I followed her instruction, and the last thing I saw
was the mask descending. Then I was enveloped in a seamless
veil. If it weren't for all the stones those shits throw at me,
it might even be okay. I could compensate in other ways. The
smells, the slaps, the moans, the hair tugging. But they keep
on to the end. Do they get tired of it too? I shouted louder,*

squealing like a pig. Every cell of Nelly's body was at fever pitch. I would give anything to see her at the final explosion. Even if it was just once. Just one time. Ten days left to see if I fall to one side or the other.

Luckily, the three of us are back together again. Sao and Pascual think the campaign thing is fun. They've appointed themselves discourse and image directors, and Bramsos' studio is our campaign headquarters. Which is good, because that way Nelly can only come round on official business. I showed them Orquídea's document on our first meeting, and all the complicity of so many other, earlier conspiracies returned. We look at each other as if the bad times hadn't existed. All three of us understand that just because it was more real, it wasn't any less a game. Just the reverse.

Pascual started designing the logo straight away. On a piece of card, he drew an open sore of varying depths, with transparent pus oozing from it. The pus is falling onto a smooth surface on which the sore is reflected. But the reflected image is very clear. It's a symmetrical, precise sore, you could say, well dressed and with impeccable manners. Sao passed him a sheet of paper with the campaign slogan and Pascual inscribed it below in defiant lettering:

Do you really want to know what you already know?

When Ponce's rehearsed outburst had ended (Who did I think I was? They could crush me in quarter of an hour. Didn't I remember what had happened to the last one?), he said something

I didn't completely understand. It was as if he was implying that boundaries are created by the lack of barriers. Armed, as ever, with his figures, he embarked, like a man possessed, on a monologue. He spoke of the millions generated by the image of the most handsome revolutionary in history, said the children of marijuana-smoking parents were incredibly snobbish; he gave a cackle when one of his charts whispered to him that kids who lose their virginity with a whore have never squeezed an orange with their own hands; he assured me that, on average, social activists have 42% more flab on their necks than workers in bonded assembly plants, that 66% of housewives practice dance steps with their floor mops. And so he went on for a while, without even noticing my various attempts to stand up and leave. At last, with his index finger pointing to the door of his shadowy bunker, he told me that, most importantly, there was one thing I should not forget.

"The mystics say everything is the same. The difference now is that the same doesn't include everything, and neither you nor anyone else can do anything to change that."

He bent one ear toward to his charts, and I took advantage of that situation to quickly depart with saying goodbye. I have the impression he's going to very close by all the time. I'll do whatever I can to keep out of his way.

DAY 2

Residents of Villa Miserias,

In this, my inaugural campaign speech, I should begin by thanking you for coming here to the Plaza del Orden to listen to me. And then introduce myself as your humble servant, whose only desire is to exercise authority for your benefit. Through you. For you, the residents of Villa Miserias. According to custom, I should explain that from a very young age I've felt indignant about the injustice doled out to those who have the least. I should talk of how I felt indignant as I watched my nanny on her feet, working long hours, like someone suffering a punishment in classical mythology, consumed by the need to clean, wash, mop up, cook, make the beds, and all the rest of it, from dawn to dusk, so that we could then dirty everything, leave plates of uneaten food around, throw clothes on the floor, and complain, again and again, if we found a single one of her hairs in the soup, or the food wasn't spicy enough. All this for a miserable wage. And no health insurance. No old age pension. Obliged to wear a humiliating uniform. Conversations in another language under her very nose when we didn't want her to know what we were saying. And the moment I felt that indignation, I should tell you, was when I decided to prepare myself to help all the nannies in Villa Miserias. To put an end to injustice! That became for me a moral imperative. A mandate coming from somewhere outside me. I, Max Michels, would play an active role in politics to take personal responsibility for things changing.

Once the purity of my vocation had been established, I should launch into an attack on the most recent administration. Whether from their ineptitude, ignorance, corruption, affiliation to a conspiratorial elite, heartlessness, or the many other repugnant characteristics, I would explain, they are to blame for the ills we suffer. We need change. Grassroots change, not just a pretense of it. With dramatic intonation, a frown on my brow and an accusing finger, it would be my job to tell you that I am that change, that my opponent represents the continuity of the present state of affairs. You know this. You don't want the same any longer. You want something different. Something better. In short, I should tell you that you want me.

Finally, I should lash you with a hurricane of vague, nonsensical policies aimed at the core of your well-intentioned beings. No more half-eaten quesadillas for the workers! I'll bring in reforms that will make your dreams of luxury a reality! I'll put an end to the chronic body odor of the Black Paunches! Free cosmetic surgery for all! Our children will be learning four languages from the age of six months! I'll do away with drug dealing without affecting consumption levels! I'll listen to and do something about all the needs and worries of the hundreds of residents of Villa Miserias! Because my sacrifice is for you! I won't let you down! Just put a cross against my name in ten days' time and your new lives will be wonderful. Lives worthy of the unique being each of you is. Thank you for your attention. You can now applaud and shout slogans.

I am, however, not going to do any of the above. My campaign isn't aimed at tricking you into electing me, and then later hating me until you become enraptured by the next snake charmer who really is going to pull you out of the mire. I offer you nothing more than my vision of things. I intend to show you the leeway for real action, and the obstacles in its way. You will see that we have those obstacles embedded in our deepest selves. I'll shed my light on all those corners. And I can warn you that you won't like what you see. Some of you will long for the return of darkness. To those who do, I recommend you vote for my opponent. Those of you who decide to follow me should have three central points clear:

ONE. I'm not participating in this election for you. My motivations for becoming president of the board are selfish. In that respect, I'm no different from anyone else. Not even the self-sacrificing altruists. The fact that their pleasure is based on a consciousness of their goodness, the delight engendered by the notion of saving lives, doesn't make them any less egoistical. I too have a hole inside me that needs to be filled. And what can fill it is the power to make decisions about matters that concern everyone. There is no addiction that enslaves humans more strongly than the addiction to power. Strictly speaking, all politicians are megalomaniacs. The lives of many of them show the inverse relationship between the external mask and internal self-esteem. The cruelest dictators feel themselves to be the dregs of humanity. Their worst atrocities deepen the abyss they were called to fill.

What I will say to you is that my ghosts are not the horrific kind. My ambitions can be classed as mediocre. This is good news for you, because statesmanlike characteristics are a thing of the past. We live in the managerial era. The color gray has never before shined so brightly.

It's not true that ideology has died. Quite the reverse. The dominant ideology has settled into structures that are no longer even questioned. It's not even necessary to express it. If it's not visible, that's because it's everywhere. There's no need for justification, it simply is. Denouncement of its very horrors is an essential part of the ideology of the times. The honor of doing this is reserved for a tiny, illustrious elite. The most committed go on demonstrations and shout slogans. There are even some who sign letters in the centerfolds of newspapers. It's part of the system.

Far from living in a post-ideological era, we are witnessing the empire of a flattened vision of the world, an empire that is proclaiming the end of all other epochs. It's announcing that after centuries of barbarism, we are finally reaching our goal. Luckily, history buried its capital H along the road. There are no more agitators to question the foundations. The new overlords are very nervous, given to flight when the panic starts. That's why they need only administrators to make sure the bonds are never tied too tight. I have no problem with being an administrator. It's important you know that.

TWO. The other great lie has to do with you. Your awareness of periodically taking part in making the decision about who will be the next president of this colony has an important psychological function. Above all, it allows for a return to the everyday bubble of real worries, the ones that eat away at our existence. Why rack your brains trying to understand complex, abstract, sometimes indecipherable social norms? It's such a bore... What's the use of stopping to think about anything below the surface? Voting for the most convincing slogan does away with all that. The messiah Ponce has demonstrated that 94% of voters wouldn't be able to complete the most basic questionnaire about the platform of their candidate of choice. And those levels of ignorance aren't related to social class, they are very similar for both rich and poor. It's completely natural for the latter not to care a fig. The rich, on the other hand, put themselves forward as having most interest in public participation: but their commitment to democracy is nothing more than a mechanism for diverting attention from their terrifying concentration of wealth.

Despite all this, when there are elections, no one talks about anything else. The vote is a great social insignia for a gathering of the clans. Putting a cross on a ballot paper allows one to give up any idea of personal coherence. Political creeds are just that, political creeds, without practical implications for life. The idea of living the way you vote is as absurd as asking a girl to practice a religion that decrees she must still be a virgin when she marries. In both cases there's a tacit understanding that they are not the sorts of rules that have to be observed.

It's not uncommon to see those who have the whip hand voting for those who, at least in their speeches, defend the people who suffer the lashes. Or for people on the margins of society to vote for politicians who talk about marginalizing those who don't fit the norm. You almost certainly know young people earning a fortune in companies that utilize highly dubious business practices, who nevertheless support candidates decrying those same companies and their highly dubious business practices. Or women who turn up to vote in chauffeur-driven cars, who are strongly in favor of greater social equality. You must have heard of cases of manual laborers supporting anti-union platforms. Of women who vote for conservative candidates who set limits on the choices available to their gender. I could go on all night.

What's happening in those cases? Are those people really voting against their own interests? No way. At some level, it's common knowledge that the basic inertias don't come into play at the ballot. Voting has become a more social than political affair. There was a reason why the apostle of the noble savage postulated that the only way for the communal will to be expressed was for voters not to communicate with each other, not to influence each other. Can you imagine what he would think of the dictatorship of opinion polls? Is there any point in going along like sheep to validate what statistics have already predicted with scientific precision?

Let's dispose, once and for all, of the illusion that voters decide anything relevant. So, just what is it they do decide? Which of the handful of options they don't really understand is best for making decisions about the options they have no idea at all about? On a future occasion, I'll address the topic of how prospective candidates are filtered out. But let me offer one fact now: in the entire history of Villa Miserias, there has never been a candidate who did not own an apartment. All of them, without exception, have been homeowners. That simple fact locates them in a different class than the vast majority of those they pretend to represent. Can you call being obliged to choose between hunger or thirst an election? The only possible democracy would have, as a fundamental point of departure, voters with full stomachs. It seems to me crueler still to saddle them with the blame for always having made the wrong decision. If I haven't been indulgent with my own motivations, neither will I be with the level of participation you actually have under the current model. Voting for me, as for any other candidate, is voting for a specific way of thinking that, even if unwillingly, corresponds to the interests of those who are like me, and not like the majority of you.

THREE. So, we're all complicit in this tragedy. But that doesn't mean we're all equally responsible for it. It can't, however, be denied that every vote, regardless of which box is checked, is a vote in favor of the existing order. You might object, citing examples of extreme regimes—well- or ill-intentioned— that have transformed things after gaining power through the ballot. For some time now, that is exactly what money has taken upon itself to prevent. Nowadays, the armor plating protecting money from the ascent to power of anyone who goes against its interests is invincible. The beardies who took to the hills with a few rifles had an infinitely greater chance of success than any contemporary Quixote who defies capital. Anybody whose name appears on the ballot slip has already made an unspoken pact with the owners of wealth.

I think I can guess what some of you are thinking. If the ballot box isn't the right way, the modern equivalent of the beardies with their rifles seems the only other option. Am I right? Yes, but the Black Paunches are already heavily armed, you might object. Subtlety isn't their strong point, as they have demonstrated on the various occasions that have acted as effective warnings. I'm deeply sorry, but I don't intend to offer you an easy way out.

Big Brother once explained that the word sabotage derives from the wooden shoes known as sabots. A group of workers in an occupied country wrecked an armaments factory, used to supply the army of the crooked cross, by jamming the machinery with their clogs. According to Big Brother, this demonstrated the capacity of the ordinary man to derail the train of the most effective death squad ever created.

Nevertheless, I can assure you that nothing like that will happen. Being part of a community involves not wearing sabots. Inequality rests on the small strikebreaker we all carry within us. That's why the usual, worn-out forms of protest are just grist to the mill. They allow those with the power to say, "See? We tolerate dissidence here. Right boys, your moms are waiting for you at home. It's time for things to go on as normal."

I once attended a lecture on social relationships in a center for people with Down's Syndrome. The speaker, a handsome doctor with the bearing of a pelican, explained that, due to the immense range of possibilities of the syndrome, the patients created their own boundaries to distinguish themselves from those with lower levels of ability. The ones who could move around unaided didn't want to be put in the same category as those who were wheelchair bound. The guys in the center with girlfriends laughed at those with no sexual experience. Far from forming a fellowship of disabled people united against a world that segregated them, they reproduced the hierarchical structure in which everyone has their correct place. I have never seen a better example of that base trait of our species.

What does all this have to do with my campaign, I hear you ask. The answer is that egalitarian discourse—the non-recognition of the barriers of blood, birth, mother tongue, strength, physical beauty, intelligence, and so on—is the great modern balm for perpetuating the worst inequalities ever seen. On positing that we are all equal, the responsibility for this failure is passed on to each individual. Not being like those who are equal has nothing to do with things decided before birth. No sir. Here among us we have the example of the darkest-skinned president of the board in our history to remind us that the only thing needed is sufficient effort.

Even the much-vaunted concept of being equal before the law isn't as clear as it might seem. One of the few non-reactionary jurists once explained that equality before the law involves accepting the inequalities the law recognizes. A pregnant woman does not have the same rights as a convicted pedophile. Their equality before the law consists of being under the protection of different norms. We are not equal before the law precisely because the law recognizes the importance of us not being so. The juridical and social norms regulating social life are a reflection of our most deep-rooted prejudices. The fact that some cases seem positive and others abominable doesn't change the basic fact one iota. We are a tribe whose social organization is based on the recognition that, in the view of that society, some members are more equal than others.

It's no coincidence that an age notable for its enormous gap between haves and have-nots should be the first to posit, within its discourse, that each individual is equally important. Who among you here is ready to look in the mirror and accept himself as a bastard? Who is able to admit that she prefers to satisfy the insatiable before another's hunger? Who can accept that horror is only worthy of being called by that name when it is experienced in one's own flesh?

Allow me to end by paraphrasing an aphorism by the long-suffering man with black shadows under his eyes who understood better than anyone the prison of invisible bars that was constructed during his lifetime:

Not democracy, but the idea of democracy.

Thank you for being here tonight dear residents. We'll see each other soon, at the next event.

Why can't I see?

Who's writing this?

Who's asking who's writing this?

What really drives me crazy isn't even not seeing her. It's realizing that, whatever I do, I'll never see myself reflected in her eyes.

I had one eye fixed on her during that whole speech. What was she writing in her notebook? She didn't even raise her head once. At times it seemed like she was drawing something. I'd rather not imagine what. And then there was the distance: Nelly was in one of the reserved seats in the first row, and I was trying to gauge the reaction of the crowd with my other eye.

Leaning over the empty seat separating them, Ponce and Orquídea were whispering together, satisfied. The chief was supposed to be arriving at any moment. But in the end, he didn't turn up. My opponent was there, camouflaged by a string of former and present officials. When I said the part about drugs, Maso pointed his two-finger pistol at me, fired six times, blew on the smoking finger and practically dislocated Mascorro's sternum with a slap celebrating his own joke. Taimado sniffed his armpit at the allusion to his hordes, and then an unpleasant expression broke out on his face as he nodded his head. Poor Candelario sat through the entire speech, as wooden as his impassive bench. I think he was afraid the saws would arrive; this time to cut me up. They'd left him useless for much less.

Behind them, the rows were arranged by coefficient. The strange thing was that the ushers didn't have to guide people to their places. Everyone already knew where to sit. Waiters min-gled among the front rows, offering drinks and snacks. The next tier could give their orders at a side bar erected for the occasion. Then, its territory marked by Juana Mecha's broom, came the beige mass. The regulations permit them to attend political acts in exchange for just one thing: they cannot change out of their uniforms. Apparently this is for their own good. It's a matter of saving them from the humiliating confusion of being mistaken for residents.

It was more like a communal meditation session than the opening of a campaign. If any single breath went astray, the others returned it calmly to the common rhythm. Sao and Pascual had helped me to lay a few bombs. They were all primed. I thought when I finished the plaza would empty, as if it were assembled from interlocking pieces that had been put back in their box.

When I'd thanked them, the members of the audience came out of their collective trance. Fists thumping the air, whistles swal-lowing, and spitting out confetti. I came down from the podium, looking for Nelly, and was swept away by a tidal wave of effusive backslaps. Among the shouts, I heard that it was about time, that someone had to say it, that they were with me all the way. Shit. The pink lipstick on my white shirt must have come from the usherettes asking for a photo. Ponce held out his hand to me before leaving with one of them. Nelly was nowhere to be seen.

Sao managed to extract me from the mob with a hug. We were supposed to meet up at our campaign headquarters for an analysis of the event. The thing is...it's...I couldn't articulate an objection. She understood immediately. "Don't worry," she said.

"I'll tell Pascual my father isn't well and I have to relieve him at the laundry. Get some rest." I'll never understand how she does it.

I ran off before it was too late. They were already fucking with my head. What if she isn't there when you get back? And what if she is? Let's see how you get out of this one, you moron. Why bother? She's already mad at you. At that moment Juana Mecha appeared to sweep us out of the way:

"Even if the arrow's pointing skyward, if the box is upside down, that's where Hell is."

When I arrived it was already dark and Nelly was watching television. We weren't due to be cordial enemies again until the next day. I waited for a commercial break to see if she would say something: I was anxious to hear her opinion of my speech. In her television program, a tangled affair involving the brother of the friend of the ex-girlfriend of one of the juvenile characters who were now older—or something like that—was on the point of unraveling. Nelly knew how it turned out: she'd already watched it several times. The break arrived but she was still silent. I thought that maybe she meant to talk over my speech at length, not just limit herself to a brief interlude. I asked if she was hungry, but she simply shook her head, so I went to the kitchen to get something to eat.

I shouted an offer of a whisky: it was answered by canned laughter. I had to be up early the following day, so best make the most of the time I had left. As I couldn't decide whether or not I was hungry, I just sat down to wait for the program to end.

I didn't remember those episodes being so long.

I returned to the bedroom as the theme tune was playing in the background. Nelly was looking for something else to watch. That was when I exploded. What the hell's wrong with you? I screamed. Why did we always have to watch the programs she liked? She'd never once asked what I'd prefer. When I chose something, she always, by coincidence, fell asleep.

At some point in my rant she switched off the set. After that she lay face down on top of the sheets and buried her face in the pillow. Once again I was moved by the crease formed by the juncture of her ass and her back. I stamped out of the room.

It soon became obvious that Nelly wasn't going to come and make up. I was afraid my shouts might have woken the Many, but apparently they had placated them. Attempting to distract myself by thinking about the campaign, I took down Pascual's painting to face the family axiom. If there's no truth but the most convenient lie, what use was Ponce & Co.'s planned experiment? Supposing that anyone really cared, or even that such a thing as an awakening actually existed, then what? The charm of those sets of concentric dolls is that each is more or less exactly the same as the one before, if a little smaller. Who'd want a series where the next one was toothless, with sagging breasts and a clubfoot? It's not the same for a prisoner to receive a sentence of 1322 years as to get life. Doctors who have carried out emergency operations at the front advise that if there is no real anesthetic available, a placebo should be administered. Anything that comes to hand. Why do they now want to install the complete lack of illusions as an illusion?

Had Nelly fallen asleep? The light was still on. Without insulting me, one of the Many made my situation clear. What did you expect? An "Oh Max, that was the most intelligent speech ever. I admire you so much". Come off it. Be a man and apologize the only way you can.

The asshole was right. If only they always addressed me in those terms, I'd be more receptive to their fucking slaps in the face. I went back into the bedroom with the pig mask on. You can get used to anything. Nelly lay still, giving to understand she was sleeping. I slid down the bottom half of her pajamas in an attempt to sort out the misunderstanding. She must still be mad at me. Or maybe she really was asleep. I set about my task until she removed my hand. Then she turned and grimaced in disgust at the sight of my pig-face. "Ugh, Max. Take that off. I don't feel like it tonight." I obeyed, resigned to not sleeping. Then she stretched out a hand and took something from her dressing table. It was a sleep mask. "Guess what? This time it's me who doesn't want to see you." She donned it and began to fulfill her campaign promise. We were all so happy that we didn't care when things went dark again. Nelly, and everything else. Thanks to the mask, there was no way she could tell. Maybe I should get angry more often.

DAY 3

THE DUEL OF THE PROPHETS
Nelly López

Candidate Max Michels continues to offer a pretty strange campaign. Of course, voters like a bit of fun, but perhaps enough is enough. If he goes on this way, the residents might very soon get tired of him and his theatrics. Maybe it would do him good to remember everyone is replaceable, and a lot of people would like to be in his shoes. He has nine days left to show he's capable of taking advantage of the enormous opportunity that's been offered him.

His campaign team put up posters all around Villa Miserias, inviting people to a duel of prophets. It must have caused a lot of morbid curiosity because, at the given time, Plaza del Orden was really crowded.

The first thing to be seen on arrival was a clever stage design. At the back of the pavilion was a sheet painted by Pascual Bramsos showing a mountain split in two. The sky on the right had black thunderclouds with vultures circling round below, and the mountain was surrounded by barbed wire. On the other side of the scene the weather was more pleasant. The sun was resting on clouds like cotton wool balls. On the mountain, there were loungers with lettuces scattered around on them. Some of the lettuces were drinking a sort of reddish cocktail. In the center was a metal staircase separating the two halves. I have to say that the stage design made us all curious about what was going to happen next.

Suddenly, the daughter of the laundryman appeared disguised as a priestess of ancient times, holding two large tablets. She went up the staircase as if going to the summit of the mountain and stood there motionless for quite a while.

Next, Michels and Bramsos came on stage. The candidate was wearing a white tunic, a curly wig, and had a false beard. Bramsos' hair was uncombed, he was wearing round spectacles and a long-sleeved, checked shirt. They walked around the set for a while like they were lost. Then they tried to go up the stairway, but kept pretending to slip back. The audience began to tire of this and there was a murmur of what sounded like desperation.

When some people had already left in search of something better, the two of them fixed their eyes on the laundryman's daughter. As if obeying an order, they each went up his own side of the stairway. The girl gave each of them his own tablet. Max Michels' said "Ten Recipes for Dominating the World," while Bramsos' said "The Decalogue of the Good Progressive." So finally we knew what the duel of the prophets was about. They went back down the staircase to address the crowd. One began to read out a proclamation, and then the other followed, like they each wanted to attract the listeners to their own side. Here are the proclamations they exchanged:

PB: If everyone was like me and mine, the world would be a marvelous place.

MM: Prices must be kept as low as possible. There is no more implacable tyrant than the consumer.

PB: We must support every noble cause. Reality is complex

enough already without expecting something to happen.

MM: Advertisements must always address members of the target audience in an intimate tone.

PB: There's no point in arguing with people who think differently. They will never admit they are wrong.

MM: There is nothing more lucrative than fully exploiting a sense of lack.

PB: People like us are characterized by the number of permanent furrows on our brows.

MM: Even those who don't have enough to dream of it have to be put on the property ladder.

PB: Everything must happen in the most organic way. All intense experiences will be described as either awesome or demonic.

MM: It is permissible for companies owned by thousands of anonymous shareholders to be ruthless in their search for profit because the blame can't be put on any single person.

PB: Brute force is for brutes. With my cigar and my coffee, I have all I need to bring in the police.

MM: The most efficient mechanisms of normalization are shareholders and the stock market. They can sink millions into poverty at just the press of a button.

PB: The masses are not at fault for being the masses, but for how they are the masses.

MM: Crime adapts to the level of sophistication it has to confront. It will never disappear, only be transformed.

PB: Rich white women are not more attractive per se, it's just a coincidence that they are the ones I like most.

MM: The more a politician presents himself as one of you, the greater the community's toleration of the pain he inflicts.

PB: The fact that they are better looking and smarter than the next person has nothing to do with them being my children.

MM: It only needs a very few examples of social mobility for anyone to think it's just as possible for him.

PB: Come what may, our hopes lie in our kids. They represent the eternal tomorrow.

MM: The slogan including all other slogans: "The voter is always right."

While they were sparring over proclamations, the members of the crowd were uncertain which prophet to listen to, until they finally plumped for one or the other. When they had finished, Michels had twice as many supporters as Bramsos. Then something really strange took place that only those of us present can believe actually happened.

At some point in the duel, the daughter of the laundryman came down the staircase and started handing out balloons filled with what looked like water. The people on Michels' side got orange ones, and on Bramsos' side they were gray. Then she went back to her place on the mountain and shouted at the top of her voice, "Balloon war!"

The audience obeyed without a second thought. When the first balloons burst, we realized they were actually full of the orange or gray paint. As Bramsos' band was smaller, they were soon soaked in orange paint. Michels' followers were covered in gray, but less completely. Some lunatics tried to steal balloons from the enemy camp. But I couldn't believe it when I saw the reason was to burst them over their own heads. Those of us who were neutral ended up splattered with paint of both colors. We went home with our clothes soiled by the war between the two bands.

To put an end to the madness, the prophets called a halt to the war by giving each other a long hug. They helped the daughter of the laundryman down the staircase, and the three went happily away. The members of the audience had already got into the groove, so some stayed bursting balloons until there were none left.

The campaign is just beginning, and there's a lot of time left still, but I think at this rate Michels won't even make it to the end.

This time, running off to my dark enclosure wasn't an option. Not that I was anxious to go there. Just in case, I'd made sure the paint wasn't the sort that doesn't wash out. As I knew Nelly wouldn't see the funny side of being splattered, I'd thought about warning her the night before. But wasn't it she who'd declared the cordial enmity during the campaign? The layers in my head are so muddled I no longer know which are mine. The Many aren't as stupid as they seem: I've caught them mimicking my ideas. They know how my mind works. They're capable of adding just that extra grain of salt so I won't claim them as my own. They delight in using my confusion as their principal weapon for ensuring their continued existence. When they go too far, I can catch them out: Who thought that? And the automatic reply: Not me, me neither, not a chance, I might have. Aren't I you? No, no, no, you're not me, no way, okay, it's our fault, it's better for us all this way, but at heart you know... It's exhausting. It reminds me of those fairground games where you have to hammer down moles that pop out of holes. My personal fairground is so perverse that the one who wields the mallet is also the mole and vice versa. Luckily, we've got the chocolate brownies tomorrow. That stupefies the Many for a while, though then they come back even more furiously, emboldened to the point of breaking all connection with me. It could be a good day for trying out the pepper gas trick. There's a long way to go yet. If I at least knew for sure there would be an end to it somewhere. Could this be the end? Nelly says relationships are very complicated. But that wasn't scripted in my black fairy tales. How long can eight days last?

Sao and Pascual were ecstatic. I gave the impression I was too, but Sao was surely aware that, at heart, I couldn't care less. Everything went to plan. The fact that Ponce didn't say anything must be an indication that we have their blessing. Otherwise the chief would have acted. I thought I saw him in the crowd, but in the end it was just an illusion. It's strange, just now I went over things with my two friends: I know they'll help me anyway they can, but they also have their own motives for taking part of the campaign. Sao's interested in patterns, she wants to find out how two particles, thousands of miles apart, are linked. The problem is clearing away the chaff. She thinks, once that's done, models of behavior as immutable as the laws of physics will appear. That's why the environment we act in is so fundamental.

Pascual, on the other hand, is convinced that any form of politics is an aesthetic. The monotone, the flat, the consensual untruths, the exaltation of the banal, are all, however abominable it might seem, still aesthetics. For him, what's crucial is capturing the intention behind the appearance. The chosen wrapping must not be considered as a decisive piece of data, you have to take a step back. In that sense—or so it seems to me now—even obesity is a political act. I guess they're right. I guess I should be more passionate. I guess I should be concerned, like them. They are terrified by the Ponce Questionnaire. Terrified by the possibility that the script consists of nothing more than us going as far as possible off-script. Who? Why? Sao asked. I don't know, I don't know, I replied. Sorry, I'm very tired. My other active frontline awaits me. Or that's what I believed.

What I found was in some way a relief. The Many had been

insinuating worse: including a terse farewell note. It wasn't that bad. Her dirty clothes were dumped on the apricot sofa. It's no big deal, we've already talked about having it reupholstered. It makes Nelly feel insecure. She wants to be the only one to have shared it with me. I put the bundle of colors in a plastic bag. If I bring it back clean tomorrow, maybe she won't be so mad at me. I hope the other laundry is as good. Sao will understand if she finds out.

What those fucking Many were right about was that she'd locked the bedroom door. I've got a duplicate key here somewhere, but that's not what matters. I put them to sleep with whisky, and when there was only me left standing, I slumped onto the sofa. Now no one is listening, I can say you sleep better here.

DAY 4

HELPING IS SO NICE!

Nelly López

Yesterday, the group of women who run the Leonardo RU arts center held their charity dinner. The guest speaker was Max Michels and, it goes without saying, he turned up with his campaign team. At this stage, it's hard to say whether the pandemonium that breaks out whenever they appear is accidental or planned. The annual dinner is usually very quiet, even boring, but, coincidentally, this time it ended in a riot. The authorities are attempting to identify the culprits.

The act began just as normal. The chairwoman of the arts center's board went to the podium to offer words of welcome. There was a buffet including shark fin soup, snails, anteater pâté, frog legs, roast quail, iguana filet, and other odd dishes. On the desert table were some chocolate brownies that looked inoffensive. None of us knew they were possessed by devils.

The chairwoman explained the rules of the event. In the center of the room was a tombola drum containing the money raised by ticket sales. If they got the urge, the diners could donate more during the evening. Each time that happened, the electronic board would announce the name and the amount donated. The chairwoman asked us all to applaud when someone added another donation. She explained that everyone there asked themselves the same question every day: What can I do to help correct what's wrong with the world? Finally, she explained that when the event was almost over, there would be a vote to decide which cause to give the money to. She had to pause several times in her speech because people had started calling out, pretty loudly, Helping is so nice! Helping is so nice!

One important thing the chairwoman explained was that charity was not the same as it had been in the past. Happily, now it has nothing to do with guilt. It's much better that it's fun, even sexy, and that those who donate receive public recognition. She added that it's really good for society to have its best members acting as guides, because that way ordinary people will want to be like them and copy their behavior. The important people in Villa Miserias were always telling her that they wanted to return to the community all the things they had received.

In addition to Max Michels, she said there was another A-list guest, a very intelligent gentleman, who had come a long way to be there: Dr. Seeman. He would be sitting on a wooden chair so anyone could go up and talk to him. Before the chairwoman left the podium, people had already begun to shout, and with increasing fervor. Helping is so nice! Helping is so nice!

In the meanwhile, without anyone knowing it, people were falling into the trap that had been laid for them. They were eating the chocolate brownies, unaware that they had been spiked. The authorities still don't know what was in them, but it was something that caused attacks of uncontrollable laughter. There were women in evening dress talking to snail shells, as if asking forgiveness for having eaten their former inhabitants. An elderly couple let their hair down, kissing each other like they were twenty, and they had to be ushered out. And if only that had been all. But it wasn't. The worst was yet to come.

Dr. Seeman was sitting on his wooden chair. He looked very calm, as if it was only his body in the room with us all. Suddenly, there was a line of people wanting to talk to him to see if he'd share some of his wisdom. At the head of the line was a young girl. When the doctor simply asked her, "How are you?" the kid started doing a really strange dance, her whole body contorting backward and forward. She was wiggling her hips as she danced in a trance toward the tombola drum. The board began to celebrate her donation.

Something similar happened to the next guests to greet Dr. Seeman. Well, that's how it seemed, but afterwards we found out that it was only the people who had eaten the brownies. The point is that the electronic board went on announcing more donations. The tombola drum was getting fuller and fuller and the donors were gyrating around it in a circle. Dr. Seeman stayed in his chair, even when there was no one in line.

The only good thing was that the chairwoman didn't eat any brownies and so was able to keep her calm. She went back up to the podium for the most important act of the night. The slips of paper with the nominees for the donation had all the usual categories: street children, mothers with AIDS, old prostitutes, and people with mental handicaps. Before the voting started, another woman from the committee whispered something in the chairwoman's ear so that she could pass it on to the other guests. What she said was more or less that it wasn't really fair to give the money to any of the groups because, despite the fact that they might help some particular victim, others would still be in the shit. But it would also, she said, be unfair to us, because we'd have to go on seeing the ones who remained in poverty. Then what she proposed was to give everyone the chance to feel better about themselves.

The idea was to create a center for appearance and good manners for the less privileged groups. It would be easier for them to bear their misfortune if they were clean, well-groomed, perfumed, and dressed in the residents' cast-off clothes. They could also have a bit of training in how to talk properly so that they would have better manners when they were begging. Almost everyone dancing in the circle voted in favor of the new proposal. The tombola drum continued to rotate, as if it was happy too, and everyone there joined together again in shouting even more loudly the slogan of the night: Helping is so nice! Helping is so nice!

How far am I willing to go to continue hiding? Maybe I should say something to Nelly. She'd be sure to understand. And if I do tell her? That would mean my downfall. I bet the ones before me enjoyed her for hour after hour. It was only natural. I was really lucky today, but I should try to find less drastic ways of covering up. I was frightened by the permanent blindness, by not being able to see Nelly or anyone else. I've got to get through to the end of the campaign, come what may.

Pascual is surprisingly brilliant. Configurations speak to him in another language. When he suggested that thing with the chocolate brownies, I thought it was crazy. I imagined women throwing up, foaming at the mouth. Panic attacks. Everyone would know it was us. I envisioned Taimado arresting me. The fantasy only stopped when he started searching Sao. I don't know what they added to the mix, but the dose was perfect. Dr. Seeman's visit was the ideal element for taking things over the threshold. He acted as an unwary guru.

My father was right to despise his body in that way. It encapsulated all the truths he fled from during his life. His theoretical framework was just a defense. I hope, some day, I can feel sorry for him. For those couple of hours, I had it all clear. Pity it was because of the brownies. How do we get those permanently buried things to come to the surface? They'd need to be translated into language. The dance would have to be spoken in words.

I can see now I'm fucked. There's no going back. No way out. For me, that would be like entering all over again. How could it be any different? Any political action on a grand scale has the same objective: denying to the point of annihilation the certainties that pulse in the body. Life is an unbearable threat to life. Our age considers itself the most liberated ever. But it's no coincidence that it's also the one putting most effort into denying the body, stifling it with goals, objects, and personas. It's a matter of drowning out the pulse with a slogan.

As I was witnessing the event, it became clear to me that the essence of philanthropy is hypocrisy. It's like creating a gold statue dedicated to a thief who's giving back part of his booty. And each and every time it's defended by the same quandaries: would you prefer all those people not to have medicines? Something's better than nothing. If everyone adds his grain of sand... The same recycled claims: a little hunger is preferable to a raging thirst. Who's going to argue with photos of mutilated children? The result is to make any kind of meaningful discussion about its lasting impact impossible. If you donate a coin toward paying off the community's huge debt, it counts as the equivalent of exactly nothing. In contrast, if you construct a hospital without doctors or medicines that can, in any case, only take in a minute percentage of those in need, lots of photos have to be taken. If I get to be president of the board, I'm going to take two measures. The first is that donations won't be tax deductible, so they have to fork out real money, not just what they have to pay to the community anyway. The second, to prohibit making donations public. Then we'll see just how great their generosity is.

The pepper gas really frightened me. It was as if a thousand burning maggots were devouring my face. And my eyes. Blindness again. Past experience told me my sight would eventually return. But this time I wasn't so sure. The Black Paunch who sprayed me was high as a kite: he must have eaten quite a few of the brownies. It was easy to provoke him into reacting. It seems their training has worked. Without missing a beat, the stream got me straight in the face. But then, confused by the squealing of a downtrodden mollusk, he even managed to fall on top of me. Nelly ran up, screaming at him to get off. I had to persuade her not to report it in her article, to say it had been an accident, my own fault.

She dumped all her stuff—she could come back for it later—and took me by the arm, walking very slowly, trying to calm me, telling me the effects wouldn't last long. Her voice projected a facet I'd never seen before. The armor had vanished. She blew on my face to ease the burning. Although that actually made it even more unbearable, I had no intention of saying so. It would have been agreeing to the endless repetition of those smoky exhalations. The truth is, I've never seen that side of her.

Back home, she applied an ointment that gradually closed my molten pores. A damp bandage returned sensation to my eyelids, and I realized that I would recover this time too. Nelly guessed the disc that would best fit the moment. Another scene I'll return to forever. I was fighting with all my strength to stay awake. Although they would never admit it, I knew that even the Many were spellbound. So much so that they didn't notice the change in her caresses. None of us expected it. Anything I have to say on the matter would be an insult to what happened. For the first time, we made love.

DAY 5

THE LS' DINNER PARTY
A Comedy in Three Acts
By Sao Bac-Do

DRAMATIS PERSONAE
l1 LACKEY ONE
l2 LACKEY TWO
l3 LACKEY THREE
L1 LORD ONE
L2 LORD TWO
L3 LORD THREE

ACT I

(*In the basement of a house with two upper stories, l1, l2, and l3, impeccably dressed in their long-sleeved waiter's shirts, black trousers, and highly polished patent leather shoes, are carefully making the necessary preparation for the Lord's dinner party. A dinner jacket with all the accessories hangs on a hat stand. The stage set is austere. Beside the kitchen utensils, the only noticeable prop is a large red vase.*)

l1:   Hurry up! The Lord will be here any minute. He might bring a lady. How stupid I am! You know what I mean. I'm referring to a gentleman. Anyway, we have to have everything in order. Remember the fuss he made the other day when there was no ice in his glass.

l2:   I'm pleased by your diligence. A shame it's not my turn today. At least not on the first floor. I do, however, feel obliged to point out your lack of self-criticism. I seem to recall that the person who committed the gaffe with the ice bore a suspicious resemblance to you.

l3:   It's not my place to arbitrate in disputes yet. I've got fifteen minutes left. At least let me enjoy them. I will, however, admit that there's a pinch of truth in what you say. Kicking up a fuss about nothing is the Lord's prerogative. That's in the contract.

l1 and l2 (*in unison, surprised*): What contract?

l1:   As if you didn't know we were forced to sign our letters of resignation in advance. If there was a contract—and you know very well there isn't—it would be no use at all. The day they feel like it, we'll be kicked out on our asses without a word.

l3:   Listen to you! The language purists. It's just a manner of speaking. Like everything else, in fact.

l2:   I don't know what right you have to give us lessons. At least for a few minutes you're just one more inhabitant of the underworld. Even if you're wearing the other clothes. Not even your slicked-down hair can make you into a Lord while you're down here. Appearances are deceptive. Until you've walked upright through the door and watched us crawl in through the cat flap, you'll still be lower case. And don't forget it.

l3:   True. And that reminds me: Whose turn is it to give my attire a rigorous inspection? Because the last time…

(*l1 picks up the vase and brandishes it as if about to smash it on l3's head.*)

l1:   The last time what? Go on, say it. I'm begging you.

l3:   Calm down, calm down. There's no need for that. I'm not insinuating anything. The dinner jacket was impeccable. I'm only saying there could have been a bit of fluff on it. Just the idea is repugnant.

(*l1 puts the vase back in its place.*)

l1:   That's better. Come on, it's getting late.

(*l3 takes off his lackey's uniform. l1 and l2 wash his body with a kitchen scourer. Then they methodically dress him. When they have put on his hat, he pushes them away from him. The curtain closes.*)

ACT 2

(*The first floor of the house. A table is set for two. The room is decorated with elegance, but no taste. The same red vase. There is a hat stand holding identical garments to the ones L3 is wearing. The latter enters through a wide doorway. He stands with an annoyed expression on his face, repeatedly checking his pocket watch. When he hears footsteps, he hurries to pick up the handset of the telephone and puts it to his ear, although the phone has not rung. He pretends he is answering a call. l1 and l2 crawl through the cat flap. They are carrying trays on their backs. They laboriously help each other to place the trays on the table. L3 puts down the handset.*)

L3:   I'll be eating alone after all. The dog ate the keys of the lady who was going to dine with me. She begged me to let her take a cab, but that's very dangerous. I had to refuse.

l1:   Did milord call the lady "a bastard"?

L3:   Lady? Did I say lady? I must be worn out. I meant my friend, a man of very important affairs. He's got a cold. I had to be firm and stop him from coming. I can't risk contagion. The vulgar expression you referred to is a sign of our close friendship.

l1:   If milord says so.

(*l2 shoulders l1 out of the way to stand next to L3.*)

l2:   Dinner is served. Without wishing in any way to influence milord's decisions, he should be aware that it was a servant who devised the whole menu.

L3:   What's for dinner?

l2:   Cheeseburgers and french fries.

(*L3 picks up the plate and dashes it to the floor.*)

L3:   You know I hate burgers! When the fuck have you ever seen me eating one? Sometimes I don't know how I put up with this.

(*l2 turns to l1.*)

l2:   Wretch! The burgers were your idea. Is there no limit to your brown-nosing? You'd do anything to get in the room with the fireplace.

(*L3 continues to talk, as if to himself.*)

L3:   I allow you to live in my home, eat from my icebox, receive calls on my telephone, have an afternoon off a week, and this is how you repay me. The two of you are completely incompetent. And to think I have to chose between you. Never did a king have to rule over such idiots.

(*l1 is about to smash the vase on l2's head. He stops to listen to L3's last words, then runs over with the intention of shattering the vase on his head. L3 starts talking again and l1 pauses.)*

L3:   No. It's not your fault. We belong to different species. My rank means I have to make sacrifices. It's my responsibility to be patient with you. Educating you is impossible. I can only try to minimize your ignorance. Would you make me some little ham and cheese sandwiches with a bit of mayonnaise while I make my decision?

(l1 and l2 rush to the cat flap, and nimbly slide through it. When they have left the scene, L3 rings a small bell to summon them. They return on all fours.)

L3:   forgot. I'd also like a nice little glass of red wine.

l1 and l2: Yes, milord. Immediately.

(They exit again on all fours. Less effusively this time. L3 rings the bell once more. l1 and l2 return. They find it more difficult to get to their feet.)

l1 and l2: Yes, milord?

L3:   There's something else I want, but I can't remember what. Go away while I try to remember.

(l1 and l2 crawl back trough the cat flap. The bell summons them again. They crawl back in and move to one side of L3, making no attempt to stand.)

L3:   All this coming and going has taken my appetite away. I'm going up to the lounge for a whisky. I'll let you know my decision.

(l1 and l2 look at him expectantly. L3 adopts a distracted air. He pokes a finger in his ear and, on removing it, examines the wax and then wipes his finger on the tablecloth. He stands up, stretches his arms, and slowly cracks his knuckles. He begins to jump up and down, opening

and closing his arms and legs as if doing a warm-up drill. l1 and l2 stand stock still, their heads bowed. He eventually approaches them with a solemn expression and silently points a finger at l2. l1 and l2 leap to their feet. l2 hurriedly puts on the dinner jacket, l1 picks up the vase and hesitates between smashing it on l2 or L3. He is undecided. Finally, he puts it back in its place. With his body language displaying exhaustion, he exits alone through the cat flap. The curtain closes.)

ACT 3

(On the second floor, L2 and L3, holding a glass of whisky apiece, are seated in adjacent armchairs. A fire burns in the hearth behind them. They are laughing uproariously. They turn to slap each other on the back. The laughter dies down, the backslapping grows less frequent. Silence eventually falls. l1 is standing by the table on which rest the tray of sandwiches and the whisky bottle. The red vase stands to one side. As soon as L2 and L3 have emptied their glasses, he quickly refills them. Every so often he offers them sandwiches from the tray. They give no sign of noticing his presence.)

L2:   Yes, old boy, it's hardly possible to live these days. The way prices have gone up is atrocious. You only have to go to the supermarket to see. I send him with the same amount of money as before, and each time he comes back with fewer bags. I know because the trembling in his arms is less pronounced than it used to be. At first I thought he was stealing from me. Now we check the receipt together to avoid suspicion. And he prefers it that way, so he doesn't fall into temptation.

L3:   Oh, the cost of living. It's such a bad sign that we even have to mention it. In less vulgar times, our peers wouldn't have had to worry about it. If a well-bred gentleman behaved with propriety, life gave him the reward he deserved. Well... Cheers my friend. To the complex times we live in.

L2:   By the way, have you got your cloak ready for next week's meeting? The brothers have bought some beer mugs that hold up to five pints.

L3:   I'm devastated, but I can't be there. I leave the day before.

L2:   That's a shame. It promises to be a very special occasion. Where are you going?

L3:   To root for our Hopscotch World Cup squad. We've got the best selection in our history. This time we really are going to win.

L2:   The hopscotch championship...you do live it up. Although I don't have a wife, I can imagine how she'd feel if I announced my intention to go. It's the sort of plan she'd detest. She'd make my life impossible, harping on about it for months. I'm sorry, old boy, I'd love to accompany you, but just the implications pain me. We'll miss you at the lodge.

(L3 sits lost in thought. He has just realized something. He holds up his glass to be freshened, despite the fact that he has only drunk half his whisky. l1 moves quickly to fulfill the request.)

L2:   Is something wrong, old boy?

L3:   It's just...I don't know how to say this...(*L3 switches into Spanish.*) ¿No te parece que no deberíamos hablar de estas cosas enfrente de él?

L2:   ¿Por qué? ¿Quieres que seamos personas distintas?

L3:   No, para nada. Es sólo que preferiría no mencionar estas
        cosas en su presencia. Podría darle ideas.

L2:   Claro. Como tú digas, compadre.

(*L3 stands up again. Something has just occurred to him.*)

L2:   ¿Qué pasa ahora, camarada?

L3:   ¿No crees que sea capaz de entendernos?

L2:   Estoy seguro de que sí. Después de todo, los tres fuimos a
        la escuela juntos. Creo que incluso él se graduó con
        honores.

L3:   Cierto, cierto. Et si je parlais come ça?

L2:   I didn't understand that last bit, old boy.

L3:   E si parlo cosi?

L2:   I hear your voice, but I don't speak that language either.

L3:   To be honest, neither do I. Just picked up a few phrases
        somewhere.

L2:   So…Cheers.

(*l1 moves almost imperceptibly to stand in front of the Lords. He is
holding the vase in both hands. The Lords continue their chat, waiting
for him to leave. He stands stock still, not saying a word. When they can
no longer bear the tension, they finally turn to look at him.*)

L2:   We're fine for the moment. We'll let you know when we
        need you.

l1:   Milord could address me differently. Don't forget that, up to
        a short time ago, we were equals.

L2:   Equals? A short time ago? There's nothing before the
        present moment. I don't remember it. And what if I did?
        What difference does it make? Something that happened

a second ago is as irretrievable as something that occurred a thousand years ago.

l1: Those conceptual games are easy when you're a Lord. But scourged flesh has a longer memory. I'm very close to helping you remember. (*l1 claps the vase tightly, doing his best to control himself.*)

L3: So you did hear us? That's precisely what we want to avoid. All this paraphernalia—our suits, the expensive whisky, the fireplace—all of these things have, in essence, a principal aim: to help us forget that, however much we might pretend it's not so, our existence is just as vain as yours. Now, go. Leave us in peace!

l1: Milords are very, very intelligent. You know about these and other matters. I could well have been one of you. It's just a trick of fate that I'm not. So you could show a little more empathy.

L2: That's precisely what leads us to despise you. The consciousness we could be in your place, live your life, wear that ridiculous uniform, sleep badly in your cot, have to shit in your toilet. Not being you is the best incentive I have to go on being me.

(*A loud bang is heard and the lights go out. L3 stands up and begins to tremble violently.*)

L3: You imbecile! The fuses! How often have I told you to change the fuses?

(*l1 loses his cool. He breaks the vase over L3's head. L3 falls to the floor. L2 struggles with l1, eventually pulling out a clump of his hair. l1 hits L2 with the remaining half of the vase. He goes on hitting them both*) *until he kills them with the last solid shard of the vase. He undresses them with the same parsimony he had once used to dress them. Then he combines various parts of the two sets of clothing until he is dressed as a Lord. He pours himself a whisky, rehearses a profound expression, and sits down on a sofa. Holding up his index finger, he begins to babble nonsense, nonexistent, fragmented words, only stopping to take a sip of his whisky. When he has finished his drink, he stands up.*)

LI: Who'd have thought it? The whisky tastes exactly the same.

THE END

The excitement came to nothing. The night before, I'd thought we were making our way together through the shadows. I'd fallen asleep with the bandage still in place, partly through exhaustion, but also because I didn't want to change the slightest detail. After so much violence, I thought, I'd discovered the unreachable Nelly. The one so many dreamers had hoped to capture. Even before the deadline, fate was pronouncing in my favor. The descent had been worth the effort, a new Max was emerging, things would be different, the Many and I would be reconciled, and endless shit like that. I never tire of getting it wrong. Unless the errors belong to reality, and it's reality's cowardice that prevents it from accepting them.

But in the morning, I still asked Nelly to take off the bandage. She snipped at it with a pair of scissors, asking why I couldn't do it myself. Said she didn't have time for all my ceremonies. Or something like that. I wanted to explain what had happened. The imperceptible turn of events. When I came back from the shower, she'd gone. One of the Many had a frightening idea. I went to the wardrobe to show how wrong its malicious tale was. To show it that Nelly had slept badly, or was feeling stressed by the campaign. After all, she was as new as me to this game. The asshole was right. Nelly had taken a suitcase of clothes. But she's left others, I attempted to argue without conviction. I can't bear the Many's condescending silence. The fact that they feel sorry for me pisses me off more than their frontal attacks.

I went to Pascual's apartment to rehearse the play. Sao offered to find someone to take my role at short notice. She offered me a dignified way out, saying I should rest, because there was still a long way to go. Pascual pretended not to be listening. I can understand it: for him this is as serious as any other installation. The person writing this agrees.

The ones who live packed in the hole within my brain don't. They can't come to an agreement. Some wanted to keep pressing on. Others suggested putting an end to it all, including the campaign. Between all the pushing and pulling, someone close to me learned his lines. The scene with the vase made my blood run cold. I can't even describe the image that exploded in my head a second before.

The number of residents supporting us is growing. As is their fervor. Sao didn't even tell Pascual and me about the provocateur she'd infiltrated into the crowd. The Black Paunches dragged him out kicking, frenetically shouting, "It's a leg pull. His realism is a lie." People wanted to kill him. They silenced him with insults. The confusion ran over onto the stage.

When it was over, the three of us confessed to a pretty similar experience: at the moment when we were most fully in character, it seemed like the action was taking place offstage. That the audience was there to entertain us, to shake us out of our torpor for a while, and not the reverse. Our miniscule staging was part of the theater known as Villa Miserias. While the action's going on, no one ever asks who wrote the script. When the curtain closed on the last act, they applauded all three actors equally, as if it was unfair to take the side of an isolated element within the obvious order of things.

I returned home, expecting to sleep alone. Nelly, however, was waiting to have dinner with me. She'd changed her clothes; her hair was damp; she asked about my day with genuine curiosity. So she hadn't attended the play. I gave her a rough outline of events to gain time while finding the courage to ask the obvious question. How interesting, she said. She would have loved to be there, but had had a meeting with her aunt and the chief. Naturally, she couldn't tell me the details. But he was such an interesting man. If she hadn't been ashamed to do it, she would have taken notes right there. Everything he said was like an aphorism with different depths.

It seemed she had material to keep going like that for quite some time, so I asked why she'd showered at her aunt's and not here in our apartment. Her eyes lost their black gleam. She went to her suitcase and took out a pair of muddied jeans. Her shoes were also soaked. Was I satisfied, or was I going to keep on with my frigging suspicions? I felt like a complete idiot: I'd been caught in the mid-afternoon downpour as well. She left her meal half-eaten, and when she went to the bedroom, didn't even bother to close the door. Such was the measure of her disillusion. I went to the sofa and discovered that it wasn't so easy to sleep straight through as I had thought the other night.

DAY 6

Residents of Villa Miserias,

Many thanks for being here again with me tonight. We are at exactly the halfway point of the campaign. In the end it will be you who say where you want to take things from here. But allow me to be a little more precise: the direction our community moves in will not be decided here. Villa Miserias is an insignificant component in an automated assembly line. As I have said before, the only thing I will not do is deliberately deceive you. Neither my adversary nor I can choose any path. The plans have already been drawn out on a larger scale. What you, the voters, have to decide in five days' time is if you intend to walk the plank with your eyes open or blindfolded.

Electoral campaigns are the most visible component of the present day political mask. That mask is made up of millions of small faces content to feel, every few years, that they are participating equally in the collective whole. True. However, if we look behind the façade of equality, we find an extremely obese creature, with insatiable appetites, that will do anything to achieve its single aim: to always possess a little more of everything. The main function of the political eggshell of equality is to protect the most unequal economic base ever known.

Not even the most ambitious conqueror ever dreamed of the power that money has gained in our day. This scrap of paper with its delusions of grandeur has taken on a life of its own to the extent that ours are mere appendages to its uncontrollable instinct for reproducing itself. It has reduced human beings to nothing more than interchangeable objects on which a price can be placed. Aren't we always hearing people talking about the importance of knowing how to "sell yourself"? Even the majority of artists openly admit a willingness to sell their work to the highest bidder. Money is the source of its own system of values and it admits no competition.

Look around you. Look in the mirror. Life has become one long advertising campaign. And the product to be advertised is oneself. By assuring itself of ideological adhesion, money has managed to close the circle of the most tyrannical dictatorship ever known to mankind. Representative plutocracy is the ideal means of maintaining its rule. Can you imagine a warrior who is able, with just a few phone calls, to overpower whole nations? Money subjugates countries without the need to fire a single shot.

Its generals are anonymous: even those of the highest rank look no different to anyone else in their jeans and jackets with patches at the elbows. They're one of us. The only difference is that you will never have a super-yacht in which to sail the seas in the company of spectacular models. But that's an unimportant detail. Money's foot soldiers are no more than glorified death squadrons in that polymorphous abstraction known as "the market." Under the pretext of infinite plurality, a single code of conduct is imposed. There is only one basic way of existing in the world: theirs. After a long historical process, I can tell you that code is already, in essence, also ours.

Those bodiless barons aren't content with just the unlimited accumulation of material possessions: they also use blackmail, extortion, and usury to ensure that vast communities yield to their demands. They are particularly interested in language, although they themselves are often unaware of this. Like all tyrannies before it, the tyranny of money has understood that the best way to make its dogmas unquestionable is through the eradication of any concept that allows them to be questioned. And this is where the supreme importance of euphemism comes in. If the concepts used to name certain things are eradicated, the possibility of discussing them—even thinking about them—is automatically negated. They are not the first people to understand this, they have just put the idea into practice with amazing effectiveness.

Rather than calling them exchanges that benefit the owners to the detriment of the workers, they talk about "making the labor market more flexible." The right of the most powerful to control increasingly larger portions of strategic sectors is called "economic liberalization." The abolition of the right to unionize is known as "increasing efficiency." Usury is the price to be paid to calm nervous markets, so that a society can pay today's debts with promises of a better tomorrow.

Who are these malign beings determined to make life an affair without nuances or colors, a funereal dance involving interchangeable objects? They aren't as invisible or distant as they might seem. In fact, they are here, nearby: each and every one of us is them.

The principal mechanism for achieving hegemony is the same one in which we are all most complicit. Its most concrete contradiction is the adoration of low prices, conveniently draped in the luxury goods that situate each of us in his corresponding stratum.

The wholesale collapse of prices is only made possible by the removal of mediation, the destruction of the chain of profit margins produced by the common need to meet basic necessities. The ideal situation is a world where one single man buys each product at a price close to the cost of its production. The sales volume achieved by the sum of minute profit margins translates into fortunes greater than the wealth of entire nations. The theology of prices sanctions practices until now confined to organized crime. For example, selling below cost to bankrupt rivals is legal, always under the protection of its benefit for that implacable dictator known as the consumer. Who worries about the poverty-stricken smallholder growing tomatoes when it comes to making a small saving on the cost of the next day's salad?

Flattening everything in their path, low prices are the ideological weapon that destroys the production chain. The ultimate objective is for the chain to be composed of only two links, of just two types of person: a world divided between the rich with access to luxury goods, who increase their wealth by selling to others—to the poor—at rock bottom prices, using methods that only contribute to perpetuating their poverty. As one important businessman in Villa Miserias' commercial zone confided to me, "My business is selling cheap to the bottom of the pyramid." The tendency toward the elimination of the cost-price ratio sounds the death knell for the added value that allows intermediate producers and tradesmen to subsist. They are left with only the minimum necessary to avoid starvation, and to persuade them not to stop producing basic necessities. The problem isn't the low prices in themselves, but the concentration of wealth through which they are achieved, sweeping aside every obstacle between the monopoly of the few and the end consumer.

The duct between the two new races is organized charity. As donations are tax deductible, the rich are in charge of the competition within the public sphere to decide how the percentage of their profits that should have been handed over to the tax authorities should be employed. And then we're supposed to go down on our bended knees before their immense generosity. When did that child with worms in his guts ever dream of receiving a kiss on the forehead from the most beautiful women on the planet? The most perverse of status symbols is belonging to a club so exclusive it only admits people capable of throwing crumbs from mountaintops. That act alone is enough to forgive them for the practices that allowed them to accumulate their fortunes in the first place.

Residents of Villa Miserias, it's no coincidence that what we pray for at the moment is growth, but never an equal distribution. But what use is a larger cake if the new slices are always enjoyed by the same people? Let's not fool ourselves: the food each and every one of us needs to live is in the hands of vultures. Legal drugs are the only things that keep the factory running. We've become cannon fodder, zombies doped to produce the riches we're supposed to dream of, but never attain.

I promise you one single thing: if you elect me, I will do everything in my power to perpetuate this system. There will be a constantly increasing number of stores where you can buy an enormous variety of products, the majority of them cheap, but also the very expensive ones that will mark the differences between you.

I'll negotiate worse and worse conditions for the workers in the estate, until they get it into their heads that they are pieces of trash clogging the machinery of growth and progress.

Elect me, and I'll give you what you want: an electoral democracy that allows us to rid ourselves once and for all of the bonds that constrain us in the economic sphere. Because every consumer has the inalienable right to dedicate his life to attempting to buy everything. Let's do away with the communal restrictions that stop us doing just that. I won't be the one to oppose the most secret desire of every one of you.

We're close to coming out of the tunnel into the light. I just need one more push from you to guide you through.

"Hey Max, have you thought about what you'll do if you win?"

The question caught me off guard. I stood there staring into space as if considering the answer. In reality, I was attempting to work out who it was that was now sitting in my living room, with yet another beautiful face. I'm finding it hard to decide if it's she who changes, or if it depends on which of all those voices inside me is shouting loudest at that moment. I'm not just saying that. I really do try to limit the annoyance all this might cause her. I sometimes wonder how I'd feel about having a clown inspecting me the whole time, as if I were a statue. But I don't always resist it. I venture into the black caves without a torch to see how far I can go. I still haven't found any fissures, but the number of cracks fogs my mind. I know the pupil must be there somewhere. If only it would allow me to set up a base camp. Every time I think I've reached a summit, the mountain has moved and I find myself back on the foothills.

"Like, really, Max. Have you thought about it or not? What are you going to do if you win? The thing is that apart from the number of people who came to hear you, they seemed different from before." For the first time, Nelly was expressing some enthusiasm for the campaign.

"I haven't had time to give it any thought. Winning wasn't really my aim. I'm still not sure what it is, but that would never have occurred to me. I'm conscious of being one more variable in the questionnaire." This new inversion was casting me in the role of a nonbeliever.

"I'm really sorry. I can't give you any details, but there's one thing you should hear: they're nervous. The other day, I saw Taimado hanging around here. Like, please be careful, Max. Just remember nothing's a secret from them."

Did she really say "secret"? The word set the Many swarming. As I wanted to continue the conversation, I did my best to ignore them.

Judging by the uproar, some of them thought Nelly knew everything. And not just that, but would be willing to betray me. I'd be known as the candidate who spoke the truth to cover up his own blindness. His humiliating blindness. The least conservative of them would use much worse adjectives. Better to silence them by speaking:

"I've only done what I was asked to. They thought the residents were ready to dispense with the sweeteners. The document didn't specify how to get the message across. I've got a right to choose how. And no one's trying to hide my friends' role. I doubt if the chief is naïve enough to believe that story about the truth."

The tumult continued. Now the frigging Many were saying I was pretentious. The night before Nelly and I had slept in separate rooms. I had a feeling she wanted to call a truce, but was afraid the bastards would make life unbearable. There was nothing for it but to knock them out.

"Jeez, Max. That's just the problem. You know all about the questionnaires. You know that if you go on talking about things they don't want to come out, I don't know if they'll put up with it. Like, please Max, there's only five days left. Do it for me. You've shown what you can do. And don't try to pretend, I bet you've even enjoyed yourself. If you want, we can change things when this is over. I'm begging you not to just throw it all away."

Come off it, you lying bitch! Are you really dumb enough to believe that poor-little-me stuff? If one single word of it were true, there'd be no need for us.

I abruptly tugged Nelly's arm and she floated toward me like a newly fallen leaf. The Many were so caught up in their clamor, they didn't see the trick coming.

When we were naked, I raised my eyes to check that Nelly was still there with me. Or rather, I was there with her. I put my hands to her throat to slowly strangle her: without losing a glimmer of their black intensity, her eyes began to grow bloodshot. She slapped my face hard, asking for more. The Many were dumbfounded. Who's the wimp now, you fucking shits? Suddenly, Nelly was strangling me back.

The last thing I saw was her adept turning of the tables. Then I was in the shadows. Nelly set the standard by squeezing my throat with increasing force. Like a signal prompting us to wait for the right moment, our coughing made us both ease off a little. When we were both really struggling for breath, we knew the time had come. I heard a single, shared cry that seemed to go on forever, leaving my fingers without the strength to seal the pact for good. The cry was silenced by blackness falling over everything else. I don't know which of us passed out first. At some point, Nelly's body spilled over onto my own numbed sensibility. I have no idea how long we remained unconscious. Nor who came round first. All I know is that when Nelly recovered, she went to fetch a bedspread. We were feeling colder than the room temperature merited. When I saw her again, I held her close until I fell asleep, this time naturally. Without the need for either of us to say it, we knew the countdown had begun. We had five days to discover if there was space for a new principle.

DAY 7

NO ONE KNOWS WHAT'S GOING ON
Nelly López

Anyone who considered Max Michels' campaign to be just a stunt should think again. The truth is that his circus is pulling in more and more people. The residents at least give up their time to listen to and watch his proposals. The main problem is that no one, including himself, it seems to me, knows whether his shadow-theater spectacle is actually showing us anything or is in fact hiding something.

The Plaza del Orden had changed overnight into a gigantic board game. The territories of the world represented on the board looked like something, but who knows what it was. Michels' team had drawn the frontiers in gray, and also written some of the customs and characteristics of the various countries within their boundaries.

Half the map was dominated by Pascual Bramsos, who looked very handsome in his red beret. Candidate Michels headed the other half. He was wearing a backwards baseball cap. His discourse director was elegantly dressed, and was apparently the leader of an assembly discussing what was happening on the board. When necessary, she went to the podium to make pronouncements. Sometimes she urged them not to overdo the aggression, but they didn't usually take much notice of her. In fact, it seemed like her function was to authorize the chaos we all witnessed.

At first it seemed like the point of the game was for each side to amass the greatest number of territories. When curious residents turned up to see what was going on, either Bramsos or Michels assigned them territories. As weapons, they were given a set of giant plastic dice. In addition to giving territories to the newcomers, the leaders ran around, checking the loyalty of their troops, taking over new territories with a throw of the dice, or making pronouncements from the podium about some of their opinions. They went on like that for quite a bit until Michels came out on top. The problem is, it's not clear what he won.

Summarizing everything that happened is very difficult. The residents only saw a chaotic scene of territories being taken over by others. The dice gave orders like "swamp a neighboring country with arms until there is a massacre," or "install a military dictatorship capable of smashing kneecaps by the thousand," or "bomb reservoirs to cause famine among the population," or "organize a summit meeting to inform the locals about your practices." A few allegiances were also formed by the offer of an umbrella. But people who received the umbrellas were disillusioned to find, when they tried to open them, that only the spokes were left.

Bramsos and Michels' methods were completely different. Bramsos forced his followers to memorize a set of ten commandments, whacking them with an iron rod when they made mistakes. Some of the residents went off in a rage because the red-bereted leader took his role a bit too seriously. To calm them down, he offered a swig of some very strong liquor that knocked more than one of them out. Michels, on the other hand, won followers over with porn mags, sodas, candies, or autographed photos of celebrities. He gained territories by getting the first round. Then he asked for all their natural resources in exchange. The officials who administered his colonies stuffed themselves with hot dogs while looking at photos of blonde bombshells.

The discourse director mainly divided her time between meetings and writing drafts of speeches. But whenever one of the leaders tried to get hold of a particularly valuable territory, he'd first try to gain her approval. They mostly said they were invading because there was no respect for human rights in the territory, or no freedom of expression, or that they treated women badly, or had hostile policies. The discourse director would then consult a table of equivalences that clarified which die authorized the invasion. Each time Michels argued that civilians in his country had been attacked, she ruled that the enemy forces should be wiped out.

While this was going on, Bramsos' territories rebelled. I think the population got tired of being beaten with iron rods. And they were jealous of the fun their neighbors were having. As he was unable to put down the rebellion, Bramsos took to drinking the strong liquor. When he was completely drunk, he started concentrating the wealth of his former bloc in the hands of a few of his loyal followers. Left in the lurch, the other inhabitants tried to copy what was being done in Michels' territory. Although they didn't feel the least nostalgia for the iron rod, they began to realize that the gum they chewed in Michels' countries wasn't any great shakes either.

By the time this reporter had to leave to file her report, the board was in total chaos. No one knew who belonged to which bloc. For more than an hour, the discourse director had been giving a speech no one listened to. The giant dice were scattered all over the board. Michels was going back and forth, trying to read what was left of the gray writing to see if he had any countries left to conquer. Bramsos fell into a drunken stupor on a bench. There's no doubt that something very intense happened in Plaza del Orden, but the problem is that no one knows just what it was.

The board game left us completely exhausted, and not just physically. I'm not sure if Pascual went over the top by accident or on purpose. Sao helped him throw up before taking him home. This time she didn't even have the energy to smile: her role had left her without hope. We'd established a number of basic rules at the beginning, but had agreed to let everything else run its natural course. It's hard to make any judgment on the day: what had to happen, happened. To think otherwise would be to just perpetuate the sham.

I was thinking of leaving when Ponce turned up. Nelly was right: Taimado was not far behind him. They can look where they like, there's only one hole full of emptiness. Not even Nelly knows she knows that. Or I hope so. It's different now. Maybe the blindness was what happened before I could see her. Maybe it's only when Nelly goes dark that I can see her. Maybe I haven't got any fucking idea. I need to get through the next four days.

"I thought you'd got past the adolescent stage," said Ponce, looking down at my outstretched hand. "You know better than anyone what the chief is capable of. He's coming here, by the way. If you wait a few minutes, you'll finally meet him."

"I'm only doing what I was asked to," I replied, hoping he couldn't smell my fear. "You can say the same thing in different ways. Gridding out existence is just one of them. Your questionnaire doesn't cover as much as you all think."

His dark glasses misted with rage. "That remains to be seen. I'd like to give you a final recommendation: look in your pathetic father's book. On one of those pages there's the story of the sorcerer's apprentice who unleashed uncontrollable forces. The chief has spent years muddying certain dimensions of the residents' lives. We wanted to help them understand there's no other truth than the one communicated in cash. We're not going to run risks because someone's acting stupidly. Am I right, Taimado?"

"Uh-huh. We're only giving you one last warning, for your own good."

"Don't be fooled, Max. We've already got the missing piece. And soon we'll know where it fits. Let's go, Taimado."

How did he know about the blank book? Could Nelly possibly be the missing piece? I thought I'd better ask her to dispel my doubts.

The moment I got home, I called her name time and again. There was no answer. There was no sign of her. Then, when I'd stopped shouting, I heard a sob. I walked quietly so as not to lose the trail: it was coming from the closet. When I slid the door open, Nelly shrunk from the light. In a shaky voice, she asked me to get in there with her and shut the door. She was leaning back against the wall, wearing only a loosely wrapped bathrobe. Her eyes and nose were red. I sat beside her, the two of us sealed off from time in the darkness.

Whenever Nelly tried to say something, the tears came faster. I pressed her to my chest, begging her to calm down. She refused to explain what was wrong, but managed to sob that she was a fool, was very sorry, she hadn't known. She clung to me, pressing my body more tightly against hers. Her proximity made me feel like a monster. I'd never managed to see her because I didn't deserve to. Behind that beautiful armor was a frightened woman. Why hadn't I realized that before? Worse than anything were the ideas that came into my head at that moment. It was the perfect setting, but Nelly was a wreck. And so was I.

I swear it was she who took the initiative. At least that's what I think. At this stage, it doesn't really matter. Afterwards I lay with her head resting on my chest. She'd stopped crying. The heel of a shoe was digging into my back as I tried to persuade her we should move. We left the closet like two strangers, and lay as far as possible from each other on the bed. I waited in vain for her to say goodnight: she was most probably waiting for me to do the same. After a prolonged debate with the Many, I fell asleep before I could utter another word to her.

DAY 8

You have thirty seconds to respond, with anything that comes into your mind, to the following twenty quotations. That means a maximum of ten minutes in total:

"To see another thus. I know not what to say. I will not swear these are my hands."
Who's asking and who replies?

"…an admirable evasion of whore-master man, to lay his goatish disposition to the charge of a star."
It makes no difference if the star is outside or inside a person.

"He's mad that trusts in the tameness of a wolf, a horse's health, a boy's love, or a whore's oath."
We're taking a step backward. Calling them wolves and whores isn't acceptable any more.

"All that follow their noses are led by their eyes but blind men…"
Blind men can see the difference between shades too.

"The art of our necessities is strange, that can make vile things precious."
The wheel of need turns eternally on the same thing.

"This cold night will turn us all to fools and madmen."
Let's hope at least that we're wearing expensive clothing when it falls.

"Who's there, besides foul weather?"

The ones who are always there. The Many.

"Is there any cause in nature that makes these hard hearts?"

Blow up the environment to see if they soften.

"...yet nature finds itself scourged by the sequent effects: love cools, friendship falls off, brothers divide: in cities, mutinies, in discord; in palaces, treason..."

A man doesn't stop being a man just because he can vote.

"...know thou this, that men are as the time is: to be tender-minded does not become a sword."

Blood flows very slowly in the arteries of numbers.

"And my poor fool is hang'd!"

There are many of them nowadays, but they aren't made the way they used to be.

"'Tis the times' plague, when madmen lead the blind."

They don't want to believe there's nothing there except what has already been seen.

"...man's nature cannot carry the affliction nor the fear."

Betting on catastrophe is the source of huge fortunes.

"Why, then, your other senses grow imperfect by your eyes' anguish."

I'd give up everything else just to see her once.

"What, art mad? A man may see how this world goes with no eyes. Look with thine ears; see how yond justice rails upon yond simple thief."

Ears are no less vain than eyes.

"When the mind's free, the body's delicate: the tempest in my mind doth from my senses take all feeling else save what beats there."

On the road to the abyss, unexpected scenes appear that will never abandon you.

"The quality of nothing hath not such need to hide itself."

Lungs process the only air at their disposition.

"You have seen sunshine and rain at once: her smiles and tears were like a better way: those happy smiles that play'd on her ripe lip seem'd not to know what guests were in her eyes; which parted thence as pearls from diamonds dropt."

Nelly, Nelly, Nelly. That's Nelly.

"The prince of darkness is a gentleman: Modo he's call'd, and Mahu."

And Selon Perdumes.

"...I am ashamed that thou hast power to shake my manhood thus; that these hot tears, which break from me perforce, should make thee worth them."

I know now that manliness only exists through its absence.

Sao was very serious about the test she'd prepared. She says it's a relaxing warm-up for the debate. In the end, the drama about the king who dethrones himself only to see his daughters betray him comprises all other dramas that followed it, including present ones. The one thing still clear to me is the corrosive power of the naked truth. Deception is the basis of a happy beginning: an inability to lie unleashes generalized disaster. Sao is right when she says no one has ever again formulated a more profound psychology of power. She'd like to have all the candidates take the test. She quite rightly thinks it might save us unpleasant surprises.

The pretense of transparency articulates the new deception. The illusion of knowing everything allows what is most fundamental to remain hidden. Ponce's model claims that for every scandal exposed, 235 others are never discovered. What's pertinent here is thinking we're not being tricked any longer, even though we know that, by necessity, we are. Who would really want to know his partner's erotic fantasies? Romantic relationships would be impossible. I envy those who manage to believe they're the only one.

It's the same with poverty, ignorance, corruption, racism, snobbery, and all the rest. They're not just mishaps in the process of being eliminated: they're endemic to the present social organization. The man who analyzed the Great Transformation stated clearly that the main difference between the past and the present is that before, when there was enough for everyone, it was inconceivable that some would go hungry. With the exaltation of egoism, many were condemned to become the basic ingredient in the march of the machine. The mass production of poor people ensures that they accept being exploited by those able to exploit them, to divest them of everything but the minimum needed for them to continue producing at low cost. And they'd better be grateful for the chance to serve.

Millions don't even have that, and so are willing to accept much worse conditions. Official discourse and the charitable foundations try to salve guilty consciences: the cripple with the gangrenous leg, thrown out into the street, is not a pretty sight for anyone. Patience. The time will come. We just have to progress a little further. The more the very few amass, the more crumbs will fall to the ground to be fought over to the death. Is there enough for everyone to live the way I do? The answer to that question puts you on either the side of the thieves or the dispossessed.

The trick is for everyone to be united in denunciation. Admitting to the existence of the rot guarantees its perpetuation. I remember the concert organized in Villa Miserias to buy new shoes for the workers. They didn't raise enough for even a tenth of them. The real situation didn't interest anyone. What was important was to express concern: "You know what? I'll just do another line of coke to relieve my suffering."

This time a truce wasn't even tabled. Nelly shut herself up to go over her notes. I tried asking her what she'd been referring to the night before, but she didn't know what I was talking about: "Oh, Max, forget it. You might not believe it, but I was crying about something that has nothing to do with you." Really. It's the truth. And she'd got a lot of work to do. She was under pressure. I went to bed and watched television so not to miss her presence. It was her who slept on the sofa. I had an awful night. Nelly got up early, looking very rested. I'm becoming more and more alone. I can't even count on my sofa now.

DAY 9

THE CREAM PIE DEBATE
Nelly López

With only three days to go, the election debate finally came around. Max Michels' eccentric campaign made us think we'd see something different there too. But no one expected what did happen: his opponent, Modesto González, received a barrage of cream pies. Michels neither confirmed nor denied that he'd planned the attack. And his only declaration didn't make anything clearer: "If you're determined to go on sweetening the cesspit we live in," he warned after the second cream pie had landed right in the middle of Gonzaléz's face, "it's only to be expected that some people will decide to carry things to their logical consequence."

The most surprising thing is that the other candidate didn't raise a hair. During the whole debate, he acted as if he was a shop dummy with pre-recorded cassettes inside him. He repeated the same old policies in the same old tone, and made automatic gestures, never showing the palms of his hands. He didn't even clean the cream off his glasses after the attacks, just went on speaking as if nothing had happened, expressing his good intentions with a cream-pie face.

The audience wasn't willing to identify who had thrown the missiles. When the event had finished, the Black Paunches licked the fingers of suspects they picked out at random, but nothing. To judge by the sour looks of the Paunches, the residents were using their ingenuity to protect themselves. In the end, there were no arrests.

And there was no need for them anyway. González was celebrating with his followers in a marquee set up right next to the main stage. His team released a shower of gray confetti as he was making his triumphal entry, and the bits of paper stuck to the cream on his face. With his hands laced over his head, he went on wagging his elbows in celebration for a few minutes until all his followers left.

A pretty obvious change has taken place in Michels during the campaign. His standpoint has become more and more obscure, like he feels more and more comfortable in the dark. His campaign promises are like maxims. In the debate, he said he'd bring in policies that separated the residents further from each other. He also told them he'd fulfill his promise to make them self-reliant. To no longer have to feel guilty because they have more than the bunglers, the people with no ambition, the lazy bastards (dear readers, forgive my language, but that was the term he used), the idlers, the weak, and the dregs of society in general who don't want to add their push to the progress of Villa Miserias. The most powerful words of that night were when he said that if you can't bear seeing the workers eating leftovers, then don't go to the canteen at mealtimes. Period. He finished off the debate with a pronouncement that showed no pity for anyone: "Forget apologizing for being what we are! I'm not offering the best for each one of you, only for those of you who are able to get it."

The residents gave him a wholehearted ovation. Some of them were waving around cardboard axes with what looked like blood on the blades, very probably handed out by his campaign team. So maybe the tide has turned and Michels has won over the dark side of the residents. At least that's how it seemed during the debate.

There's no going back now. The borderline used to seem to me a punitive concept, more like a warning than a reality, until I suddenly crossed it. That image of not stopping when going downhill is incomplete. It forgets to mention that first you have to scale the huge desire to run headlong down the slope. I wanted to be one of the great majority who graze placidly across the plains. Not to have to confront either steep upward paths or vertiginous descents. On election day, I intend to take another look at my father's secret hiding place. We'll see if I'm destined for martyrdom or villainy. That's if I have the guts to find out.

I hadn't realized the managers were cream-pie proof. There's no way of stopping them. Modesto González spoke about the importance of selling the best of Villa Miserias. Maximizing the profitability of our image. Taking full advantage of the brand. Each new layer of cream made him stronger. Anonymity gave him a more clearly defined character. Big Brother mentioned the importance of a flesh and blood figure that could attract emotions. The wheel hasn't moved on, but it is still turning. We are no longer monitored from any specific center. We're kneaded into shape by abstract forces, emphatic maxims, mysterious, remote entities. The law always favors those who make the rules. Feelings are numbed. The protest is always the same, the photo of a woman covered in blood. This time they've gone too far! And then, back to reproducing the chain of subjugation at every level.

The bosses make corporate retreats to encourage unity with the workers. That complicity authorizes the later trampling underfoot. Those at the vanguard of thought have as many as three mansions. Union leaders say that seeing them arrive in luxury cars raises the workers' morale. The talking cream pie was right when he said it makes no difference which of us wins. And although he didn't state it openly, the reason is obvious.

Political struggle is a form of entertainment floating over an implacable economic base. The workforce is so flexible that it's not even a workforce anymore. Just cheap pieces of machinery, discarded without the least ceremony.

The front row of notables was there, with one empty seat, as usual. The chief wouldn't be long in coming: until, once more, he didn't. To calm my nerves, I tried finding differences between them, but they just melded together like a shapeless gob of spit. I shook my head gently to settle myself back in my mind. That apparent lightness of a liquid allows it to spread unhindered, and it's not until you try to stand up that you understand its incredible weight.

Sao and Pascual are as fed up as I am. We're not going to meet up again until election day. Even though I still haven't finalized the precise details of my plan, they mustn't suspect what it is. Sao would be too frightened. She knows me better than anyone, but not well enough. I really don't want to cause them pain. What they don't know is that I've still got more doors to open.

I was so absorbed in my thoughts when I left the debate that I almost tripped over Juana Mecha's broom. She must have been waiting for me. I gave her a huge hug to stop myself crying. She examined me with her hands on her chin, as if trying to work out who was standing before her. I think it's the first time I've seen her dismayed: "The eye that sees and is seen by the dragon's gaze ends up seeing and being seen by the dragon's gaze." She kissed my cheek before returning to her sweeping. Her shift had ended some hours before.

I turned the key and kicked open the door. A deal's a deal. It was late already, too late for that committed journalist air. The darkness of her eyes made me reckless. There were only a few nights left before the final cavern.

Without uttering a word, I pulled Nelly toward the bedroom. She asked in a whining voice what was wrong with me. I responded by practically dragging her along, with her struggling to free herself from my grip. I planted myself in front of her, pressing her to me with both arms. She shook her head as if begging me, but all I could hear were the orders of the Many, who were, by then, massively overexcited, out of control. I threw her onto the bed and unfastened her belt. Her body was struggling so fiercely against me that all I managed to do was break the belt in two. That's when she gave me the slap that prematurely blinded me. With her scratching and kicking, I tore off her jeans. Panting with fear, she pleaded with me to stop. But every moan aroused me a little more. Grabbing hold of her hair with one hand, I stood to take off my own clothes. I was going to possess her, whether she liked it or not. She took advantage of my distraction to stretch out a hand in search of some object. I was already down to my briefs when I felt a stabbing pain in my thigh. A pair of nail scissors had drawn a glob of blood. When I pulled the scissors out, it hurt more than the original injury.

With blood-splattered horror, I began to mutter pusillanimous apologies. I wasn't myself. I didn't know what I was doing. I pleaded with her to forgive me. She snarled, angrier than ever before. Then she leapt into the bathroom and returned with a roll of bandage. "So, you sorry excuse for a man. Don't even move." She wrapped a strip of the bandage around my wounded leg and used the rest to tie my hands behind my back. Next, she finished undressing and mounted me. Her eyes were afire with pure disdain. Then came the insults, the blows, the bites, and the caresses. I'd never experienced such an exciting sense of panic. We were so involved I didn't even notice the arrival of the blindness. My other senses were trembling in hypertrophy. Then came the calm.

As a final punishment, she didn't untie my hands for the whole night, but she did clean my wound before going to sleep, and again in the morning. I lay studying the cut for what seemed an eternity: I knew it was going to leave a permanent scar.

DAY 10

LEARNING TO SEE IN THE DARK. AN INTERVIEW WITH CANDIDATE MAX MICHELS
Nelly López

The election is almost upon us. Max Michels arrives punctually for his appointment at the news office of *The Daily Miserias*. He is limping and says he had a domestic accident. He looks evasive. Like a gambler who's seen the last card but is waiting his moment to turn it over. His close-shaven head shows his rapidly receding hairline. Looking into his eyes, you'd say he was a stranger even to himself. His destiny is on the point of arrival, but he's still in total darkness. He still knows nothing about his future. He tells me he's ready to answer the first question.

Are you going to go back to being an anonymous office worker or do you think you'll be a new kind of president?
It's not up to me. The voters make the decision. I've made my position very clear. I don't want any more deception, no matter how beautiful it is. Either we face things as they are, or you've seen the last of me. That's why there have been a great many people before me who could certainly make a better job of it.

During this campaign, you've often projected an image of uncertainty. At times it seems like you're doing the one thing you've always wanted to, but at others it feels like you despise the whole thing, and want to return

to your former life. If you could choose your future, which would it be?
I think you're laying traps with that question. By this point, I don't
have a past life. Not even in my memory. This experience has
affected every past and future fiber of my being. I'm very close to
discovering what color it will finally be. But, in any case, there's no
use pretending I'm here of my own free will. I've spent many hours
trying to discover if it started as my idea or someone else's. I don't
know if I set my sights on something I couldn't achieve, or if the
goal I can't achieve chose me, and I went along with it.

Having said the, what happens in the future depends on my
ability to be myself. If my fellow citizens accept me with all my
contradictions, we'll go ahead. In political campaigns, just as in
love, you have to make concessions. But if this becomes official, the
situation changes. I can't do my job under the constant threat of
being replaced by someone better. Neither my soul nor my body
could bear it. It's time to speak straight. I'll soon know if my song
wants to be heard, or if I should take it somewhere else.

Don't you think that's just the easy way out? You're passing the buck.
Either they accept you as you are or nothing. That way, you've got both
success and failure covered, and neither of the two are your responsibility.
Do you think you're so exceptional that we'll accept blackmail?
I don't think I'm exceptional. Just the reverse. I don't have any
exceptional traits. I'm sure there are plenty of others capable of
offering what we already know all too well. It's very likely they'd
be better bets. What makes me different is the fact that I don't consider myself to be superior. The only thing is that if I'm going to
continue along this road, I won't have any part in deliberate farces.

I might accept the bleakness of the environment, but that doesn't mean I don't think there's a part that shines, that makes me think it's worth staying here. But what I don't want to do any longer is to use kindly stereotypes to describe the darkness.

It's so easy to spout logical theories that finally translate into violence against the weakest. But be careful, because the naked truth can be more brutal than a deception that works for both sides. How can we be sure you'll manage to maintain order without crossing your own boundaries? I think physical violence is just the most unsophisticated expression of violence in general. True, psychological terror is more bearable, but it's also true that it compensates for its lower levels of intensity by its lasting effects.

Do you think revealing relationships can lead to outbreaks of violence? I'm sure you do. What I would ask in this case is why you concentrate only on the visible violence and not on the violence underlying it. If the slave rebels when shown the whip, is the person responsible for that act of rebellion the one who taught him he was being whipped?

People who know about these things say there are always dissident voices in any form of order. The typical agitators who threaten the status quo with their protests. And what's more, it's common for them to disrupt the functioning of an important part of society. How do you intend to deal with those voices that disagree with the direction you've taken? It's been a long, tortuous road. I've already, in fact, had to confront the shrieking of innumerable cowardly voices. They know my weakest points well, and can sense the moment when they'll face least resistance to their main objective. They want to maintain the chaos that provides them with their particular way of life. Let me give you an example. Throughout this whole phase, an anonymous group has been determined to confuse me by means of aggressive pronouncements. At every opportunity, they have questioned my ability to meet the challenge I decided to take on. They have resorted to the lowdown method of offering whatever bait they can come up with, knowing that some of it will be taken.

If I may, I'd like to take advantage of this space to tell them, straight out, that—for practical reasons rather than some personal belief— I intend to tolerate those voices, learn to live with them, rather than attempting to silence them. I've realized that frontal attack only strengthens them. So, I intend to use my energy to differentiate between the constructive voices and the sadistic ones. Since I have no choice but to listen to all of them, it will be my privilege to decide which ones it's important to enter into negotiations with, and which will have to be ignored until no one can hear them any longer.

It seems like there's no place for compassion in your vision. Although it might appear contradictory, when you see a person who's hurt you has a pair of scissors stuck in his leg, you might feel like helping him. Don't you think your crusade for the unvarnished truth will, in the end, lead you to see reality just in terms of black and white?

Once again, it's just the opposite for me. The black and white are produced by the need to see everything as rosy hued. The majority of people concerned about general well-being are in fact more worried about their concern than general well-being as such. A sharp musician summed it up in an incontestable definition: "Cocaine Socialism."

Renouncing what is unnecessary for life is achievable. What's standing in the way of living with what we need and sharing the rest with others? Quite simply our thirst for capturing the infinite in each moment of existence. Compassion functions as a modern form of the selling of indulgences, except now you don't have to wait for death to receive the key to paradise. Every act of charity sates more guilty consciences than hungry stomachs. Every year, Villa Miserias breaks its own record for charitable donations. But has the chronic poverty that charity is there to combat diminished? Not in the least. The differences are increasingly insulting. It's lucky for clear consciences that absolution has a price, a price each one of us sets, and that, on the whole, doesn't in any way affect our ability to enjoy life as we wish. By just handing over a check to people we wouldn't share a toilet with unless it'd first been disinfected, we tick the box of social responsibility.

It's very easy to heal the wound caused by a pair of nail scissors. But more complicated to make a serious examination of the structural causes of that all-out warfare. Stabbing with scissors is a legitimate defense to a cowardly act. But even so, you can't avoid the explosion of violence by just repudiating it. An understanding of the reasons for its existence is also necessary.

In my vision, it's the nuances—the different layers of reality— that stop us putting off until tomorrow the possibility of finding a better way of living together. Let's accept that all we have, each day, is the present moment. And for that succession of presents to produce a different panorama, we first have to take a look at ourselves in the mirror that our ideas, norms and institutions want to permanently cloud.

If things had started differently, they wouldn't have ended this way. When I lost my self, we were both lost. Unless at the bottom of the hole there's a different reality, with more than one tone. My father's dead and gone. Forget the idiotic stories. I'm almost ready to find out what's left for me to do.

When I entered her aunt's apartment for the interview, I saw Nelly's suitcases. She claimed it wouldn't be ethical for us to sleep together on the day of the election. Her professional coolness showed me yet another facet of her personality. Even the Many repented their excesses. We joined forces in turning back the clock. The scissors came out of the wound. The blood went back into the vein. Instead of being thrown onto the bed, Nelly sprang at me like a panther. Each reversal of events added a portion of clarity to the shadow. Rather than strangling each other while trying to piece together a completely black jigsaw, we were composing a photo in which only Nelly and I fit, with no place for Perdumeses, Ponces, Taimados, Bramsoses, or Candelarios. What could all the stupidity matter to us when we were capable of looking at each other that way? Both the beginning and end of the ball of wool were present in that first moment. The Many accompanied me in the lament: if only we'd known how to roll it…

The interview was a fencing match with rubber foils. I hadn't expected what came afterwards, so it didn't occur to me to wear a mask. The basic function of our unflagging conflict was made clear. So many scenes we could have avoided if we'd accepted what anyone else could have seen. Juana Mecha warned me from the very first day. But I didn't then know I was already blind. A home built on mutual resentment is astonishingly durable. Each blow adds a new layer to the walls, isolating it from contact with other possibilities, until they become so thick that only an enormous implosion can bring them down. Which of the two of us will have the courage to set off the device?

Perhaps as a final act of revenge, or maybe a final penance, Nelly decided she wanted some idea of what it meant to see nothing. It was almost a scientific experiment, making me recall the scraping sound of my mother's pencil as she made notes on insects. Nelly undressed in front of me, taking time to fold her clothes. Her black eyes were fixed on mine with no intention of deviating. I too undressed as if about to undergo a medical examination. Nelly began trying out cause and effect variants, making careful note of what my eyes reflected. A sense of imposture prevented me from relaxing before each new technique. I think she came to the conclusion that the crossover point was further on. She lay beneath me to try it in the traditional position, without the need for fireworks. The last thing I saw was her eyes closing. Even the sounds we made creaked like rusty metal. Throughout the torment, I could sense the palm of her hand feeling out the boundaries of my darkness. She passed it in front of my temporarily nonfunctioning eyes, opened my eyelids, pressed my temples as if trying to reactivate something, anything. A feeble wail dented my eardrum. I was in no mood for crying out anything: neither the truth nor lies.

I lay face down, waiting the usual period for the blindness to pass. Nelly took her folded clothes and went to the empty study. I dozed for a few minutes, trying to gather the energy to go home. The sun was still in the sky. I noticed concerned expressions on the faces of residents, surprised to see me walking around barefoot, my shirt only half buttoned. Just one day to go. My destiny anxiously awaits me in my father's hiding place. Maybe he already knows which way the chips will fall.

DAY II

Residents of Villa Miserias,

Tomorrow will decide if I'm talking to you here for the last time. You all know who I am by now. And at the given moment I'll hear the decision about my future.

The first man to encapsulate society in an air-conditioned bubble explained that laws are a reflection of the collective consciousness. Crime and other transgressions express a rejection of the established order. In that way, they have the important function of modifying the rules in relation to changes in the communal pulse. The profound change in the politics of our times has consisted of individualizing the act of taking that pulse. We are not to be a whole made up of innumerable interlinked parts. Instead, each part wants to be a small whole in perpetual expansion. Politics must limit itself to allowing each and every one of those wholes to float or sink, according to their own abilities. We have to state the obvious: the other, as such, is irrelevant; in the majority of cases, it is nothing more than a fly with an irritating buzz. Its only importance is as an appendage to satisfying personal impulses; as a component in a micro-fiefdom headed by each individual. Society has to understand itself as a pact between swarms of those fiefdoms, seamlessly armored against ties that oblige them to be interdependent.

Just as in other times, homosexuality offended sensibilities—and was punishable by imprisonment—within a few years, formally recognizing the presence of others will be equally anachronistic.

The notion of minimum rights will be sentimental hypocrisy, a criminal attack on the satisfaction of purely egotistic desires. G.B.W. Ponce has demonstrated that for 93% of residents, the person most loved and admired is himself. The consequence of positing individualism as the highest value is the insatiable need to express ourselves to others in increasingly shameless ways. The supreme vector is exclusivity: only I and very few others can enter here, and those that do must share my characteristics.

Like any other political mask, the present one covers an economic base involving highly diverse relationships, including, of course, contemporary variants on slavery. Because what else do you call a relationship in which one side works an extra seven hours without being paid for them; in which his wages are lower because he lives and eats in a dark corner of the gilded cage he has to polish every day; in which he lacks medical insurance or a pension for his premature old age; in which he is ridiculed for his appearance, habits, and language, both on television and in person; in which he is punished for eating the high-class food destined exclusively for the bosses and their offspring? The language that abolishes differences of caste operates as a sedative force against outbursts of unrest. Considering the servants as "one of the family" allows the person who does so to trample those servants underfoot and say it's for their own good.

Speaking of equality between unequals, the transparency of the dark, the freedom of prisoners, justice for the illiterate, and, above all, the democracy of the elites, are all supremely effective cover-ups. Positing these concepts in the abstract, expressed solemnly in flowery speeches, is a means of allowing the reality that contradicts them on every street corner to be ignored. Just as in personal relationships, it's a matter of fooling ourselves into believing no one is cheating on us. Shutting your eyes and pretending things are just the way we want them to be. While playing our role as vigilant citizens, we're living the fantasy of the mother who thinks that, by spying on her son every day, she really knows his deepest secrets.

The cost of campaigns is constantly increasing. Consultants go into every detail, plan every gesture and phrase. Slogans are more and more just slogans. When faced with such perfectly produced candidates, can we really believe we learn anything relevant from our mass-produced contests? Ponce has shown that 67% of electoral promises are broken, 74% never fully put into practice, and, on average, 49% of what candidates say is lies. Do any of you have a problem with that? Does it weaken your desire to go to the polling booth tomorrow? The performance has to be played through from the start every time the big top is raised. What would the circus be without its enthusiastic spectators?

What I propose, then, is an administration without precedents in words, if not in deeds. I'll gladly accept the task of increasing the tax levels of the lower strata. I'll cut unproductive spending on such anachronisms as curing illnesses, and so-called spiritual activities that are no use to anyone. Our task will be to construct the market stalls, install electricity and a water supply, organize a transportation system so stall-holders and customers will flock there, and equip the Black Paunches so they can prevent any questioning of the rules of the game. After that, each one of you is on your own. You'll soon see that one can get used to anything.

We'll add new layers of normalcy over the preceding ones. There'll be no nostalgia: the only past will be the present, flanked by the specter of a future that threatens to be always worse.

I offer to put politics at the service of the economy. The rational consumer will be supreme. Exalting the consumer in this way also means exalting the entities, businesses, candidates, entertainers, intellectuals, and sportsmen most skilled in producing cohesive majorities. The more adherents a cause has, the more it can weave them together with the most visceral impulses. Our motto will be to give less and less so it stretches further. It's the triumph of the unlimited satisfaction of individual consumption over the perverse Utopia of providing essential needs for everyone. Every vote for me is a vote for ostentatious consumption. I promise the floor will be below ground level for the vast majority. Don't worry, those of you who get a foot on the ladder won't be able to see them, even with binoculars.

Let's get it straight, once and for all: poverty is not an evil to be eradicated by development. On the contrary, it is a vital component of the present social fabric. It is the fuel that keeps society productive. While there is need, there will be no limit to how low we set the standard of what is acceptable. It has to be combated in theory, with crumbs, but never from the structures that create it. Think about it for a minute: how can the millions squandered by the authorities to promote their image be justified in the face of so much basic lack? The poor are an enormous blessing for our societies. It's about time we at least got that clear. The notion that the market corrects excess is an absurd fallacy: the market is excess. It's our inalienable right to live any way we want, without limits being imposed by the miserable existence of others. Can you imagine what it would be like if there really was universal higher education? Who would clean up the shit of those able to pay not to have to do it themselves?

Big Brother said that the best way to get possession of something is by stating it belongs to everyone. Our age has gone further, it has managed to move beyond the fetish of property: money has understood that the best way to govern in the interests of the few is by convincing the others that this, in fact, coincides with the well-being of the whole. Any sacrifice is justified if it keeps those few safe. As long as they go on getting drunker and drunker, the sweat of their hangovers will drip from their brows. Let's be ready with a cloth to clean up the wake they leave as we watch them pass at high speed.

One final warning: there is no other Wonderland than this. Let's stop projecting its fantastic features onto the one we have constructed together. Let's dare to look at our own side of the mirror, and no longer fear to confront our own gutted image.

Tomorrow will tell if we shall see each other again.

In the meantime, thank you.

I got back, hoping she would have changed appearance. What would it be like to break the rules for the umpteenth time? I looked around for some article of clothing that smelled of her, but only found my mental snapshots. It seems that the Many have softened their stance. I think they do this so as to be able to go on giving me shit. Now they're presenting her to me as irresistible. Kind. They're converting my anxiety into pure longing. Why did I let her go? There will never be another like her.

I soon tired of listening to them. I needed to open my father's secret compartment. I went to the bookcase in the living room and removed two heavy books in Latin—a language as unintelligible for him as their content—to reveal the sliding wooden panel. I carefully checked the gun: it was lighter than I remembered. It seems to be in perfect order, the bullets are ready to obey orders. I still have a little time to decide whom to fire them at.

EPILOGUE

"Anyway," Howard, the old fellow, said, "anyway, gold is a very devilish sort of a thing, believe me, boys. In the first place, it changes your character entirely. When you have it your soul is no longer the same as it was before. No getting away from that. You may have so much piled up that you can't carry it away; but, bet your blessed paradise, the more you have, the more you want to add, to make it just that much more. Like sitting at roulette. Just one more turn. So it goes on and on and on. You cease to distinguish between right and wrong. You can no longer see clearly what is good and what is bad. You lose your judgment."

The Treasure of the Sierra Madre

B. Traven

I

Max Michels woke up a few minutes before the alarm clock sounded. It was still completely dark outside. And inside. He made an effort to return to his last dream. Its content was blurry, but he yearned to prolong the sensation. Even though it was present in his consciousness, in reality it had disappeared. He opted for getting up and moving.

This key decision was as critical as having registered as a candidate. You could say it was his deformed sister, hidden in the basement to protect her from her own abomination. The years of being locked up had made her unpredictable. Max had no illusions about his ability to control her. He would be an active spectator to the last moment. After that would come the uncertain tones. The only sure things were the background colors.

He attempted to slip past the mirror on his way to the shower. His reflection, however, was waiting to force him to stop. He imagined himself as he had so often been, his nose painted purple. The difference now was that his complexion was less soft, his eyes looked out over dark bags, and there were indelible lines on his forehead. The ink of that tattoo his father had made had sunk into the deepest layers. No treatment could remove it, unless he was prepared to slice off his own skin down to the arteries. Max and his reflection shrugged simultaneously. The book with its blank pages was about to be closed forever.

Before leaving, he put on his beige raincoat. Although the weather didn't merit wearing it, it was the only item of clothing in which he could hide the gun for the whole day without arousing suspicion.

He inspected Bramsos' purple boat. The inverse gravity that kept it in contact with the wave seemed weaker, tired of struggling to avoid the fall into the void. Looking closer, Max believed he could see an almost imperceptible crack separating it from the wave.

Only an act of faith had prevented its fall.

He took down the painting to confront the axiom inherited from his father and ran a finger over each letter, as if wanting to discover if this tactile reading would offer a different meaning, some alternative interpretation that would make him veer from his collision course. There was no alternative. The decision was undaunted. He repeated the sentence aloud before slamming the door: "The measure of each man lies in the dose of truth he can withstand."

As he was going out of the building, he met Juana Mecha and immediately noticed that something was different: there were no bristles on her broom to sweep up the waste. With a melancholy air, she was scraping the handle against the ground with a sound that set Max's teeth on edge. Without interrupting her mechanical movements even to raise her head, Mecha whispered a half-hearted barb:

"If you puncture the dark, all you'll do is surround yourself with blacker, louder lightning and thunder."

2

He walked uncertainly to Plaza del Orden. The unwritten rule was for candidates to abstain from participating in the electoral assembly of their own buildings. Etiquette required them not to muddy what should be a foregone conclusion: only Severo Candelario had achieved the feat of losing on his home ground.

Max stopped before entering the territory where a part of his future would be decided. The outcome would not weaken his resolution; it would be simply an additional factor that inclined him toward one of the possible sides. At least that was what he thought at that moment.

He stood observing the forty-nine battalions tearing into each other at the tops of their voices. It was going to be a long day. To judge by appearances, the assemblies had more than enough orators. When the last resident of each building had vented his desire to express an opinion, they would proceed to the ballot box. After that came the count that would determine who had won. $uperstructure would be in charge of the final computation, weighing up the relative wealth of the voters. As he watched a Black Paunch haranguing his troops, Max smiled affectionately, knowing Building B's vote didn't even count for a twentieth part of the weighting of the wealthiest buildings.

He went on his way without removing his hand from his pocket. If the lead came out on the side of the chosen target, Max would be absolved of responsibility, although the sin would still have to be atoned for. If there was anyone left standing capable of atonement.

But first, he had to make a few visits. He smiled to see Candelario in the distance, sitting on his bench. Just as he did at every election, the former schoolmaster was mounting a guard of honor for his fallen tree. Max imagined a series of photos showing Candelario taking his portrait of the tree at the same time each morning. He had aged with dignity. And if his shoulders were slightly shrunken, they could still bear the weight of the head always turned in the same direction.

When Max sat beside him, attempting to maintain silence, Candelario gave him an affectionate pat that Max interpreted as an apology: If I still believed in all this, I'd undoubtedly vote for you, my boy. In exchange for these words, Max asked the schoolmaster to do the thing that gave him greatest pleasure: to tell, one more time, the tragic story of his tree.

Candelario gladly gave himself up to the memory of his only passion. He was unstinting in the details of his description of the willow. Muscular but sensitive. It had a wise lightness of spirit. It hadn't given those Paunches the pleasure of seeing it shed a single tear. Its wood had died in the serpentine form of the glowing embers that had burned in so many hearths around Villa Miserias.

As the story washed over him, Max thought that, in the end, Candelario had triumphed over his executioners. His tale opened a hole in time: he was capable of seeing the tree with absolute clarity. Once again its flesh was torn by the Black Paunches' toothy grins. Severo Candelario had achieved the only variant of immortality given to the human species. When Max stood to express his sentiments with an embrace, the former schoolmaster offered him a firm handshake and, to Max's perplexity, a concise explanation:

"They destroyed me by slicing up the trunk. But they've done something worse to you. They pulled out your roots until you became something different from what you could have been."

3

He walked on to the fountain that had so often gotten him out of a predicament. The deeper his tribulation, the clearer its waters seemed. The problem was that now, even the least trickle threatened to swamp him. Max was unsure if he was raising his head for air, or if the movement in fact tended to pull him down and so diminish any instinct to resist. What could have once been considered lifesaving gulps seemed, at that moment, more like artifices for prolonging the existential torture. Fear of sinking meant remaining, of his own free will, in the liquid mud. The effort needed to get out and breathe wasn't worth it. Was that you? he silently asked the Many, more from genuine curiosity than any desire to get involved in an argument.

When Max arrived at the laundry, he took the poem that sealed his pact with Sao from the pocket of his pants. After so much rough handling, the words were almost indecipherable. The passage of time had, however, preserved them in his memory: he had no need for his eyes. He crushed the sheet of paper in a trembling hand then, sensing its weight against his fingers, relaxed the pressure that was asphyxiating it. Looking around distractedly for a trash can, he was relieved not to find one. He couldn't risk that paper falling into the wrong hands.

He began tearing it up and then patiently swallowed every last scrap. Inside, Sao was diligently going about her work. To Max it seemed that the different stages of her task were reduced to one. Even when she was focused on her work, her almond-shaped eyes held an indelible smile. Max stood unseen, quietly observing her from a distance. Everything necessary was there within her. Both the questions and the answers. Who? Why? They were more a method than a destination. When she opened herself to the outside world, Sao provided a channel for a profound impulse, and Max understood how lucky he was to be one of the recipients into which that generous impulse flowed. The least he could do in return was not cause her any more harm. He would stop being an ulcer in perpetual need of her care. He stopped short when it occurred to him that saying how sorry he was would put an end to his plans. He thought it over for a few seconds. When Sao lifted the handset to answer a phone call, Max took advantage of her distraction to flee.

4

Max's hand, fed up with the vacillation of the person who normally controlled it, rapped on the door of Pascual Bramsos' studio. The artist appeared, covered from head to toe in plaster: he was putting the finishing touches to the mold for a bronze sculpture to commemorate the campaign experience. He was thinking of calling it "The Torments of Elias."

The plaster mold consisted of a line of three life-size figures of varying heights, and in a variety of postures. The first was a man, standing looking down another who was kneeling before him with a bowed head. Together they formed the traditional image of the conferral of a knighthood. What distinguished this scene was that, rather than lightly tapping the man's shoulders with his sword, the standing man was digging dozens of barbs into his subject's curved back. To one side, a third, smaller figure was observing the scene from above, his head raised. He was on his knees, one hand resting on the surface of the enormous box to which he was attached by a chain around his neck that allowed him a little room for movement. This man's free hand was occupied in sticking similar barbs into his own back, which was even more densely pierced than the other's. And he was digging them in deeper as he was instinctively aware of where they would cause most pain.

Max contemplated the scene, freed from his former envy. That was what he had come to say. Despite competitive complexes, the thing that had united them since childhood still existed. At some point, Max had unconsciously strayed off track, and had begun to believe his own calumnies against his friend. He didn't want to miss the opportunity to explain this.

"Pascual, I've been behaving like a jerk."

"Why do you say that, Max?" asked Bramsos in surprise, smearing more plaster onto his brow as he wiped off the sweat.

"Because I let myself be carried away by real chickenshit feelings. And I didn't know how, or didn't want to block them."

"Max, I can guarantee that's no worse than my own judgment of myself. Or the way I've felt about you."

"You forgive me, then?"

"There's nothing to forgive. One secondary effect of our times is that our images of ourselves are so fragile. We idolize ourselves through the approbation of others. I'm more conscious than anyone of my baser instincts, but I can't eradicate them. All I can do is to keep them in check. There's no more egotistic love than the one that demands perfection in the other in return. Go ahead, tell me your gut feelings about me. It doesn't change a single thing." Bramsos had noted Max's sweating palm moving to the pocket of his raincoat. "What are you thinking of doing with that?" he asked, as if inquiring about any other fun plan.

"Something. I'm not sure what yet."

"I'm not smart enough to make you change your mind about anything. Just think carefully about whether it's worth obeying those calls. You'll always be Max for me."

A contented silence fell over them. Whatever happened, the three paper boats were united at the cusp of their powers. If their respective falls were horizontal, vertical, bumpy, brilliant, light, cushioned, or bloody, it didn't change anything. As if wanting to convert himself too into a plaster statue through human contact, Max hugged Bramsos tightly before heading off on his way.

5

Max was handed a free copy of *The Daily Miserias* and, from habit, immediately looked for Nelly. He leafed through the paper from front to back several times, but she wasn't there either.

What he found was a colorful celebration of the moment

everyone had been waiting for. At last! The day had come when the community would be free. The assemblies were concrete expressions of the permanent mandate of those kings for a day. They were at the peak of the ongoing festivity that was living in democracy.

As a demonstration of its authentic impartiality, *The Daily Miserias* had designed an impeccable front page. The two faces of the candidates had been evenly divided into four parts, and democratically recomposed into a single image. Max had the areas around the left temple and the right jaw, while Modesto González had the opposite corners. Under the photo of this collaged political monster appeared the command issued by its creators.

RISE UP AND WALK!

A disinterested revision of the issue allowed Max to learn that 34% of men with dandruff who were fans of field hockey, and had a caged salamander as a pet, still hadn't decided how to vote. An elderly man with a generic name looked back bitterly on the old days, delighted his grandchildren would have opportunities he'd never even dreamed of: "In the past everything was the same, but nothing was equal!" To reiterate its commitment to its readers, *The Daily Miserias* offered information about the deployment of an army of reporters in each assembly. It clarified that while all the buildings would receive the same attention, they would double their personnel in those with a greater weighting. The express aim was to reflect the overall opinion while, at the same time, concentrating on the most decisive ones. Orquídea López declared she was confident of achieving that precarious balance.

Max realized he hadn't eaten anything during the whole day. He put the newspaper under his arm and considered his options. He had no money with him, and didn't want to return to the apartment for fear of having to shut himself in there. He opted for the workers' canteen. It would be good for him get a firsthand impression of it after having heard hundreds of stories about its ill repute.

He was lucky enough to arrive a few moments before the official mealtime. In spite of the fact that the canteen was busy, he didn't find it as packed as usual. He considered asking permission to eat there, but didn't know from whom. None of the diners acknowledged his presence. He therefore went straight to serve himself from the ample buffet of leftovers set out at the back of the room.

The remains of some slightly stale enchiladas with black huitlacoche corn fungus caught his fancy. He added a portion of rice sprinkled with tiny slices of octopus, and lined up to reheat his meal in the communal microwave. He then squeezed himself into a space on a long table at which a silent group of beige uniforms was already seated. He wondered whether his raincoat was camouflaging him, or if the workers actually preferred to enjoy their food in silence. Even a more immaterial specter than him would have aroused some kind of reaction.

He took a couple of distracted mouthfuls of rice: the octopus had the consistency of chewing gum. Robotically, he put a piece of enchilada in his mouth. He wanted to get through this alimentary chore as quickly as possible. Something repulsive, synthetically sweet and sour landed on his tongue. When he tried the huitlacoche, they smelled of expensive perfume. At the first sign of retching, he put his face closer to the plate, and discovered the remains of dark red lipstick on a bitten edge of his enchiladas. A second gastric contraction bathed the delicacy in vomit that then splashed onto his neighbors' sleeves, leaving a lumpy smear, tinged with the black of the mushrooms and Max Michel's bile on the tabletop.

He expected a chain reaction since not even he could bear the stink of his vomit. But his table companions continued eating as calmly as ever. The last thing that registered in his brain was a woman in beige hurrying up with a pail of water. She was apparently intent on wiping away all trace of his semiliquid shame.

6

The repairman examined Max's revolver carefully, removing the bullets to inspect them one by one. He looked down the barrel to see if there was anything obstructing it. The minutes ticked by. Max longed to hear there was nothing to worry about, that everything would go the way it should. The repairman, however, was punctilious about maintaining his professional standards: it was impossible for him to cede to his customers' emotional needs. After stretching Max's nerves to breaking point, he finally gave his verdict:

"It appears to work, but it's no use. Are you sure you need it?" he asked Max, trying not to sound paternal.

"I've tried everything I know to plug the holes," Max apologized, anxious to make a good impression.

"In that case, allow me to adjust it for your specific needs." Without waiting for a reply, he went to his laboratory for a few moments, the revolver in his hand. On his return, he handed the gun to Max intact. The repairman then looked at his watch until the second hand reached a pre-established point.

"Done. Now, my fee please."

7

Max was in the mood for a walk under the shelter of the typical Villa Miserian dusky pink evening sky. Around him, the residents were returning home, exhausted but satisfied. The assemblies had finished: it was now a matter of waiting for the computation to discover who had won.

It was time. The question with no answer began to thrash and kick in Max's inner dark cavern, demanding to be immediately released. He put his hand to his forehead in an attempt to calm the reverberations, closed his eyes and breathed deeply. Dust. Dust. Dust. Max allowed it to enter through every pore. The particles were unhurriedly coming together to form a figure: after his sinuous meanderings, he finally had a solid outline before him whose shadow had no beginning or end. There was only one way to deal with it. He opened his eyes to check that the dusky pink sky had disappeared, put his hand in his pocket and set off at a brisk pace.

8

Selon Perdumes opened the door as if Max was the last guest to arrive at an exclusive dinner party dressed up as an informal gathering. The obvious people were already there: G.B.W. Ponce and Orquídea López, plus—unfortunately or otherwise—Nelly. Perdumes poured the tea he had prepared for his guests. There was exactly enough to fill the five cups on the living room table.

The host calmly bore the newcomer's scrutiny. After so many mishaps, Max could now put a face to the name. Or was he just a concept? Today he's in a grayish, slightly moth-eaten skin, thought Max as he compared what he saw with the idea of Perdumes he had fantasized. But he did have the unmistakable alabaster smile. Max could sense its glimmer even when Perdumes had his mouth closed. In contrast, his by now probable ex-boss was quietly watching him from behind his dark shades. Orquídea was balancing a saber: despite having positioned her finger at the juncture of the hilt and the blade, the sword seemed to be weighted down on the side of the latter. It was only by tilting her body in the opposite direction that she succeeded in producing the illusion of horizontal equilibrium. Max fixed his eyes on Nelly, attempting to work out how she managed to look more beautiful every single time he saw her. In protection, he blurred his eyes until she lost definition and became a blob obstructing the tranquility of the empty space. Without clear features, she was equivalent to any of the other bodies. Max stroked the gun hidden in his right pocket. He had to be sure that it hadn't decided to change sides at that precise moment.

"Oh, Max. Like, I don't know how to explain, but this isn't what you think," said Nelly, recovering her shape. "We were asked here to get the results of the election."

"I don't think anything any more, Nelly. I'm tired of so much thinking."

Well said, enough talking, let's have some action, exclaimed the Many in unison. Max was relieved to find he wasn't alone at such a decisive moment. At last, they were united against a common enemy.

"There's no need to be like that," said G.B.W. Ponce, easing the tension. "We're proud of you Max. You've excelled in carrying out the task you were assigned. Impossible to imagine a better candidate. Would you like to know if you're going to be the new president of the residents' association?"

"I couldn't care less. The truth I'm facing isn't in the order of the social structure of lies. You all used me. You've known everything right from the start. At least for a short time, I'll be master of my present. I couldn't give a fuck about what happens afterwards." The steel felt increasingly less cold in his hand. It was slowly reaching melting point.

"Now then, Max. Calm down a little. Can't you see that you livened up a really dull process? *The Daily Miserias* achieved record advertising revenue. The residents had the time of their lives. From now on they'll be demanding campaigns at least as entertaining as this one has been." It was Orquídea's turn to try to defuse the ticking time bomb.

"Exactly. You made me into a preprogrammed clown. There's only one way to remedy the situation." The Many's patience was running out. At any moment they might turn on Max and precipitate a different ending. If he didn't act soon, he'd have to face the consequences.

With the bull raging from the wounds that also weakened it, Selon Perdumes sensed it was time for him to enter the ring.

"Wonderful! Welcome, Max. We've been waiting for you. Do you like the tea? It's a mixture of herbs from remote, secret places. Only I know the correct proportions to produce a chaotic harmony between their various properties."

"It tastes the same as it always has. The trick is in presenting it in a new way each time. I'm not going to put up with being manipulated any longer."

"Stupendous!" replied Perdumes from the most expansive version of his alabaster smile. Max had the impression that as he spoke, his color was improving. That wasn't possible. Or was it? "Just tell me one thing. You feel you've been used. Manipulated. A puppet horrified to discover the strings that move it. Can you explain who forced you to do things against your will?"

Max turned as if by reflex to Nelly's pair of burning black caverns. He wanted to tell her they could forget everything, make a new beginning, the two of them and no one else. He could spend the rest of his life in the dark.

"No one. The power of seduction lies in the fact that it is voluntary. I'm not so blind as to be incapable of recognizing that. But it doesn't change the fact that you are masters of pressing the buttons of inadequacy. Knowing we can shake them off doesn't change the reality of the shackles that negate any form of movement."

Without a word from a single one of the Many, Max was able to guess what they were thinking: there was no use trying again with Nelly. The umpteenth new beginning would only lead to the same ending.

"Marvelous! I see you include the residents in your fury. Since I've been a visible presence in Villa Miserias, can you give me any example of aggressive coercion? The Black Paunches only enforce the laws agreed by us all. Is it my fault they're happy to apply what you call shackles? Do you know of any time when men wandered the world without cares? Even the people who made up that story did so only to immediately legitimize the need to submit to a determined order."

"OK. But according to you, your laws and the order that underlies them are neutral and make no distinction between unequals. True, the chains of servitude are as old as the human race. The difference is that in the past the links in those chains had names. It never occurred to anyone that the people at the top were called the same as the ones below." The sweat in his palm challenged Max to act. Each additional drop made the revolver more slippery.

"Genius. Absolute genius!" Perdumes turned to Ponce, his teeth now almost transparent. "The perfect choice!" He turned back to Max to continue the chess game. "Young man, you are well aware that what's important is the mold, not the material its made from. To be exact, we wanted you to help us verify if they were ready to dispense with their idols. What difference does it make whether the gods are lightning, rain, the dead, emperors, monarchs, soldiers, footballers, actresses, freedom, democracy, or any other of their future incarnations? Every dogma is tyrannical.

They all demand unconditional submission. All except one. Only money, as the supreme entity, offers us the chance to be the person we want to be. Or rather, are capable of being. Up to now, it has had to remain hidden behind a few noble ideals. Ah, justice, equality. The words only have to be set down on paper for people to assume they exist in reality. Look around you. Do you know of any society where they even come close to being real? Try convincing someone who can afford an expensive lawyer to be represented by a public defender. Explain to a middle-class left-winger that his luxuries aren't morally superior to those of his snooty neighbor. Suggest he swaps houses or wives with his much-vaunted proletariat. I can guarantee he'll tell you where to go. Reason is useful for detecting other people's abominations. By definition, one locates oneself on the right side of the frontier between the just and the evil."

Max could have sworn the teeth were beginning to vanish. He couldn't allow their gleam to defeat him now.

"Positing the absence of ideology is the most infallible ideology in history. It's an attempt to install it as the definitive one. It's a closed system containing within it all possible objections, just like the religions it replaced. Money isn't value-free. Your own henchman, here present, has demonstrated the enormous similarity of patterns between the different strata. The unrestricted freedom to accumulate is just as enslaving. And as you rightly pointed out, the Black Paunches exist to rein in those who don't want to be part of the flock, a flock that is allowed to choose between different incarnations of the same shepherd."

The gun in Max's pocket was running out of breath.

"Magnificent! Your material religiosity is magnificent! You still think something different exists in another dimension. Allow me to convince you that this isn't the case. Didn't your beloved Big Brother say the great ills of society would possibly never be righted, but that no one was ready to accept this? We're offering to do that once and for all. Behind the façade of money, there is just more money. And then a bit more. For a very small number of residents, the only thing that makes them angry about large fortunes is that they don't belong to them. The rest consider them as natural as the length of their penises.

"We will be eternally grateful to you for helping us spread the new gospel. There is nothing hidden behind the appearance other than incarnations of new appearances. If you map the journey of each coin, you'll discover not one of them is clean. And, following the same line of thought, I challenge you to show me a politician unwilling to kiss money's ass. They know that refusal would be suicide. They would be unable to govern, or even be elected to power in the first place. Let it go. You're better off enjoying the beautiful Nelly than resigning yourself to watching how others with a higher capacity for ignoring all those things that torment you, do just that."

By the time Perdumes had concluded his speech, his complexion was almost purple. He let his alabaster smile hang over the room while he waited for his opponent to make a decision.

Max Michels clearly heard the snap of the inner safety catch connecting him to the familiar forms among which he'd being tiptoeing all his life. He released the revolver from the claustrophobia threatening to turn it against himself. At least the first shot would hit someone else's flesh. He first pointed the gun at Orquídea: she had been the original standard bearer. Then he moved on to Ponce: he'd frigging love to check if those dark glasses were bulletproof. Finally, it was Nelly's turn. With her, he'd descended into the well from which he would never return as himself. He allowed himself the luxury of imagining them as two lead characters in a classical tragedy. Too great a passion for a cold world. He could leave with her right now. He could…

"Heavenly! Max, leave them out of this. Particularly the girl. It's not her fault. This is between you and me now."

Perdumes' face seemed the color of bone. The ubiquitous smile had called in missing. It pained Max to realize that, once again, the man was right. He was itching to know the color of the blood that ran in his veins. Maybe pale green. Then the Many pointed the revolver at Max's temple: put an end to all this now, you'll be able to take a rest, even from us. The hand oscillated between the two possible targets, unable to decide, but finally came to rest in one direction. Max closed his eyes before pulling the trigger. The notion of his whole life filing before his eyes made a brief appearance. But there wasn't even time for that.

A deafening explosion was heard just at the moment Max felt the truncheon blow that left him lying on the ground paralyzed from the waist down. The smoke-shrouded shadows were still standing, unperturbed. Before the hail of kicks from a squad of Black Paunches hit him, Max heard Joel Taimado giving his report to Selon Perdumes.

"Hey boss, looks to me like these bullets are just toys. They've got jam inside."

9

With great difficulty, Max opened his eyes. His lids felt as heavy
as if they had been closed from his birth. His body was a rotting
raisin, held in one piece by an arsenal of bandages, gauze, stitches,
adhesive tape, shattered bones, and stabbing pain. But anyway,
he'd been lucky. Before losing consciousness, he'd heard hyster-
ical screams halting the furious onslaught of black boots. They
had pounded him without completely breaking him. That same
metallic voice, now in a sweetly wary tone, was attempting to wake
him from his dream. It took Max a little longer to come out of
the place of refuge he believed himself to be in.

"Oh, Max. Like, what are you saying? Your nanny died years ago.
Don't you remember?" The sound of Nelly's voice corroborated
the information given by the walls: Max was in his apartment,
recovering from a brutal beating. His tongue told him he was
missing half of two front teeth. His left knee was swollen with
liquid: a ligament must be torn. He asked Nelly for a mirror to
see how this new chapter in his life would begin. His nose, with a
new bump, looked like a continuation of the slash that ran down
from his hairline, cutting through his eyebrow on its way. Was
this the face of the new president of the Villa Miserias residents'
association?

"Jeez. It's...I don't know how to say this...you got trounced.
You didn't even win in your own building," wept Nelly disconsolately, as if she was condensing the whole gamut of earlier
experiences in her tears. Her shoulders were shaking, with no
apparent intention of stopping. It was one uninterrupted wail

that didn't admit any other possibilities: neither past nor future. The two people present there in that room were prohibited, for reasons they would never understand, from continuing to struggle to be in each other's company.

Max allowed himself a dark smile. He was finally returning to the point of departure, only more deformed in body and spirit. Since his childhood, his father had instructed him in the edifying properties of pain. Perhaps he would be satisfied now. He felt Nelly carefully molding her body to his. He didn't have the strength to look at her, but caressed her thick hair with the few fingers that had escaped uninjured.

Floating in a restless sleep, Max initially thought he was taking refuge in a dream. Yet the tenacity of the human contact gradually convinced him this was not the case. Now there was no doubt, Nelly was naked. With extreme care, she was removing the thin dressing gown covering his bruised skin. It was as if she was trying to heal every corner of him with fire: it was a pleasurable operation. Max deliberately avoided opening his eyes. Seeing. Not seeing. The difference was more a matter of grade than class. He wanted to allow Nelly to continue without distractions. What truth could his gaze arrive at that his body couldn't? Nelly's wails had become whimpers. Max suspected she was ready to cross the boundary into a region where he could no longer see her. More gently than was usual, she rolled on top of him. It made no difference whether or not he opened his eyes now: Why bother? Better to sail with her through less anguished waters.

The timbre of Nelly's breathing became heightened until it crystalized into a mantra Max refused to obey: Look at me, look at me, I'm begging you to look at me. He grasped her buttocks more tightly in an attempt to distract her: Nelly continued to emit that command camouflaged as a plea until, unwillingly, Max opened his eyes so as to continue being unable to see her.

Nelly appeared immediately, arching back her body: Max could see her as clearly as he had felt her touch. Her black hair was falling over her shoulders. Her sweating body belonged fully to Max. At last. The expression on Nelly's face was one of jubilant ecstasy: she knew it was different this time. She didn't even take her gaze from Max at the moment they climaxed simultaneously. She lay above him, breathing, for a few minutes more. Outside, night was falling. They fell asleep in silence. A moment before doing so, in his inner self, Max articulated the thought that there might, after all, be a new chapter in the book with blank pages. The wimp had triumphed. The Many hadn't even had the balls to recognize their resounding defeat.

The following morning, Max woke embracing the empty space where Nelly should have been sleeping. With great difficulty, he got out of bed. It—everything—had been worth the effort. The thorny path only made the arrival more unique.

He found Nelly standing in front of the painting in the living room. Her hair, tied back, gave her a demure air. As soon as he saw her, Max knew it was all over. There was no need for explanations. And Nelly did not seem disposed to offer any either. She gave him one last look, allowing him to imprint in his memory the image that would torment him.

"Oh, Max. There's nothing left to say. Goodbye. And best of luck with everything."

Before Max had even had time to embrace her, Nelly had quietly closed the door, as if, with that considerate gesture, she was erasing the wake of her fleeting irruption into the life of Max Michels.

Max took down the painting to torture himself for a moment with the hidden axiom. He read it again and again until it was empty of meaning: reduced to a random collection of letters that could have taken any other form. Any form at all. Suddenly, they flooded onto Max's internal screen. They didn't coincide with the words on the plaque, either in number or order, but were, even so, trying to say the same thing. Max limped to the bedroom to dress. He needed to unload the burden of this new certainty onto his enemy. He would go in peace to visit Selon Perdumes.

10

When he left the building, Max noticed something had changed. He was used to seeing the dust floating in the sunbeams filtering through the trees. But now this phenomenon seemed to have gone into reverse: the dust was clouding the halos of light, now tired of putting up resistance. Hearing the familiar trsssh, trsssh of Juana Mecha's broom, he went up to her in the hope of hearing some enigmatic comment that might clarify the situation.

"Good morning, young Max," she said with her sweeper's courtesy.

Disconcerted, Max made his way toward the Villa Miserias administrative offices, where Selon Perdumes would undoubtedly be present at the swearing in of the new president. When he arrived, the ceremony had just ended: Modesto González had taken office. Perdumes was nowhere to be seen: perhaps he was just late, or had, for some reason, decided not to attend the ritual investiture of his new mascot.

With a sense of foreboding, Max asked if anyone knew where he was. Who? Selon Perdumes. Never heard of him. One after another, the officials and curiosity seekers looked at him as if he was unhinged, noting his bruises but not daring to ask if he was out of his mind. Convinced this was just another of Perdumes' perverse games, Max proceeded, in his ungainly gait, to the absent man's apartment.

The residents he passed on his way were in on the joke. They seemed genuinely shaken by his mention of the stranger with an unpronounceable name. The poor defeated candidate! He'd had some accident that had addled his wits. They wished him a speedy recovery before continuing on their way.

Breathing painfully, Max rapped on the door of the apartment. An alarmed, middle-aged woman appeared, clearly getting ready to leave for work. He demanded to see Selon Perdumes, but received the same answer: Who? Never heard of him. Are you feeling all right?

Max shouted out the name, as if trying to force his enemy out of his hiding place. Terrified, Señora Eloisa Roca asked him to get out her home. That gentleman had never lived there. The family photographs were proof that the apartment had been kept unchanged for many years, in memory of the original owner, her mother, the widow Inocencia Roca.

Beaten, Max Michels shambled through the streets of Villa Miserias in search of some explanation. The residents watched him with pitying disinterest. He stopped and looked around him. They all had a common trait that outshone any other of their facial features: as they hurried past, they offered him an alabaster smile.

EDUARDO RABASA studied political science at Mexico's National University (UNAM), where he graduated with a thesis on the concept of power in the work of George Orwell. He writes a weekly column for the national newspaper *Milenio*, and has translated books of such authors as Morris Berman, George Orwell, and W. Somerset Maugham. In 2002 he co-founded Sexto Piso, recognized as one of Mexico's leading independent publishers, where he currently serves as editorial director. *A Zero-Sum Game* is his debut novel, published in Mexico by Surplus Ediciones (Sur+), in Spain by Pepitas de calabaza, in Argentina by Godot Ediciones, in France by Éditions Piranha, and in the US by Deep Vellum. In 2015, he was selected among the best 20 young Mexican contemporary authors in the Hay Festival's *México20* project.

CHRISTINA MACSWEENEY is a literary translator specializing in Latin American fiction. Her translations of Valeria Luiselli's works have been published by Granta and Coffee House Press; Luiselli's *Faces in the Crowd* was a finalist for the Best Translated Book Award in 2015, and *The Story of My Teeth* was a finalist for the same award in 2016, and won the *Los Angeles Times* Fiction Prize. Her work has also appeared in the anthologies *México20*, and *Lunatics, Lovers and Poets: Twelve Stories after Cervantes and Shakespeare* (And Other Stories, 2016). Her most recent published translation, Daniel Saldaña París's *Among Strange Victims*, was published by Coffee House Press in spring 2016, and a short story, "Piñata," by the same author was included in the 2016 National Translation Month publications.

Thank you all
for your support.
We do this for you,
and could not do
it without you.

DEEP
VELLUM

DEAR READERS,

Deep Vellum Publishing is a 501c3 nonprofit literary arts organization founded in 2013 with a threefold mission: to publish international literature in English translation; to foster the art and craft of translation; and to build a more vibrant book culture in Dallas and beyond. We are dedicated to broadening cultural connections across the English-reading world by connecting readers, in new and creative ways, with the work of international authors. We strive for diversity in publishing authors from various languages, viewpoints, genders, sexual orientations, countries, continents, and literary styles, whose works provide lasting cultural value and build bridges with foreign cultures while expanding our understanding of how the world thinks, feels, and experiences the human condition.

Operating as a nonprofit means that we rely on the generosity of tax-deductible donations from individual donors, cultural organizations, government institutions, and foundations. Your donations provide the basis of our operational budget as we seek out and publish exciting literary works from around the globe and build a vibrant and active literary arts community both locally and within the global society. Deep Vellum offers multiple donor levels, including LIGA DE ORO ($5,000+) and LIGA DEL SIGLO ($1,000+). Donors at various levels receive personalized benefits for their donations, including books and Deep Vellum merchandise, invitations to special events, and recognition in each book and on our website.

In addition to donations, we rely on subscriptions from readers like you to provide an invaluable ongoing investment in Deep Vellum that demonstrates a commitment to our editorial vision and mission. Subscribers are the bedrock of our support as we grow the readership for these amazing works of literature from every corner of the world. The investment our subscribers make allows us to demonstrate to potential donors and bookstores alike the support and demand for Deep Vellum's literature across a broad readership and gives us the ability to grow our mission in ever-new, ever-innovative ways.

In partnership with our sister company and bookstore, Deep Vellum Books, located in the historic cultural district of Deep Ellum in central Dallas, we organize and host literary programming such as author readings, translator workshops, creative writing classes, spoken word performances, and interdisciplinary arts events for writers, translators, and artists from across the globe. Our goal is to enrich and connect the world through the power of the written and spoken word, and we have been recognized for our efforts by being named one of the "Five Small Presses Changing the Face of the Industry" by *Flavorwire* and honored as Dallas's Best Publisher by *D Magazine*.

If you would like to get involved with Deep Vellum as a donor, subscriber, or volunteer, please contact us at deepvellum.org. We would love to hear from you.

Thank you all. Enjoy reading.
Will Evans Founder & Publisher Deep Vellum Publishing

LIGA DE ORO ($5,000+)

Anonymous (2)

LIGA DEL SIGLO ($1,000+)

Allred Capital Management
Ben & Sharon Fountain
Judy Pollock
Life in Deep Ellum
Loretta Siciliano
Lori Feathers
Mary Ann Thompson-Frenk
   & Joshua Frenk
Matthew Rittmayer
Meriwether Evans
Pixel and Texel
Nick Storch
Social Venture Partners Dallas
Stephen Bullock

DONORS

Adam Rekerdres
Alan Shockley
Amrit Dhir
Anonymous
Andrew Yorke
Anthony Messenger
Bob Appel
Bob & Katherine Penn
Brandon Childress
Brandon Kennedy
Caroline Casey
Charles Dee Mitchell
Charley Mitcherson
Cheryl Thompson
Christie Tull
Daniel J. Hale

Ed Nawotka
Rev. Elizabeth
   & Neil Moseley
Ester & Matt Harrison
Grace Kenney
Greg McConeghy
Jeff Waxman
JJ Italiano
Justin Childress
Kay Cattarulla
Kelly Falconer
Linda Nell Evans
Lissa Dunlay
Marian Schwartz
   & Reid Minot
Mark Haber

Mary Cline
Maynard Thomson
Michael Reklis
Mike Kaminsky
Mokhtar Ramadan
Nikki & Dennis Gibson
Olga Kislova
Patrick Kukucka
Richard Meyer
Steve Bullock
Suejean Kim
Susan Carp
Susan Ernst
Theater Jones
Tim Perttula
Tony Thomson

SUBSCRIBERS

Alan Shockley

Aldo Sanchez

Anita Tarar

Audrey Mash

Ben Fountain

Ben Nichols

Bill Fisher

Bradford Pearson

Charles Dee Mitchell

Chase Marcella

Chris Sweet

Christie Tull

Courtney Sheedy

David Christensen

David Travis

David Weinberger

Dori Boone-Costantino

Elaine Corwin

Farley Houston

Ghassan Fergiani

Gregory Seaman

Guilty Dave Bristow

Horatiu Matei

James Tierney

Janine Allen

Jeanne Milazzo

Jeffrey Collins

Jessa Crispin

Jill Kelly

Joe Milazzo

John O'Neill

John Schmerein

John Winkelman

Joshua Edwin

Julia Rigsby

Julie Janicke Muhsmann

Karen Olsson

Kasie Henderson

Kimberly Alexander

Kristopher Phillips

Kurt Cumiskey

Lara Smith

Marcia Lynx Qualey

Margaret Terwey

Martha Gifford

Meaghan Corwin

Michael Elliott

Michael Filippone

Michael Norton

Michael Wilson

Mies de Vries

Mike Kaminsky

Neal Chuang

Nick Oxford

Nicola Molinaro

Owen Rowe

Peter McCambridge

Ryan Jones

Shelby Vincent

Stephanie Barr

Steven Kornajcik

Steven Norton

Susan Ernst

Tim Kindseth

Tim Looney

Todd Jailer

Tony Messenger

Whitney Leader-Picone

Will Pepple

William Jarrell

COMING FALL/SPRING 2016–2017 FROM DEEP VELLUM

CARMEN BOULLOSA · *Heavens on Earth*
translated by Shelby Vincent · MEXICO

ANANDA DEVI · *Eve Out of Her Ruins*
translated by Jeffrey Zuckerman · MAURITIUS

JÓN GNARR · *The Outlaw*
translated by Lytton Smith · ICELAND

CLAUDIA SALAZAR JIMÉNEZ · *Blood of the Dawn*
translated by Elizabeth Bryer · PERU

JOSEFINE KLOUGART · *Of Darkness*
translated by Martin Aitken · DENMARK

SERGIO PITOL · *The Magician of Vienna*
translated by George Henson · MEXICO

EDUARDO RABASA · *A Zero-Sum Game*
translated by Christina MacSweeney · MEXICO

BAE SUAH · *Recitation*
translated by Deborah Smith · SOUTH KOREA

JUAN RULFO · *The Golden Cockerel & Other Writings*
translated by Douglas J. Weatherford · MEXICO

ANNE GARRÉTA · *Not One Day*
translated by Emma Ramadan · FRANCE

YANICK LAHENS · *Moonbath*
translated by Emily Gogolak · HAITI

DEEP
VELLUM